The Headmaster's Darlings

STORY RIVER BOOKS

Pat Conroy, Editor at Large

The Headmaster's Darlings

~ A MOUNTAIN BROOK NOVEL ~

KATHERINE CLARK

Foreword by Pat Conroy

The University of South Carolina Press

© 2015 Katherine Clark

Published by the University of South Carolina Press
Columbia, South Carolina 29208

www.sc.edu/uscpress

Manufactured in the United States of America

24 23 22 21 20 19 18 17 16 15
11 10 9 8 7 6 5 4 3 2

Library of Congress Cataloging-in-Publication Data
can be found at http://catalog.loc.gov/.

ISBN 978-1-61117-538-7 (cloth)
ISBN 978-1-61117-539-4 (ebook)

Photograph of Carl Martin Hames on the dedication page
courtesy of Dalton Blankenship

This book was printed on recycled paper with
30 percent postconsumer waste content.

This book is dedicated to the memory of Carl Martin Hames, teacher and mentor extraordinaire, who, in the words of Ralph Waldo Emerson, endeavored "not to drill, but to create . . . and set the hearts of . . . youth on flame."

FOREWORD

All cities have their secret venues known only to insiders or the native born. Every Southern city has its own splendid enclave of privilege where the very rich build their mansions in earthly paradises that block most intrusions from the rowdiness and havoc of the outside world. Katherine Clark grew up in the magical kingdom of Mountain Brook, a forested chapel of ease that looks like God's own dream of a suburb. It is Alabama's answer to the Garden District in New Orleans, or Atlanta's Buckhead or Charleston's South of Broad. Overlooking the battle-scarred city of Birmingham, it remained aloof and barely touched by the brutal struggles of the protestors for civil rights against police dogs, fire hoses, and all the shameful laws in the Jim Crow South. When the explosion at the Sixteenth Street Baptist Church killed four black girls dressed in their Sunday best, my friend, the novelist Anne Rivers Siddons, was staying at a sorority sister's house in Mountain Brook. When Annie heard the news, and questioned the parents of her sorority sister about what had happened on the streets of Birmingham, she was told again and again, "It's nothing to worry your pretty little head about, Annie."

That is Mountain Brook. It's the second most important character in Katherine Clark's marvelous debut novel, *The Headmaster's Darlings*. And what a powerful character it becomes in her satirical view of the pampered location of her childhood. Looking down on a city of steel and iron, it served as an island of reprieve for the honored families lucky enough to inhabit its grand estates. It was built beneath the canopy of a hardwood forest and rose up as a communal ode to perfect taste. Like an Umbrian hill town, Mountain Brook can wound an outsider with its uncommon beauty, its inlaid tastefulness, and its proud rebuttal to all forms of excess or lack of restraint. This is a place that will always possess a quiet sublimity that maintains its own love story to a vanishing South. With its manicured gardens and sloping lawns and the lush, green rivers of golf courses cutting behind the margins of its famous houses, Mountain Brook would seem to be the happiest place to grow up for a white child in the South. It is an elegant, cutoff world of such languorous, slow-moving beauty that it appears as isolated and innocent as the Shire in Tolkien's fantasy universe. Children spend summer days by the pool at the country club in sight of a golf course as green and well-tended as they are. In the evenings there are debutante balls where young women celebrate their fresh flowering into womanhood and young men dazzle in the sheer glory of their prime under starry Alabama nights. But the town, in all the directions of the compass, finds itself surrounded by a real world that lies in wait.

Though Mountain Brook provides the setting for this novel, it has little to do with its prodigious heart. That belongs to the novel's central character, the art and English teacher at Brook-Haven School, the outrageous and unforgettable Norman Laney. In a nation that does all too little to honor its teachers, Katherine Clark helps us to remember how a single man or woman in a classroom can light immeasurable fires in the imaginations of a whole generation of grateful students. Our teachers lead us by the hand toward the secrets that enlarge our vision, the deep mysteries of poetry, art, history and mathematics. They place us on those hidden pathways where our truest selves lie ready for awakening.

Norman Laney is the most magnificent teacher I've read about since I read A. S. Neill's *Summerhill* in that impressionable year before I became a teacher myself. But I think now that Norman Laney is a far superior educator to A. S. Neill and I would have given up a year of my writing life to encounter such a man. As it was, I was taught English by three giants in their field: Joseph Monte, Gene Norris, and Millen Ellis. If I'd finished off my high school education with a year monitored by Norman Laney, I would have enjoyed the finest high school education in the beauties of the language of any boy who ever lived. Laney seems to extol the whole world in every breath he draws and opens that world to anyone he meets, student or adult. The world is his to give and savor, whether you have the willingness to accept his generous vision or not.

In many ways, Norman Laney serves as the anti-Mountain Brook, a poor white fat boy from a lower-middle class section of Birmingham who is called upon to teach in the most prestigious private high school in Alabama. He is a man of voluptuous, uncontrollable appetites, a great hippopotamus of a man. His obesity seems almost superhuman; his hugeness is a necessary ingredient in a personality that is loquacious and flamboyant to a fault. There is nothing trim or ship-shape about him. You come to believe while reading this Laney-esque novel that a small body could not contain such richness and raw fabulousness of a life well-lived, that a thin vessel could not contain such energy. Normal Laney, several hundred pounds and gaining weight by the chapter, hovers over this book and the souls of his students like the triumphant archangel casting Satan out of paradise.

It is his encounter with Mountain Brook society and its sons and daughters that forms the solid core of this work. He finds he enjoys life among the rich and he takes Mountain Brook by storm. But it is Laney who recognizes that he and his fellow teachers at Brook-Haven have a sacred responsibility to open up the possibilities of the outside world. For him, it is a credo that his students know there is brilliant, radiant life teeming with enlightenment and fulfillment outside their home state. He is indefatigable and can't stop teaching from the time he wakes up in the morning until he puts his enormous girth to bed at night. He is sexless, but comes across as sexy and charismatic as he moves with ease and grace through the living rooms and salons of Mountain Brook. Yet individuals such as Norman Laney always have a hazardous gift for drawing ground fire from their enemies.

Like her unforgettable main character, Katherine Clark moves with ease through the dinner parties and soirees of Mountain Brook society. She was raised as a Southern belle in the 1960s and didn't know until high school that her native city was one of the great battlegrounds of the Civil Rights Movement. She didn't have a clue where the jail was in which Martin Luther King, Jr. wrote his magnificent letter. But she has spent a lifetime reading and reflecting, not to mention four years at Harvard getting a college education. Now she trains that well-read, well-educated mind onto Mountain Brook, and what she has done is to create a world. This is something I always look for in fiction: Did the writer make me a world? The great writers know how to build a world for their readers, like Dickens does with London, Saul Bellow with Chicago, William Faulkner with Yoknapatawpha County. Katherine Clark knows how to capture a world, turn a phrase, tell a story, and write a comedy of manners that peels the beautiful layers off Mountain Brook society and shows the rancor and ugliness and tragedy below.

Story River Books is publishing *The Headmaster's Darlings* with great pride and a serious commitment to Katherine Clark's talent. This is the first of many novels that we are calling the Mountain Brook Series, the first of many that will bring to life the world of Mountain Brook and chronicle the fates of Norman Laney and his various darlings. Katherine Clark will write her name in the book of great Alabama writers, and she will long be remembered as the creator of Norman Laney, the greatest portrait of an American teacher I have ever read, immortalized, as I believe he richly deserves, by one of his golden girls, one of his darlings. Here's how good this book is—for the rest of my life I will also be one of Norman Laney's darlings.

PAT CONROY

~ PART ONE ~

Fall Semester
The Brook–Haven School
1983

SEPTEMBER

~ 1 ~

When he emerged from his office, the hush of the library suddenly became the silence of the tomb, as everyone thought it best to hold their breath, stifle their coughs and delay any page-turning until his gaze had completed its searchlight sweep of the room. The only one making any noise was Jimmy Kuhn, who was seated at the reference desk with three of his female classmates, none of whom were in a strategic location to observe any sudden eruptions from the assistant headmaster's office. The girls were highly amused by whatever Jimmy was saying, and Jimmy was as oblivious of Norman Laney's looming presence as he was of the total quiet that had descended over the rest of the student body gathered in the library, or even the general pall that had hung in the air all morning because of the news that Karen Ritchie's mother had died unexpectedly last night at age forty-five. With three deliberate steps forward, Mr. Laney curtailed the giggles of the girls, and the abrupt end of their delight with the unsuspecting Jimmy caused him to turn around and face the seething fury of Norman Laney's enormous bulk.

"Jimmy Kuhn!" screamed Mr. Laney. "WHERE ARE YOUR BOOKS?"

Caught off guard, Jimmy stammered. "Locker," he sputtered. "They're in my locker. The bell rang and I—"

"HOW DARE YOU COME TO STUDY HALL WITHOUT YOUR BOOKS!" thundered Mr. Laney. "It IS true, isn't it, that you DO know how to read?"

Scattered tittering erupted throughout the library, but if Mr. Laney had wanted to, he would not have been able to pinpoint any of its sources. Instead he remained intent upon Jimmy. "You HAVE achieved LITERACY in the course of your high school education?"

"Ah—yes," Jimmy said, as if he weren't entirely sure what literacy was or whether or not he had achieved it. But he had the instincts of a true performer, and playing dumb was a role that came quite naturally to him. "Yes, sir," he repeated more affirmatively. "I have definitely achieved—" he paused. "What did you call it?"

The students now broke out in open laugher, and Jimmy turned around to smile gratefully at his audience.

"THEN PROVE IT!" roared Mr. Laney. "OPEN THE FIRST BOOK YOU CAN FIND AND STICK YOUR HEAD IN IT! PERHAPS SOME OF ITS ERUDITION WILL SINK INTO YOUR BRAIN THROUGH THE PROCESS OF OSMOSIS!"

As Mr. Laney set off down the hallway leading out of the library, Jimmy turned back to the girls. "What's up with Fat Boy?"

"Karen Ritchie's mother died last night," whispered Tina Johnson.

Jimmy shrugged. He may or may not have achieved literacy, but he definitely had not achieved the maturity to understand what either death in general or the death of Karen Ritchie's mother in particular had to do with him. It was doubtful if he ever would. "I don't even like Karen Ritchie," he said. "Frizzy haired little Jewish girl."

The girls giggled as appreciatively as they dared.

* * *

Near the end of the hallway, Norman Laney turned right abruptly and entered the office of his colleague Elizabeth Elder. She had not so much an office as a sanctuary in which fluorescent lights had been banished and a large Oriental rug completely covered the linoleum floor. At her own expense, she had arranged for the ceiling tiles and strip lighting to be removed in exchange for a smooth, painted surface. In the rich glow of the desk lamp which was the primary source of light in the room, all her mahogany furniture looked even more antique than it was. Three of the walls were covered with reproductions of Gobelins tapestries. On the wall by her desk hung stern portraits of ancestors whose grim faces were illuminated by spotlights overhanging the frames. (The joke among students was that she used these portraits as models for her own grim visage, and needed them nearby so she could practice between classes.) The anomaly in her décor was the plush leather armchair which could withstand the girth of Norman Laney much better than the straight-backed needle-pointed chairs she indicated for any other visitor.

Mr. Laney plopped down in his chair and simultaneously produced an apple. As he bit savagely into it, he looked more horse than human, with his lips peeled back to reveal a formidable row of large, bared teeth. Juice from the fruit flew as far as Elizabeth Elder's desk. It was clear that the apple was not only a mid-morning snack, but also an object on which he could inflict his vengeance. Elizabeth Elder remained unflinching, and waited patiently for

Norman Laney to speak his mind, her steady, piercing gaze trained intently on him above her reading glasses.

She was quite well aware that Norman's atrocious eating habits and table manners were deliberately exaggerated to help him separate his friends from his enemies. Those in Mountain Brook who accepted him, loved him and believed in him were invariably inclined to overlook his grossness. Those who disliked him, distrusted him, feared him and generally believed he had no business being accepted in Mountain Brook society often betrayed their true feelings when forced to witness Norman's gluttony. Although Elizabeth had been a proven friend for decades, she knew better than to irk him at a time like this by even the slightest movement of a single facial muscle. She kept her face perfectly blank as she watched him devour the apple.

Still he didn't speak, but extended his left leg and rocked it back and forth in agitation.

"So he finally killed her," he said, taking another savage bite of the apple.

"I wouldn't talk like that outside this office," Elizabeth Elder warned him.

"Well that's what I'm saying to everybody I know," he replied, with another defiant bite. "He killed her," he said, through a mouthful of apple.

"I wouldn't be surprised if she killed herself."

"Same thing. Living with him was murder. Or suicide. Whatever you want to call it. But he's the one who killed her."

There was a moment of silence in which Elizabeth Elder's exasperation ultimately took the form of speech.

"Really, Norman," she said. "You could get yourself in a lot of trouble with loose talk like that. That man would love nothing better than to vent himself in some kind of lawsuit against you."

"He'd never win." Norman's leg rocked more rapidly back and forth.

"Oh, yes he would. You'd go bankrupt in a week from legal fees. That's all the victory he would need. And how well do you think our beloved head of school would handle this kind of complication?"

"You're right," he conceded in a reversal that would have surprised anyone who didn't know him as well as Elizabeth Elder did. She was equally unfazed by his abrupt change of subject.

"Franny has agreed to do *Raisin in the Sun* for Theo," he said. "I'm still looking into it, but I think it'll be the first time any school in the state of Alabama has put on the play. That's good for a *Birmingham News* story, and Theo will be a shoo-in for Yale. I'm going to send a videotape as supporting material."

"It's not the play Theo wants."

"Who cares what Theo wants?" said Norman. His voice rising, he leaned forward in the chair and narrowed his eyes, as if Elizabeth Elder were his adversary and not his dearest friend and colleague. "I am not going to allow Theophilus Jackson to play a British aristocrat in the voice of a Southern Negro." He elongated the vowels of this last word to such an extent that it sounded like "knee-grow," and he rapped his knuckles on Elizabeth's desk.

Unruffled as ever, Elizabeth said calmly, "He's going to accuse us of being opposed to color-blind casting."

"Who's opposed to color-blind casting?" Norman snapped back. "This has nothing to do with color-blind casting. This has to do with the fact that *The Importance of Being Earnest* is not going to be the fall play. *A Raisin in the Sun* is the fall play. If Theo Jackson plays that role as brilliantly as I know he can, he might find himself accepted into one of the finer Ivy League institutions in this country despite his low B average and abysmal SAT scores." Norman's foot rocked violently, as if trying to match the vehemence of his tirade.

"What if Theo refuses the part?"

"Let him. We have plenty of other students who could play that part."

"No other male students who also happen to be African American."

"Exactly!" Norman almost shouted. "Then Theo will see that this has nothing to do with color-blind casting, but about getting himself into Yale. And hopefully, it won't be too late."

He thrust his hands on the arms of the chair and hoisted himself up. Elizabeth Elder's eyes followed him as he rose ponderously. "Norman," she said, in the voice of a mother bringing a wayward child to account.

His eyes met hers as he stood upright in front of her desk. "Who's going to see about Karen?" she said.

"I am, of course," he said, adopting for his part the voice of the aggrieved child who has been wrongly accused.

"Let me know what you find out." She shook her head. "It's a bad way to start the school year."

He turned to leave, but then looked back. "Incidentally," he said. "What's Jimmy Kuhn still doing here? I thought he wasn't coming back."

Elizabeth sighed. "His mother was up here last week, begging Tom Turbyfill for one more chance."

"But why?" Norman turned back around to face Elizabeth fully again. "He's perfect Mountain Brook High School material."

"I think that's what his mother's afraid of." Elizabeth pursed her lips.

"I will not have this school used as a babysitting service for spoiled rich kids!" said Norman, wagging his finger at Elizabeth as if she were the culprit. "You and I have worked too hard to turn this school into something else. I'll just have to try harder," he said, turning again to leave. "The boy is so obtuse he doesn't even know when someone is making his life miserable."

"Only two more years to go," Elizabeth said with another sigh.

"No!" Norman declared bluntly. "He's got to go before next year. I refuse to be associated with the school of which Jimmy Kuhn is a graduate. Let me know if you hear anything." He left the office with as little preamble as he'd entered.

* * *

Back in his own office, Norman Laney discovered a yellow Post-it note which must have just been placed there by the secretary from the main office while he was talking to Elizabeth Elder. "Midge Elmore called. Wants you to call back." Normally Norman might have waited a day or two before subjecting himself to a phone conversation with Midge Elmore, but today he seized the receiver and jabbed fiercely at the buttons as he would have liked to jab his fingers in Jimmy Kuhn's idiot eyes. If anyone knew the details of what had happened last night, it would be Midge Elmore.

"What have you heard?" he asked as soon as she answered, not bothering to greet her or identify himself.

"Oh, Norman," she said. "I've just come from there."

"You've been to the house?" he said, temporarily taken aback. But yes, he recalculated quickly, this was why he loved Midge Elmore. She was one of the few people he knew who could do the simple, obvious thing without hesitation. It was she who would do what would either never occur to anyone else, or be immediately dismissed as impossible, unthinkable.

"I called Brody's as soon as they opened," she said. "But I thought it best to take the tray myself rather than have it delivered. I didn't think they'd want just anybody coming over there."

"Midge, you are a miracle of Southern womanhood," he said.

From the sound she made in reply, he could tell what deep satisfaction she got from this compliment. And he meant it too. Times had changed, even as far south as Birmingham, Alabama, where it often seemed there was no such thing as change. But sometimes it *did* happen, for the better as well as the worse, and now the news of a death did not automatically summon the world to your door with condolences and trays of food. Especially if you were as universally and thoroughly disliked as Warren Ritchie, whose family wasn't even from Birmingham anyway. Even worse, Warren's people had come from "up North," and try telling anyone in Birmingham that not all "Yankees" were "Jews." Norman himself had tried and failed repeatedly over the years. Once he had even brandished the *New York Times* obituary of Warren's father, which made it clear that the family wasn't even Yankee, let alone Jewish. Although Warren's father more or less moved to the Northeast in prep school, his family came from Chicago. But the response he got was always the same: Of course Warren denied being Jewish—who wouldn't? In Alabama, the New York *Times* was not a source deemed trustworthy or even noteworthy. Besides, anyone who had ever met Warren Ritchie had the most crucial and conclusive evidence right in front of them: everything about his conduct and personality was completely "Jewish." And Birmingham was a town where Jewish people had to go to their own country club.

However, Midge Elmore had always been a direct and untrammeled conduit for the culture in which she lived, and that culture told her that when somebody died, you took over food. Her society was the authority which dictated her life, and she was its most faithful minion, carrying on traditions and ideas long after they'd been discarded by almost everyone else. God love her, thought Norman, with her beauty parlor helmet hair, fluffed and teased and sprayed with rigid regularity three times a week, as if it were indeed a form of protective clothing, or battle gear, she needed in order to face the world. She couldn't have been more different from Susan Ritchie, the California girl with her long straight hair and aviator glasses. It was a credit to both of them, Norman thought, that they had forged such an unlikely alliance.

"I wanted to let you know," she continued, in the bolder voice of a woman who had just been recognized as a miracle of Southern womanhood, "that I told them it came from the school."

"You told them it came from the school?" he asked, momentarily confused. "The food? You said the school sent it?"

"I thought it would mean more to them that way."

"Brilliant," he said. "Absolutely brilliant. What do we owe you?"

"Nothing," she said. "I wanted to do it."

In gratitude, he lowered his voice and adopted the conspiratorial tone Midge herself used when exchanging gossip. "What happened? Did she kill herself?" He leaned over his desk as if Midge were on the other side and he was straining to hear her reply.

"Oh, it's awful, Norman," she said.

He sighed inaudibly and leaned back in his chair, wondering if he would have to pay the full price of a conversation with Midge Elmore. When she devolved into non sequiturs, the outlook for receiving quick, direct information was not promising.

"How's Karen?" he said.

"To pieces," she said. "They both are. I've never seen him in such a state, ever. I didn't even want to go inside—just leave the tray and tell them we were all thinking about them. Norman—" here she lowered her voice to her trademark tone of secrecy. "He pulled me inside the house and would not let me go. *I was the only one there and he would not let me go. He kept me there for three hours.*"

"That's what he gets for being such a jackass," said Norman, biting into his third apple of the day. "Was it an accident, or did she deliberately take too many pills?" The time had come to prod the conversation along.

"He did tell me that she *was* on Valium. But you're not going to believe this—"

He found himself leaning forward over the desk again as she lowered her voice even further. Naturally he had suspected, but had not known for sure what sort of medication Susan Ritchie had been taking in order to live in the same household with Warren.

"He took me into the bathroom, Norman," she said. "Showed me the bottle and counted out all the pills right there on the counter. Said every pill was accounted for according to the prescription and the date it was picked up. He saw her take one pill last night, just like she did every night at bedtime. None are missing from the bottle. He made me look at the label and read the date. Then he insisted I read the date out loud. He was distraught."

"Do you know what I heard?" said Norman, with his mouth full. "When one of his suits wasn't ready at the cleaners, he called them up and threatened to sue. Said he was trying a case the next day and wanted to wear that suit, and if he lost the case they could expect legal action. Can you imagine? Is that true?"

"They wouldn't take Susan's business anymore," said Midge by way of reply. "She had to start using another cleaners."

So it was true. He bit thoughtfully into the apple.

"Warren wasn't even sure she was—gone—until the ambulance came and the paramedics couldn't resuscitate her. The doctor at the hospital said they'd need to do an autopsy to find out what happened."

"Is he going to?"

"Yes."

Norman leaned over and threw the apple core into the overflowing waste basket beside his chair. The interest and usefulness of this conversation were

11

almost over, and he stood up at his desk as if to signal the end. "Can I rely on you to do me a favor, Midge?" he said, as if she were the only one he could trust with an important request.

"What is it?" she said.

"Call over there and tell Karen that she needs to come up to school this afternoon and get her assignments."

Midge was scandalized. "Oh, no, Norman," she said. "Her brothers are flying home today and that child's not in a fit state to go anywhere. I was going to come get her books and whatever the teachers want to send home and take them over to her. She can't leave the house. She's incapacitated."

"Tell her to CAPACITATE then," he snapped, his voice approaching the decibel level he used on the likes of Jimmy Kuhn. "She needs to get out of the house and away from that man. The sooner she gets back into the school routine, the better off she'll be."

"Maybe I could pick her up and bring her," said Midge dubiously.

"You do that then," said Norman sternly, knowing full well that Midge liked nothing better than an unequivocal directive from a respected authority. "Why don't we say three-fifteen. Just after school's out. I'll see you then."

"I'll see what I can do."

"Three-fifteen. I'll expect to see you both in my office." He softened his tone and became the co-conspirator once more. "You'll let me know anything you hear," he said. "Oh—and Midge?" he added. "One more thing."

"What is it?"

"What was on the tray from Brody's?"

* * *

No sooner had he hung up the phone than Tom Turbyfill appeared at his open door, tapping gently to announce his presence. Norman began rifling through the papers on his desk, as if so absorbed in his work that he wasn't aware of his visitor.

"Sorry to disturb you, Norman," said Dr. Turbyfill.

Norman looked up from his desk, as if just noticing the headmaster's arrival. "Come in, come in," he said, with the deliberately false joviality of a much too busy man trying to act cordially nevertheless.

"No need. No need," said Dr. Turbyfill. "But I just wanted to let you know—it has been brought to my attention—that we should do something to show our sympathy for the Ritchie family at this most difficult time."

"Already taken care of," said Norman, trying hard to keep the loathing and contempt from creeping into his voice as the headmaster's words echoed in his ears. It would be hard to say what grated most; the list was long. For one thing, there was the pompous delivery of one cliché after another. Then, the way he skipped a full beat between each word, so he sounded more like a robot than a human being. Worst of all perhaps was his scrupulous avoidance of any linguistic contractions, as if this testified to the learning he had acquired over many years.

He calmed a bit after noticing that Dr. Turbyfill was indeed impressed with Norman's foresight. "Food tray from Brody's," he said in answer to the raised eyebrows. "The works. Delivered this morning." He sat down and began searching in one of his drawers, as if he really did not have time just now to prolong the conversation.

Tom Turbyfill pursed his lips. "We will have to look and see just how much we have budgeted for expenditures of this nature."

We? thought Norman Laney. Would that mean Dr. Turbyfill and Mrs. Hessler, the accountant? Dr. Turbyfill and Norman Laney? Or was that a more royal we?

"Didn't cost the school a dime," Norman shot back, briefly meeting Tom Turbyfill's eyes before resuming the search of his drawer. "I got Midge Elmore to donate the tray on behalf of the school."

"Excellent. Excellent," said Dr. Turbyfill, his round full moon of a face expanding even further as he beamed his head-of-school smile. "I can see that you are way ahead of me. I will count on you to write the appropriate notes to the Elmore and the Ritchie families. Thank you, Norman."

Yes, I'm way ahead of you, thought Norman, all but slamming the desk drawer in disgust as Tom Turbyfill walked back down the hall.

Just then he happened to remember that Elizabeth Elder's husband had been a suicide many years ago. It had happened long ago, before he knew her, and she never spoke of it to him, so he had no idea how much pain the memory could still cause her. One thing he was sure of, however: Elizabeth was not the block of stone she could make herself appear to be. She was simply a woman of decorum and discipline and above all, professionalism, who did not allow her private self to infiltrate the performance of her professional duties. In other words, she was the opposite of himself, and he did not know how he could get along without her.

* * *

That evening when he got home, Norman was greeted by the strong smell of his favorite meal—a leg of lamb—which was too expensive and too much trouble to be served except on special occasions. Dropping his bulging briefcase down in the hall with a sigh, he said, "Thank you, Mother."

"I heard the news," she replied in her familiar rasp. "When I got off the phone with Phyllis, I called the Pig and put in my order. Phyllis took me down there after lunch. I knew you'd need a boost." She exhaled a large cloud of smoke from her twenty-third cigarette of the day.

Sitting there in her established place on the sofa in their tiny living room, she looked the exact opposite of both the willowy silhouette associated with her Virginia Slims cigarettes and the pen and ink Picasso nude hanging on the wall above her head that had been left to him in Bella Whitmire's will. What the seventy year-old Norma Laney most resembled was in fact a toad. Her short, squat body sprouted incongruously thin arms and legs, and her head seemed to peer out just above her collar bone, her neck having disappeared some years ago, along with her girdle, which could no longer contain Norma's expanding contours. A large fleshy mole on her left cheekbone and the customary croak of her voice completed the effect.

She was the person most dear to Norman Laney in all the world. From earliest childhood, his monstrous obesity had set him apart, not only from other children, but from all other human beings, including his own father, as if he were not exactly a member of the human race. He had grown up with the instinctive knowledge that he would never be able to live what is called a normal life. By the time he was an adult, he had long understood that he would never get married, never have children, and never have a family other than the one he was born into. But if even a fraction of the gossip he heard on a daily basis could be believed, his domestic situation was far better than that of most married couples in Mountain Brook. He gave his mother the full credit for that, and considered it a privilege to share a home with her.

In honor of the meal she had prepared, they opted to have dinner in the miniscule dining room wedged between the kitchen and the living room. Calling it a room was going a bit far, as it was really more an alcove of neutral space buffering the two larger rooms on either side, but it just did allow for a small table and four chairs. It was only when this furniture was put in place that Norman and his mother had realized how completely it obstructed the passage between kitchen and living room, especially for people of their size. They now had to use the hallway when going from one of those rooms to the other: an aggravating but necessary inconvenience for those who wished to live like civilized human beings.

To Norman Laney, there were only two types of people in the world, and these types had nothing to do with race, social class, ethnic origin, financial position or even formal education. In his classification system, you were either a civilized person or you were a barbarian. Of course, the particular

14

Southern society in which he now made his home was filled with barbarians who considered themselves civilized people. But this was infinitely preferable to the Southern society he came from, which was filled with barbarians who didn't even try to act like civilized people.

The elite, all-white enclave of Birmingham where Norman lived was populated by wealthy, well-educated citizens who lived their lives according to certain standards of sophistication. They shopped at Saks in Atlanta and Neiman-Marcus in Dallas. But despite the advantages of living in their little pocket of privilege, "the Tiny Kingdom" of Mountain Brook, far too many of them shared the same backwards mentality and values as the rest of their underprivileged state. While they would never use redneck or white trash language like the "n" word, many still regarded black people as either niggers or freed slaves who were lucky to get paid what they did. When Martin Luther King, Jr., had written his "Letter from the Birmingham Jail" twenty years ago, they had been mixing martinis up on their mountain, just like they always had, just like they always would. They appeared not to notice the Civil Rights Movement. It was just something that happened downtown, a place where they didn't live. However, it was probably too much to hope for, that they would be affected by the Civil Rights Movement when they were living in a place designed to look like it hadn't even been affected by the Civil War: a lush Garden of Eden modeled on the image of the Old South, where every house was a mansion, every woman was a belle, and every darkie was happy to work there as a maid, a yardman or a waiter at the country club. The refinement of this genteel world of Southern ladies and gentlemen was strictly cosmetic; underneath was all the ugliness of the unenlightened ideas and beliefs from the dark ages of Southern history. As far as Norman Laney was concerned, discrimination based on race, religion, gender, and all the rest was uncivilized behavior. Unfortunately, Mountain Brook was devoted wholeheartedly to perpetuating all these forms of discrimination, because without them, their country clubs and debutante societies would have been meaningless.

Norman figured his job, as an outsider who had gained extraordinary entrée into this exclusive world, was to introduce true civilization in place of its thin veneer. Lots of people thought he was just a social climber. Lots more hated him personally, resented his intrusion, were disgusted by his appearance and looked forward to the day he would die of the heart attack they all predicted. But just as many loved him and welcomed him, even if they didn't always know what he was up to. At any rate, he got invited to all sorts of wonderful parties and received piles of Christmas presents. And as a lover of life on a scale as grand as his own girth, he found that he tended to love most people in that life, especially if they dressed well and served good food at their parties, which, in Mountain Brook, they invariably did. Nevertheless, he had a higher calling. If he had been asked to define his own personal mission in life, he would have said he was trying in his own small way—or rather, in his own large way [laughter]—to lead a charge against the ranks of barbarians who dominated and controlled his world. He conducted this campaign as a crusader for Art and Culture, which were the most powerful forces in the war against barbarians.

Who are the barbarians? he was often asked, and to avoid antagonizing his enemies even further, one definition he frequently provided applied mainly to residents of New York City. Barbarians were easily identifiable by any number of criteria, he would say, one of which was: if you didn't have a dining area in your home, you were a barbarian, or at least, you were living like one. He had even used this example in the classroom last spring, when teaching the stanzas about the typist and the house agent's clerk eating food out of tins in "The Waste Land."

"Instead of preparing a meal, they're just opening cans of food!" he had proclaimed, pounding the desk with his fist. "Rather than creating an evening ritual of beauty and grace, they're just gobbling down the groceries!" He had pronounced it "gro-ce-ries," with equal accent on all syllables. "There is no spiritual or emotional exchange of any kind! It's just an animal act-i-vi-ty, followed by further animal act-i-vi-ty, all on the same sofa! If televisions had been invented by the time T.S. Eliot wrote his poem, they would have been watching TV while they ate their dinner!" Confident that at least half the members of his classroom had dinner in front of the television, he had made it sound like the ultimate act of barbarity. Of course—although Norman and his mother would never eat food that came out of a can—they usually ate their own dinner on TV trays while watching their favorite programs in the den. But tonight's meal deserved a place on the dining room table, along with one of those particular bottles of wine he had been saving for Christmas time.

"Honestly, Mother," he said, chewing thoughtfully over her question about Karen's state of mind. "She looked more frightened than anything." The image of Karen's face as it had appeared that afternoon in his office rose before him. The delicate white skin was even more pale than usual, and the fine network of blue veins at the temples seemed to throb as if in fear of imminent attack. She had uttered hardly one syllable, which was unfortunately typical of her, and her big brown eyes were glassy with terror. Norman was used to seeing terrified students and even junior faculty quake before him in mortal dread. The magnitude of his body combined with the thunderous roar of his wrath could strike terror into God himself. But Karen had no reason to fear his fury. She was that student who was so quiet and self-contained you forgot she was there until you graded the papers and realized she'd scored highest on the exam or written the best essay in the class. But this was in itself a different kind of problem. Usually with students of her intellect, he was able to form a deep bond that went far beyond the normal relationship of teacher and student or even protégé and mentor. He became almost a surrogate parent who helped these special pupils navigate the shoals of adolescence, explore their intelligence, contemplate their futures and finally hurl themselves into their independent lives with all the force of his weight and good wishes behind them. But not so with Karen. He had never even been able to strike up a real conversation with her, let alone a meaningful connection. Much as he tried, she had never become one of his darlings; she remained only a diligent and dutiful student with him, and he had never succeeded in reaching the individual within.

What had happened that afternoon in his office was only one example of his overall failure to communicate or connect with her. Asking Midge Elmore if she would collect Karen's schoolwork from the front office, he had then turned around and told Karen he didn't give a damn when she handed in that work or how many days off she had to take from school. That wasn't the real reason he'd called her up to the campus. What he really wanted was to see how she was doing and give her a chance to talk to somebody if she needed to. In reply, she said nothing for so long he was beginning to think she was never going to open her mouth the whole time she was there. When she did respond, it was clear she hadn't understood him at all. She seemed to think he was angry that she'd missed a day of school and might have to miss one more, for her mother's funeral. He had merely sighed, and she continued to stare at him as if in abject terror.

Norma's eyes narrowed exactly as her son's did when possessed by some fury of either emotion or thought. "He doesn't beat those children, does he, Norman?"

"Oh, no, Mother," he was quick to reply. "He's not that kind of barbarian. Sometimes I wish he was, though."

"Norman, you don't mean that."

He ate for some moments in contented silence, sopping up the rich gravy with one of the Sister Schubert's dinner rolls and complimenting his mother on the mint sauce which she made herself from the fresh mint leaves he grew out back on his little postage stamp of a patio.

"What I mean is: I'd know exactly what to do, and I can assure you, I would not hesitate to do it." Spearing a bite of potato, carrot and lamb, he continued to speak with his mouth full. "You know I've had to do it before, and I would not hesitate for one second to do it again, just because this is Mountain Brook."

His mother nodded, remembering quite well the incident of child abuse in her son's first year of teaching at the public high school in Pratt City, the blue collar enclave just west of Birmingham where she had spent her married life and raised her two children.

As Norman continued to enjoy his leg of lamb, even picking it up to get with his teeth those tender morsels that liked to cling to the bone, he contemplated the problem of a different kind of abuse, which left no telltale bruises or broken bones, but had a child apologizing for missing school on the day of her mother's death and shaking in her shoes when someone who would be her friend tried to offer sympathy and comfort. He had no idea how to combat this kind of abuse any more than he knew what had made her father such a barbarian in the first place.

"Well, he *is* Jewish, you know," was the Birmingham explanation, but besides the fact that Warren wasn't Jewish, his parents had been kind and gentle people whose primary failing appeared to be their liberal social conscience, which had brought them to Birmingham in the first place. Apparently they were a childless couple in their forties when Warren came along unexpectedly and miraculously, years after they had ceased to hope for children. Of course they had doted on their only child, and obviously had spoiled him with their worshipful attention to his every need and desire. That was Norman's explanation.

"He's not Jewish," he had said to somebody on the phone that afternoon. He couldn't remember who—so many people had called him to gossip about Susan's death that day. "He's not Jewish; he's a narcissist." "Oh," Grace had replied vaguely. Had to be Grace. "I didn't know we had any of those in this town."

Well, Norman had thought grimly to himself, we have at least one in this town: he was fairly certain that was Warren's particular form of barbarity. Warren now wanted the undivided attention and admiration of the world, which simply wasn't to be had in Birmingham, despite his many accomplishments. However polite people might be to him in their Southern way, they would not ask him to their parties or invite him to join their country club. But Warren would never stop trying to ascend to those heights, and everything was put in service to this grand ambition, including his wife and

18

children. Of course he got it all wrong. For example, no one cared that his children went to Ivy League schools. Even if his daughter went to the best college in the country, she would never be one of Birmingham's debutantes. And it wasn't what college your children went to; it was the sorority or fraternity they pledged at Bama. Yet Warren's ego made him a fool despite his supposedly high IQ. He believed that a forceful demonstration of his own supcriority—reflected of course by his wife and children—was all he needed to endear himself to those who were so clearly his inferiors in intelligence, education and professional achievement. His failure to penetrate the inner sanctums of Mountain Brook society only made him try harder in all the wrong ways to gain friendship with people who had nothing to offer him except admittance into their exclusive social world, which was committed to nothing so much as to keeping people like him out of it.

"Can I get you some more?" said his mother.

Norman shook his head.

"Do you think you could ask Midge to step in and look after Karen this year?" she asked.

Interesting idea. Midge would do it, if he asked. But it gave him another idea. A better one.

"No, Mother," he said, laying down knife and fork with sudden determination. "I think *I'm* going to step in."

Shaking her head, Norma pushed up from her chair and began clearing the table. "I don't know what you're thinking," she said, "but I hope it doesn't put us back in Pratt City."

This was her favorite and most effective way of warning her son against the excesses to which he was prone. Their hometown of Pratt City was located near what had once been the state's largest coal seam, and the town had begun as a mining community which supplied that coal to the steel mills in the post-Civil War industrial city of Birmingham. Norman's great-grandfather and grandfather had both worked in one of the mines. His father had worked in the nearby blast furnace, where he'd been killed in a deadly explosion. Norma's dearest dream for her bookish and freakishly fat son was for him to somehow obtain a college education that would be the only thing capable of catapulting him into a world more suited to appreciate his special gifts of mind, soul and even body. Not only had he been granted that college degree, he had also been granted unheard-of welcome into the aristocratic world of Mountain Brook and its most distinguished and select private school. It behooved him to be content with that, because there were plenty of people who thought he had no business being in Mountain Brook in the first place, certainly not at dinner parties or the country club. But he constantly pushed for more, more, more. It had ever been his way.

Naturally it took a lot to put the brakes on the world's largest Puck when he was determined to make mischief, but whenever Norma felt the need to apply those brakes she said, "I'll be waiting for you in Pratt City when they finish kicking you out of here." This was a prospect guaranteed to get him to think twice before committing his next act of folly or derring-do. Norma's vexation with her son's foolhardy bravado was matched only by her boundless love for his valiant heart and princely soul, which galloped full speed ahead in its ridiculously fat beast of burden, while tilting at every windmill and leaving the world a better place than he found it. She lived in constant dread that he was headed for a fall.

OCTOBER

~ 2 ~

When Mr. and Mrs. Vernon arrived on campus for their mandatory meeting with the guidance counselor, they thought at first they might have come to the wrong place. Although their daughter had been a student at the school for the past four years, they had only been on the campus themselves once before. It was too far away from where they lived and worked in Ensley, and any visits to the school would have required substantial time they couldn't afford to take away from their jobs. If Mrs. Vernon's sister had not been able to drive their daughter to school and pick her back up every day, she would never have been able to accept the full scholarship she'd been offered. The memory of their sole visit from four years ago was too dim to counter the strange spectacle that confronted them when they tried to head up the drive where the sign had indicated the school buildings were located. Orange traffic cones blocked their path and all they could see ahead were a series of paint cans and a group of surprisingly young workers in overalls—female as well as male—bending over with brushes as if painting the road.

Mr. Vernon was in the process of telling his wife that they must have taken the wrong turn by the sign, when one of the young workers came up to the car and directed them toward a gravel parking lot. Smudges of orange paint, the same color as the traffic cones, were on her nose, ears, and all over her fingertips. These were not workers but students, the Vernons learned as they walked toward the main building. And they weren't painting the road; they were painting on large white canvases.

"This is for our 'Art in the 20th Century' class," explained the paint-smudged student who was escorting them. "Somebody made the mistake of telling our teacher that anybody could paint like Jackson Pollock, and he challenged us to try. So here we are."

The Vernons nodded as if they knew who Jackson Pollock was and understood this unorthodox assignment perfectly well. They didn't trust themselves to enter into a conversation, however, and were relieved when they came in view of their daughter waiting for them beyond the double glass doors of the school's entrance. With her in the foyer was the fattest man—white or black —they had ever seen in their lives. Next to her was what looked like a large piece of scrap metal, from which smaller pieces dangled dangerously close to their daughter's face. It was all the Vernons could do not to look at each other in dismay and distress. Students in overalls painting in the street? A man so fat he could be a freak in the circus? Junkyard debris parked in the entrance? What was this school they had allowed Mira to attend for four years? Had they somehow been led astray? They'd been told it was the finest private school in the state of Alabama, but it wouldn't be the first time white folks had deceived unsuspecting black people.

Although Mira had told them Mr. Laney was fat, it was hard to believe that this human monstrosity was actually the well-respected assistant head-master and guidance counselor they had heard about. He had insisted on this meeting with the Vernons, although the family had already decided that Mira could go to the University of Alabama on the National Merit Scholarship she'd been offered after her junior year. Tuscaloosa was not so very far from Ensley; she could take the bus home every weekend; it was only four years; and if Mira's teachers thought she needed to go, her parents had agreed not to stand in her way or ruin her "chances," although they had no idea what her "chances" were, and nobody in their family had ever been to college or gone so far away from home.

When they arrived at the entrance, Mr. Laney was pacing the floor impa-tiently, scanning the walkway for signs of the Vernons as well as his students' progress on their Pollock projects. He didn't dare go outside the building to in-spect their canvases more closely, because it was a hot day in October and he'd sweat through his undershirt in less than a minute. He did not want to be drip-ping like a melting snowman during his conference with the Vernons, who— unlike most of the other parents—knew him not at all. He never would have made this assignment in October if he hadn't needed to arrange something for his students to do while he met with the Vernons during his "Art in the 20th Century" class period. Next year, he thought, if the assignment proved successful, he would build it into the syllabus and schedule it for December, when the weather was cool enough and he was actually teaching Abstract Ex-pressionism instead of Cubism. Two days ago, a student's throwaway remark had inspired the idea just after he'd received word from the office that the Vernons could only meet with him at 11:00 on Wednesday.

He was chagrined to see that the student who had landed the task of intercepting the Vernons and leading them to the office was not one of his best and brightest, but one of the slut circle. The overalls he had stipulated for today's project were the tightest she could find, and conformed so closely to the contours of her crotch that the "W" outlined between her legs looked painful rather than desirable. Clearly she was catering to her target audience of adolescent boys, who were not equipped to be deterred by such subtleties any more than they could be turned off by what struck him as outright so-licitation. The girl could not have promoted her female parts more blatantly if the crotch on her overalls had a sign with an arrow saying "Enter Here." Why she was even taking this class was a mystery to him, unless the word had trickled down that he'd designed the course as an easy elective for his star seniors who deserved a break because of all the essays they were writing for their college applications. Lori Wagner would not be writing any such essays, and it would be all he could do to get her to fill out the form for UAB just so he could uphold the school's catalog copy: "100% of our graduating students apply to college; 100% receive acceptances." Whether she actually attended or not, he wouldn't have to know or care. By then she'd be a graduate, and she would be the one who had to live with her statistics.

As he hastened to open the door for the Vernons, his eyes couldn't help but be drawn to that part of Lori Wagner's anatomy she so explicitly empha-sized, but he managed to refrain from wincing and broke into a big smile of welcome for two people he'd never seen before in his life. Although he had arranged their daughter's scholarship, he'd been in Europe the summer they had come to discuss the details, and Elizabeth Elder had been the one to meet with them. Elizabeth had described them as "lovely people," and no doubt they were. But in the eyes of Birmingham, they would appear to be a janitor and a maid. Lee Vernon was wearing his uniform from the auto repair shop where he worked in Ensley, and his wife was wearing a floral smock over white polyester pants like any maid in Mountain Brook, though in fact, she was a nurse's aide at the VA hospital. With a curt nod to Lori for her trouble, he put an arm around each of the Vernons and led them quickly to his office before some idiot like Tom Turbyfill read the name label on Lee Vernon's uniform and asked "Vernon" if he were here about the toilet overflowing in the boys' bathroom.

Once all were seated in his office, he felt his disadvantage immediately. The Vernons were clearly as taciturn as their daughter had proved to be, and were obviously disconcerted by the Matisse Blue Nude poster from the

MoMA exhibit hanging on the wall behind his desk. Since he had never taught Mira in even one course during her four years at the school, he hardly knew her at all. With other students who had steered clear of his classes for one reason or another, he had often been able to manage an acquaintance just through chance encounters in the hallway. Intimacy came easily at a small school like theirs. But Mira was so shy, quiet and polite as to be utterly self-effacing. She made herself invisible, and he literally never saw her in the hallways. After four years, he was convinced this was her natural personality and not simply some protective pose she'd adopted to survive amongst the affluent white student population at the Brook-Haven School. In fact, her skin was almost as white as everyone else's, which had caused him a good deal of disappointment when he first laid eyes on her. "Some luck," he had said to Elizabeth Elder, "that our first black student is not even all that black." In the pictures for the school catalog, it was impossible to tell that hers was actually the face of a black person. And he wanted his (white) students as well as their parents, who usually never encountered a black person except for a maid, a yardman or a waiter at the country club, to be fully aware that they were dealing with a BLACK person on terms of equality. Although schools in the South had been integrated twenty years ago, the public school system in Mountain Brook had no black students because Mountain Brook had no black residents. So Mountain Brook, which was incorporated as a city for exactly this kind of reason, had been able to ignore racial integration just like it ignored anything else it wanted to ignore about the larger city of Birmingham and even the larger world outside Birmingham. With the Brook-Haven School, Norman Laney figured he had his golden opportunity to bring black students into a lily-white institution in a lily-white suburb. Except for the fact that Mira Vernon didn't look very black, he'd had no cause to regret taking the advice of his former colleague from Pratt City, now an administrator in the Ensley system, who had proposed Mira Vernon as an ideal recipient of the minority scholarship he had worked so hard to establish.

The teachers who did have her in their classes had always spoken highly of her. Gayle Naughton in particular was most fond of Mira, probably because she had the same virtues as Gayle herself: she was studious, industrious and impeccable in her work. If Mira had ever been his student, it would have been his business to tap into the rest of her. As he saw it, this was his main job as a teacher. But Mira had either avoided or escaped him, and he was temporarily at a loss as to how to reach her at this most crucial juncture. The stone faces of her parents gave him little to work with there as well.

Norman Laney was never at a loss for long. If there was one thing he knew how to do, it was put on a show, and impromptu performances were his specialty. Pushing back suddenly from his desk, he stood up and broke into his broadest grin. When he smiled in this way, his face became filled with teeth, punctuated at either end by a large, rosy ball of flesh. It was a clown's happy face, and it usually had the power to dispel any oppression and charge the atmosphere with the exuberance of his outlandish personality.

"Well," he declared through his smile. "This is a happy day. A happy day indeed!" Looking now at the floor, he began pacing rapidly back and forth behind his chair. "When a black girl from the most segregated city in one of the most segregated states in the most segregated part of a country cursed with the original sin of slavery can graduate alongside fellow students from the whitest and wealthiest suburb of the most segregated city in a segregated state, we have come a long way indeed!" He paused in his pacing to face his audience, who looked more alarmed than impressed. Grabbing the back of his chair, he leaned over it and proclaimed, "This is a day such as Martin Luther King dreamed of!" He assumed they had heard of the Reverend Dr. Martin Luther King, Jr., who had graced the city of Birmingham with his presence on more than one occasion; but if they had any knowledge of that great man and his achievements, they gave no sign of it. Mr. and Mrs. Vernon even shrank back a bit in their chairs, as if in further alarm.

It wasn't working. Perhaps he was just too fat for them. He sat back down.

"With her grades, Mira can go anywhere in the country she wants to go to college," he said simply. "Where shall we send her?"

Mr. and Mrs. Vernon exchanged glances with one another while Mira looked down at her lap. Tentatively, Mr. Vernon said that Mira would be able to attend the University of Alabama if the scholarship was as good as its word.

"Oh," said Norman, waving his hand as if he could literally dismiss the idea. "Mira can do much better than that. This girl is headed for the Ivy League. That's where she belongs."

Confusion as well as apprehension spread across the Vernons' faces before they became more impassive than ever. He was failing to reach them, and they were shutting down. He sighed. It was his fault. This was his job and he had failed to do it. He should have been working on Mira long before this. As soon as it had become clear that she was a stellar student, he should have sought her out, buttonholed her in the hallway, called her into his office, and filled her ears with the Ivy League. The reason he hadn't was because she was—well—BLACK. He had been so afraid of making a mistake that he'd done

27

nothing except hope everything would fall magically into place when the time came. Well, the time had come, and nothing was falling magically into place. His failure would be huge: this girl and her parents seemed to possess not the faintest inkling of the future that could be hers.

In other words, they were innocents. Norman had always been more appalled by the innocents of the world than by the schemers who milked the system for whatever they wanted. Of course, the schemers often got more than they deserved, but the innocents often got nothing. And there *was* a viable third way, which was to know as much as you could about the system and work it as judiciously as possible. Judicious use could be achieved through two simple rules. Number One: you did no harm. (This was, in fact, his golden rule in life, and a much more feasible one than Love Thy Neighbor. Also, if it was good enough for the neurosurgeons, then it was good enough for him.) Second: take only what you really needed and most wanted. In today's world, greed was punished more often than pride.

"Let's see what Mira thinks," he said, looking pointedly at her. "Mira, where do your ambitions tell you to go?"

She shook her head briefly in embarrassment, as if that would suffice for reply. Refusing to let her off the hook, he stared more pointedly at her until she was forced to speak.

"I've never thought of applying to a place like Harvard," she said, in the soft-spoken voice of an almost ethereal being.

"Why not?"

She looked helplessly at her parents for a brief moment before turning back to him.

"Why not?" he persisted.

"It never crossed my mind that I'd ever be accepted."

"I'm the guidance counselor here!" he barked. "It's my job to know whether or not you could get in, and I'm telling you that all you have to do is fill out the application and pack your bags. You're in."

This prospect obviously gave her no pleasure, and her parents looked like their daughter had just received a terminal diagnosis.

"Wouldn't you like to go to Harvard?" he asked, softening his tone.

She looked at her parents.

"What's the matter?" he said, his voice sharpening. "Well?" (The bullying approach might work better in the given situation. But if all else failed, he could insist they have a second appointment at a later date with Elizabeth Elder. She had a quiet, steady force in complete contrast to his flamboyant one, but it penetrated just as deeply and might be much more effective with the Vernons.)

"I doubt my parents could afford it," she said, so quietly he could barely hear her.

"They have full scholarships up there just waiting on somebody like you to grab them. They'll have work-study to provide for your books, your plane fare, living expenses. They'll take better care of you than the University of Alabama, believe me. How can you walk away from an opportunity like this? What's there to be afraid of?"

She looked again at her parents.

"I'm not asking your parents," he said. "I'm asking you. Tell me. What's there to be afraid of?"

"I'm not sure I'd do very well—"

"Nonsense!" he thundered, causing them all to jump slightly in their seats. "The hardest part about Harvard is getting into the place! Once you've done that, then you're a Harvard student! And Harvard students, by definition, do not fail! Harvard sees to that."

It was clear she didn't believe him, though she said nothing.

"We've got some of our students there now," he continued. "One's a Phi Beta Kappa. (The other he didn't mention.) Some of your classmates right now will most probably be going there next year. They'll do very well and so would you. This school you're about to graduate from can take its place among the finest prepare-a-tory schools in the country. You couldn't be better prepared."

When she glanced at her parents yet again, it occurred to him that his best shot at Mira might be to get them out of the room. "Excuse me a moment," he said, rising abruptly out of his chair. As he moved swiftly toward the door, his massive poundage undulated in waves that threatened to engulf the Vernons. He didn't care if he crowded them or even brushed up against them slightly as he passed by. In fact, he wanted the Vernons to get a close look at every bit of the weight he would bring to bear on this situation.

When he opened the door, the hum from the library ceased instantly, as it always did. Surveying the room, he spied one of the sophomores he was bringing along and beckoned for her to come in the office. Although her friends looked worried, she knew she was about to be honored, not bawled out for chatting instead of doing her homework. Sure enough, Mr. Laney asked her to take Mr. and Mrs. Vernon to the Orange Bowl and give them a tour of the gallery's latest exhibit. She was happy to comply and get out of study hall, while the Vernons seemed very glad to get out of the assistant headmaster's office.

"Now," said Mr. Laney, settling back down in his chair and facing Mira alone. "I want to know the real reason you hesitate to apply to any Ivy League schools. Is there something you couldn't discuss in front of your parents?"

She shook her head and looked down at her lap.

"Speak up!" he said sharply.

"No, sir," she said, in the cowed voice of a black defendant before a white judge.

Trying to forestall the verbal explosion he could feel rising within him, he rose along with it and began pacing the room, as if venting his frustration through steps rather than words. His anger was literally visible in the quivering flesh which accompanied his agitated movement. If there was one thing he hated (actually there were hundreds), it was timidity. And he abhorred meekness, especially when, as in the case of Mira, there was every reason for honest pride. If the school had not taught her that much then it might as well have taught her nothing. A bitter sense of failure surged through him like the gastric acid from his utterly empty stomach. (It was almost lunch time and hours since his last bite of food, as he allowed himself no snacks whatsoever during these conferences with parents.) He forced himself to sit back down and pretend to be calm.

"Why would you think you couldn't get into an Ivy League school? Your grades are among the best in the class. You stand an excellent chance of being this year's valedictorian."

"But my SAT scores," she said, looking down again at the hands twisting nervously in her lap.

"Look at me when you're talking!" he commanded. "Look at me like the young woman of intelligence and dignity that you are! I forbid you to sit there cowering like some ignorant, terrified field hand brought before the plantation master! Look me in the eye, and do it like you mean it!"

He made his gaze as steely as possible and waited until she met it, but with nowhere near the force he would have liked to see. (It was a real shame, he thought, that he had never had her in a class before. What he would have taught her had nothing to do with book learning, and was far more valuable, far more necessary. If he could, he would see about putting her in his senior English class next spring, instead of Gayle's AP. Gayle would holler, but she'd get over it.)

"Now what did you say?"

"My SAT scores."

"What about them? Speak to me in complete sentences!"

"My SAT scores are not good enough." Her voice was so low he could hardly hear it.

He sighed with exasperation, not just with her but with the limited amount of time indicated by the clock on the wall. "Your SAT scores don't matter," he said bluntly.

She said nothing, but at least she continued to hold his gaze, her eyes widened with surprise.

"You don't believe me?" he continued. "Just trust me. SAT scores are the last thing any Ivy League school is going to care about as far as you're concerned."

It was clear she neither believed him nor understood him, and was still (dammit) too terrified to communicate with him. Glancing at the clock, which showed he had about three minutes left before the bell would ring, he leaned across the desk. "Mira, tell me this," he said, waiting until her eyes locked with his. "What's the color of your skin?"

She didn't seem to know whether it was a joke or a trick, and said nothing. It failed to cross her mind that he was completely serious.

"What's the color of your skin?" he repeated, leaning back now.

Still she didn't answer, although her eyes remained locked with his.

"Let me put this as clearly as I can," he said, leaning intently across the desk once more. "With your grades and your skin color, you can get into any Ivy League school in this country. I dare you to prove me wrong."

"You think they'll accept me just because I'm black?" she said, shocked into speaking without hesitation.

"NOT JUST BECAUSE YOU'RE BLACK!" he exploded. "Have you heard a word I said? You've got straight A's! You will have glowing recommendations from all of your teachers at the best college prepare-a-tory school in the state of Alabama! And you're a black woman! The Ivy League schools will be knocking each other over to get to you!"

It was hard to interpret the look she had on her face, but she appeared taken aback—at what, he wasn't sure.

"What's wrong?" he said. "Are you ashamed of being black?"

She shook her head.

"Then don't be ashamed to use it!"

The ringing of the bell provided an emphatic punctuation, but he sat there as if he hadn't heard it, as if she better pretend she hadn't heard it either.

"All any of us can do," he said more gently, "is to use whatever we've got."

Still she was silent. He decided to try another tack, and also allow himself a small snack since it was technically lunch period and it wouldn't be long before his stomach began to sound like a volcano.

31

"Have you ever read *Their Eyes Were Watching God?*" he said, unwrapping a Baby Ruth bar and gazing at it fondly while Mira shook her head. "Baby Ruth, meet Norman Laney!" he declared before biting off one third of the chocolate bar. He wasn't sure, but he believed the tiniest of giggles might have erupted from her mouth. The hope that flared through him tasted as good as the Baby Ruth.

"We're reading that novel this spring in my senior English class," he continued, although up until that moment, he had not planned on that book in his syllabus. "I want you in that class this spring." He searched her eyes and she nodded obediently. "Zora Neale Hurston," he repeated, shoving another third of the Baby Ruth into his mouth as chocolate particles rained down on his desk. "Black writer. Female." With one more bite, the candy bar was gone, and he swept the crumbs off his desk with a magisterial flourish.

"There's a passage in there I want you to read before next spring. While you're applying to colleges. You'll know it when you get to it: two black women talking. One explains to the other how the black woman is *the mule of the world.*" He waited for this to register, and leaned across the desk with more intensity than ever.

"Elmira Vernon, let me tell you this: for the first time in the history of civilization, the black woman is no longer the mule of the world. The tables have turned, and the black woman has a chance to go straight to the top. How dare you betray centuries of slavery and servitude by your forebears and fail to seize the moment black women have been working for since the beginning of time?" He stood up as if transported by the rising tide of his own eloquence. Her eyes followed him obediently. He was getting to her, he thought. He was nearing a breakthrough.

"This is your moment," he pleaded with her. "The black woman is having her day. Take it! Run with it! As far as you can go. It won't always be this way. It won't always be your moment. The world will move on to something else, and I want you to have your Ivy League degree before it does. Do you understand me?"

She nodded. He unwrapped another Baby Ruth and bit into it.

"Let me just state the obvious, and then I have to go get some lunch or the headlines in tomorrow's paper will show that an honor student was killed in a freak accident when she was crushed to death after her English teacher keeled over from malnutrition."

She couldn't stop herself from laughing outright. He knew he had her then, and took a moment to savor his achievement along with his chocolate bar. (It was not going to be necessary, after all, to bring in Elizabeth Elder.) Throwing away the wrapper, he stood before her.

"The only cards we can play are the ones we are dealt. You happen to be holding an ace in your hand, and there's nothing wrong with playing it. You follow me?"

Again she nodded.

"I know exactly what I'm talking about, because I've done it all my life. Look at me and tell me what you see," he said, thrusting his gargantuan stomach even closer to her face. "Go on. Tell me."

A blush spread slowly across her pale coffee colored skin.

"You see fat," he said cheerfully. "You see the fattest human being you will ever see in your whole life."

As she smiled he bent over to bore into her eyes. "My fat could have stopped me," he said. "And it *has* prevented me from doing many things I would have liked to do. Early in life, I had to give up all ambition of ever entering the pole-vaulting championships." (This was one of his favorite and most effective lines, which he assumed she'd never heard before since she'd never been in his class.) "But in return, I have learned how to use my fat." He rotated his hips like an elephant doing a hula dance, and his colossal hulk rolled back and forth in comical crosscurrents. He was rewarded with her helpless laughter. "To the best of my ability, I have taken advantage of my fat in every possible way and done everything I can to make my fat work for me." He continued to gyrate so his churning fat did indeed look like it was working. "Who would blame me? Are we understood?"

She nodded, trying to stifle further laughter.

"So," he concluded. "This is the plan. Are you listening?"

She nodded.

"Good. You are going to apply to at least one of the Big Three. If you're doing this for yourself, pick whichever one you want. If you're doing this for me, then apply to Harvard. In six weeks time, I want you in my office with the completed application, and we'll go over it. Agreed?"

Instead of nodding for the final time, a shadow of doubt clouded her face.

"What is it?" He glanced impatiently at the clock. It really was lunch time.

She hesitated.

"Out with it. I'm here to help. What is it?"

"I'm not sure my parents have the money—"

"I've already told you we'll get you a scholarship!"

"No," she said in her soft voice. "I mean for the application."

"If that's all," he said, lumbering back to his desk. "I can solve that right now." Retrieving his wallet from a locked drawer, he plucked out two tens and a five. "Here," he said, the bills fluttering in his hand across the desk. "Take it," he ordered, staring at her until she reluctantly did so. "Now let's get out of here before your parents begin to wonder if I'm attempting sexual congress!"

He hoped Mrs. Hessler was eating lunch in her office, because he needed to get that $25 back from the discretionary fund before he left school in the afternoon. And with her tiresome rules about receipts and invoices, he needed to start working on her right away.

* * *

Norman did not intend to slight Warren Ritchie when he sallied forth from his office, grinning hugely in triumph, with one arm around Mira, his latest convert, the other poised to shake hands with the Vernons, who were waiting just outside his office. Much as he despised the man, he wanted their conference to go smoothly, for his own sake as well as Karen's. But Warren's appointment wasn't until one, and Norman had no reason to expect to find him waiting along with the Vernons at twelve-fifteen, and in fact failed to notice him until he bounded eagerly forth to shake the hand Norman was extending to Lee Vernon. He couldn't help but put the man in his place. It would have been nothing less than a cosmic insult to the Vernons if he had failed to do so.

"Excuse me," he said to Warren's outstretched arm. "I was just saying good-bye to Mr. and Mrs. Vernon." The grin frozen on his face, he shook hands vigorously with both of them, while his eyes darted from them to their daughter without once straying in the direction of Warren. But it was primarily for Warren's benefit that he added to Mr. Vernon: "Mira is going to be one of our Ivy League applicants this year. Harvard, I think. I'll see you out." Still he did not greet Warren Ritchie, but nodded at the sophomore who had been chaperoning Mira's parents. She could go to lunch now.

He could almost hear the unrequited self-importance seeping dangerously out of Warren Ritchie's bristling body. That everyone would now suffer from the release of this toxic gas was not Norman Laney's fault, and he refused to take responsibility for the consequences. Instead, he found himself wondering, as always with Warren: "Who the hell does he think he is?" Had the man literally not seen the Vernons standing there? Or had he assumed that they were part of the custodial service and couldn't possibly be parents like himself with a daughter applying to college? Whatever the case, their patient humility was no match for Warren's impatient egotism, and Norman had no regrets about his handling of the situation. The nerve. He could sense the consternation in the man's footsteps as he hurried after them down the hall.

"I thought we could get a head start," he was saying to Norman's retreating back. "I've got clients coming—"

"I'll see you at one," snapped Norman, whipping his head around to address Warren for the first time. Then with icy, letter perfect politeness, he said, "Feel free to wait in my office, or take a tour of the Orange Bowl Gallery downstairs, if you like. We've got a new exhibit."

Couldn't be helped, Norman thought. The man had the social instincts of a spoiled six year-old brat who assumed that every occasion was his own birthday party, and that all the assembled were there to pay homage to him and defer to his every wish. And when such deference and homage were not forthcoming, he raged like a toddler having a tantrum.

Norman would never forget the first time he'd really met Warren Ritchie, not quite ten years ago, when their oldest son had been a senior at the school. Warren Jr. was one of the first from the school, in Norman's experience, to apply to the Ivy League, because his mother and father had both attended Harvard—had met there, in fact—and wanted their son to follow in their footsteps. Back then, the school hadn't really had a "guidance counselor" like he was today, but Norman had stepped forward to shepherd the application of Warren Jr. to Harvard.

The whole idea of Harvard excited him enormously. It wasn't the prestige of the Ivy League, or the academic curriculum, or the great minds gathered there to teach. In fact, Norman Laney's private opinion of Harvard was that if ever there was a big fat emperor sitting on its big fat ass with no clothes on, it was Harvard University. But publicly, Norman knew better than to speak of big fat emperors with no clothes on. More importantly, what excited him about Harvard was the idea of a young person on the verge of adulthood being suddenly plunged into a new world. He himself was a living testament to the transformation that occurred when a young person went away—really away—from home to college. And he had gone only a few miles, from Pratt City to Birmingham, when he won (thank God) the scholarship to Birmingham-Southern College. But so vast was the difference between the two places that he might as well have crossed oceans. Like Thomas Wolfe going to New York, it was the making of him. "The unspeakable and incommunicable prison of this earth" released him finally, into the world, and even somewhat out of the prison of his own infinite flesh.

When he had returned to teach in the same Pratt City school system out of which he came, he had tried in all ways to indicate this journey that his students might take, away from home and out into the world. Over the years he had even come to see this as his job—not to teach so much as to lead his students out of the womb and into the world. It was up to him to pry his students out of the iron grasp of their parents and their culture and let them loose. Southern culture in particular held its people in a very tight fist. But no matter what the home was—whether it was Pratt City or New York City—the mere fact that it was home meant it had to be left behind. You had to leave that which had given birth to you and raised you—it was an incontrovertible law of human growth and development. He could always recognize in an instant those stunted souls who had never left home. It had to be done. Even if it was just for a few years. When you came back, you would be a changed person, and you would inevitably introduce those changes into the home you came back to, whether you came back for good or just for visits. This was how individuals matured; this was also what made communities grow and change for the better. This was the recipe for progress. And progress was at the root of civilization, because anything that didn't progress would eventually stagnate, and anything that stagnated would eventually fester. And if there was any place in the country that needed to grow and change for the better, any place that needed to be transformed by progress, it was the state of Alabama.

The field trip to the Birmingham Museum of Art he had arranged for his seniors at Pratt City High was the first time most of them had been to the city—or so far away from home. He would never forget—it had become one of his favorite stories—when one of his students had pointed to the statue of Vulcan atop Birmingham's Red Mountain and remarked that they must have taken a wrong turn, and arrived in New York, because there was the Statue of Liberty. Only one or two of those students ever got out, and they didn't go very far. Not many in Pratt City ever headed to college.

But the Brook-Haven School represented a different opportunity, and he had to credit the Ritchies with showing him the way. Susan Ritchie was the vice president of the Harvard Club of Birmingham and the head of the committee which interviewed all Alabama applicants and sent the admissions office detailed letters about each one. Most of those who applied from Alabama—and there weren't that many of them, Susan said—were children of parents who had attended themselves. "But do you know why they get in, Norman?" she had asked. "Not just because their parents went there. Not just because they're bright," she said. "If that were all that mattered, Harvard could fill its freshman class each year just from the Andovers and the Exeters in its own backyard." His pulse had quickened; he must have known he was on the verge of a turning point in his life. "They get in because they're from Alabama." His jaw had dropped.

"Harvard is committed to diversity," she had intoned, like the mission statement from a glossy brochure. "Racial, ethnic, religious, and—" she had paused so long that he began to think she'd forgotten the final prong of diversity. Then she came out with it: "Geographic!" she proclaimed, giving him a moment to absorb the significance of Harvard's commitment to "geographic" diversity. "This is the reason our own children have attended Brook-Haven," she continued confidentially, as Norman felt his jaw dropping again. "Warren's first thought, of course, was that his children should attend the same prep school up North that he did. But when someone told him that they actually had a better chance at the Ivy League coming from Alabama . . ."

Norman was speechless; he hadn't known what to say. It was bad enough that someone had been more cunning and calculating than he, but it should have been illegal for someone to employ that amount of cunning and calculation for his own selfish purposes.

Susan must have sensed some of what was passing through his mind. "Every year the admissions office begs us to send them more applicants from Alabama," she told him defensively, as if she and Warren had done the admissions office a favor by sending their children's applications. "But most students from here don't even dream of Harvard; they'd sooner think of flying to the moon. And our interview committee is not in a position to reach them. But you are. Maybe you can reach them, Norman."

It was his clarion call to action. Although the students in this private school, unlike the ones in Pratt City High, all assumed they would go to college after they graduated, for most this meant either Alabama or Auburn. Sometimes it meant Vanderbilt or Sewanee, and occasionally the University of Virginia. But as Susan Ritchie pointed out to him, there was no reason they couldn't do much, much better. Norman instantly conceived a new role for himself, one which suited him perfectly, of teaching his students to aim high and THINK BIG.

Executing this new role was not nearly as automatic. The Northeast was viewed with suspicion and distrust, if not abject hatred, and the Northeastern universities were considered subversive institutions that catered to and promoted extreme liberals, Jews, and lesbians. Mountain Brook was full of living proof that no one needed an Ivy League degree to obtain extraordinary wealth or social prominence. On the contrary, such degrees were much more hindrance than help in a place like Mountain Brook. Yes, there were some very well thought-of men in town who had attended these Northeastern universities, usually out of deference to a father and grandfather who had also attended before them. So for these people, it was a family tradition that must be maintained and honored. But most went no farther than the University of Virginia, which constituted "going North for college" to those in the Deep South.

Norman's breakthrough had come a few years ago, with Caroline Elmore, the oldest child of Perry and Midge. Caroline was slightly overweight, refused to wear contact lenses instead of glasses, insisted on defiantly short hair and was otherwise not very attractive. All she ever did was read, read, read, said her mother, who despaired of this impossible daughter so completely unlike herself. The only hope for Caroline, she thought, was the University of Alabama, where she might be able to pledge Kappa if Midge pulled enough strings and called in enough favors. After all, Midge was an active Kappa alum who had written hundreds of letters on behalf of everybody else's daughters. Now it was time for people to come through for her. And of course they would.

Considering the mania of sorority rush, Norman thought the only hope for Caroline was Harvard. For her, getting into an Ivy League school would be easier than getting a bid from a top sorority at the University of Alabama. Harvard had nothing on Kappa Kappa Gamma when it came to rejecting unsuitable candidates. Although usually the sororities at Bama took any girl from Mountain Brook, he suspected they would make an exception at the prospect of Caroline.

"Why don't we just send in an application to Harvard and see what happens?" he had suggested blithely during his conference with the Elmores in the fall of Caroline's senior year. "Stephen Ritchie is applying there this year, and Caroline is every bit as smart; her grades are every bit as good."

Midge had been aghast.

"Of course, she probably won't get in," Norman had assured her. "Most people *don't* get into Harvard, you know. But I'd like to see what happens. Just as my own little experiment." As an afterthought, he'd added, " I don't think the Ritchie children have anything our own boys and girls don't have."

A spark of competitive fire had flamed in Perry Elmore's eyes. As a defense attorney who had graduated from the University of Alabama law school, he was disgusted by the way Warren rubbed his huge plaintiff's settlements as well as his Harvard Law School degree in everyone's faces. He relished the possibility that Warren might not be the only one who could play that Harvard card. So Perry had given his hearty approval for his daughter's application, and graciously (also fortunately) dismissed Norman's offer to pay the application fee himself.

Harvard accepted Caroline Elmore. That was the easy part. The hard part was: would the Elmores accept Harvard?

Midge's father called to thank Norman for the honor Harvard had paid his granddaughter. His daughter was going to frame the acceptance letter so Caroline could hang it on the wall and show it to her own children one day. But it was out of the question for a Southern girl from a good family to go to a place like that; Harvard was too full of "nigras" and Jews.

Midge's father had worked for J. Edgar Hoover's FBI, and had been dispatched on "investigative missions" targeting "nigras" and Jews twenty years ago, in the 1960s, during the days of the Civil Rights Movement. He was the perfect illustration of why Southern girls and boys from "good families" needed to go to places like that.

While the family debate raged on, Caroline sent in the letter securing her place in Harvard's freshman class. Norman had taught her better than he realized.

Poor Midge was utterly devastated and prepared to be completely apologetic and defensive in public. She had so clearly failed as a mother. But then the strangest thing happened. When she went to parties, people now came rushing up to talk to her rather than easing gently away. Now one of her children had done something that actually *was* startlingly unique and worthy of lengthy discussion. For the first time in her life, Midge found herself an object of interest and curiosity. She was at the center of an unfolding drama; she had a starring role in a developing situation. Midge Elmore's *daughter*—of all things—was going to Harvard—of all places. Nobody had ever heard of such and everybody wanted to hear the story and learn the latest from Midge herself. Soon enough, Midge was nothing but Harvard, Harvard, Harvard.

Instead of an enemy, Midge became his staunchest ally, and Norman's new strategy for bringing civilization to the Deep South was launched. Still, he couldn't deny that it was Susan Ritchie who had planted the original seeds that had blossomed into his big ideas. And it was when he was invited to the Ritchie's house for dinner to celebrate Warren Jr.'s acceptance at Harvard that he'd had his first real encounter with Warren himself. Warren Jr. opened the door, and Norman could see Karen—who was then eight years old—and the other boy, Stephen, hovering nervously in the foyer behind their older brother. He was somewhat surprised not to be greeted by either of the parents, but he could hear the maternal murmur of Susan's voice soothing a whining child in a nearby room. Something about a particular shirt not being available to wear.

"I didn't realize there was another brother or sister," he said politely. "For some reason, I was under the impression there were just the three of you."

As these three were exchanging glances, a sudden uproar burst forth from the room where Susan was trying to calm the fussing child. Except this was no child, Norman realized; this was Warren Ritchie shouting at his wife at the top of his lungs because the shirt he'd intended to wear was not ready. His three children stood paralyzed in dismay, and Norman was similarly frozen in disbelief. Soon they could all see a parade of garments being flung from the room into the hallway off the foyer. Apparently Susan was producing these as possible substitutes, and Warren was rejecting them in no uncertain terms. His fulminations traveled like bolts of lightning from anger to accusation to recrimination and finally to the insistence that his wife should iron the shirt again and he would not leave the room until she did so. Throughout this tirade, Susan's voice had remained at its steady murmur, until she left the room to go comply with her husband's order.

"Shall we have a seat in the living room?" suggested Norman, as if he were the host and the three children his guests.

They were only too happy to be told what to do in this awkward situation, but too abashed to respond to Norman's determined effort at small talk. Even Warren Jr.'s upcoming attendance at Harvard failed to jump-start the conversation. Eventually Norman gave up and wandered over to the bookshelves. He'd been told Warren Ritchie had an impressive collection of first editions.

A full thirty minutes after Norman's arrival, Warren Ritchie burst into the living room with a hearty welcome as if nothing untoward had occurred. Instead of apologizing, he was beaming with pride—at what Norman couldn't possibly guess. The elation now lighting up his face seemed as inappropriate as his bellicose petulance was a half hour ago. The disconnect was so stark, and so complete, that Norman couldn't help but form an instant dislike for the man. Here was a person, he thought, who could start off his day by deliberately running over the neighbor's barking dog—or even the neighbor himself—and arrive at work as if nothing had happened.

Warren shocked him further by dismissing all the children, one of whom was supposedly the cause of the evening's celebration. The younger brother, Stephen, was now a student at the school, and Norman would have liked this opportunity to get to know the boy better. He normally didn't have much to do with the younger pupils. And Karen, the youngest—he assumed she would be attending the school in due course and probably applying to Harvard as well. It appeared that all the children were expected to attend their parents' alma mater. These were interesting and intelligent young people—interesting and intelligent young people were his life's work—and he certainly had not wanted them banished from the room. If they had truly been mere children, he could have seen the point.

Susan was nowhere to be seen either. He had caught just a glimpse of her before Warren began his effusive grand entrance, resplendent in his crisply pressed polo shirt and khaki pants. She had not wanted to catch his eye, and Norman could certainly understand why, but he had expected her to follow her husband into the living room. Instead, the sounds he heard from the kitchen indicated that she would not be joining them. Norman understood now: this was to be the Warren Ritchie Show. The other members of the family were expected to disappear as the nonentities they were.

For most of the next hour, Warren proudly showed off his book collection without noticing that his guest was about to collapse from the prolonged effort of supporting his massive weight, and was still clutching the bottle of wine he'd brought as a gift. Nor did Warren think to offer Norman anything to eat or drink while they waited for dinner. Of course, these people were not Southerners, he knew: Southerners would never allow a guest—especially an extra large guest—to stand for an hour without food or drink, first editions or no first editions. Though technically Warren had been raised in Birmingham, his parents were from elsewhere, and it really did take a Southerner to make a Southerner, Norman thought. It wasn't just a matter of being born here. But it was one thing not to be a Southerner, and quite another to be a barbarian. And while normally he would have swooned over the signed first editions of Faulkner, and fainted on the spot at the Thomas Wolfe, he found himself strangely unmoved. It wasn't just the lack of food or drink either. It wasn't just that Warren showed no interest in or appreciation of the actual texts of these books, and it wasn't just his all too transparent effort to co-opt them as symbols of his superiority which he could use to browbeat innocent guests who had been cruelly deprived of food and drink. It was his odious air of ownership, as if he actually owned these authors and their works in a way that no one else ever could. Faulkner had not written his masterpieces for the delight and edification of readers all over the world, but for the glorification of one Warren Ritchie's living room. It was intolerable. All the Geneva Conventions of hospitality had been brutally transgressed. Bring in the Red Cross.

When Susan came in to announce dinner, Norman found himself shocked yet again, although he had never known her to wear make-up of any kind, and her figure had always been that of a skeleton. But her absolute drabness seemed almost deliberate, and was a complete contrast to the spruce appearance her husband had insisted on for himself with such childish truculence. No other woman in Mountain Brook would have invited him to dinner and then worn baggy old blue jeans and a yellowed tee shirt with an arthritis camp logo on the front. But then, he remembered, it wasn't Susan who had invited him. Warren had actually called and issued the invitation. Norman began to fear for the worst; all hopes of a decent dinner disappeared. Wine, he prayed. Let there be wine. Mustering a big smile for the downtrodden Susan, he proffered the bottle he had brought with him and said, "Well!" with a heartiness he didn't feel, "Let's celebrate!"

"What's this?" said Warren, intercepting the bottle which he had apparently just noticed for the first time, although his guest had been standing in front of him holding it for the past hour. "Susan," he said, turning accusingly to his wife. "Did you ask him to bring this?"

Silently she shook her head.

"I don't drink red wine," said Warren, discarding the bottle on a side table.

The wine he did drink turned out to be a ghastly liebfraumilch that Norman could barely swallow, although he forced himself to choke down several glasses as the only hope for conviviality. The dinner, however, was another surprise: veal piccata with tiny, tart capers and tender cutlets dusted with just the merest hint of flour and lightly sautéed to perfection. It was not the kind of meal most Southerners would normally produce. Even in Mountain Brook, the instincts of the cook—who was usually the black maid—were for heavy breading and deep frying. Southerner though he was, and poor man that he definitely was, Norman hated that kind of poor Southern cooking, which was designed for tough, inferior cuts of meat that had no taste to begin with and never would. Susan's veal was a true delicacy and a rare delight, and he made sure to let her know it.

Instead of replying, Susan looked over at her husband, who said offhandedly, "Oh, we eat this way every night," as if the fairies came by to prepare their meals. Susan had clearly worked much longer in the kitchen than just the one hour he had waited. He would have to get to know her better, he thought, this Harvard graduate from California who spent a good portion of her day at the stove and the ironing board. It was no wonder to him now that the Harvard Club and the interview committee were so important to her, apart from the fact that she was obviously expected to raise not just children but Harvard students. And as for these children, they might as well not have been at the table. Harvard material though they might be, they said not a word during the meal and kept their eyes on their plates. Even Warren Jr., whom he'd come to know quite well, replied only in monosyllables when Norman spoke to him, and then looked back down at his plate.

Nevertheless, Norman's good humor returned with his enjoyment of the meal, and the occasion seemed to be turning out better than he'd expected at the disastrous beginning. But then he dropped his guard—caught up as he was in his veal—had to ask Warren to repeat his question, and then rendered a hasty opinion about—he couldn't even remember what it was about now— a book, a movie, even a political figure it could have been. What he really wanted to talk about was where Susan had found that veal and those exquisite little capers, and what seasoning she'd used when sautéing. He'd lost all interest in Warren's conversation and wasn't paying close attention. Perhaps it was this itself, or Norman's failure to properly mirror Warren's own opinion, but in any case, Warren had suddenly unleashed a torrent of heated, unintelligible words. With his face becoming red and contorted, he looked like he might be suffering a seizure of some kind, or possibly even a stroke. But when Norman looked around in alarm at the others, they were looking down in distress at their plates.

This was no seizure; this was just Warren. With her eyes Susan signaled the children, who all jumped up at once to clear the table. This maneuver succeeded in defusing Warren's outburst until Karen, in the haste of embarrassment, accidentally knocked over a glass of wine into her father's lap. His pants soaked, Warren leapt up in a wild rage and berated the poor child so harshly that she ran to her room crying openly.

At this point Norman himself rose from the table to say he really had to be going; it was a school night for him and he had lots of work yet to do on the graduation program. Susan rose as if to walk him to the door, but Warren had become the genial host once more.

"No, no," he said. "You must stay for dessert. We always have dessert."

He showed no awareness of his recent blow-up, his sobbing child, or the wet stain on the crotch of his pants. For the sake of Susan and the children, Norman stayed for dessert, but vowed it would be the last time he ever did anything at Warren Ritchie's behest.

* * *

The conference with Warren Ritchie and his daughter actually began smoothly enough. When Norman reappeared in his office, Warren had jumped up from his chair and stood almost at attention, stiffening and drawing up his body as if trying to impress a superior officer. He pumped Norman's hand with such enthusiasm that a forelock of his dark hair fell down on his forehead. He really would have been handsome, Norman thought—with his dark hair and enormous, even darker eyes—if he hadn't been such an ass. Not too long ago, Norman had arrived early at a party to help the hostess with her preparations, and found Warren standing in the foyer in this same posture of military attention. He had been the first to arrive—dreadfully early—the last to leave—dreadfully late—and utterly oblivious to the fact he'd only been invited because everyone more than half suspected him of murdering his wife. Those who had spent their lives shunning him now wanted to get a good look at him. In Birmingham, as in many places, you could get away with it if people suspected you of murdering your wife, but not if people suspected you of being Jewish. One was socially acceptable; the other was not.

Pulling out his chair, Norman did his best to suppress his own loathing for the man in front of him. He mopped his brow with the handkerchief from his pocket and tried to clear his mind as well. Unfortunately, he'd made the mistake of going outside after seeing the Vernons off, because most of his students were still working on their canvases. He'd forgotten that he'd given permission for them to work through the lunch period if they wanted. He hadn't really expected them to do so, and was intrigued to find that most of them were, even Lori Wagner. (Although she might have stayed just for the opportunity to show off her rear end while bending over to paint.) The temptation to take a look at their work was too great, and he'd spent a full thirty minutes going from canvas to canvas in the hot noonday sun of October in Alabama. The assignment was producing some fascinating results. But this left only ten minutes for lunch, and he did not want to be late getting back to Warren Ritchie. He didn't have to start early, as Warren had wished, but he sure as hell couldn't be late. Not only had he wolfed down his food—sloppy Joes today—but he'd eaten much more than he would have if he'd had more time. He always ate too much when he ate too fast. The heavy meal and the hot sun his body had absorbed were now causing him to sweat profusely.

Warren appeared not to notice his discomfort. "I have some good news," he said proudly. "Tim Lomax is going to take over as head of the Harvard interview committee. He knows all about Karen, of course, and there shouldn't be any problem." Warren puffed up like a young boy telling adoring parents of some successful exploit.

So much for Susan, thought Norman, his blood pressure rising and his spirits sinking. He stole a glance at Karen, who was trying to make herself small by shrinking to the corner of her chair. This should be her moment, he thought angrily. Mopping the back of his neck, he hoped his supply of clean handkerchiefs was not depleted in the drawer.

"We all know that Karen will most probably be attending Harvard," said Norman in a scrupulously polite voice. "But I do hope you'll agree to send her on the college tour this fall. It's New England this year. There's still time to sign up."

Warren frowned slightly and shook his head. "Why spend the money? She's visited both of her brothers several times and is quite familiar with the campus. We'll be going up again in the spring, you know, for graduation."

Norman's phone rang, and though normally he wouldn't answer it during a conference, he welcomed the interruption. Just those five seconds of exchange with the secretary helped keep his blood pressure from rising further.

"We'll be doing much more than looking at schools," he said evenly. "We're seeing *A Chorus Line* in New York and the de Kooning exhibit at the MoMA. In D.C., we'll be touring the Capitol and going to the Vietnam Memorial. Don't you think Karen deserves to go along? She's worked so hard for four years."

Warren frowned more darkly and appeared on the verge of losing control. "I think it's better if Karen sticks with her schoolwork and doesn't miss class," he said. "What's her GPA? Is she still at the head of the class?"

"Actually, we have several students who stand an excellent chance of becoming valedictorian," said Norman, with faultless courtesy. "One of those is the African-American student you saw just a moment ago." He stole another glance at Karen, who looked stricken, and hoped she would forgive him.

"You told me at the end of last year Karen was at the top of her class!" His face turning red, Warren rose half-way out of his chair.

"Sit down, Warren," Norman said, rolling up his shirtsleeves. "And behave."

Sheepishly Warren did so. Norman could see Karen's eyes darting in alarm back and forth between him and her father.

"What matters is that all of Karen's recommendations from teachers will attest that she's always been at the head of her class and could well be the valedictorian. By the time we know for sure who that will be, Karen will have been accepted at Harvard. That's what's important. Let's keep our focus."

Warren brightened and glanced over at his daughter with obvious pride.

"But who knows?" said Norman abruptly. "If Karen were to go on the tour with the rest of her high-achieving classmates, she might find a college she prefers to Harvard."

Father and daughter were both shocked and Warren was even rendered speechless, until he realized it was a joke and started chuckling.

"I'm perfectly serious," said Norman with as much frostiness as his sweating body could muster.

"Where else would she go?" said Warren, still chuckling. "Not Princeton. And certainly not Yale." He barked with laughter at the absurdity of these prospects.

"Actually I was thinking of RISD," said Norman, toying idly with a pencil and trying to signal Karen telepathically with his eyes to keep quiet.

"RISD?" said Warren, caught off guard. "What the hell is RISD?"

"Rhode Island School of Design. After all, her grandfather did win a Pulitzer Prize for photography, and I think Karen may have similar talent." (Actually he thought no such thing. Although he did teach Man Ray in his "Art in the 20th Century" class, photography was not his favorite medium and he was a poor judge of its practitioners.) "Did you see your daughter taking photographs of my students working on their canvases? It's for a possible article in the *Birmingham News*." (Actually it was for the yearbook.)

This was all too much for Warren. He jumped out of his chair and began shouting. "I know what you're trying to do! You're trying to get Karen to go somewhere else so that colored girl can take her slot!" His face was red and contorted in that way Norman had come to know so well. "I won't have it!" he shouted. "I won't have it! Karen is going to Harvard!" He took several menacing steps toward the desk, and shook his finger in Norman's face so hard that the forelock of hair bobbed up and down in the angry V of his frowning scarlet forehead.

In reply, Norman picked up the phone, pretended to buzz the front office, and inquired about the arrival of his next appointment, although at two he would be teaching his "From Giotto to Talleyrand" course, and didn't have another conference for the rest of the day. He dropped the phone in its cradle with a sigh of exasperation, as if his next appointment had indeed arrived and he was so sorry to conclude his delightful conference with the Ritchies. Over the years he had learned it was best to act as if Warren's outbursts had never happened. After all, this was how Warren himself handled them. As soon as he had broken all rules of civilized discourse and polite society, his good humor returned and the outburst disappeared into the ether, instantly forgotten.

"I was actually thinking Karen should apply early decision to Harvard," said Warren in the wheedling whine which was his other standard mode of communication.

Norman rose from his desk. "I don't think that's wise."

Warren's face reddened further and he moved closer to the desk. "I knew it!" he shouted. "I'm right! You *are* trying to take Karen's slot away from her!" Spittle reached Norman's face.

"No one has a guaranteed slot at Harvard," said Norman with punctilious sanctimony that was lost on the frenzied Warren. Slowly he made his way around the desk.

"You know what I mean!" said Warren, coming face to face with Norman. "Harvard takes two from our school and we know they'll take the Elmore boy!"

Norman shrugged in utter nonchalance. "There are no quotas," he said, looking down at his desk as if bored. "We could have two acceptances; we could have three; we could have zero."

"What are you talking about?!" said Warren, dangerously enraged, his face now literally "in Norman's face." "I graduated Magna cum Laude with Highest Honors! I was on the Harvard Law Review! I give them thousands of dollars every year!"

"Yes," Norman nodded thoughtfully. "I'm sure Karen will get in."

It was the kind of soothing remark his wife Susan might have made, and Warren was instantly mollified. He drew himself up. "Early decision," he said.

"I'll agree to that on one condition," said Norman, heading for the door. It was fortunate that when Warren lost control of himself, he also lost any sense of time and appeared not to realize that there was a half hour remaining in their allotted appointment.

"Who says you have to agree?" said Warren, following closely behind.

Norman turned around and paused, looking with deadly intent into Warren Ritchie's eyes. "Early decision applications are a lot of work for the staff and the faculty," he said. "All that paperwork, all those teacher recommendations. It doesn't happen early unless I make it happen early." He narrowed his eyes and drilled his most malevolent gaze into Warren Ritchie's face.

"This is blackmail!" shouted Warren.

"This is life," said Norman, shrugging slightly.

"It's your job!"

"I'm the one who decides what my job is," said Norman in a voice of steel.

"What condition?"

"I think Karen needs to go on that college tour," said Norman with polite formality, turning once more to the door.

"Why should I send Karen on a useless college tour just so you can have a free trip to New York?" said Warren, nipping at Norman's heels like a yapping terrier.

Norman opened the door of his office and ushered Karen and her father into the library. "Bring me the form for the tour with a $500 check by the end of next week, and we'll get started on Karen's early decision application to Harvard," he announced grandly. Smiling now, he shook hands with Warren and patted Karen on the back. (He would make it up to her later.) Warren looked startled but compliant. Just then Norman's phone rang again, allowing him to suggest that Karen be the one to see her father out before returning to class.

Alone in his office, Norman got down one of his travel books and began trying to figure out how to add RISD to the itinerary of the college tour. "Colored?" he thought to himself. "How does a Harvard graduate use the word 'colored' in 1983?"

* * *

That night after dinner and *Dallas* with his mother, Norman told her what Warren Ritchie hadn't bothered to ask.

"I don't think Karen Ritchie will get into Harvard early decision," he said.

His mother was aghast. "He'll have your head," she said, blowing cigarette smoke. "Why won't she?"

The answer was simple, but he wasn't sure his mother would understand. He tried her anyway.

"Karen has no X factor," he said.

"Like Dylan Elmore has Sanskrit."

"Exactly!" Norman almost shouted.

"Like growing up black in Birmingham. What's that girl's name?"

"Mira," he said. "Mira Vernon."

"It's really not fair, is it?" she mused, leaning toward the ashtray.

"What do you mean, it's not fair?" he said sharply. "The least our country can do after ENSLAVING THE BLACK RACE is to send a few black people to Harvard! Especially those who make straight A's at the Brook-Haven School in Birmingham, Alabama!"

"Oh, get off your high horse, Norman," said his mother, leaning back. "I didn't mean that. Just that there are worlds of girls and boys who would do well at Harvard, but only a few will get the chance. Doesn't seem right, if you ask me. Seems like anybody who can do Harvard work ought to have the chance to get a Harvard degree."

"That would hardly be feasible, Mother. The campus can only accommodate so many."

"Just like the Mountain Brook Country Club," she said, plucking a fresh cigarette from the pack beside her.

"What on earth are you talking about?"

"Why doesn't the club take on anybody who can pay the dues?" She struck a match and observed him over the flame. "Because they're a *small* club, they say, and can only accommodate so many members."

"Mother, really. Harvard tries very hard to be as inclusive as it can be, but it can hardly take on every qualified student in the country. At least it does its best to have a student body that looks like the United States of America. Meanwhile, the Mountain Brook Club tries very hard to be as *exclusive* as it can be. To give rich white people one more reason to congratulate themselves for being rich white people. I hardly think it's fair to compare Harvard University to the Mountain Brook Country Club."

"Maybe not," she said, wagging her finger at him. "But I still say: If Harvard really cared about education and diversity and democracy and all those things, they'd be working on a better way to make themselves available to anyone who's qualified." She inhaled deeply on her cigarette, as if it were the first, rather than the twenty-first, of her day. "Like the Elmore child teaching himself Greek from that correspondence course at Duke."

Norman was not sure what a correspondence course at Duke had to do with Harvard, but this reminder of Dylan Elmore and his X factor brought him back to the subject of Karen Ritchie, who lacked any apparent X factor and showed no sign of intellectual curiosity or passions. She was good in all her subjects, but had no particular love for any of them. A dutiful achiever is what she was. He didn't know where the rest of her was, or even if there was any more to her. The father had forbidden her to take any electives or "extracurriculars." She had to focus strictly on academics and making straight A's.

It was Norman who had suggested that she take up photography, and proposed her as editor of the yearbook. Since her grandfather had been a photographer and reporter for the *Birmingham News,* and won a Pulitzer Prize for a series on steel workers in Birmingham, it was a natural activity to suggest. Karen had gone along willingly enough. If there was one thing she'd learned from life with her father, it was the habit of blind obedience. Her father had agreed only because his wife had confirmed Norman's point about "the well-rounded student."

"Surely," said his mother, dragging deeply on her cigarette, "considering that her grandparents and parents all went there, and now with one brother about to graduate from the law school, the other at the college . . ." she paused to blow smoke, "surely Karen has nothing to worry about as far as Harvard is concerned."

"I don't know, Mother," said Norman. "Did I tell you that Stephen is on academic probation?" With much more force than necessary, he clicked off the television with the remote control.

"No, you did not tell me that," said his mother, shocked.

"Well he is," Norman snapped, becoming furious all over again. How dare that boy take the opportunity of a lifetime and squander it like he had when so many others would have given anything to be in his place and made much better use of it? How dare he disgrace the reputation of the Brook-Haven School and jeopardize the chances of any other of its applicants to Harvard? How dare he endanger Norman Laney's good credit with the admissions office? How dare he? How dare he?

"How could this possibly happen, Norman?"

"Stephen is a barbarian, Mother," he said. "That's how it happened. He is making A's in all those courses he needs to get into medical school, and making D's in all the others. When the time comes, he won't even graduate with a major in any subject. His degree will be in General Studies. The medical schools won't care. He is a complete and total barbarian and I hope never to need medical attention in whatever specialty he decides to go into."

"Do you mean to tell me that someone can graduate from *Harvard* without a degree in *anything*?" His mother glowered at him as if this were his doings.

Although Norman objected to the hypocrisy of Harvard as much as she did, he didn't want to give her the satisfaction of knowing it, nor did he want to discuss it at the moment. Unfortunately, she still did.

"Even in all those junior colleges George Wallace scattered all over Alabama to buy the redneck vote, you have to major in *something*," she pointed out.

"No you don't," he snapped. "That's the whole point of junior college."

His mother just rolled her eyes and puffed in silence for a while, shaking her head and blowing her smoke up at the ceiling. Norman turned the television on at a much lower volume. There was nothing he wanted to watch, but he needed the distraction.

"You don't really want Karen to go to the Rhode Island School of Design," said his mother. "Don't you think Harvard will take her eventually?"

"Yes," Norman sighed, clicking the remote control again. "When it comes down to it, they'll take her eventually."

"Norman," said his mother in a voice of warning. "You don't expect her to say no to Harvard?"

"What I want, Mother," he said irritably, "is for her to say no to her father. Same as our Southern girls need to learn how to say no to their mothers. Karen needs to find out who Karen is."

"Plenty of time for that when she gets to Harvard," said his mother emphatically. Stubbing out her cigarette, she heaved herself up from the couch. "And I want you," she croaked, wagging a finger at her son, "to stay out of that man's way. He's dangerous. Do you really believe what he said about the autopsy report?"

Norman kept his eyes on the blank television screen and ignored his mother's wagging finger. "It's not just what he says, Mother. Valerie Whitmire saw the report with her own eyes. She has her clinic at the hospital."

His mother began stacking the dishes from the TV trays. "Arrhythmia my wrinkled rear end," she said. "That sounds exactly like what somebody would say when they're trying to cover something up."

"Arrhythmia is the only thing they've come up with, Mother. They didn't find anything else. No overdose. Nothing."

"Well if it *was* an arrhythmia, it came from the stress of living with him. He sure would make *my* heart want to stop beating. I say he's a dangerous man and you just stay out of his way, Norman Laney. Don't you dare go head to head with him. Get Karen into Harvard and let her take it from there."

NOVEMBER

~ 3 ~

Norman Laney's phone had been ringing constantly since ten o'clock, which is when he had an "administrative hour," and all his friends as well as his mother knew to call him then if they wanted to reach him in the office. In addition to the congratulations pouring in for last night's triumph—plastered across the front page of the paper—all of Mountain Brook was abuzz with news of the Keller divorce.

Frank Keller was principal shareholder and CEO of Coca-Cola Bottling; in other words, he was one of the richest men in Mountain Brook. His wife Felicia—or Fee, as she was affectionately known—was one of the most beautiful women in Mountain Brook. She and her sister were both such famous beauties in their youth they'd been nicknamed the Gabor girls, whom they greatly resembled. Given Frank's wealth and Fee's looks, they were considered a perfectly matched married couple, despite the well-known fact that they had absolutely nothing in common. Fee was still a vivacious woman who wanted parties, parties, parties so she could show off her face, her figure, her clothes and her jewelry before it was too late. Accordingly, she was on the board of every major charitable organization in Birmingham, and greatly valued for the way she channeled her glamour and her husband's money into all these worthy causes. But her husband came home exhausted in the evening and wanted only his drink and his dinner before going to bed. However, no one had dreamed it would all end in divorce. Even more shocking, the woman who was "getting" Frank Keller was their neighbor, whose husband had died six months ago from cancer.

"Poor Fee," said Libba Albritton, the sixth person who had called so far with the news. She spoke as if her friend had a terminal disease from which she would soon be dead rather than merely a pending divorce. Poor Fee, indeed, thought Norman. In a way, she would soon be dead. In Mountain Brook, a woman of her generation who was spurned by her husband lost both her so-cial and her sexual currency in one fell swoop. Fee's many dearest "friends" had not loved her so much as the place she occupied in their universe. Alliances that had lasted for decades were already shifting to the incumbent Mrs. Frank Keller.

But what Libba had called about was something quite different: she and her husband Milton wanted him to come to New York again and help them negotiate the sale of another Miró painting. It was to be the same as last time: a week in New York with a chauffeured limousine, two or three nights at the theater for shows they wanted Norman to choose, dinner at La Côte Basque and La Caravelle.

"Summer is out," he told her flatly. "But what about this spring?" He flipped rapidly through the school year calendar on his desk. "Spring Break starts on March 15th," he told her.

Libba said she'd check with Milton and let him know.

All in all, he thought, this was turning out to be a much better school year than he'd thought possible after that dreadful beginning with Susan Ritchie's death. This could be the best senior class he'd ever worked with: the way the applications were shaping up, he could have as many as a third of his class accepted into Ivy League schools.

Just then Tom Turbyfill tapped on his door and asked for a minute of his time. Norman had been expecting the headmaster all morning to offer his congratulations and thanks for getting the school's name in the paper in such a prominent and flattering position. Norman had worked hard to make it happen, but had not known till he opened his paper this morning that the photograph of Theo Jackson in the Brook-Haven School's produc-tion of *A Raisin in the Sun* would be on the front page, above the fold. And Theo—thank God—had a black face that showed up black in a flash photo-graph. The article itself ran in Section C, but was not the usual fluff found in *Living*. When being interviewed, Norman had made sure to mention at least half a dozen times that Theo Jackson and Mira Vernon—another of the play's stars—would be the first African-American graduates the school had produced, and both were applying to Ivy League institutions for college. The reporter had duly noted these facts and worked them into the story. Feeling flush with his p.r. coup as well as the prospect of a luxurious trip to New York, Norman found himself in a generous and expansive mood, and motioned with unaccustomed friendliness for Tom Turbyfill to come in and have a seat. But Tom wanted him in his office. This was a bit unusual, but Norman assumed there was a parent in the headmaster's office that Turbyfill couldn't handle.

However, there were no parents and only the most perfunctory congratulations for the success of the fall play. Then the headmaster pursed his lips,
formed a temple with his fingertips, and said this was the most difficult moment he had experienced at the school since coming on board two and a half
years ago.

"What do you mean? What's happened?" said Norman sharply. "Elizabeth
and I can take care of anything you need us to. You know that."

Tom Turbyfill pursed his lips more firmly and said, "I am afraid this is a
problem of a different nature."

"What is it?" said Norman, with growing impatience. He could hear the
phone ringing in his office, and hated to miss his share of either the glory or
the gossip that had been pouring in all morning.

"It is hard for me to say this Norman," said the headmaster with madden-
ing deliberation, "but the problem, it would appear, is with you."

"What problem? What are you talking about?"

"I think it best if I do not vocalize it, and we do not discuss it. With a
little reflection, I am sure that you will know the matter I am referring to."

"I assure you, headmaster, I haven't the faintest idea what you're talking
about, and won't be able to address the problem until you tell me exactly what
it is." Norman's momentary good will toward Tom Turbyfill had expired.

"The only way you can adequately address this problem is by giving me
your resignation." Tom Turbyfill spoke in the bland, neutral tone of a funeral
parlor director, for whom even the death of a loved one was a business best
handled without stressful emotions.

Norman blundered to his feet like a wild beast staggered by an unexpected
arrow. "My resignation!" he was almost shouting. "Have you lost your mind?
What are you talking about?"

"Sit down, Norman. Sit down," said Dr. Turbyfill. "I would lower your
voice too, so we can keep this conversation strictly between the two of us.
That is my every intention."

Grudgingly Norman did as he was told.

"I have given this matter a great deal of thought over several weeks,"
continued Dr. Turbyfill, "and decided that the best course of action for all
concerned is for you to give me your resignation before the end of the school
year. If you do so, I will never have to mention this matter to another soul,
and I will be able to give you the highest of recommendations in your search
for another position."

Dr. Turbyfill paused, and Norman stared at him as if the man had indeed
lost his mind. But the headmaster's composure was as unruffled as his hair,
which looked like a toupée, although it wasn't.

"If you do not give me your resignation," he went on, "I will be forced to go to the Board in the spring and tell them why your contract should not be renewed. Then the matter will be public record—and public knowledge—and I will not be able to offer you any recommendation at all. You can save yourself a world of embarrassment, not to mention your career, and save the school a possible lawsuit, if you do as I suggest. The choice is yours to make, although I believe it is a clear one."

"It's not clear at all," said Norman in a voice of ice. "You cannot mean that I am to resign without even knowing why I'm resigning?" It was laughable, and after the initial shock had worn off, Norman's first instinct was actually to laugh. It really did seem as if the headmaster had suffered some break with reality and was speaking out of a temporarily deranged mind. The conversation had become absurd, and Norman saw no point in continuing it. Tom Turbyfill had gone off the deep end, and he and Elizabeth would need to put their heads together quickly to figure out how to get through the rest of the year without an administrative earthquake.

"You know as well as I do why you must resign from this school." Tom Turbyfill's voice remained toneless and uninflected, even sort of friendly in that openly artificial way of institutional blather.

"I assure you, I don't," said Norman, rising again. "How can I defend myself when I don't even know what you're accusing me of? This is outrageous!"

Tom Turbyfill remained seated. "There is no way for you to defend yourself," he said with continued calmness. "And *I* am not accusing you of anything. The issue was brought to me and I am simply acting upon it as I see fit in my capacity as headmaster."

"Who came to you and what did they say?" said Norman, narrowing his eyes.

"I beg you not to make me reveal that information, Norman. If I have to, I will, but only at the annual meeting of the Board in the spring. If necessary, the other party to this matter will go before the Board as well at that time."

"You're acting like I've committed some unpardonable crime! Some unmentionable sin! Like I've assaulted a parent or fondled a student! I ask you again: Who came to you and what did they say?! Because I know, no matter who came to you, no matter what they said, there is no proof of ANYTHING because I HAVE NOT DONE ANYTHING!! Much as I might have wanted to strangle a dozen parents, I have refrained from doing so, and I wouldn't begin to know how to fondle a student even if I wanted to, WHICH I DON'T! So why don't we just clear this up, RIGHT HERE, RIGHT NOW. Who said WHAT?!"

Tom Turbyfill simply looked down at his desk and shook his head, as if telling his reflection in the polished surface that Norman Laney had chosen the most self-destructive course of action available to him.

When the bell rang, Norman flung open the door of the headmaster's office and plunged furiously into the throng of students crowding the corridors between classes. The heat of all the human bodies and the enormity of his anger made him feel almost faint as he marched directly to the classroom where he taught "Art in the 20th Century" and wrote a topic on the board for an in-class essay: Discuss the meaning and the results of your attempt to paint like Jackson Pollock. "If anyone so much as sneezes while I'm out of this room, so help me God, I'll have their hide and nail it to the door as a trophy!" he warned. The students looked at each other in complete surprise. After last night's play and this morning's front page, they had counted on the best of his moods, when he made no demands on them and told stories instead. (He had yet to recount his experiences at the premiere in Hollywood.)

"Laney's on the warpath," he could hear the students whisper in the hall as he made his way to Elizabeth Elder's office. When he closed the door she always kept open, she knew something was greatly amiss, and accordingly removed her reading glasses and let them rest on the shelf of her bosom. But it was only after he'd told her what happened that he himself began to register the magnitude and seriousness of his encounter with the headmaster. Elizabeth's hardened countenance told him at once that he was headed for a struggle rather than the simple mutiny he desired.

"I was afraid this would happen," she sighed.

"Do you know who it is? Do you know—"

She held up her hand. "No, I don't know that, Norman," she said. "But I do know he's wanted you gone from the moment he got here. You know that too."

"Yes, but why? Why?"

She shrugged. "Uneasy lies the head that wears the crown when everyone knows it belongs to someone else."

"But I'm no threat to him. If I'd wanted his job I would have taken it two and a half years ago when they offered it to me."

"You should have taken it," she said sternly. "I told you at the time you should and that we'd both live to regret it if you didn't."

"I have absolutely no desire to be the headmaster and never will," he said.

"That's exactly why you'd make such a good one," she said tartly. "The best administrators are those who don't want to be administrators. Anyone who actually wants such a job is inherently unsatisfactory."

"The fact remains that I am not the headmaster and have demonstrated beyond doubt that it is not a position I seek."

Elizabeth smiled like a parent indulging the ingenious excuses of a clever child. "But you *are* the headmaster, Norman. You run this school. You know that, he knows that, everybody knows that."

"So what's the problem? He gets the title and a salary several times what mine is. All he has to do is perform the administrative duties relevant to a person who has no degrees in any academic subject whatsoever."

"I guess he's not happy to play the puppet. Didn't you see this coming?"

Miserably, Norman shook his head. "I didn't think he could afford to cross me! *I'm* the one who knows everybody! *I'm* the best fundraiser! I'm a one-man public relations department! *I'm* the one who gets our students into Ivy League schools! *I'm* the one who increases enrollment year after year! *I'm* the one who makes this school what it is!"

"And that's exactly why he wants to get rid of you."

"Why would he want to get rid of the best employee he's got? I'm the one who makes him look good!"

"It's precisely because you are the best that he wants to get rid of you."

Norman shook his head. "Obviously you understand something I don't." He was beginning to get annoyed with her.

"Norman," she said, looking down the length of her nose at him. "You can't really believe you make him look good. You make him look irrelevant."

"He *is* irrelevant! The school is what matters, and I make the school look good. What's more important, you and I make this a good school. Who cares how he looks?"

"Tom Turbyfill obviously cares how he looks."

Norman stared at her. "What are you telling me? That he would do something that jeopardizes the school's welfare if it makes him look good?" He shook his head. "I don't see how that works. If the school goes down, he won't look good for long."

"How long do you expect him to stay here, Norman? Tom and Brenda have not exactly been asked to join the country club. They're nobodies from Macon, Georgia, and that's all they'll ever be here. If I've heard the rumors, I know you have too. She is far from thrilled with their move here."

"Fine," he snapped. "They can move back where they came from."

"He doesn't want to move back. He wants to move up."

She paused to give Norman a chance to explode. But he seemed strangely paralyzed all of a sudden.

"I'm afraid that's what this is all about," she continued with a sigh. "He knows he must distinguish himself in some way here before he can move up to a better position somewhere else. And he's realized that with you around, he'll never be able to accomplish anything he can point to."

Norman remained thunderstruck. It had never occurred to him that an individual hired to lead an important institution would simply use it for his own advancement without caring if he destroyed it in the process, as long as he could move up afterwards. Despite the hundreds of thousands of faults Norman knew he possessed himself, one of the few he did not possess was small-minded selfishness, simply because he had always known that lifting himself up from where he came from meant doing the same for everyone else around him. How could any individual thrive or flourish in the midst of others who were struggling and failing? Norman saw himself as a member of the community, where his own well-being was part of the larger, general welfare. If life was just every man for himself, everyone else be damned, then that was the jungle. Norman wanted civilization. He had always wanted *civilization.*

What a fool he had been! He had thought all they needed as headmaster of the Brook-Haven School was a simpleminded figurehead who could perform all the boring duties smarter people like himself and Elizabeth didn't have time for. So Tom Turbyfill didn't want to be a mere figurehead. But he was still a simpleminded idiot, far too dimwitted to accomplish what he was trying to do on his own. Rapidly Norman scoured the mental list of his known adversaries for the likeliest candidate to be in cahoots with Tom Turbyfill. Elizabeth's mind must have been thinking along the same track. Often this was the case, which is why they made such a formidable team.

"You have no idea who could have gone to Tom Turbyfill?" she said. "What complaint might have been made of this seriousness?"

"No idea." He shook his head. Of course, he'd always had the feeling that he was getting away with something, and that one day he would cease to be able to get away with it and might even be held accountable for all the ways he had exceeded his mandate. Nevertheless, he shook his head even more emphatically and said, "I have absolutely no idea what I could have done."

"You can't think of a thing?"

"Of course there are hundreds of things!" he exploded. "You know me! I'm guilty of everything! It could be anything!"

"What about Warren Ritchie?" she suggested.

Norman considered. Ironically, Warren Ritchie was actually thrilled with Norman at the moment, because of Karen's interview during the college tour with an admissions officer on the Harvard campus. These weren't always granted when a student had already been interviewed by the local committee. Warren had been beside himself with gratitude, even inviting Norman for a thank-you dinner. Norman had even been tempted to accept, because Warren was now doing his entertaining at Highlands Bar and Grill; but in the end he had politely declined. However, at least they were back on terms of neutrality. The unpleasant conference last month seemed totally forgotten in that way Warren had of totally forgetting.

"It's not Warren," he told Elizabeth finally. "I'm afraid it's someone in Mountain Brook who wants me out of here. Who doesn't like what I'm doing with this school and has joined forces with Tom Turbyfill to get rid of me."

"Then who? Think."

He thought. Well, on the college tour a few weeks ago, in Washington, D.C., Sally Lindgren had sneaked into Malcolm Fielder's hotel room and given him a blow job. Unfortunately, this had occurred on the same night that Norman was having dinner with Miranda Newcomb, one of his darlings from a few years ago, now a junior at Georgetown. Although he adored her grandmother Grace, he was not on good terms with her parents, whom he had defeated in mortal combat over their daughter's choice of college. Now their worst fears were coming true, and they had demanded Norman undo the damage done to their daughter. Bent on joining the Peace Corps and going to Zanzibar when she graduated, Miranda was still very much in her "I-hate-the-South-and-I'm-never-going-back-to-Alabama" mode. And she was stubbornly, adamantly refusing to be among this year's debutantes in Birmingham. If she didn't change her mind soon, the opportunity would be lost. This would be a crushing disappointment to her family, and would have serious repercussions in the future. Whenever Miranda got married, her engagement announcement in the newspaper would not be able to mention that she had been presented at the Krewe Ball, the Ball of Roses, or Redstone. Norman had promised to do what he could, although he had also promised never to leave the parent chaperones alone in charge of the students on the college tour.

But he really needed to have this conversation with Miranda, and not just because her parents were up in arms either. Nor did he go for the elegant dinner—paid for by the Newcombs—and the opportunity to have a drink— okay, several drinks plus a bottle of wine—on what was supposed to be an alcohol-free trip. He went to deliver his own message to Miranda. Which was: As much as he wanted his students to transcend their origins, he also wanted them to know that after they had done so, they couldn't forget their origins, reject their families or turn their backs on their community. For all he had encouraged Miranda to go to Georgetown and applauded her decision to join the Peace Corps, she still had to return to Alabama, at least occasionally, to bring a bit of the outside world back with her to inject into the hermetically sealed cocoon of her hometown. Unfortunately, Miranda had proven as intractable as her parents had described, and his outing had lasted longer than anticipated. Finally he had exploded at her:

"Of course it's STUPID, SILLY, and MEANINGLESS!" he had shouted. "So why don't you just do it then?!"

For the first time all evening, Miranda had no righteous speech to make. In fact, she was speechless. Ultimately, she had said slowly but accusingly: "You are asking me to betray *my* principles, *my* ideals, that I worked so hard to establish, that *you* helped me to carve out in opposition to the role my parents want me to play—"

"I'm not asking you to betray anything, dammit!" he had shouted, and actually pounded his fist on the table so hard that a glass of ice water jumped and threatened to tip over. They both reached out to grab it, and the contact of their hands broke the tension.

"Darling," he said, gently now, his pale blue eyes indicating the vast reservoir of kindness that lay behind them. "There *are* no principles involved in this. It's not as if you're expected to choose your future husband and announce your engagement at the end of the debutante season, like your grandmother was expected to do. All *you* have to do is fly home in February for one weekend, put on a pretty dress and walk down a piece of red Astroturf—or whatever it is—at the Civic Center. Then in June you walk down a piece of green Astroturf in another pretty dress at the country club. That's it."

"That's a lot!" she had shot back, her brown eyes blazing again under the curtain of her heavy blonde bangs.

He had always loved that black-eyed Susan look she had, the vivid contrast of the brown eyes and the blonde hair. One of the many ironies of the whole situation: if she *did* agree to make her debut, she'd be the prettiest girl there.

"You are asking me to participate in a degrading ritual that treats women as objects and second-class citizens whose only purpose in life is to get married and serve some man as her lord and master! I can't believe I'm hearing this from you, of all people! The only one I had on my side when I wanted to get away! Why are you joining forces with them? How can you ask me to do this?"

He sighed. "Degrading ritual": this was the "I-hate-the-South" Southerner's attempt to play to the liberal Yankee crowd. It bored him in the extreme.

63

She had a long way to go. "All I'm asking you to do is give back," he said wearily.

She stared at him, unyielding but also uncomprehending. He took this opportunity to say, "A minute ago, you said the whole thing was stupid and meaningless. Now you're calling it a degrading ritual. It can't be both, you know."

He took a hard-earned victory sip of wine. He had scored a major point, and they both knew it. She sulked and remained silent. Letting her stew for a moment in outrage, he treated himself to another, larger sip of wine. Both the triumph and the wine went to his head a bit, and emboldened him further.

"You know," he said, pontifically, swirling the wine around in its glass, "it's bad enough that so many people in Mountain Brook don't understand that with great wealth comes great responsibility." He paused and took another reflective swallow of the excellent Cabernet. "But it's also important to understand that with great education comes responsibility as well." He set down his wine glass and bored into her eyes with his own narrowed ones. "Responsibility to give back from the enlightenment we've gained from obtaining one of the best educations available in the country. You want to help Zanzibar, but you won't help Birmingham?"

She leaned back and crossed her arms aggressively across her chest, as if she weren't prepared to give one iota of her position or herself. "I fail to see how making my debut can help lift Birmingham out of the dark ages," she said icily. "How is that giving back?"

"For one thing, it's giving back to your family. That's all your parents are asking. And considering what they're paying for you to attend Georgetown, I don't think it's a lot to ask. If you come down off your perch for a minute and think about it, I believe you'll realize there are precious few ways to show your love and gratitude in return. And if *this* is what they really want from you, consider yourself lucky. You can make them happy without giving up anything except a few evenings of your life. As the beneficiary of so many advantages and privileges, it's important for you just to get into the habit of giving back," he concluded grandly.

Suddenly she broke down and began sobbing into her hands. "It's just that I fought so hard to get away," she said, her shoulders heaving. "I don't want to give up anything I've worked so hard to achieve."

He extended his hand across the table, palm upward, until she reluctantly placed her own hand in his. Squeezing it, he waited until she looked him in the eye. As soon as she did so, he abruptly withdrew his hand and adopted a brisk, businesslike tone designed to put an end to the conversation. Waiters

64

were hovering impatiently in the near vicinity, and they were the only diners left in the restaurant on this Monday night.

"You wouldn't be giving anything up," he said emphatically. "When you *graduate* from *Georgetown* and join the *Peace Corps,* you'll be a *former debutante* who's going to *Africa.* Believe me, you'll be making a much more powerful statement that way than you would be by making a SILLY and MEAN-INGLESS refusal of this one small request from your family. When Birmingham's debutantes start doing things like graduating from Georgetown and joining the Peace Corps, this tells Birmingham it better re-think its notion of women. Isn't that more important than trying to impress your classmates and prove how liberal you can be?"

"I'm not trying to prove anything!" she answered hotly, but he could tell she was stung.

"You know Valerie Whitmire?" he said.

"I know who she is." Miranda took a sip of water and refused to meet his eyes.

"Could have taken a job anywhere after her fellowship, but came back to Birmingham and runs the indigent care clinic for the Health Department," he continued.

Miranda nodded wearily, as if bored and tired, or else threatened by some other Mountain Brook woman's refusal to be the usual Mountain Brook woman.

"She thought I was either kidding or following her mother's orders when I told her she should join the Junior League. But I do not take orders from Adelaide Whitmire, although Adelaide's the only one who doesn't know that, and I was perfectly serious."

Miranda looked up in surprise, and he seized her eyes with his own narrowed ones. "When women like Valerie join the Junior League, it will have a chance to be what it's supposed to be, and not just some excuse for a social gathering of idle women. Plus, plenty of those idle women don't want to be so idle; they just don't know how not to be, because no one has shown them." He twirled his empty wineglass and contemplated the tablecloth, keenly aware that he had Miranda's full attention, but not wanting to blow it by capitalizing on it too obviously. "If you really want to bring about change, you have to work within the system," he said lightly, as if dispensing casual advice about the most trivial of subjects. "You'll find that out in Zanzibar if you don't know it already. Nobody likes a carpetbagger," he concluded emphatically, slapping the table for emphasis and also beginning the process of rising from the booth, where his weight had dug a hole almost impossible to get out of.

Although Miranda still seemed inclined toward a silly, meaningless and stupid statement of protest, he believed he'd made headway and done a good night's work. It wasn't until the next morning he learned what had taken place in Malcolm Fielder's hotel room at the Iwo Jima Inn. Norman had chosen to handle it by pretending he hadn't heard a word of the gossip and knew nothing about it. He failed to see how he could have been at fault. The curfew was clear, the chaperones were all in place, excepting himself, and no one could be expected to mount a twenty-four hour guard against adolescent hormones anyway. So he had simply reiterated the rules of the road, and threatened anyone who broke them with the next plane out. He had a soft spot for Sally Lindgren, because she was overweight and needed to prove herself. It wasn't easy being a fat girl in Mountain Brook, and he hoped the incident would be forgotten by the end of the trip.

But the gossip had persisted long afterward, probably because students at the Brook-Haven School didn't usually date one another. With only thirty to thirty-five students per grade, everyone felt like family; dating each other would have seemed incestuous. So the Malcolm-Sally liaison was big news, especially when—on the weekend after the trip—Malcolm "went back to" his girlfriend Kate Dexter, president of TKD at Mountain Brook High School. Sally was distraught and humiliated, missed a whole week of class and talked of dropping out. Anyone who had not heard about the blow job on the college tour knew about it now.

Sally's mother Jan had stormed into Norman's office blazing with indignation over her daughter's humiliation, as if it were all Norman's fault and all his responsibility to put it right. Norman loathed Jan Lindgren, and was fairly certain this loathing was fully reciprocated. He was also certain that Jan had come straight to the school from the beauty salon, because her hair, clothes and makeup were worthy of a Hollywood star staging her big scene.

He wouldn't be a bit surprised if Jan hadn't gotten more mileage out of her get-up by prancing into Tom Turbyfill's office and cooking up the drama with him. Because Norman had not been overly sympathetic. He had simply pointed out that what happened proved his point about Sally needing to go to Middlebury, where the Yankee boys would be lining up to ask her out. Then he'd shown her the door. Afterwards, he'd grabbed the phone, called Sally at home, and told her he expected to see her in class on Monday morning. (When it came to playing the 600 pound gorilla, he was a natural.)

But it could just as easily be the Newcombs instead of the Lindgrens who had gone into the principal's office demanding Norman's ouster. Miranda had still not agreed to be placed on the debutante list, and the deadline was nearing. Or what if, say, Midge Elmore's father, now a retired FBI agent with lots of time on his hands, had taken it into his head that Norman Laney was engaged in dangerous and subversive activity which must be stopped? He had never forgiven Norman for getting his granddaughter into Harvard. Despite the fact that Caroline had not become a lesbian and even had a boyfriend who was not a Jew, the J. Edgar Hoover crowd wasn't the kind to drop a grudge or a suspicion. As all the world now knew, they could stalk people they didn't like for years, especially those who were trying to do the least little revolutionary thing. And these people often ended up mysteriously dead. Could it be that Norman was now the target of a retired FBI agent's final case? In truth, any parent or grandparent of any one of his students—past or present—could have figured out what Norman was doing and realized he was guilty of the worst sort of treason. And they didn't have to charge him with something he'd actually done. They could always make something up; they could always just say he'd pawed some student, God forbid. He wondered: if someone *were* to accuse him of molesting a student, would it be a male or a female they'd put him with? Either way, if they wanted him gone, they could easily get rid of him. He was only where he was on their sufferance. It wasn't a comforting thought.

The bell rang for lunch.

"We'll talk about this more on Saturday," said Elizabeth, gathering her handbag.

"Saturday?" Norman drew a blank.

"We have a date," said Elizabeth in consternation. "The symphony."

"Oh, yes," said Norman. "Of course. The symphony. You must forgive me. My brains have turned into scrambled eggs."

"You're not going to stand me up again, are you?"

Fortunately, there would be no need to. The Alabama Crimson Tide was playing a game on Saturday night, and that would literally be the only game in town. No other event dared compete with that one, and the only parties would be those devoted to watching the game. These were a strange spectacle indeed: wealthy white Southerners gathered around a television set cheering for big black males whom they would have feared, hated and reviled under any other circumstances. The only way he could make sense of this was to consider it a remnant of those not-too-distant Alabama days of black slaves and white masters, when the slaves carried the burden, as in this case the ball, for the white society. But this was a thought too terrible to contemplate. It was definitely not a sight for *his* Saturday night. He had long since stopped being invited to these occasions, having made it clear years ago that neither his ego, his identity, nor his sense of well-being were dependent on a certain team of brutes winning more games than any other team of brutes; and he had never found himself so bored or desperate as to watch a football game from start to finish. But everyone else he knew, except Elizabeth, would be either watching the game or attending it. It never mattered whether the Tide had a good team or a bad team; one thing they would always conquer each and every autumn was the Birmingham social calendar. The joke was: you better not plan on getting married or passing away during football season, because no one would come to either your wedding or your funeral; they'd all be at the game. No bride in Birmingham ever dreamed of getting married in autumn.

"Of course I'm not going to stand you up," he said indignantly, as if he'd never once done so.

"Then why don't you come for dinner at six?" she suggested. "We'll figure this out then."

* * *

Back in his office, Norman waited impatiently on the phone while holding for Valerie Whitmire.

"Hey, darlin,'" he said when she finally picked up. "Something's happened and I've got to talk to you. But this is not a conversation I can have on the telephone."

"What about dinner tonight?" she suggested. "Highlands Bar and Grill."

He looked at his watch. It was only ten after twelve, his mother never began her preparations for dinner until well after lunch, and he adored Highlands Bar and Grill. Still, he hesitated. It was not just the best, but the most expensive restaurant in town.

"On me," she said. "I'm dying to hear about the premiere, and quite able to pay for the privilege."

Gratefully he accepted and said he'd be there on the dot of seven.

Not counting the myriad ways in which he pushed against the boundaries of who he was, what he was, where he was and what he was supposed to be doing on a daily basis, there was only one actual "firing offense" he'd committed since Tom Turbyfill had been at the school. It had happened about two years ago, and almost no one knew about it, not even Elizabeth Elder or his mother. One of the few who did was Valerie Whitmire, and he had to talk to her as soon as possible.

~ 4 ~

The dot of seven, he had said. Valerie Whitmire looked at her watch. 7:09, it said, and no Norman Laney. But when she looked back up, it was to see his prodigious face plastered against the glass, peering in at her and grinning hugely. Valerie found herself grinning back and waving eagerly, her heart leaping strangely within her as if it were the love of her life planning to join her, rather than this freak of nature, this human leviathan lolloping toward her. But in fact he was a love of her life, and she felt lucky to be sitting at the table that was his destination for the evening.

It was taking him a while to reach it, however, because he seemed to know someone at every table, and with Norman, there was no such thing as a casual greeting. For one thing, his very size prevented it. He had no way of slipping past anyone with a brief nod. When he came by, chairs had to be shifted, men had to stand up, and tables edged slightly this way or that. Norman knew how to revel in the commotion he caused whenever he entered a room. His preposterous fat was as good as celebrity, and just as effective as beauty. All heads turned in his direction; there was no way not to notice him. Female voices shrieked in delight and called out his name. His smile had a mega-wattage as outsized as he was while he shook hands with the men and embraced the women he knew at every table. Everything about him was outsized: his appetites, his laughter, his enjoyment. Larger than life, he filled up the room, and not just with his bulk, but with his enormous good cheer. He was an instant party in and of himself.

On this Thursday night, the restaurant had been half-empty, quiet and subdued when Valerie first came in, but when Norman arrived, the restaurant was suddenly crowded and loud, the air was instantly electrified with the excitement of something rare and wonderful. In a split second, his tremendous presence transformed the hush of a weeknight in a provincial city into the feverish mirth of a festive, gala occasion in a glittering world capital. By the end of the evening, anyone in the restaurant who had never before heard of Norman Laney would now know who he was.

Even when Norman finally reached her table, Valerie was obliged to share him there as well. After all, Norman Laney was a kind of public property, especially for the ladies. No sooner had he ordered his whiskey than these ladies came over to tell him the latest, ask him one more question, inquire after his mother, issue an invitation, or beg for a time to get together. Norman was the benevolent and magnificent king on his throne, holding court for adoring subjects who couldn't wait to pay him homage.

"Naw, darlin'," he drawled to one in the exaggerated Pratt City accent he sometimes reverted to. "I'm too old and too fat to spend one more summer of my life in a hell-hole like Montgomery. Never again!"

"But you were wonderful! Absolutely wonderful!"

"They just wanted my body!" (He had to wait for the giggles to subside.) "Falstaff is a role I was born to play!" he boomed in a voice loud enough to be heard all over the restaurant. "I'm glad I did it. I was happy to donate my carcass for such a good cause. And it was a privilege to be on stage with those other actors. The Alabama Shakespeare Festival really is one of the best in the country, and I was honored to be asked." He rapped his knuckles on the table for emphasis. "But never again! One summer in Montgomery is all I can do, even for art and culture! Somebody else will have to do *Part Two*. No, this summer, I'm off to Europe!"

"I'm seeing her tomorrow night as a matter of fact," he said to another in much more confidential tones. "I'm taking her to the March of Dimes gala."

"You *are*? She's going? How is she?"

"Fine, fine. I think it's going to be an amicable divorce—best for everyone involved." (This is the tack he would force Fee to take if it killed her.)

Only when the waiter materialized to take their order did the stream of visitors subside. It was a waiter unfamiliar with Norman Laney, and he made the mistake of pointing out the restaurant's signature starter: grilled shrimp on a bed of garlic infused grits.

"Don't dare talk to me about grits or green tomatoes!" Norman blustered in mock outrage. "If I want grits, I can fix 'em myself! Give me somethin' I cain't fix at home!"

Rapidly he scanned the menu while the waiter hovered in trepidation, unsure whether this mammoth of a man was genuinely irate or only pretending to be angry. Throughout the restaurant, diners were chuckling among themselves: Norman Laney was a one-man show.

"Foie gras!" he announced, just as the pioneering chef/owner of Birmingham's premier (and only) fine dining establishment arrived at the table. With a nod, the chef dispatched his hapless waiter, who promptly scampered to one of his colleagues and begged him to take over the table.

Meanwhile, the chef was offering Norman a dish not on the evening's menu, a spécialité prepared just for him—veal scallopine with red-eye gravy on a bed of wild rice flecked with kale and collards. It was that perfect marriage of haute French cuisine and down-home Southern cooking that was Frank Stitt's brainchild and would make him famous one day, Norman had no doubt. He responded by showering the chef with his most effusive compliments and begging him to hang on, to give Birmingham a chance to catch up, become civilized and stop being barbarians who ate nothing but barbecue. In a way, he and Frank Stitt were engaged in the same important enterprise. Stitt was doing with food what Norman Laney was trying to do with his school, and that was, make an entire city GROW UP.

"If it weren't for you, dear boy, we'd all be sitting in the country club trying to cut into some tough old T-bone and wondering how long Lula Pet's ash was going to grow before it fell on her steak!"

Laughter came from several tables, especially those whose occupants had been at the club the previous evening and would be there tomorrow night, watching as Lula Petsinger's cigarette ash littered the plate containing her uneaten steak. Lula and her husband Big Pet ate out every night at the Mountain Brook Country Club, except for Mondays when it was closed, and Lula never ate a single bite of the steak she invariably ordered. She still adhered to the debutante code of decades ago, which stipulated that a girl should never let her escort observe her eating with any appetite, or eating at all if she could help it. Apparently, Lula was afraid to break this rule although her current escort had also been her husband for at least forty years.

"Now, darlin'," said Norman, scraping his chair noisily across the floor so that he was facing Valerie exclusively with his back to the rest of the restaurant, signaling the official end of the open audience with the king. As much as he worshipped Highlands, he couldn't bear to watch the spectacle at the bar any more than he could tear his eyes away from it if facing that direction. The restaurant had only been open a year, and while it was definitely gaining patrons, those who came to sit at the gorgeous marble slab of the bar were the marginalized members of Mountain Brook. The divorced, the disgraced, the over-dressed and overly made-up who were obviously and desperately grasping for some quick escape or even redemption from the current failure of their lives. This evening there was a woman sitting at the bar whose plastic surgeon must have trained under Michelangelo: her breasts were literal monuments to the art of sculpture. Since Norman was a huge fan of Michelangelo's work, he couldn't help but be fascinated by the statuary now affixed to this woman's chest. Obviously, no flimsy fragment of lingerie could be expected to support such massive stone cuttings, and she was obliged to rest them on the lip of the bar top. The man lighting her cigarette appeared to be debating whether he could cushion the blows life had recently dealt him in this woman's hard bosom later on in the evening.

Nothing less than an entire soap opera unfolded every night at Highlands' bar. Since Norman was also a huge fan of soap opera, the only way he could keep from watching it was to make it physically impossible to do so. Tonight especially, he had to turn his back on it and focus on the young woman in front of him, because his own life was in danger of turning into just such a soap opera.

Shaking out his napkin, he said, "Tell me why you're available to have dinner with a fat old man like me."

Valerie laughed, but Norman's pale blue eyes were looking at her with genuine concern. She was touched.

"You're going to start sounding like my mother," she said, chuckling.

"You're right. I am," he retorted with good humor. "I kept her quiet through Duke and medical school, but now I'm ready to share her point of view. It's time for you to make love and make babies!"

"Can't do it alone," she said cheerfully.

His eyes narrowed. "You're not seeing anyone?"

She shook her head and took a sip of her drink.

"Hard to believe," he muttered, rattling the ice in his glass.

"I'm fine," she protested. "I don't have time to meet anyone, and the clinic is so busy I wouldn't have time for anybody I did meet."

His eyes narrowed further and he leaned across the table. "Are you trying to tell me you don't have time for a sex life?"

She blushed.

"If there's anybody who's in a position to know all the good reasons for not having a sex life, it's me," he announced, in a voice a shade too loud for Valerie's comfort. (He was rarely content with an audience of one.) "You can tell me you don't like it, you don't want it, you don't need it, or you can't get it, but you cannot tell me you *don't have time* for it. How old are you?" he said abruptly, knowing very well exactly how old she was. "Twenty-eight?"

"Thirty," she said, blushing more deeply.

"Get busy," he said, leaning back in his chair. "Love and work. Love and work." He rapped his knuckles on the table. "You've got one; now go get the other."

Valerie leaned forward to take a silent sip of her drink.

"Whatever else you can say about the man, he had that one right. It all boils down to love and work. You've got to have both."

"So how's *your* love life?" said Valerie, an impish twinkle in her eye.

"Oh, darling," he said. "I have a great love life, because I'm in love with thousands of people. And you're one of them. But I don't have to explain why I'll never go so far as to ask anyone else to join their life with my body. There's hardly enough room in my life—not to mention my small apartment—for my own impossible self. You, on the other hand, need to get with it."

"You can't just go out and get a husband like you can a medical degree," she said, defensively.

"Used to be the other way around," he mused reflectively.

"Thank God for progress."

"If you're sitting here with me in ten years, I don't know if you'll call it progress," he said.

She was silent.

"There's a handsome young teacher in my school I'd like you to meet," he said on sudden inspiration. "This is his second year with us. Might be a bit younger than you, but not much."

"What does he teach?"

"English," said Norman, losing restraint and seizing the bread. "Seventh and eighth grade English. He's leading the Reading Seminar too this year. I'll tell you what." He chewed thoughtfully.

"What?" she said.

"When the movie premiere's in Birmingham, I'll bring him along. You can meet him then."

She neither assented nor demurred, but took the opportunity to change the subject.

"So how was Hollywood?" she said.

"Oh," he said, suddenly bored. "Grand, I suppose." He really did not want to get into his trip this evening. Normally, he could have regaled her through dinner with his Hollywood experience, but tonight he was not in the mood to alchemize the dross of his trip into narrative gold. The weekend in Hollywood had mainly been a disappointing anticlimax, and not simply because the movie itself turned out to be so bad. As far as his own role went, he was pleased with his performance and the editing of the scenes in which he appeared as a disruptive night-club patron who goes berserk when the stripper refuses to give him a lap-dance. He'd had fun filming his scenes a year ago, and that was that. There was really nothing else to tell. As far as being "in" a movie with Arnold Schwarzenegger: he had filmed no scenes with the star and barely even met him before he was whisked away in a limousine from the party after the premiere in California. This party he had looked so forward to was more about cocaine than conversation, and he was extremely sorry to see that Valerie's cousin and his former pupil James—on whose book the movie was based—was as heavily into the cocaine as everyone else. It was not Norman's scene.

"Since I was neither thin nor snorting cocaine," he said to Valerie, "I had nothing in common with anyone there. L.A. really is the capital of the barbarians."

Surprisingly, he had told her not the story of his trip, but the absolute truth of it, and she was more interested and impressed by this, he saw, than if he'd tried to dress it up for her. She really *was* a special creature, he thought. Ellis might not be good enough for her. But then, nobody would be. And she must get married. He would insist on that. Smart and successful as she was, there was something sad and defeated about her too, he thought. Was it simply the sadness of the unfertilized female? That could be part of it, he admitted, although there was something else as well. All that intelligence, all that education, all the hope and promise of a bright young life, and it all ended up inside the four walls of the examination rooms where she spent her days. Even though the work she did was necessary and important, even though the world needed good doctors, and God knows, the poor people of Alabama needed good doctors, it still didn't seem like enough. Something was being squandered; something was being lost. What it was he couldn't quite say, other than to point to his long-held belief that those who lived for Art and Culture had the greatest chance of fulfilling the best part of themselves.

"I can't wait to hear what it is you couldn't talk to me about on the telephone," she was saying.

But just then their first course arrived, and wait she must, Norman insisted. He did not want to get into "all that" while trying to pay his respects to the glorious food in front of him.

"All that" had occurred two years ago, when one of his seniors, Alexandra Sanders, had appeared unexpectedly at the door of his office one afternoon just after the final bell, asking if she could speak to him privately. No sooner had she sat down than she burst into tears. Eventually he gathered that she was pregnant. At first he was flabbergasted: he would never have picked her as someone likely to engage in the kind of activity that could get a young girl pregnant. She was a special kind of student, a gifted musician, something of a prodigy with the cello, and a frequent stand-in with the Birmingham Symphony Orchestra. She attended all the rehearsals, took lessons and made decent grades in all her subjects at school. She was hoping for a spot at Juilliard, and had won an audition scheduled to take place next month, when she would fly to New York. Normally students with her kind of artistic ability attended the Alabama School of Fine Arts, but her mother was a friend of Norman Laney's and also wanted to make sure her daughter had a well-rounded education.

"What do you want to do?" Norman had asked.

Still sobbing, she had shaken her head helplessly.

Norman had to think for a minute and meanwhile, found her a clean handkerchief from the supply in his drawer. He got up to give it to her and began pacing back and forth across the room while he continued to think.

"Let me put this another way," he said finally, stopping to look at her. "Do you still want to go to Juilliard next year?"

She nodded through her tears and dabbed at her eyes with his handkerchief.

"I take it you don't want your mother to handle it, or you wouldn't have come to me in the first place," he stated flatly.

She nodded again.

"Okay," he said, moving back to his desk and pulling out his chair. "Here's what's going to happen. In a few days' time, you will get a phone call from an alumnus of this school. She's young; she's a doctor. Her name is Valerie Whitmire. She'll make arrangements to meet with you, and she'll take it from there."

The word abortion had never been uttered in his office. When he had called Valerie from the security of his own home, he had also avoided any use of that word and even steered clear of the concept itself. "What exactly do you want me to do?" Valerie had asked him. "That's between you and Alexandra," he had said. His fingerprints could not be found anywhere on the scene of this crime. Nevertheless, the truth of the matter was, he had arranged for one of his students to get an abortion. The procedure had been performed, Alexandra had been accepted at Juilliard, and had been flourishing there for the past two years.

He had believed any danger was long past. And after all, he had made no appointments at any abortion clinic; he had paid no money for a student at his school to get an abortion. He had never even said the word to anyone involved. And he was a good Catholic who technically did not believe in abortion. He did not know or want to know who the guy was, though he assumed it was one of the older musicians in the Symphony.

But if Alexandra had ever told her mother or the father of the child, and word had gotten out . . . there was at least one powerful (meaning extremely wealthy) member of the Board who would see it as his Christian duty to expel Norman Laney from the Garden of Eden and place him on the road to perdition. Or what if it was Alexandra's mother who was furious?

Valerie was adamant that she had never breathed a word. She had not seen anyone she knew at the clinic. Planned Parenthood did not ask for identification, and Valerie had paid in cash. Most important, she was absolutely certain that Alexandra understood the need to protect those who had come to her rescue.

"Why is it an issue all of a sudden after all this time?" she wanted to know.

Norman had not decided whether to tell her, although if he were to tell anyone, it would be her. After all, it was the Whitmire family he had to thank for getting him a job in Birmingham all those years ago, when he'd been a tour guide leading a group of old ladies from Mountain Brook through Europe one summer. What began as a nice way to earn extra money and see Europe on his schoolteacher's summer vacation ended up changing his life when the old ladies, especially Bella Whitmire, had fallen for him as if they were a group of schoolgirls and he was the handsome captain of the football team. In a way, this is how they made each other feel about themselves.

He got along wonderfully well with what the world called old ladies, not just because he lived with his mother and had daily practice, but because he did not make the usual mistake of assuming that just because they were old, they had no life or desire for life. People made similar assumptions about him all the time because of his obesity. Being fat was just like being old—you got written off. People assumed you lived in abeyance, beyond the parameters of normal existence. But he actually preferred old ladies and often found them much more fascinating than younger women, who tended to be caught up in husbands, children, lovers, divorces or affairs. Older women were no longer in thrall to their sexuality, and could discuss a concert or a play or the glories of Europe with enthusiasm equal to his own.

At the end of that first trip to Europe, Bella Whitmire had deplored his return to Pratt City, and began plotting to get him out. Bella wanted him not only for next summer's tour; she wanted him at her parties. And—with her immense fortune and the influence that went along with it—if there was something Bella Whitmire wanted, she was usually able to get it. Not for nothing was she the principal benefactress of the private boys' school which her grandson James was attending at the time. This school was originally founded as a segregationist academy for white students who lived in the Birmingham city limits rather than Mountain Brook, where there were no black people. Over the years this segregationist academy had not evolved much from its origins, except that it now attracted plenty of students from Mountain Brook because of the discipline it administered to unruly rich boys whose parents were often in Europe. Still, it was far better than the public high school where Norman taught in Pratt City. He knew his main chance when he saw it, and the school was quite happy to offer it. If he could handle those rough Pratt City kids, he might be able to work wonders with the spoiled Mountain Brook boys. He had certainly worked a miracle in his own life and that of his mother, who was happy to leave Pratt City although her other son remained as the manager of a rental furniture store.

No one in Mountain Brook had ever seen anything quite like Norman Laney before, and there were whispers at first. But there were two things Norman Laney would never be accused of being: one was a lap dog, the other was a pet poodle. And it would never occur to anyone in Mountain Brook to consider Norman Laney "a little mule," although historically, the men like Norman's father, grandfather and great-grandfather were the "little mules" who supplied the labor for the "Big Mules" of Birmingham's iron and steel industries. Despite his origins, Norman had his own kind of claim on being called a "Big Mule." When you weigh as much as he did, you were quite capable of holding your own, as he was fond of saying. Bella Whitmire might have gotten him in, but he was more than prepared to take it from there on his own. Perhaps the best way in which his fat had worked for him was to make him one-of-a-kind; people were instinctively drawn to the power of the original. If he was anything, he was an original. And if he could make it as a fey fat boy in Pratt City, Alabama, he could make it anywhere.

In less than a dozen years, Bella Whitmire was gone, and so was the boys' academy, which decided to merge with its all-girls counterpart and form the Brook-Haven School. No one could predict what would come of this venture, and everyone was nervous about a two ton force meeting an immovable rock, about Norman Laney's oil to Elizabeth Elder's vinegar. But the school had succeeded beyond anyone's hopes, including those of Norman Laney and Elizabeth Elder. Not only had they transformed an institution designed to keep a hidebound city mired in its dubious past: they were now using it to help transform that city itself.

It was an irony too great to be believed that a casual outsider like Tom Turbyfill would usurp their creation and exploit it for his own personal benefit with utter disregard for its importance to an entire community. But he was not yet ready to tell anyone other than Elizabeth, until he had a better idea of what he was up against and how he wanted to handle it. What was he was up against? What was being turned against him? What had he done?

"Is something wrong, Norman?" Valerie looked at him quizzically.

"Someone is trying to get rid of me," he said.

~ 5 ~

It was an inexpensive imitation of a corporate office, designed to impress. It failed utterly in this intent, and still probably cost way too much. The ficus tree standing in one corner of the room was obviously artificial, clearly plastic rather than silk, and its pot was not solid brass, just a thin veneer already flaking off. The dark, heavy frames on the wall contained generic prints of nothing in particular. The desk was so highly polished that its glossy sheen easily revealed the lack of any true hardwoods in its surface. Norman felt like he was in the manager's office at a car dealership.

Of course, that could have been because he *needed* to be in the manager's office at a car dealership, as his old battle tank was utterly decrepit and long overdue for its final breakdown; but truly, there was absolutely nothing in the room he was now sitting in to indicate that it belonged to the chairman of an English department. Not only were there no bookshelves, there were no books in evidence anywhere in the room. No filing cabinets, no stacks of papers. No hint of clutter anywhere. But also no hint that the life of the mind was lived within these walls or that anyone anywhere in the vicinity even knew what was meant by the life of the mind. Although Norman realized that the immaculate surroundings were supposed to imply the height of professional excellence, the result was the opposite of its intended effect, and Norman felt his spirits plunge.

Still, the head of the department was a decent man with wide-ranging interests beyond his degree in Rhetoric and Composition. He usually attended both the fall and the spring productions at the Brook-Haven School, which is how Norman had first met him several years ago. Occasionally Norman ran into him at the symphony or Smith & Hardwick bookstore downtown. Last summer he'd spotted him in the audience at *Henry IV, Part One* in Montgomery. He couldn't remember exactly when Larry Plumlee had first broached the subject of a position for Norman in the English Department at Shelby

State community college. In the beginning Norman had not taken him seriously, but Dr. Plumlee brought it up nearly every time they came across one another. "Don't forget there's a place for you in my department if you ever want one." At first Norman had treated this as a joke, then an elaborate compliment, and finally as the serious overture he now needed it to be.

Norman knew that Shelby State was trying to raise its profile and attract a higher caliber student from the local area. But beyond that, Norman suspected that Plumlee wanted him to direct the school's theatrical productions. Shelby State didn't have a drama department, and the plays they occasionally managed to put on had been directed by an English professor who left three years ago. Plumlee appeared to have a genuine love for the theater, which dovetailed conveniently with the school's desire to refine its image. If you put on a play, you could almost count on at least a photograph and a caption somewhere in the *Birmingham News*. It was free publicity, and nothing signaled cultural engagement better than Shakespeare.

Never having given it much real thought until now, Norman was floored by the actual details of the position Larry Plumlee had held out to him over the years. For one thing, his salary would be almost double what it currently was at the Brook-Haven School. And if he directed a play during the semester, he would receive a "two course reduction," meaning he would teach only one course in addition to putting on the play. Norman had a hard time simply nodding his head as if he were not entirely flabbergasted by the terms: almost twice the money for less than half the work. There would be no administrative duties, either, and if Norman preferred, he could teach his classes—or his one class—on Tuesdays and Thursdays. What this would do for his Mondays, Wednesdays, and Fridays was almost too exciting to contemplate. What this would do for his life was almost beyond his power to imagine.

Norman drove in a daze back to his own campus. If he took this job, it would transform his life. He and his mother might even be able to afford a house finally—not in Mountain Brook, of course, but he cared nothing about living in Mountain Brook. More important, it would mean liberation.

"I don't know how you've kept up the pace all these years," Dr. Plumlee had chuckled. "Frankly, I don't know how anyone does it. But you in particular. With all of your activities outside the classroom," he had hastened to add, lest Norman assume his weight was being referred to.

Norman need not have worried about what reason to give for his sudden interest in a position at Shelby State. Dr. Plumlee had simply assumed that Norman had finally grown weary of the sheer daily grind of being a high school teacher, as anyone would, not just a man who was both morbidly obese and on the wrong side of forty, who also led a hyperactive social life, traveled to Europe at least every other summer, and made an imprint as large as he was on the entire cultural scene of his community.

And Norman was indeed existentially exhausted with the routine of his job. Every day an eight o'clock class in senior English, followed by a nine o'clock class in senior English. His administrative hours at ten and at one were more often than not filled up by conferences with seniors and their parents. "Art in the 20th Century" at eleven; "From Giotto to Talleyrand" at two. After school meant paperwork and faculty meetings, sometimes even more conferences or students just showing up at his office. Often he didn't get home till six, sometimes seven.

And it wasn't the physical fatigue that wore him down—although for a man of his size, the strain was considerable. But the most punishing thing was the lack of time between getting home in the evening and his eight o'clock class the next day. How could he renew himself? There was simply no time to lead the life of the mind on which his occupation depended. Without that, he was simply a workhorse, a job-holder—not a true teacher. With all the extra hours—my God, the extra days—he would have to himself if he taught at the college, he could become a real intellectual once again. And get paid for it. Get nicely paid for it. In the excitement of that thought, he almost ran a stop sign.

And yet, he didn't really want that job at Shelby State. It was fun to entertain the fantasy, and thrilling to know that if he had to, he could jump into an alternative existence as early as next fall. But he didn't really want that alternative existence. It was like daydreaming about winning the lottery and retiring to the South of France. He had the good sense to know that the South of France worked only as a fantasy, and would not make him happy for more than two days if it became reality. He would only be happy as long as he had his own chosen work, and that work didn't exist in the South of France. Or at Shelby State.

His arrival back at the Brook-Haven campus—just in time for the two o'clock bell—showed him immediately one reason why. Students were flooding the halls as they moved noisily from one classroom to another. At Shelby State, he had seen almost no students. Of course, it had been lunch time, and of course there were hundreds of students, many more than at the small private school where he taught. Shelby State's enrollment was in fact way up, as the "post-industrial" city of Birmingham was now flourishing as a medical center rather than languishing as it had for years with the demise of the steel mills. But at the college, there was no sense of that student body as a whole.

Naturally, the campus was larger and the buildings were scattered, so the students were dispersed throughout. They trickled here and there; there were no throngs jamming the hallways all at once. In fact, there were no hallways. Many classrooms could be entered directly from the sidewalk on one side or the quadrangle on the other. He'd never be happy teaching at a place like that. He needed the coming together of the student body once every fifty minutes. It was like the heartbeat or the pulse of the school. It pumped the blood into what he was doing.

Which was what? He didn't entirely know, and didn't have time to ponder. As soon as he breezed through the glass doors of the foyer, Ellis and Priscilla Bradley rose up from the sofa where they were sitting. Ellis asked nervously for a minute of his time. Norman looked at his watch: he was already five minutes late for "Giotto." Couldn't this wait? Ellis colored and said the issue pertained to the Reading Seminar, which was meeting in one hour at the end of school, so he needed immediate resolution of an issue which had just cropped up. Norman looked at Priscilla; she wasn't even participating in the Reading Seminar. But something about the look on her face made Norman realize he better not let the issue wait. He told them to go sit in his office while he went to speak to his class.

As he approached the classroom he could hear the mild uproar which inevitably developed in a teacher's absence. His brow contracted. He was not in the mood for either this or Priscilla Bradley. Although the noise ceased instantly when he entered the room, he lost the upper hand as soon as he had to ask them to wait quietly for another few minutes. Not just the upper hand—he had probably lost them for the class period. When he came back, it would be too late to begin the day's lesson. He knew it, and they knew it. It was even conceivable that he'd lost them for the rest of the semester. Christmas vacation was just a few weeks away. Their foretaste of freedom would be hard to suppress, given the sense of defeat and failure he'd suffered since his encounter with the headmaster. In a wretched moment of dismay, he could feel it all slipping away: not just his students and the semester, but his job, his life's work.

In his office he glowered at Ellis and Priscilla Bradley. Ellis apologized for taking up his class time; she looked smug.

"What's the problem?" he barked at them without preamble as soon as he reached a position of power behind his desk, where he remained standing.

Priscilla drew herself up in righteous indignation. "The problem is *The Ginger Man*," she informed him with prim sanctimony. "It's scheduled to be next month's Reading Seminar selection."

"What's wrong with it?" Norman frowned darkly.

"Mr. Laney," said Priscilla, brimming with zealous piety. "I want you to know: That novel has scenes depicting *oral sex.*"

With a slap of his palms, Norman Laney thrust himself across the desk until his face was just inches away from hers. "How would you know?" he snapped at her ferociously.

She shrank back as if in fear of the menacing jaws of an alligator about to snap her head off. Best of all, he had taken the wind right out of her self-righteous sails, and she was rendered utterly speechless. But he had learned from experience not to go for the kill. Sometimes the victims didn't re-enroll at the Brook-Haven School for the next school year. Regaining a vertical posture and a professional demeanor, he advised her not to be concerned about a reading list for an extracurricular activity in which she did not participate. To his dismay, Priscilla regained her holier-than-thou posture and sanctimonious demeanor, and then proceeded to demand that the reading assignment be changed to "something more suitable for high school students."

Ellis quickly launched into his rebuttal, but Norman cut him off just as immediately. He didn't need to hear it; he knew it already. Yes, the Seminar selections were supposed to be edgy and off-beat. Yes, he had approved the syllabus at the beginning of the school year. And yes, Priscilla was an insufferable Baptist crusader who would never be harmed by a book she had not—supposedly—been reading, especially since she was not a member of the Reading Seminar. However, Norman realized that he himself could be harmed by Priscilla and her all-too-Christian family. Accordingly, he reproved Ellis for his lack of judgment and assured an increasingly triumphant Priscilla that the book had never been submitted for his approval and would be taken off the list. All members of the Reading Seminar would be notified of the change this afternoon. He thanked her for bringing the matter to his attention, and told her she could now go back to class.

"I couldn't fight this one," was all he said before dispatching Ellis as well. He had no patience at the moment for Ellis and his outrage, which was almost as annoying as Priscilla and her outrage. He would be making it up to Ellis anyway, he thought, when he introduced him to an attractive young woman named Valerie Whitmire, who, in addition to being an established physician, was also an heiress. If Ellis had any sense at all, he would make love to her immediately, marry her soon afterwards, and be profoundly and happily grateful to Norman Laney ever after.

But Ellis was a young man, a relatively new teacher, who had not yet encountered certain humdrum realities that impinged on intellectual freedom, like what it meant that Priscilla's father was now a member of the Brook-Haven School board. Ellis thought his ideals and principles were all that mattered, that *The Ginger Man* should prevail over Baptist sensibilities, that literature should run roughshod over arrant nonsense. In a perfect world, he was right, but in an imperfect world, *The Ginger Man* might need to be sacrificed to the larger struggle to maintain the integrity of the school against the threat of barbarians.

Baptists were often the worst sort of barbarian, and there was often no Baptist so bad as one with money. Lots and lots of money, million upon million, Norman had been told, made through a chain of self-storage facilities. Lots of money brought guilt to some Baptists—not enough to make them sacrifice their money, but enough to make them sacrifice their lives in the attempt to show how worthy they were, in the Baptist sense, of the money they made, how it was in fact God's reward for their sterling souls.

Priscilla's mother was a member of the Eagle Forum, and her daughter took after her: she was always on a Baptist rampage for some issue she could use to demonstrate her own sanctitude. They always had to prove themselves; they didn't want Jesus to take away their money on earth or their throne in heaven. Don Bradley was apparently not a zealous sort of man; he was a money-making sort of man. But his wife had harnessed him to her piety and his money to her causes. They had made headlines last year with a donation to the First Baptist Church for its new youth center. In hopes of a similar donation for a new performing arts center, Brook-Haven had ill-advisedly invited Don Bradley to become a member of the board. Norman thought him less likely to give the school money than to find fanatical fault with academic matters that were none of his business. This is what his daughter did, and no doubt both husband and child had been issued their instructions and set on a mission to convert the school to Jesus.

Norman had not yet decided what tack he would take against Don Bradley, which was just as well, since Tom Turbyfill had now radically altered the equation. Norman needed to save himself first before he could take on anything else. And for all he knew, it was Don Bradley, or his wife and daughter, who had brought the complaint against him to the headmaster. It was not inconceivable that they had somehow learned of Alexandra Sander's abortion or his role in it, but even if they hadn't, most of Norman's numerous activities could be called "un-Christian" according to the strict Bradley family definition.

As for the daughter, he hadn't even tried; he had simply suffered her presence for the two years she'd attended the school. In an irony hackneyed enough for a Hollywood movie, she had transferred to Brook-Haven after her sophomore year, when one of the teachers at her Christian school was discovered having sexual relations with a student she was tutoring after class. Of course, in order to demonstrate their purity, the Bradleys had removed their daughter from the school where sin had been committed. Norman knew at a glance that two years was not enough time to pry open a mind warped so tightly shut. He would never succeed and would get no thanks for trying. He'd made not a murmur when the Bradleys announced in the conference that they intended for Priscilla to attend Samford—the small Baptist college in Birmingham Theresa Bradley had herself attended—although with their money, they could have sent the girl anywhere. But this particular struggle wasn't for him.

Fortunately he felt that way about *The Ginger Man* as well. It wasn't one of his favorite novels and he did not think the students would be shortchanged by a last minute substitution. Funny, he thought as he opened his classroom door, how his job was being threatened on all sides by oral sex. First Sally Lindgren and Malcolm Fielder, and now *The Ginger Man*.

But the smile on his face was a careless mistake. He should have been frowning at the level of noise coming out of his classroom instead of smiling as if he'd just had a good gossip on the phone while his students waited for him to come teach their class. He knew quite well what they thought of him at this moment: that he preferred gossiping to teaching, that he was—if not a barbarian—then a fraud, a charlatan, a hypocrite. Of course he was! he shouted at them in his mind, the frown and the ill-humor descending quite naturally on his countenance. Of course he was! He made no secret of it, and there was no embarrassment in it either, as far as he was concerned. When these untried young people were more mature, and entrenched in their own adult lives, they would understand it too: there was no way to attempt something meaningful in life, and at the same time pursue a reasonable amount of pleasure, without resorting to a certain amount of deception and hypocrisy. It wasn't just for politicians and criminals; it was how everyday people who were good but human reconciled their ideals, their dreams, their needs and their desires with the intractable realities of their lives. It was either that, or Valium. He thought of poor Susan Ritchie.

But there was only one way to reclaim these students for the here and now, and possibly for the rest of the semester. He looked at the clock.

"Put up your books!" he said gaily. "It's too late for the lesson I had planned for today," he admitted confidentially as he moved toward his desk. The mood of the classroom swung instantly in his favor.

"Did I ever tell y'all about my trip to Hollywood?" he inquired, as if trying hard to recall, although he'd deliberately withheld this material until a moment came when he really needed to use it.

"No!" they clamored. "You didn't! Tell us!"

He was amused to see that now he was the best of teachers—their very favorite, in fact. His smile grew as he pulled out his chair. Students shifted in their seats with impatience and anticipation; Laney looked like he was shifting into high gear.

"Well," he began. "As you must know by now, I am no particular fan of Arnold Schwarzenegger's acting, but when I met him at this party in Los Angeles . . ."

* * *

He was in no mood for David Allison and his father, and had in fact forgotten this appointment until he sank gratefully down in the armchair in Elizabeth Elder's office, only to be told by her that the Allisons were waiting for him in his office. Shaking his head with a sigh, he heaved himself up and left without a word, as if it were all Elizabeth's fault. One of the beauties of their relationship was that he need spend no formalities on her, and it was going to take all his remaining strength to summon a smile for the Allisons.

He tried first for an embarrassed laugh before breaking out in his big smile. "I normally don't have this problem," he admitted to them, trying to sound sheepish. "In fact, I don't think I've had to say this once in all the years I've been guidance counselor at this school. But these essays—" he smiled again in embarrassment while father and son leaned forward—"These essays," he repeated, "are just too good."

Out of the corner of his eye, Norman was watching Edward Allison closely, and when he beamed with satisfied vanity and intact ego, Norman knew his supposition was correct. Edward, the father, not David, the son, had composed these application essays. And they were the worst of any he'd seen so far this year.

Edward Allison was a pompous little Brookie with very blond hair, horn-rimmed glasses and a bow tie. He had that self-satisfied, self-congratulatory air Norman had noticed in almost every graduate of UVA he'd ever met. The way they dined out for the rest of their lives on their degree from the University of Virginia, they were worse than the Princeton people. And what it was they believed so superior about UVA was beyond him. But this was part of that secret knowledge they didn't consider it necessary to share with the mere mortals who'd attended any other school.

To top it all, Edward was one of those attorneys who fancied himself a writer. He compiled briefs, he sent letters, and he had majored in English at

UVA. So he was a writer. At parties he would talk about the novel he'd write one day if he ever had the time. Even worse, he'd actually written this novel—a "legal" thriller—and succeeded in placing it with a New York publisher. Norman read it in one night when it came out a few years ago. He could honestly say that it was the worst book he'd ever read in his life, because usually when he encountered a book this bad, he didn't even get to the end of the first page. If he'd liked Edward Allison at all, he would have been embarrassed for him. Since he didn't like him at all, it was absolutely galling, especially because the best Norman had been able to do with his own short stories and poems was to win a few second places in Birmingham's Hackney Literary Awards.

Edward's writing style, lauded on the jacket flap as "forceful, direct prose," was comprised of one short, simple sentence after another. Norman's high school students could write with similar competence, and some with much more grace. There was no attempt at character development, which created no motivation for the totally inexplicable behavior of the main characters, one of whom committed a bizarre murder. The ridiculous plot resolved at the end with an even more ridiculous deus ex machina maneuver. If these subtleties were lost on those who bought the book, Norman suspected that was because they never actually read it. If you bought the book, you had paid your dues to loyalty and friendship. If you complimented the author, he wasn't going to quiz you about what you liked most. The best thing about the book, as far as Norman was concerned, was that it appeared to mean Edward Allison didn't need to write another one. He'd written a book, so he was a writer. His novel took its place of pride in his office along with his framed degrees from UVA as another trophy proclaiming his superior intelligence.

The purple prose of his son's application essays had been immediately suspect. In Norman's experience, few seventeen year-old boys were ever that concerned with "helping others," and if they were calculating enough to write about it anyway, they would have fabricated a different profession besides the law in which to fulfill said ambition. It was just the kind of mistake Edward would make. He seemed to think that writing was an exercise in stringing together one received idea after another until the necessary space had been filled, and that these ideas need bear no relation either to each other or to reality. The "others" Edward "helped" in his own law practice were the big insurance companies. And he "helped" them to deny the help their customers had paid for in premiums.

But Norman needed to tread carefully with Edward Allison, who occupied the rather unique position of being neither one of Norman's friends nor one of his enemies. Normally Norman did not inspire neutrality: people either loved him or hated him, and made no secret of it. With Edward, he didn't know where he stood.

"Don't get me wrong," Norman said, holding up his hand. "I'm not accusing David of plagiarism. But I think he probably had a lot of expert assistance, and if I can sniff that out, trust me: the admissions committees will too. They take a very hard line with this sort of thing, and it could ruin David's chances."

Father and son looked at one another.

"What do you suggest, Norman?" said Edward.

Norman pretended to ponder. "I think," he said, speaking as slowly as possible to convey the impression of an idea he was gradually evolving. "I think that David needs to write these essays without any assistance." He paused as if he were still trying to piece together his thoughts. "Then he should bring the essays to me. Over the years, I've developed a knack for helping students polish these up without overdoing it."

This was precisely the course of action Norman had advised almost two months ago to all of his seniors, but Edward was nodding as if Norman were speaking some abstruse wisdom only he was capable of understanding.

David himself was a nice enough boy with good enough grades who would probably get in at least to Vanderbilt or Sewanee, if not UVA, because of his tennis.

* * *

Elizabeth had assured him she would still be in her office, working on recommendations, and indeed she was. She was always as good as her word, never said one thing and did another. For the second time that afternoon, he sank gratefully down in the armchair she'd installed especially for him. As soon as he did so, he could hear the phone in his office ringing. Elizabeth raised her eyebrows, but he was determined to ignore further interruption.

And yet, while she waited patiently for him to speak, he suddenly felt disinclined to do so, although ever since his interview with Dr. Plumlee, he had wanted to share this news with her and see if she could tell him why he wasn't at all interested in a job that paid twice as much as he made now for less than half the work he was currently doing. The whole topic was overwhelming and distasteful, and he wanted only to wallow like a beached whale in the ambient glow of her desk lamp and the comfort of her good will.

"Who are you working on?" he said finally.

She looked at him for a moment before answering to let him know she wasn't fooled. She knew he had not come to her office to ask this question.

"Glenn," she said.

"I thought you finished him last week." He yawned.

"That was my first draft," she said, with a hint of warning creeping into her voice. Now was not the time to remind her that there were plenty of other recommendations she needed to be working on.

"Your rough draft is anyone else's masterpiece," he said, yawning again.

"I'm not taking any chances," she said.

"He'll get in wherever he applies."

She stared at him stone-faced, as if to forestall further discussion. But he had no intention of re-visiting their debate about Glenn Daniels. Glenn was hers and Norman was not going to interfere, although he still thought Glenn should at least apply to Harvard and Yale. To his surprise, Norman found himself expressing this exact thought, despite his best intentions to leave the subject alone.

"I really don't believe you came in here to pick this particular fight," said Elizabeth, more stony-faced than ever.

No, indeed, he had not, but suddenly and strangely, he wanted to pick this fight. Glenn Daniels had a chance at any college in the country, and Norman believed he ought to be in full possession of the best of those chances. But Harvard and Yale were not good enough for Elizabeth Elder's protégés. She had rigorously high standards for what an education should be, and Harvard and Yale did not measure up. They were universities, they were research institutions. They were not dedicated to the education of the undergraduate. She wanted her students going to schools where there was nothing less than a professor doing all the teaching and the grading in every single course. Not for her the big names packing hundreds of students into big lecture halls. That was entertainment; that was not education.

He'd had it out with her in the fall over Glenn Daniels, and had bowed to her wishes. It wasn't often that Elizabeth had a student who took to her as completely as Glenn had. Elizabeth Elder was many things, but "fun" was not one of them. She never came late, left early, told stories or said anything remotely hilarious. She could never be jollied out of a lesson or conned into postponing a test or assignment. Most young people were too easily put off by her rigid demeanor, her unapologetic, un-permed short gray hair, and her defiantly unfashionable clothes, which did nothing to flatter or even minimize her stout, awkward figure, which moved laboriously through the halls as if her support hose were too tight.

But Glenn loved her as he loved the history and political science classes she taught. And his parents were not typical Mountain Brook parents; in fact, they didn't even live in Mountain Brook. The mother was a social worker and the father was a civil rights attorney who also drove to Tuscaloosa three days a week to teach at the law school. They had adopted Elizabeth's point of view, that Harvard was more flashy degree than solid education. After researching Williams, Amherst and Swarthmore, they were happy with these choices Elizabeth had suggested for their son. Norman had decided not to press his case then.

So why did he want to create a conflict out of it now? He didn't know why; he just felt compelled to do it.

Elizabeth sighed wearily. "I'll be happy to continue this discussion after you've told me what you really came in here to talk to me about."

He echoed her sigh and glanced at his watch. The phone began ringing again in his office. He sighed again and grabbed hold of the arms on his chair to pull himself up. For some reason, he wanted to answer his phone rather than continue his conversation with Elizabeth, and left her office without a word.

She looked back down at her desk and resumed work on her recommendation for Glenn Daniels.

* * *

On the phone he learned that Valerie Whitmire had made him an appointment with UAB's new bariatric specialist and surgeon for the following Tuesday. It was the price he had agreed—jokingly, theoretically—to pay for her silence about his conflict with the headmaster. For the past few years she had hounded him about having gastric bypass surgery and spelled out the ills he could expect if he didn't: diabetes, heart attack, stroke, kidney disease. It was a miracle, she said, that he was still walking around, but he wouldn't always be if he didn't do something drastic about his weight. In fact, exactly how much did he weigh? she was always asking him. She never believed him when he said he honestly didn't know. And he really didn't know. Because they didn't make a bathroom scale that could take him; because he joked with any nurse or doctor who tried to tell him his number; and because he really didn't want to know. He knew enough: that he weighed way too much. Once or twice over the years he had actually called to set up appointments with a surgeon, but always hung up indignantly because it was impossible for him to plan to be at a certain place at a certain time six months in advance unless the destination was Paris or Florence. But Valerie had assured him she could get him in with the new doctor in just a few weeks. They had shared two bottles of wine, plus drinks before dinner; he was well-fed, he was tired and he had school the next day, so he agreed and forgot about it. His primary worry was over losing his job, not losing his weight.

But Valerie had seized her chance and put him in the position of having to show up for that appointment or cause her a great deal of embarrassment. He would never risk that, and she knew it. Besides, she had assured him, it was merely a consultation. It wouldn't cost anything and he wouldn't be committing himself to anything either. He didn't have to go through with the surgery if he didn't want to. Promising to be there for the appointment seemed an easy enough way to get off the phone, so he did and hung up without thanking her.

Immediately after he could hear the sounds of the Reading Seminar breaking up in the library. Then here came Ellis heading for his office and looking like he wanted to throw down a gauntlet.

"Just the man I was looking for," said Norman.

"What?" said Ellis, caught off guard.

"What are you doing on Monday, January 2nd? The night before we start back to school?"

"I have no idea," said Ellis, increasingly puzzled. "Nothing, I'm sure."

"Good. I want you to come with me to a little movie premiere and a party afterwards. Mark it on your calendar and don't forget."

Sweeping past Ellis on the threshold of his office, he closed and locked the door, and swept away down the hall with the Seminar students, leaving Ellis standing there with his mouth slightly agape, gauntlet still in hand.

DECEMBER

~ 6 ~

"It was all her idea—she'd been wanting out for years," said Norman Laney into the phone cradled on his shoulder.

"When they hit it off, it was the answer to her prayers, I can assure you." He wrote a large A, circled it, and scrawled an appropriate note in the margin.

"It's not what I *heard,* darlin', it's what I *know.* She told me so herself." He put a star next to the "Uomo Universale" in Dylan Elmore's essay on the meaning of the Renaissance Man. This was exactly the kind of touch that would earn him A's at Harvard as well as in high school. He scratched out a note to this effect, flipped to the last page, wrote another large A, and circled it.

"Nothing wrong with wanting to kick up your heels; nothing wrong with wanting to stay at home. But they weren't right for each other—*at this stage of their lives.* That's all there is to it."

Frowning, he leafed through all the pages in Kaye Beasley's exam booklet. Two sentences at the most for each question. He shook his head in as much disapproval as the telephone on his shoulder would allow, and underlined "short essay answers" twice in the directions to the exam stapled to her blue book. It didn't matter that she managed to distil the important essence of a much longer reply in those two sentences she offered for each definition term. Appearances were important too, and not only did she appear not to be following directions, she appeared not to be putting forth her best effort. And, he knew for a fact, she wasn't. He didn't know what she was getting into, whether it was sex or drugs or both. Of course, he suddenly realized, it might be nothing but attitude, designed to convey the impression that she was now one of the cool crowd. He shook his head again. No, he remembered, he had seen her coming out of the woods behind the playing field with the pot-heads who went there to smoke. She had been laughing too loudly at Philip Henderson's antics in English; he was certain it must be pot. Just as well, he thought, that she had settled on Barnard rather than Columbia, but once she got there, she better get back down to business, he thought grimly. It was a dangerous game she was playing. To his mind, drugs and sex were a pathetic form of rebellion. This juvenile kind of mutiny did not lead the way to freedom or liberation, but more often to the opposite prospects of jail, rehab, early marriage or parenthood. Then how quickly these young rebels looked for help from the very same parents and authority figures they'd intended to defy. In this scenario, rebellion usually ended in clipped wings. Stupid, stupid, STUPID. It wasn't that Norman Laney didn't believe in rebellion. He did. In fact, he believed in it so strongly that he hated seeing the rebellious force squandered, like Kaye Beasley was doing, on sex and drugs. Aim high was ever his motto. True freedom demanded lofty goals and the best of fighting strategies. If you didn't like the establishment, why waste your time and chances just shooting it the bird? Most likely you'd accomplish nothing more than shooting yourself in the foot. Leave the hated establishment to find or create something better; or stay and change it. This is what he was preparing his students for. Shaking his head one last time, he wrote a large C at the end of Kaye's booklet, circled it and scrawled "See Me" in the margin. It was high time for her to have an up close and personal encounter with him after school.

"Well for one thing," he said into the phone, "she's coming to Europe with me this summer. Been dying to go for ages, and he couldn't take her. Just too busy, he said."

Thumbing through the pages and pages written in Bebe Bannon's round, looping handwriting, he became even more incensed with Kaye Beasley. Bebe wrote forever and ever and still didn't nail down the essence of any reply as well as Kaye Beasley could in two sentences. It was a clear challenge Kaye had issued him, almost a taunt, even. Would he reward the quality of her work and forgive her defiance of directions, or would he punish her rule-breaking and ignore her merit? As far as he was concerned, it was the wrong set of questions. Kaye needed to learn that she had no business sticking her finger in the eye of any authority figure who had only her future happiness in mind. It was not only the height of rude ingratitude, it was sheer stupidity, for all her brilliant answers on the exam. Hopefully the C would shake her up and help her see further than the next laugh she might be able to get from Philip Henderson or Christopher Johns.

Circling a large B at the end of Bebe Bannon's second blue book, he skimmed back over her paragraphs and wrote a word or two here and there in the margins to indicate main ideas she had failed to incorporate. She would be perfect at Sweet Briar, and enjoy a happy, successful life. She would get the husband she wanted, have the children she wanted, and unless he was much mistaken, she would end up being the alumni director for the class of 1984. In years to come, he would no doubt see more of her than he would the brighter stars he was shooting off into the firmament, which would most probably land anywhere else on earth but Birmingham, Alabama, although these darlings always boomeranged back to him in a different kind of way.

"Listen, darlin', I'll see you next Saturday, hear?" He replaced the receiver with much more force than necessary and looked intently at the exam booklet in front of him, pretending that he had heard no tapping on his door. Tom Turbyfill was forced to tap again, more loudly this time.

"A minute of your time, please Norman," he said sonorously in the one tone he used for all utterances.

Norman looked up but said nothing and issued no greeting or invitation for the headmaster to come further into his office. Since their confrontation several weeks ago, Tom Turbyfill and Norman Laney had not had another discussion. If not for Elizabeth Elder, Norman's tendency would have been to burst into Tom Turbyfill's office a dozen times a day until he had extracted—by brute force if necessary—the name of who had complained and about what. But Elizabeth had insisted that he would receive no satisfaction from Tom Turbyfill. If the headmaster had wanted any outcome other than Norman's departure from the school, she had pointed out, he wouldn't be with-holding the vital information. He was clearly trying to use whatever he thought he had to force Norman out, so there was no sense appealing to him. It was the Board, not the headmaster, which would be his deliverance. So she had counseled him to avoid Tom Turbyfill and prepare himself for a showdown in the spring at the Board's annual meeting, which was a prolonged affair spread out over two days.

"I understand that you are considering a position with one of our community colleges," said Turbyfill pleasantly.

Ours? thought Norman. Turbyfill was from Macon, Georgia—not Birmingham. There was no "ours." He said nothing, though he was dying of curiosity. How had Turbyfill learned of his interview at Shelby State?

"I take it then, that you are following my advice?"

Norman compelled himself to try to match the headmaster's monotone. "I'm certainly looking into my options," he said, looking down at the exam in front of him. *A Renaissance man values all fields of study, and seeks to understand their interconnections,* he read silently to himself, "*instead of focusing on one area of knowledge to the exclusion of all others.*" Nicely put, he thought.

"Very good. Very good." The headmaster nodded. They could have been discussing refreshments for faculty meetings—a task the headmaster had given him at the beginning of the school year.

"*The role of the bourgeoisie was a crucial one for the art of the Renaissance, as wealthy merchants strove to obtain and demonstrate both erudition and cultivation*," he read. Whose exam was this? The writing sounded vaguely familiar, but he couldn't place the writer.

"I can expect that you will be leaving us then, at the end of this year?"

Norman shrugged and flipped back to the front of the blue book. Malcolm Fielder. Of course. No wonder the writing sounded familiar: it came straight out of the textbook. Sighing, he turned to the last page, wrote a big fat A, and circled it. Perhaps, he sighed again, after Malcolm had received his necessary degrees from the Wharton School and took his coveted place on Wall Street, he would buy some nice art for his Upper East Side apartment.

"Do not wait too long to make it official," said Turbyfill, "or you will put the school in an awkward position."

Norman looked up briefly, then turned his attention to the next exam. He had to admit: one of the fringe benefits of his falling out with the headmaster was the change in the rules of engagement. He no longer need be polite; he could be almost as rude as he'd always wanted.

"I will be happy to write you any recommendation as needed at this time," said the headmaster.

When Norman failed to look back up or acknowledge this offer in any way, the headmaster thanked him for his time as if they had just had the most cordial of conversations, and walked away. Norman exhaled the bellyful of angry breath he had withheld throughout this encounter. Given the size of his belly, it was a gale of hurricane proportion. He had to hand it to Elizabeth Elder though: so far, so good. Events were unfolding almost exactly as she had predicted when she formulated his strategy. The "awkward position" Tom Turbyfill had alluded to was at the heart of her plan. He needed to stick with her playbook; it appeared to be working. Glancing at his watch, he saw it was almost four o'clock and time for the faculty meeting. Less than half the exams were graded. With those and the letters of recommendation, it was going to be a long weekend.

* * *

Dennis Morton was the last to arrive, reeking of cigarette smoke, with his shoulder-length hair tied back in a pony tail. He knew Norman Laney disapproved of his hair, and the pony tail was his idea of a compromise, which he offered only on certain occasions, like the special faculty meeting Laney convened every December to discuss the recommendations for students applying to college. Norman half suspected that Dennis was smoking pot with his male students—who thought he was cool—and possibly having sex with Kaye Beasley. Although he had a live-in girlfriend, both she and their relationship seemed tepid at best, and did not appear to be progressing toward marriage or children. For all Norman knew, he could even be the source of the marijuana his students were smoking. There had to be some other reason—besides the long hair—that Dennis had become such a popular teacher with a certain segment of the male student body. After all, he was a math teacher, and the cool factor could only go so far. Undoubtedly there was something else fueling such wild popularity, and Norman fervently hoped it was not marijuana. Despite the hippie hair and the hole-in-the-knee blue jeans, though, he was an excellent teacher who had students performing well on the standardized tests and even enjoying mathematics. This year he had a star pupil of his own, Jason Simmons, who would be applying to M.I.T. If he was accepted, it would be a first for the Brook-Haven School. The first of many, Norman hoped, but he needed Dennis for that: math was definitely not his domain. But every day after school Dennis hung around on the sidewalk outside sucking cigarettes with some of the senior boys. Norman had a hard time believing that's all there was to it. Was he late to this meeting, for example, because he'd had to walk all the way up from the woods, where he'd been smoking pot? With his students? Irritated by these thoughts, the strong smell of the smoke, and his brush with the headmaster, Norman was in no mood for niceties—Christmas or no Christmas—and began the meeting abruptly as soon as Dennis had taken his seat.

"Our first problem is Marcia Lamont," he said. "Her parents have decided—belatedly, I know—that they want her to attend New College. She's going to need some letters."

He scanned the faces gathered around him on the various sofas and chairs which formed a loose circle in the middle of the school's spacious library. None were forthcoming; he didn't blame them. It was late in the semester—ten days before Christmas—to be asking any teachers to write letters instead of merely filling out the forms which had already been completed for the applications to state universities Marcia and her parents had decided on in the fall. Norman began pacing with his eyes on the carpet as he spoke.

"I know it's late in the day, but this is our job, and I need three of you to step up," he said.

Gayle Naughton leaned forward. God bless her, he thought. But it was only a question Gayle was offering. "Why New College, Norman?"

"Because her father believes Marcia has been held back by the traditional academic environment," he said sharply, looking pointedly at Gayle.

Gayle was shocked as only Gayle—who was the epitome of "the traditional academic environment"—could be shocked. Most of the others chuckled to themselves or laughed openly. An outright guffaw came from a male voice on his left, just out of his current line of vision. Dennis Morton was the likely source. Norman found himself yielding to temptation, as he often did when he was standing in front of a captive audience and heard laughter in the wind.

"Yes," he said, resuming his pacing, eyes on the floor. "We are the ones at fault for Marcia's lack of academic progress." He stopped and faced the majority of his faculty, seated with their backs to the large bay window overlooking the playing field, through which the afternoon sun came pouring in, even in December. "As soon as Marcia arrives in the *non*-traditional academic environment, her newly unfettered intellect will be able to soar to the heights it has always been capable of."

Except for Gayle Naughton and Elizabeth Elder, everyone laughed appreciatively. Gayle wasn't laughing because she had agreed to be one of the teachers filling out Marcia's recommendation forms to the state universities, since actually, under her strict program of daily quizzes, nightly homework sheets and specific weekly assignments, Marcia had done better work in her class than in most. But Gayle was concerned—very concerned. She could not in good conscience write a letter on Marcia's behalf and was in no mood to laugh. As for Elizabeth Elder, she disapproved of any public disparagement of any Brook-Haven student at any time, but especially this time, when Norman was in such a delicate position. She had warned him not to give the headmaster any further ammunition. But he had to give his faculty something. It was Friday afternoon, it was the end of the semester, everyone had piles of grading, Christmas was only ten days away, and here he was asking for them to go above and beyond for a student no one could champion. The least he could do was make them laugh.

Marcia Lamont was known on campus primarily for being the undisputed queen of the slut circle. Unlike Lori Wagner, who had no breasts, no hips, no rump, and thus had to accentuate the one female feature she inevitably did possess, Marcia Lamont had it all. In fact, her figure was so well-formed as to seem almost overripe, as if she were a thirty-five year old woman who had experienced pregnancy and childbirth as well as years of sexual intercourse. Her hips had a certain spread and her large breasts had a slight sag uncommon in most adolescent girls. It was impossible to think of her as a girl, and for all Norman knew, she actually had been pregnant and given birth at some point. It wouldn't surprise him.

When Marcia was a sophomore, her father, a well-known psychiatrist, had made an appointment to let Norman know that Marcia was on birth control and had complete freedom to be as sexually active as she chose. According to Dr. Lamont, this freedom would ensure Marcia a smoother adolescence and would improve her academic performance since she wouldn't need to be caught up in silly cat and mouse games with boys. Although Marcia's academic performance had not improved, at least it had not deteriorated. She remained a thoroughly bored, unengaged but dependable C student who spent most of her time whispering and giggling with the other members of the slut circle. Mainly, Norman was grateful that she did not seem inclined to share her "freedom" with the male members of her high school class. They in turn seemed strangely uninterested—even unaware of her, almost—as if she belonged to another species and they couldn't pick up her scent. They must have known instinctively that she was way out of their league, and no doubt Marcia preferred men to boys. Valerie Whitmire had once spotted her with one of the interns doing a rotation at the hospital.

Gayle—good old Gayle—was leaning forward again in her chair with all of her assiduous Yankee initiative. "What about the Reading Seminar?" she said. "Hasn't Marcia been doing that this year? Why not get Mark to write one of the letters?"

Brilliant. He made a rapid survey of the room. No Ellis. Hadn't he told him to be here just in case? Norman's newly restored good humor vanished as quickly as it had re-surfaced, and he found himself furious.

"I think he's in his office, grading papers," said Dennis, rising as if eager to go fetch him.

"He better be," muttered Norman darkly, cutting off Dennis's path by turning abruptly and thundering off in search of Ellis himself. "We need two other letters," he called behind him. "Figure it out while I'm gone because nobody goes home until we do."

Fortunately for Ellis, he was indeed in his office, and so emphatic that he'd never been told to join the faculty meeting Norman had to believe him. In fact, Ellis turned the tables somewhat by saying, "I didn't think you'd want me, let alone need me." Norman knew Ellis chafed at being an eighth grade teacher and would have greatly preferred a place in the high school, which Norman had assured him might be his one day once he gained enough experience. But the truth was, Ellis wasn't a very good teacher and wouldn't be until he accepted the reality that it was his life. It was clearly out of desperation that he'd applied for and taken the job advertised at the Brook-Haven School. A recent graduate of Columbia's MFA program, he had hoped for a position in the English Department at a university or college, or a publishing contract for his collection of stories. When neither had been forthcoming, he'd had to take what he could get. The Brook-Haven School had been the dubious beneficiary of his lack of any other option. Teaching junior high in Birmingham, Alabama was not the future Ellis had ever imagined for himself, and to prevent it from feeling like failure, he treated it as temporary.

From the half a dozen classes Norman had visited in Ellis's year and a half of teaching at the school, it was obvious that he did no preparation and put forth the minimum of effort. For each class, he had various students read aloud from the given text, and Ellis asked questions or offered explication as necessary. It was an acceptable if not scintillating mode of instruction, but the students appeared as bored with the experience as Ellis himself was. He was obviously withholding the best part of himself and drawing on it only for himself, for his fiction writing and his grant applications. Norman couldn't entirely blame him. He knew exactly how Ellis felt because he felt that way too: he simply could not turn his inner life into daily fodder for the careless consumption of his students. If he had even tried, his inner life would have deserted him completely. If he had attempted to turn his passion for literature and art into lesson plans and syllabuses, those passions would have disappeared altogether.

Nevertheless, Norman believed he had found a way to give of himself to his students, and Ellis would never make a good teacher until he found his own way to give of himself without giving himself up. This would involve the realization that even if his book did get published one day, it would certainly not change the world, and probably not change even Ellis's own life. He would still need a job, and it might as well be at Brook-Haven, where he was at least making a mark with the Reading Seminar and the literary magazine.

It would help if Ellis were settled and had a wife and at least a potential family, instead of a young person's illusion that he could step out of his present life at any time to do something else in some other place. Norman knew nothing of Ellis's personal life, had no idea what he did for sex, though he assumed he did something like most young men his age. He couldn't imagine that Ellis had trouble with women—he was tall, with wavy, sandy blond hair and pronounced cheekbones. There was something Scandinavian in his good looks. Female membership in the Reading Seminar had doubled since Ellis had taken over, and once or twice Norman had seen Marcia Lamont flirting with him. At least Ellis was as uninterested in his students sexually as he appeared to be professionally. But the time was coming for Ellis to make up his mind: either he was or was not a teacher of young people.

Meanwhile, he readily offered to join the meeting and write a letter on Marcia's behalf. "You'll have to put your fiction writing skills to good use," Norman said with a smirk, but he was secretly so pleased with Ellis's easy compliance that he told him not to bother with the meeting—just write the damn letter and have it in by Monday morning. He had feared Ellis might make this payback time for Norman's refusal to stand up for him with Priscilla Bradley.

In his absence, Franny O'Neill had come forward with the idea of writing a letter based solely on Marcia's bit part in *Blithe Spirit,* which Franny had directed two years ago. As long as she didn't even have to mention that Marcia had been in her freshman and junior English classes, Franny would write this letter. Norman quickly agreed and said sharply, "One more. Who else can step up here? We all want to go home and this is just the first item on our agenda."

Gayle was sitting with her arms folded across her flat chest and a stubborn bull-dog look on her face, as if she disapproved of everything. Norman had no doubt that she did disapprove of everything—of Marcia, of New College, of last minute decisions, sudden changes in plans, and above all of the disingenuous letters of recommendation being brazenly plotted right there in front of her. He narrowed his eyes at her; the rest of the faculty ceased murmuring amongst themselves. Something else was going on with Gayle; she was at war with herself. Norman knew these signs. She was displeased with herself too, he saw; her stern, Yankee sense of duty dictated that she should write one of these letters. He took a risk.

"I'd write a letter myself," he said, "if I didn't have all of y'all's letters to go through over the weekend. Then I'm doing the reading of 'A Christmas Memory' at Bookkeeper's on Sunday. I really can't do it all."

A low but distinct chorus of affirmation rose in response, while a deep vertical line bisected Gayle's forehead. After all, the only B Marcia had ever made was in Gayle's sophomore English class, which was actually geared toward the Marcias of the world, who would never understand the beauty of literature, but were quite capable of memorizing the mechanics. Whereas Marcia was incapable of contemplating or understanding the beauty of anything other than herself, she could parrot the definition of assonance and consonance, thanks to Gayle's endless drills and study sheets. So she had made a B. Gayle had therefore agreed to fill out the recommendation forms for the University of Alabama and the University of Georgia. All eyes were now on her. If

Norman could just bide his time for a few more moments without opening his big mouth, he knew he'd have her. Sure enough, she shook her head in disgust, threw up her hands, and muttered "I'll write a letter." A collective sigh of relief came from the faculty. "But I'm warning you, Norman," she said with piercing shrillness. "I'm not going to engage in any half-truths."

"Oh, no," he said. "Of course not." Out of the corner of his eye, he could see the very young and the very pretty French teacher, Michelle Boyer, who liked her last name pronounced Boy-A, exchange glances of amusement with Coach Riley, who taught biology and sex education in addition to coaching soccer, basketball and baseball.

"I'm not going to stretch the truth or cover up the truth," Gayle continued, leaning forward to emphasize her point.

"Gayle," he remonstrated, as if wounded. "Would I dream of asking anyone to betray their principles or integrity just to get a student into college?"

A ripple of suppressed laughter circled the ring of sofas and chairs where Norman was now sitting with the rest of his colleagues. He was pushing it—he was about to go too far, he warned himself. If Gayle took offense, she might change her mind. But fortunately Gayle was just as oblivious to the undercurrent of laughter as she was to the fact that she really ought to let the hairdresser comb out the tight curls of her permanent or that her oversized eyeglass frames were no longer as fashionable as they had been in the seventies, when she purchased them a decade ago.

"I will not sign my name to any letter that does not reflect exactly what I think," she said, her voice threatening to become shrill again.

"No one who values their sanity would dream of asking you to do a thing like that," said Norman with perfect sincerity. This time everyone laughed openly, including Gayle herself.

Yet suddenly her face darkened and her brow contracted as if she did not at all appreciate being deliberately sidetracked like this from the important business at hand. And all of her colleagues—including Norman Laney—instantly resolved into obedient silence, as if they were the guilty students who had attempted such nonsense with their no-nonsense teacher. There was a tense moment as everyone waited for Gayle's increasing agitation to express itself.

"Norman," she said finally, in a voice most often used on the likes of Christopher Johns or Philip Henderson. "What is this we're hearing about Karen Ritchie not getting into Harvard?"

The silence in the room became profound. Briefly Norman's eyes met Elizabeth Elder's, then turned back to all the other eyes fixed on him. No one dared to exchange looks of dismay with their other colleagues. (But what had possessed Gayle to bring up such a subject at this late hour? Yes, they had heard the rumors, and yes, they were curious. But not that curious at five-thirty on Friday afternoon. They wanted to go home. They did not want to be targets of an explosion of wrath from Norman Laney, and they certainly did not want to be asked to fix any further problems.)

Norman could read them perfectly as he allowed for a pregnant pause to gestate before responding. Naturally, they assumed he was distraught, and technically, he should have been. Accordingly, he took out his handkerchief, wiped it across his forehead and stared down at the floor to convey this impression.

Looking up, he began solemnly, "Against my advice," he said, and then paused again to mop his brow. "Against my advice," he repeated, "Karen Ritchie applied early decision to Harvard." He paused for dramatic effect. "She did not get in."

No one dared speak, not even Gayle, who had opened her mouth to say something and then quickly shut it again. Out of the corner of his eye, Norman could see Elizabeth watching him warily. She knew the full score, of course, which was: he was not in the least distressed by Karen's rejection and was even somewhat gratified. Yes, if she'd been accepted, he could have dusted his hands of Warren for once and for all. But that would happen soon enough anyway. Meanwhile, he had Warren sniveling and groveling—even apologizing—instead of shouting. It was he, Norman Laney, who was now shouting at Warren not to wreak further havoc by harassing the admissions committee, the alumnae committee, and the interview committee, which is exactly what Warren proposed to do, without calling it harassment. Although Norman did not usually relish moments of triumph which involved someone else's suffering, he found supreme release in venting all his own frustrations on such a deserving victim. And if Karen had been jolted out of her sleep-walking servitude to her father's boundless ego and single-minded social climbing—so much to the good.

"But what's to be done about this, Norman?" said Gayle.

Done about it? The others couldn't stop themselves from exchanging quick glances of dismay. Done about it? By them? In addition to everything else? Of course, they all loved Karen—sweet girl—though they didn't know her at all; she never raised her hand in class; never said anything; simply aced every test and made the best grades. They had always wished they could know her better, get closer to her, and after her mother's death this fall—poor girl—they wanted to do anything they could for her . . . but they also wanted to go home, they wanted to finish their Christmas shopping this weekend, they wanted to get all their exams graded by Sunday, and they wanted a drink.

"Whatever's to be done, I've already done it," announced Norman firmly.

The eyes of every single faculty member melted into pools of pure love, except for Elizabeth's which were full of amusement. Perhaps also except for Gayle's, which were forcefully impressed, but that was probably the closest she could come to love anyway.

"Karen will be reapplying to Harvard under regular admission, and meanwhile, she's got several back-ups, thanks to the college tour I insisted she go on over what I can only wish was her father's dead body. One of these back-ups is RISD. Rhode Island School of Design. They require a portfolio of creative work, and at my suggestion, Karen has been photographing and interviewing the grandchildren of the steelworkers her grandfather photographed and interviewed for his Pulitzer Prize-winning series in the *Birmingham News*. As you all know, I have a few well-placed contacts in our local newspaper . . ."

Shouts of laughter interrupted Norman's pseudo-serious little speech. Dennis Morton clapped. Coach Riley whistled in that ear-splitting way he used on the playing field. Michelle Boy-A hooped and hollered. Joyce nodded her head. Elizabeth was stone-faced, but that was because she was constitutionally wired to restrain her laughter. They were all full of relief, gratitude and fresh amazement for the ingenuity of Norman Laney, which continued to assure, year after year, that they taught at the best school in Birmingham, if not in the state of Alabama, while asking no more of them than they do their own jobs. What an extraordinary man!

Norman pretended to be perturbed by this interruption.

"I am trying my best to see that at least a portion of Karen's work gets published in the paper. I'll also be submitting the entire portfolio to Harvard as well as RISD for supporting material. I'll be very surprised if Karen doesn't end up getting accepted everywhere she applies."

He paused and frowned. (Was he going to hit them up *now*?) There was a sharp intake of breath from his audience.

"One last thing," he said sternly. His eyes swept the group, now anxiously waiting and poised for flight. "Go home, put up your feet, and pour yourself a drink!"

* * *

After this particular faculty meeting, it was always Norman's responsibility to secure the main school building, which usually involved simply locking the front door, but he was supposed to make sure that Roosevelt, the janitor, had locked all the other doors before leaving. Elizabeth had offered to help him, and as he toiled down the stairs, he regretted that he'd shooed her on home. What sort of faulty logic had led him to believe that because he had so much on him this weekend—exams and papers to grade, the recommendations to read through, the salon for "Art in the 20th Century," the reading of "A Christmas Memory"—that he might as well take on one more small burden? He was as much a glutton for misery as he was for everything else.

On the lower level he walked thoughtfully along the walls encircling the Orange Bowl, wondering what he was going to do about January's exhibit now that the artist had pulled out on him. The Orange Bowl was a peculiar sunken space with a bright orange circular leather sofa surrounding a tall white column in the middle of a large open area feeding into half a dozen classrooms. Several times a year on the walls of this space, he put on a new exhibit of works by some up and coming Alabama artist. All he asked of the artist in return was one of the works that had not sold during the exhibition. Over the years, quite a collection had accumulated, and these pieces filled every available space: the corridors, the lunchroom, the bathrooms, the main office, the foyer, even the gym. Wherever in the school his students went, they would never see the usual institutional gloom of drab walls or graffitied bathrooms or vast dead space in a cavernous gym. Everywhere they looked they would see the thrust and splash of vibrant color bringing the walls to vivid life. More important than the walls of the school, it was his students' souls he hoped to waken and bring to life. This was the purpose of art, and if it had succeeded with him, penetrating his fortress of fat and reaching the spirit buried deep within, it could succeed with anybody.

The two exit doors on either side of the Orange Bowl were locked, but Rosy had forgotten to lock the supply closet next to the art room. Norman pursed his lips: no wonder Ms. Cropp, the art teacher, had reported strange disappearances of certain materials. Turning on the light to check for signs of recent thievery, he caught sight of his students' Pollock canvasses stacked against the rear wall of the closet. Suddenly he knew exactly what he was going to put in place of January's scheduled exhibit for the Orange Bowl Gallery. The Pollock canvasses were large, and there were twenty of them. But by crowding them a bit closer together than he normally liked, he could make them all fit. Underneath each canvas, he could post a neatly typed note card containing a brief excerpt from each student's essay about their project. Brilliant! He would insist that the art critic who reviewed all his exhibitions for the *Birmingham News* write this one up as well.

The exhilaration of hatching these ideas and solving the problem of the cancelled exhibit lasted until he finally arrived back at his office and realized it would take him several trips to get all the papers he was taking home into his car. It took all his might to resist sinking into his chair like the doomed creature he increasingly felt he was since the rift with the headmaster. If he sat down, even for a minute, he might never get up again, and it would be Monday morning before they found him. If ever there were a moment for vaporizing into thin air and rematerializing in the comfort of his apartment with his drink and his dinner before him, this was it. What was for dinner anyway? With a groan of pure dismay, he remembered he'd told his mother not to bother with dinner tonight because of all her preparations for his "Art in the 20th Century" salon tomorrow afternoon. They'd order out, he had told her, or he'd pick up Chinese. He hoped she knew him better than that, hadn't taken him at his word, and had a nice hot meal waiting for him.

Perhaps, he thought, he could make it to his car in just two trips, if he could snag his briefcase after picking up the box with all the exams. There was some comfort in the thought that if he were working at Shelby State, he wouldn't suffer these indignities. He wouldn't have this many exams to grade, and he wouldn't have *any* faculty recommendations to edit. He wouldn't have had to conduct that faculty meeting on a Friday afternoon before Christmas, and he would have been at home hours ago, enjoying his leisure and looking forward to a weekend of Christmas parties instead of two days of drudgery.

He kicked open the front door and the cold December air slapped him in the face like reality. Who was he fooling? This was his lot in life. This was his burden to bear. And it was definitely a burden, this box he was struggling to hold with one hand while digging in his pocket for keys with the other. If he'd wanted to do something other than what he was doing now, he'd already be doing it. He would have made a move on his own years ago. God knows he'd had his chances. He'd always explained his reluctance by saying he couldn't dream of leaving his mother, but if he'd really wanted that job in the admissions office at Tulane, or at the Alliance Theater in Atlanta, he'd have accepted and worked it out with his mother. In the end, she would have gone with him.

Reentering the school building, he immediately broke out in a sweat from the overheated air. In the winter, he could sweat as much indoors as he sweated outdoors in the summer. For a fat person, there was no way to win. But perhaps he could take his briefcase this time, with the stack of faculty recommendations that were much lighter, and save himself a third trip. This plan succeeded until the coat he was carrying over his arm was pierced by Lin Emery's kinetic sculpture in the foyer. Ultimately he had to drop everything to untangle the jacket from the sharp point which had snared it. He'd miss that sculpture if he had to leave his job. Actually, he realized, he wouldn't miss that sculpture. He'd take it with him; it was his. Bella Whitmire had bequeathed it to him. Of course, it belonged in the school, and he'd have nowhere to put it, but he would take it just the same.

His mother would tell him to sell it and buy a new car, he thought as he finally got into his tired old Caprice Classic, which seemed to groan more and sag further and further under his weight every day. Fortunately, Norman was not one of those people who viewed his automobile as a reflection or extension of himself; on the contrary, his car was an extension of his office. As such, it was a positive junk heap, filled with student papers, glossy application packages from colleges all over the country, and sample textbooks he didn't know what to do with. The Caprice obviously did not have many more miles left in it and the Lin Emery was worth quite a bit of money. But he'd sooner pay to store it than sell it. He couldn't see it at Shelby State either: it didn't belong there any more than he did.

The truth of the matter was, he thought as he cranked up the car and lurched forward, he would not make a good college professor. He wasn't even sure he made a good teacher of young people. But they were the only students he had any business trying to teach, because the main thing he wanted to teach them was how to aspire to something. Not money or power, but something that would satisfy their soul's yearning for fulfillment and transcendence. The sad truth was, most people could not—or did not—light their own fires. But most had the capacity to be ignited if someone else lit that fire. He was that someone else. He lit those fires. He showed young people how to aspire to the top. And it was important to teach young people from a state like Alabama that the very best was not any too good for them. It wasn't just youngsters who were poor, black or from the sticks who needed to learn this lesson either. Children in Mountain Brook suffered also from the low expectations of their society, which primarily demanded that the daddy be rich and the mama good-looking. The Mountain Brook girls who had been marked out for marriage and the Junior League, the boys who had trust funds or family businesses waiting for them all needed to be drop-kicked onto the road where they could discover whatever was within themselves and in the world outside themselves. And after all, if the people who wielded the money and power and status remained mired in the ignorance of their benighted state, then conditions would never improve for anyone else.

On his way he could see the lights of Shangri-La restaurant blazing forth in a riot of neon from the shopping center on Montclair Road. A blinking red and green Season's Greetings sign competed garishly with the orange and blue sign of the restaurant and the bright pink Open sign on the front door. If he stopped in, it would take only (alarmingly) few minutes for them to fill a take-out order, no matter how crowded the restaurant. And he doubted it would be very crowded. With only ten days until Christmas, most people would not be thinking Chinese. Most people would be at a party somewhere. If not for his mountains of papers, he would be at a party himself. But he couldn't—he just couldn't. He had to make a dent in the pile. He couldn't face Monday morning if he hadn't. But he also couldn't face Shangri-La, he decided. The MSG, which they swore they didn't use, somehow wreaked havoc on his bowels nevertheless. It might well be next Wednesday before his system righted itself, and with the Capote reading on Sunday, he couldn't risk it. As he sped past the shopping plaza, he hoped he was greeted at the door with the smell of a nice pot roast or his mother's chicken à la king.

Instead, his mother herself met him at the door with the news that Libba Albritton had just called to say he must—he absolutely must—come to her party tonight: she was counting on him and it would be a flop without him. Then Felicia Keller had called in tears to see if he could pick her up and take her.

"What did you tell them?"

"The same thing," she croaked. "I said you'd be there as soon as you could."

She knew him very well indeed.

~ 7 ~

There was nothing immediately impressive or imposing about the Albritton residence. Unlike all the other houses on Grosvenor Road, it was a somewhat small single story, barely even visible through the trees which surrounded it at the top of the long winding driveway where it was located at some distance from the road. Most of the other houses were those fondly associated with the South: large white colonials with proud columns which clearly wanted to announce their presence at the top to those down below on the road. They also wanted to create the impression that Birmingham, an industrial city if ever there was one, was a product of the "aristocratic" plantation South. In contrast, the Albritton residence seemed shy and withdrawn, as if ashamed of its failure to contribute to the grandeur of the neighborhood. It was a good deal closer to the house on its right than was typical for the estate-sized lots on Grosvenor Road, and had often been mistaken for guest quarters to the larger home. In fact, it had been built on the original lot occupied by the bigger house, whose elderly and very wealthy owner wanted her son and his new bride living next to her, and accordingly built them a house for the purpose.

Only on the inside did the house cease to seem like an aberration or architectural mistake and begin to make sense. Norman Laney had known exactly what it was the first time he'd entered it many years ago. "Frank Lloyd Wright!" he'd exclaimed. Well, not entirely, he could see as his eyes swept the room. But the basic principle was now quite clear to him. The whole point was to make the house disappear into its environment and not compete with or detract from the grander homes on the street, especially the one right next to it. No doubt before the tornado had ripped a dozen trees from the front, the gray shingled house had indeed been invisible from the road. And once inside, what you chiefly saw was the rose garden out back flanked by woods all around. "It's brilliant!" he'd said.

"It's lucky," Libba had said. "The house worked out, my marriage worked out, and my mother-in-law died in a timely fashion."

111

He had roared with laughter, and they'd been fast friends ever since. One of the many, many things he loved about Libba Albritton was her utterly self-confident candor. Although she had grown up in Mountain Brook, she had not come from money and never attempted to pretend otherwise.

"I'm glad you never moved," he'd said, having heard from someone that the original intent was for Milton and Libba to move into "the big house" after old Mrs. Albritton died, and use the smaller place for guests or servants. Instead, Libba had stayed put, and converted the basement into rooms for the children and Milton's wine. The "big house" she had sold to her brother Perry Elmore for a fraction of its value.

"I'm not much of a house person," she had told him. "This suits me just fine. The less house, the better. Less to worry about while we're traveling."

Although they continued to travel extensively, especially after Milton sold Dixie Pies & Pastries to Nabisco, over the years Libba had become more of a house person, and enlisted Norman's help with buying the art. Real art. His suggestions had been modest at first, and they had gone to New Orleans to purchase an Ida Kohlmeier which now hung on the wall next to the dining table. But when contemplating the wall above the mantel, he couldn't stop himself from blurting out that what it really needed was a good Miró. Next thing he knew, he was commissioned to go get one, and stay at the Waldorf, dine at La Grenouille, and enjoy Broadway while he was at it. It had been a most delightful friendship.

This year Libba's house at Christmas made him laugh out loud as soon as he entered. There was not one festive decoration anywhere in the house, nothing red or green, no Santas, no snowmen, no reindeer, not one single acknowledgement of the holiday season except for a tiny, somewhat bedraggled Norfolk pine with drooping branches stuck in the middle of a table in an out-of-the-way corner near the big fireplace. It was swaddled and half swallowed up by an expensive red velvet tree skirt obviously intended for a much larger traditional Christmas tree, as were the ornaments weighing down the slim branches. And it was a masterpiece with Libba's signature written all over it: a Charlie Brown tree with heirloom ornaments and a Neiman Marcus skirt. It was the same way she did everything: her own way. Her style was unmistakable. A sort of "Oh, all right, I'll have a Christmas tree, but I'll do it in my own way."

The overall effect put him more in the holiday spirit than any other party he'd been to this year. Any other Mountain Brook hostess who threw a big party at Christmas had a tree as tall as the ceiling and as big as the room, with Perrino's in to string the lights, hang the ornaments and attach their trademark gold and red bows of silk organza. He could always spot a tree done by Perrino's, and had seen half a dozen so far this season. There was a playful mockery in Libba's gesture—and it was a deliberate gesture, he was sure of that. But her guests would never suspect she was mocking them, and the wretched excess of their holiday decorations, which could easily cost more than he made in a year; they would believe she was mocking herself, and her own laziness as lady of the house. They loved her for it, her refusals to be mistress of the manor or have her hair dyed and her face lifted. Appreciating neither the unconventional beauty of her house nor her looks, they appreciated her rather as one who was incontestably (as Milton Albritton's wife) one of them, yet one who chose not to compete with them. It never crossed their minds that she was ever so slyly and subtly distancing herself from them just enough to carve out her own individual space. Again, a sort of "Oh, all right, I'll be one of you, but I'll do it my own way."

He adored her. She was in on the same little secret he had known all his life: Public opinion, even in a place like Mountain Brook, was a weakling and a coward which usually deferred to the force of a strong personality. Besides, she had food. Glorious food! Until Frank Stitt opened Highlands Bar and Grill a year ago, the best food in Birmingham was found at Libba Albritton's dinner parties. He spied the pâté and made a beeline for the big round table where it lay in a splendor of crystal. With a fresh crust of baguette he scooped a large portion of the bowl's contents and stuffed it in his mouth with joyful abandon. Next thing he knew, Milton Albritton was at his elbow holding a small silver tray with Norman's drink on it. He seized it, lifted it up as if toasting his host, and took a large, grateful swallow as Milton nodded and walked away without saying one word. Milton Albritton was perhaps the most civilized man he'd ever known. Always tended his own bar, knew exactly what each individual guest liked to drink, stocked nothing but the very finest, poured like a professional and served with the quiet courtesy of a black waiter in uniform at the country club. Norman had once heard him remark that the duty of a host was to supply his guests with their favorite drink as soon as they walked through his door, and to give them a moment of peace to enjoy it before expecting even a simple hello in return. Man after his own heart! With another slice of the excellent baguette, he took a second successful swipe at the equally excellent pâté and had just crammed it in his mouth when Horace McWhorter came up and clapped him on the back so hard he almost ejected his mouthful.

"Heard you saw that crazy niece of mine up in New York," he said, lurching a bit unsteadily on his feet.

His mouth still more or less full of pâté, all Norman could do was nod at the disheveled Horace, whose clothes were always as rumpled as if he'd just woken up from a deep sleep while wearing them. His hair was equally unkempt, with little tufts at the back of his head kicking up like a schoolboy's cowlicks.

"What were you doing in New York in the middle of the semester? I thought you were supposed to be a teacher or somepin." Horace liked to affect both a deep Southern accent and a drunken leer, which thoroughly obscured the fact —to opposing attorneys from out of town—that he was one of the sharpest members of the bar in the state of Alabama, with a degree from Yale.

"College trip," said Norman, washing down the pâté with a sip from his drink.

After the tour of Barnard and Columbia, he had asked that know-nothing barbarian of a tour bus driver if they could stop for just a moment at the apartment where Horace's niece currently lived in Manhattan. When the idiot driver had grumbled about not having a place to park, Norman had just ordered him to pull over.

"On the sidewalk?!" the cretin had complained.

"Just let me out, will you?" said Norman. "This will only take a moment. I'm just going to run up and hug her neck."

It was not his fault that the elevator in her building was out of order and that she lived on the top floor. Of course it had taken longer than a moment for a man of his size to go up all those flights of stairs. But he had really only stayed long enough to hug her neck, he assured everybody back on the bus. They were all claiming that he had been gone for almost an hour, and that every horn in New York City had been honking at the backside of the bus jutting out in the street; every middle finger on the sidewalk where the bus was (mostly) parked had been aimed in their direction. The driver, the chaperones and the students were all suffering from post-traumatic stress disorder. But Diane was worth it. She was the kind of woman who made him want to block a New York City street just so he could hug her neck. And she needed it too. At the moment, she was living with a man who was 1) not yet her husband, and 2) Jewish. She had also embarked on a massive project that would take at least a decade to complete. Her family was not exactly giving her much support.

"She still tryin' to write that book?" Horace asked him.

"She's doing a lot more than trying," Norman said. "It will be an interesting day for Birmingham when that book comes out. She'll make a proud uncle out of you yet, Horace."

"Nah," he said, waving his hand drunkenly in front of Norman's face. "We'll all be dead before that book comes out. She'll even be dead before that book comes out."

"What book is this?" said Perry Elmore, Libba's brother. "Merry Christmas, Horace. Norman." He shook hands with both men. Perry, also an attorney, was as natty and composed in his attire as Horace was slovenly in his.

Horace leaned into Perry with the easy intimacy of inebriation, although he had no glass in his hand and it was quite possible he'd had not one drop to drink. "Some pile of horseshit about how all our fathers used to go to parties at the Mountain Brook Country Club and then go home, put on white robes and attend Klan meetings!" Horace's voice rose even more drunkenly as if to emphasize the absurdity of this idea.

"It's a history of the civil rights struggle in Birmingham," said Norman in his best schoolteacher's voice, turning to Perry as if the two of them were wise and knowledgeable parents while Horace was some willfully ignorant child. "And her thesis is that the leaders of Birmingham's business establishment did more than stand idly by while Bull Connor turned on the fire hoses, let loose the police dogs and whipped up the masses against peaceful black protesters."

"Poor old Bull Connor," said Perry. "I really don't believe he had the faintest idea what he was doing. I've heard he was actually the nicest man you'd ever want to meet."

"We-e-e-e-ll," said Norman, not sure about the "poor old Bull Connor" business. "I think Diane's research is indicating that the social elite of Mountain Brook were the ones pulling his strings and masterminding the whole showdown, even if they didn't put on any white robes themselves."

"Rubbish!" bellowed Horace good-humoredly, before staggering off as if he could barely stand on his feet.

Grinning at Perry, Norman shook his head as if amused by the graceless figure of Horace lumbering off. But it was more the thought that Diane's book, if she ever *did* finish it, would not make a dent in the psyche of Mountain Brook. No Brookie seemed to care that their city had gone down in the flames of racial conflagration and was only *now,* twenty years later, recovering from international ignominy and the collapse of the steel industry. They even drew the wrong lesson from the very different fate enjoyed by their sister city Atlanta, a burgeoning metropolis with a booming economy thanks to a progressive business establishment that worked hard to avoid the race wars of the 1960s by complying with desegregation and forging alliances with the black community to prevent violent conflict. Since Birmingham did not wish to be Atlanta, which had grown so large that no one would want to live there, local wisdom held that Atlanta was suffering the entirely predictable misery that came from opening itself to the wider world. So the leadership in Birmingham that had either failed to lead in the 1960s, or led in the wrong direction, had succeeded in keeping the city nice and small. Diane McWhorter's book could criticize the town's white elite to her heart's content, but it would be discounted as the sour grapes of a girl whose father was the black sheep of his prominent family. Unfortunately, if Norman had ever voiced all his own thoughts to all the people who needed to hear them, he would not have been invited to tonight's party, or any party in Mountain Brook. Consequently, he turned back to Perry and changed the subject.

"I enjoyed seeing Caroline when I was up there for the college tour," he said.

"With any luck, Dylan will be there next year."

"Oh, luck will play no part in this," said Norman decisively. "If I'm sure of anything this year, it's Dylan Elmore's acceptance at Harvard."

Before Perry could respond, they heard someone screeching "Norman!" from across the room. Anonymity never lasted long for him, even in a party as lively as this one. "You've got to tell me: Did Warren Ritchie really kill his wife?" The buzz of voices rose even higher as everyone offered their own opinion on the matter.

The two men exchanged a rueful grin acknowledging the end of any substantive conversation, and Perry Elmore seemed anxious to get away before Norman was mobbed by shrieking women.

"Oh, Norman," he said, turning back around just in time to forestall Norman's next attempt to plunder the pâté. "Got one for you."

"What's that?" grinned Norman, anticipating a good joke.

"What's the difference between the students at Harvard and the students at Duke?"

Thanks to Norman, Perry Elmore had children at both of these institutions. Norman grinned even more hugely. "You'll have to tell me, Perry."

"The Harvard students won't hold open the dorm room door for a parent struggling with his child's luggage. The Duke students will." Norman exploded with laughter as Perry said, "That's not a joke, either; that's a true story."

He extended his hand once again in farewell and gratitude. One of the Elmore children was currently attending Harvard, another was bound for there, a third was at Duke, and something equally brilliant awaited the fourth child, all thanks to Norman, who had shown them the way. Meanwhile it would behoove him, Norman thought, to have at least one more go at the pâté before trying to make even meaningless conversation with anyone. Just as he'd finished his third large helping, Jan Lindgren, one of his least favorite people, was upon him.

"You'll never guess what I heard!" she said.

"What's that?" he said, his mouth unapologetically full.

"You're going to get skinny!" she said, with the misplaced hilarity of some-one who'd had at least one more drink than he had.

"Not at this rate," he said, scooping more heaven from the crystal bowl. Thanks to him, it was now becoming a magnet for others. He better get while the getting was good, he decided, and accordingly dipped into the bowl for the fifth time in as many minutes.

"Norman skinny?" scoffed Richard Stedman. "Then who'll be Falstaff in *Part Two* this summer?"

"Not me no matter what," said Norman, licking his fingers noisily. "At least, not in Montgomery. I'll be playing the part of Falstaff for real in the European theater this summer!"

He took advantage of the laughter which ensued to help himself once more to the rapidly diminishing refreshment in front of him. His unabashed gluttony was inspiring others to loosen their grip on themselves and partake more freely. One reason he was so valued at parties was because he knew bet-ter than anyone how to eat, drink and be merry, and he led the way for others to follow.

"But I heard you saw the new doctor," said Jan. "What's his name?"

"What new doctor?" said Richard Stedman.

"You know," said his wife Andrea. "We were talking about him the other day."

"The bariatric surgeon," said Jan. "Can't think of his name. It was on the tip of my tongue a minute ago."

"You washed it down, darling, a drink and a half ago," said Norman, to further laughter. Meanwhile, the spirit of Elizabeth Elder whispered "Watch it!" in his ear. After all, Jan Lindgren could be "the one."

"Harry!" Jan called out to her husband a few feet away. "What's the name of that new stomach specialist at UAB?"

Harry failed to turn around, but Dirk Pendarvis, chairman of the Brook-Haven School board, peeled away from that group to join the one standing at the round table.

"You mean Ron Bosworth?" he said.

"That's it!" said Jan.

"Heard you met with him," said Dirk, addressing himself to Norman and the pâté at the same time, while ignoring Jan completely.

"I knew it," squealed Jan, loud enough this time that her husband did turn around.

"What's this?" he said.

"Norman's planning to have his stomach stapled!" she exclaimed.

News like that delivered in an intoxicated caterwaul like Jan's traveled fast throughout the room, and Norman felt all eyes turning toward him. The best way to neutralize Jan, he knew, was to ignore her attempt to humiliate or expose him, and pretend he didn't care about invasions of his privacy or confidential medical consultations. Instead, he should behave like she'd done him a favor and he was grateful to seize the moment she'd delivered to him.

"Is that true, Norman?" someone called out.

"Absolutely not," said Norman, biting into a gherkin for emphasis. "The doctor said I'd lose a third of my weight. So I have a clear choice between remaining morbidly obese or becoming merely fat. Thin is not in my future."

An undertone of laughter swept through the guests as they inched instinctively toward the round table and lost interest in their previous conversations. The show was about to begin, the audience was settling down and shifting its focus to the main attraction. Norman need only speak in his normal stage voice to be heard above the greatly reduced din of the party.

"Are you going to do it, Norman?" called another voice.

"Absolutely not!" he proclaimed again. "I have no desire to be fat in any ordinary way. If I have to be fat—and apparently I do—I think it's far better to be spectacularly, unbelievably, extra-or-di-nar-i-ly fat, like none other, than to be simply fat, like many others!" As if to declare himself further, he took yet another swipe at the crystal bowl.

"I have never wanted to be mediocre in anything I do!" he continued, his voice beginning to boom. "And I have never liked half-measures!" The pile of pâté on top of his baguette slice attested to the truth of this declaration. "Even when it comes to being fat, I want to go all the way and do a first class job of it. I have no intention of becoming half the man I am now!" He raised his glass as if toasting that thought, and took a dramatic swallow.

"But Norman," wailed Andrea Stedman through the general laughter. "It would add years to your life."

"Oh, darling," he said. "I'd have to give up my trip to Europe this summer. That would take away many more years of my life."

There was more laughter. All over the room the party guests were now discussing Dr. Ron Bosworth, the efficacy of bariatric surgery, and whether or not they believed Norman Laney should undergo this procedure. Many were now pressing through the throng to deliver their advice to Norman himself: they had heard horror stories, they had heard success stories, they even knew people who'd had the operation. But no one, it appeared, had met the new doctor, who had bought a house in Forest Park instead of Mountain Brook.

Birmingham, everyone agreed, was changing indeed. When the new surgeon in town didn't buy in Mountain Brook, the world was definitely changing. Norman found himself besieged on all sides with well-wishers and opinion givers.

"Heard something else too," said Dirk Pendarvis, almost under his breath. His back was now to Norman as he bent over to scrape what little remained of Libba's mushroom and chicken liver concoction. Somehow his voice penetrated the clamor as often happens when the speaker isn't trying to. "Heard you're thinking of leaving Brook-Haven." Provisions in hand, he turned around to face Norman Laney while taking a careful bite, with eyebrows raised to question the truth of this rumor.

Enough people heard Dirk's quiet bombshell and were stilled with the shock that often occurs in provincial places where people aren't expected to go anywhere or do anything out of the ordinary or change in significant ways. When someone in a prominent position flew in the face of these non-expectations, it could create a sensation of melodramatic proportions. In an instant a general hush descended so that everyone could learn what had happened.

"Oh, Larry Plumlee's been after me for years," said Norman, as dismissively as he could. "I finally agreed to hear the man out. Doesn't mean a thing," he said airily, sipping his drink with carefree unconcern.

"Smart move," said Dirk, wiping his mouth with a crumpled cocktail napkin. "We don't begin to pay you what you're worth, but sometimes the only way to get the Board to notice is to goose them like this. You're bound to be offered a raise in April. I'll personally see to it myself."

Norman shrugged as if it were all of little consequence, just as Libba, hearing a lull in the party buzz, came in to announce dinner. While the crowd began making its way like a giant amoeba toward the dining area, where Libba always had her buffet line, Norman Laney closed ranks with Dirk Pendarvis around the crystal bowl and the guests turned to one another to corroborate the impossible news they'd just heard: Norman Laney was leaving Brook-Haven??

"I think we can count on NYU," Norman said to Dirk. "But we can't forget our back-ups and Luke never brought me those applications."

Dirk nodded abstractedly while looking around the empty room as if searching for something.

"Where's Carla?" said Norman.

"Oh, she's already in Italy. We'll join her there for Christmas in two days. Luke did tell you, didn't he, that he'll be missing the last few days of school next week?"

Actually, Luke had neglected to do so, as he neglected so many other tasks, both large and small. And Norman instantly forgave him, as he always did. However, he made a mental note to give Luke what-for about both missing school and failing to bring by the other two applications. It wouldn't do Luke any good to know how easily he could get away with just about anything. He'd simply become that much more lax. Absently Norman put his finger in the bowl to scrape some of the streaks of pâté from the sides.

"You know Luke is going to be the lead in our spring play?" he said.

Dirk seemed to snap out of a reverie induced by the rose garden, now visible through the wall of windows facing the backyard. "No," he said. "Luke didn't tell me."

Probably because Norman hadn't told Luke yet, and wasn't supposed to until after the tryouts.

"What's the play?" said Dirk, following Norman's lead and excavating with a crust of bread the remains at the bottom of the bowl.

"*Rosencrantz and Guildenstern are Dead.* I'm directing. I hope Carla will be there to see it." Honestly he had no such hopes about Carla, whom he didn't know at all well because she spent most of her time somewhere other than Birmingham. Doing what? Nobody exactly knew. There was an apartment in New York and a villa in Tuscany, and no rumors of trouble in the marriage or Dirk philandering, so she somehow failed to generate gossip. Unlike Dirk, she had not grown up in Birmingham, and had managed to remain enough of an unknown quantity that people had no choice but to leave it at that. Dirk was in that magical position of having so much money and so much obvious intellect while performing so many thankless community services, that people paid him the respect and courtesy of exempting him from their gossip.

"How much are they offering you?" said Dirk abruptly.

"Oh," said Norman, taken aback at the failure of his gambit. It was usually possible to redirect any parent's attention from even the most compelling matter by bringing up the subject of his children.

"Are they going so far as to offer you an official contract?"

"I'm afraid so," Norman sighed. "I was just being polite, paying an informal visit during lunch, you know. The least I could do in return for Larry's kindness to me all these years. But apparently they *are* putting together a formal offer even though I begged them not to." He shrugged at the stupidity of bureaucratic processes. "Wonder what awaits us in the dining room?"

"Bring me that contract when you get it, why don't you?" said Dirk. "I can use it to tell the rest of the Board everything they need to know."

Norman set his glass down on the table and studied his shoes as if embarrassed. When he looked up, he said quietly, "I don't expect a small private school to be able to pay me anything close to what a growing community college can. And it's not like me to use strong arm tactics—"

"You won't be," Dirk interrupted. "I will be. And the Board will thank me for it." He nodded toward the dining room and touched Norman lightly on the elbow to indicate his readiness to rejoin the party. "Tom Turbyfill working out all right?"

"Yes—all right," said Norman, with just the slightest hesitation as the two began making their way to the buffet.

Dirk swung his head around. "Just all right, is it?" he said sharply. "I knew the man was a fool. I voted against hiring him, you know."

Norman nodded but said nothing. He well knew.

"Not giving you any trouble, is he?" said Dirk.

Norman skipped a few beats before responding, and then merely shrugged.

"I would expect you to come to me if he was causing trouble."

Norman nodded. He had thought many times about doing just that, but Elizabeth had counseled explicitly against consulting Dirk or any other Board member. It would be different, she said, if they knew what Turbyfill had on him. But since they didn't know, they couldn't appeal to the Board. Norman must *never* behave as if afraid or in need of help, she insisted, although this precisely defined the state of his existence at the moment. No matter, she said; he *must not* go to the Board and ask them for help in keeping his job. That would plant seeds of doubt and perhaps even generate an odor of guilt. Instead, he must turn the tables on Tom Turbyfill. The Board must come to Norman and beg him to keep his job, as it would in due time, she assured him. *As long as he stuck to her plan and carried it out.*

"So there's no particular problem from that source?" said Dirk, lowering his voice as they came closer to the other guests.

Instead of lowering his own voice, Norman spoke a bit more loudly than normal, as if trying to make himself heard above the din they were now approaching. "Turbyfill is no more of a problem than I expected of someone who cares nothing for art and culture and whose main qualification appears to be a lack of desire to have sexual relations with his students. Oh—and a doctorate in education."

Rather than laughing, Dirk stopped abruptly on the threshold of the dining room. "You should have taken that position yourself."

"Oh," said Norman breezily, "there will always be lots of things I should have done. But you're right," he conceded more seriously. "I should have

121

taken that position myself." He lunged forward and grabbed a dinner plate, leaving Dirk standing there alone, apparently somewhat stunned by Norman's unexpected admission.

Behind him the help was rapidly clearing the round table and setting up chairs so it could serve now as a dinner table. Even for thirty people like she had this evening, Libba believed in seated dinners. Otherwise, she said, you couldn't really enjoy the food or the conversation. With twelve in her dining room, eight at her breakfast table, and ten more at the round table in the big living area, she managed to seat everyone at the party. The dining table had been pushed against one of the walls of the room, where it served as the buffet. In the center of the room were three sturdy card tables draped with crisp white linen.

Instead of waiting in line, Dirk sat down at one of these tables in an empty seat next to Felicia Keller. Pouring them both a glass of Milton's excellent red wine from the bottle on the table, he began chatting with her as if nothing were amiss. This was the kind of public service Dirk Pendarvis was known and respected for, though most people didn't know what to make of him anymore than they did of his wife. Obviously brilliant, as an aeronautical engineer he had designed and patented a device later used by the military on its jets and made a fortune in his twenties. What that device was exactly no one but Dirk and the military could know for sure. Now he worked as a consultant and no one knew exactly what he did or who he did it for, except that he was often in Washington. Clearly he could have lived somewhere else, as his wife mostly chose to do, but Dirk remained committed to his home town and took on many a community chore, like sitting on the board of the Brook-Haven School or sitting in the empty seat next to the fallen Felicia Keller.

Since this wasn't one of Libba's more formal affairs, she didn't have place cards tonight, but everyone knew her rule that husbands and wives were forbidden to sit next to one another. However, it appeared that all husbands were reluctant to sit next to Fee. As Frank Keller's wife, Fee had been universally embraced as a dazzling social butterfly to whom all were eager to pay tribute. But as Frank Keller's castoff, she was suddenly just a foolish female, a silly little flibbertigibit who cared too much for parties and clothes and had senselessly, unforgivably ignored the most vital responsibility of any woman's life: her man. Women of her generation had been taught to marry the man who could "provide the best," and to keep him happy. In other words, marry for money and never forget that you're working for your living every day of your married life. But the work that Fee had done in recent years had been primarily for all those charities and philanthropic organizations. She had been highly respected for it in Mountain Brook until Frank Keller had let it be known that he preferred staying at home in the evening instead of attending fund-raising dinners and charity balls. Apparently a rift had been developing for years, unknown to Mountain Brook society until Frank had confided to his newly widowed neighbor: "She's been cold to me for a long time." Earlier that week, one of Norman's lady friends had summed up the divorce by saying: "All that money, and she couldn't fake an orgasm." Norman had been thoroughly shocked: he hadn't realized that any of the Mountain Brook women he knew were familiar with that particular word, let alone the concept itself. Mountain Brook ladies had always struck him as being unacquainted with ecstasy of any kind. Probably they were, but they at least knew they needed to fake it, and some were obviously more successful at this than others. At any rate, Felicia Keller was now deemed such a miserable failure that no one but Dirk could even bring himself to sit next to her.

Of course, Libba had had no choice but to invite the Kellers. They were always invited to her Christmas party, and she couldn't slight Frank: he'd done nothing wrong. Libba's Christmas party was one of the few he actually attended, since it wasn't a huge cocktail party but an intimate seated dinner where a meaningful conversation and an excellent sit-down meal were both possible. But Frank had possessed the good sense to decline this year, and the general feeling was that Fee should have done so as well, especially with her children home for the last Christmas they would have together as a family in their house. There was something both pathetic and desperate about her effort to clutch so publicly at the life which had already slipped through her grasp.

Meanwhile, Norman found a seat at the big breakfast table in the kitchen, which Libba had cleverly shielded by placing the most enormous poinsettias he'd seen this year along the butcher block island table in the middle of the room. On the other side were the roses in the garden, and it was a most pleasant effect, to be surrounded by flowers in the middle of December. He was even happy to sit next to old Dot Trimble, Milton's aunt, who had only one good ear if she'd remembered to turn on her hearing aid. It was unlikely she'd caught all the conversation earlier in the evening, and Norman had no trouble steering the talk to their upcoming trip to Europe. Dot was the only one still living of the original group he'd taken on that first trip years ago with Bella Whitmire. Apart from her deafness, she was in excellent health and less likely to drop dead in the Louvre than he was.

"Ever been to Switzerland?" said Richard Stedman. "Andrea and I are going skiing there after Christmas."

"What would I do on an alp?" said Norman. "I'm obviously not fit for either mountain climbing or skiing."

"But the scenery!" called Andrea from the other end of the table. "I just go for the view! I don't even like to ski."

"You'll never catch me gazing at mountains or wildflowers," said Norman, glad that none of her children had ever attended Brook-Haven. "I want to see paintings and sculptures! Don't give me what God can do! I want to see what man can do!"

"Now tell us the truth," said Andrea. "You're not really thinking of leaving Brook-Haven, are you?"

"Of course not," said Norman. "I just went to see the new building at Shelby State. As a courtesy to Larry Plumlee. That's all. If I'd ever been interested in teaching there I would have accepted long before now."

"Brook-Haven is so lucky to have you," she murmured, obviously disappointed that she would have no scoop to impress those who had not been at the party or even those at the party who hadn't sat at the table with Norman Laney.

For the rest of the evening, in between three helpings of moussaka, with its perfectly seasoned ground lamb and a triumphant layer of béchamel, he was busy issuing this same denial. "Oh, good heavens, no. Larry's always offering me a job. Doesn't mean a thing." Nevertheless, the news from Libba's Christmas party was deemed major if inconclusive: Norman Laney was considering having his stomach stapled and leaving the Brook-Haven School.

* * *

On the drive home, Fee was uncharacteristically quiet. Usually she was chattering, glittering, tossing her dangling earrings, and flashing her radiant smile as her beauty and charm worked their magic. In silence and stillness she deflated; her beauty and charm disappeared. She was about five years away from her first face lift, Norman supposed, not because she would need one but because she would seize on that as the answer to what had happened to her. At the end of the Albritton's driveway, where the street lamps suddenly illuminated the road, she turned her head toward the window so he wouldn't see the tears on her cheeks.

Looking both ways more than once, Norman edged cautiously and tentatively out of the driveway so he could see whether any of the high school boys were up to their tricks yet. As a result, the Caprice Classic lurched in fits and starts onto the road as if it, like its driver, had enjoyed a bit too much of Milton's superior wine and whiskey. But Grosvenor Road, with its peaks, valleys and hairpin curves, was used as a racing strip on weekend nights, and many a seventeen year-old boy was known to crash a brand-new BMW right about where Norman's car was now. Mailboxes had to be replaced two or three times a year. Now Norman wished he'd parked like the others on the street instead of up by the house as Milton and Libba always invited him to do, thinking to spare him a walk up the drive which would have him sweating like August ten days before Christmas. The last thing he needed was a head-on collision with a boy half his age, with half his brain, driving ten times his car. If that were to happen, they could forget about the emergency room and just take him straight on to John's Ride-Out's.

"I told you not to come," he said, peering one last time to his left. With sudden determination, he stepped forcefully on the gas, and the Caprice pitched with a slight screech into the road, not at all gracefully, but at least successfully and safely.

Fee put her head in her hands and stifled a sob. "What can I do?" she moaned softly. "What can I do?"

"We've already decided what you're going to do. You're going to get yourself down to Palm Beach, put on your best dress and give your brightest smile to every single man who comes to the New Year's Eve party your sister is giving in your honor. If it works out, you stay put, if it doesn't, you come to Europe with me this summer and we'll figure out Plan B."

Silently Fee shook her head, still buried in her hands.

"What?" he looked over at her sharply. "You've changed your mind?"

"I don't know," she said through her sobs. "I just don't know."

"Well I do. Your sister has already ordered the invitations. I know this for a fact because she called me about the wording. You owe it to her as well as yourself to go through with it. You can't back out now, and there's nothing left for you in Mountain Brook. Surely tonight you saw that for yourself."

Fee rummaged in her evening bag and pulled out a tissue. "I must look a mess," she said, dabbing at the corners of her eyes.

"I don't think you ought to walk through your front door looking anything but your absolute best. You've got to pull yourself together, and not just for tonight, but for Christmas and Palm Beach and the rest of your life."

The damage to her make-up was so extreme Norman was amazed she'd actually allowed herself to cry. He also hadn't realized until then just how much make-up she'd been wearing. Fee began working hurriedly to repair the damage, scolding herself for the idiocy of tears and the absence of mascara in her miniscule clutch purse. The sequins on her dress sparkled almost mockingly in the light of her little make-up mirror which she was consulting so intensely. He wouldn't be surprised if there were a thousand sequins on that dress or if it had cost that same amount in dollars.

Poor darling, he thought, wishing he had more insight to offer into her failed marriage. But the truth was, Norman knew nothing about sexual relationships. Cursed as he was with his behemoth of a body, he was at least blessed to have few urges to engage that impossible body with other bodies or force it into postures that would have made it a million times more ridiculous that it already was. He himself had been spared the problem of sex, and was for the most part happy not to be compelled into doomed, undignified encounters with someone else involving inadequate bedsprings and the inexorable laws of gravity.

On the whole, he did not feel shortchanged and rebuffed the condescension of those who pitied him for not having "a full life." According to the gossip he heard—and he heard it all—sex was problematic for everyone: the married, the divorced, the straight and the gay. (And yes, there were plenty of gay people in Birmingham, only everyone was still pretending otherwise.) But no matter what you were, there was either too much sex, not enough, or not the right kind. The two people who had once gloated to him about their sex lives turned out to be in one case impotent and in the other case sleeping in the guest bedroom. Both were divorced within a few years of making their inebriated boasts. People always chose him to be the sounding board and repository for the juicy tidbits of everyone else's private life, because they assumed he had no private life of his own and needed this form of compensation. After years of being privy to the most intimate details of so many other people's lives, he could only feel sorry for them in return. So many people spent so much time trying to get exactly what they wanted out of sex that there was little time left over for anything else. When they got what they wanted, he couldn't see that it made their lives so much more "full"—certainly not fuller than his—and no one really got all they wanted from sex—not for long anyway. It seemed to him everybody wanted more from sex than it could possibly give them, precisely because they were ignoring so many other sources of pleasure in life, like art and culture. Meanwhile it tied up their thoughts and tangled up their lives. He was more than happy to be free from that preoccupation and find his pleasures in food and drink, art and culture.

He looked back over at Fee, dabbing gently at her nose so as not to smear the newly applied lipstick. Again his heart went out to her. In a way, the same thing had happened to them both. They had simply been themselves, broken a few rules in the process, gotten away with it and assumed they always would. Until, suddenly, they didn't get away with it. You never knew when the ground you walked on was going to give way beneath you, when the rules you'd broken would be used against you. You could be the same person you'd always been, doing the same thing you'd been doing for twenty years with the world's blessing, and the next thing you knew, you were cuffed and led away.

"What did you think of Jan's dress?" Fee turned to him suddenly.

Norman smiled. She had been deeply pondering something of monumental importance: her competition. "Outrageous," he replied. "But I suppose if you spend that much on a pair of breasts, it compels you to show them off."

"She didn't have it done here."

"Can you blame her?"

Fee lapsed into silence again, but it was clear she did blame Jan, both for being younger and for taking advantage of the new rules of the game, which enabled anyone with enough money to acquire the kind of physical attractions Fee was used to possessing as her own unique birthright.

"How did you think she looked?" said Fee, biting her lip.

At first he hesitated, then decided on the brutal truth. "Damn good," he said. She'd better get used to it, he thought. She'd see a lot more of it in Palm Beach.

Glancing over, he could see Fee was again on the verge of tears, and they were almost in her neighborhood. "Jan's a fool," he told her. "A pitiful fool," he repeated, thinking of Jan's daughter Sally. Her two older girls, both as slim and pretty as their mother, had attended Mountain Brook High School and were now at "Bama" going to football games and fraternity parties. Their model for success and happiness was a life like their mother's, and in twenty years they would be getting tipsy at Christmas parties and flaunting their own cosmetic enhancements. If she hadn't been fat, Sally would have "enjoyed" the same fate. But her mother hadn't wanted her overweight daughter to be ridiculed or rejected at the high school, and had enrolled her in Brook-Haven instead. As for college, she would be happy if her daughter could go to a fat farm for four years, graduate with a degree in weight management, and use it to obtain the kind of husband her sisters would no doubt be marrying soon after college.

Norman felt his jaw clench in anger and determination. He would show Sally that being fat was the best thing that had ever happened to her. Her fat was her freedom, her ticket out. He would show her how to use it—no, by God, he would use it for her—he *was* using it for her—to get her to a better place and a better life than her parents knew how to dream of for her. Not for her the Mountain Brook curse of low expectations that she could never live up to because she wasn't born to be beautiful and thin. She would not go to "Bama." She would not become bulimic, anorexic, suicidal or slutty. And she would not end up like Fee. Without beauty or body, she would nevertheless find a happiness unknown to women like Felicia Keller or Jan Lindgren.

And the extent of the happiness she was able to achieve in her life would measure the success Norman had been able to achieve in his. This was somewhat ironic, given that once upon a time he had not even wanted the boys school he worked for to merge with the girls school that had brought all these girls into his career. At the time, he wasn't sure how his boys would handle all the girls, and didn't know what he would do with them either. But surprisingly, ever since the merger, the girls had taken over in his mind. Year after year, he found himself much more caught up in the strivings and struggles of his girls than his boys. Quite frankly, the girls needed him more. And his intervention was much more crucial to their ultimate fate. It wasn't that they were more needy or helpless, just that their society tried harder to control and shape them. This wasn't something that happened just in the South, either. Wherever you looked—past, present, near, far—women were often conscripted as the vessels of their culture. It was when those women were able to choose their own destinies that the culture often changed for the better. Also, what good would it do for the men to be enlightened if the women weren't? If the men made wives and mothers out of women who were creatures of the past, then nothing would change. So the girls were the key. And it was up to Norman to help these girls as much as he could.

"That's my mailbox." Fee pointed to a structure almost obscured by its Christmas decorations. "The one with the big pine cones."

He turned into a driveway almost as long and winding as the Albritton's.

"Is Fred here yet?"

She nodded.

All her sons had been former students of Norman's, but Fred was now an investment banker with Salomon Brothers in New York. In a few years' time, Malcolm Fielder was going to need a job on Wall Street, and Norman intended to lay the groundwork.

"Have him call me, will you?"

"The boys and their father are going to the lake house tomorrow," she said wearily. "Fishing. Then next week they're all going hunting. But I'm sure he'll call you. He said he hoped to see you."

"Good. Now take care of yourself and give me a ring if you're feeling low."

But she made no effort to get out of the car and stared straight ahead through the windshield as if mesmerized. There was something wrong with the idle on his car, which was heaving and rasping noisily as if in its death throes. Fee didn't seem to notice.

"Go on," he urged. "You need your rest, and God knows, so do I." And he needed to put his foot on the gas so his car wouldn't stall.

"You're not really going to have that operation, are you?" she asked, turning toward him.

"Operation?" he yawned, temporarily at a loss.

"The stomach stapling."

"Oh. I doubt it. I haven't got the money or the time for something like that. My insurance won't cover it and the recovery is six to eight weeks. I'd have to cancel Europe. And I have no intention of letting my old ladies down like that."

"You know Frank would happily give you the money. All you have to do is let me know. But—"

"There are far better charitable causes than my wretched hulk. I'll call you with a list tomorrow. Now get on inside and get some sleep." He yawned again. At that moment his car finally stalled out.

She seized his hand and squeezed it. "Of course you should do what's best for your health," she said. "And the money won't be an issue. It's just that—" she paused.

"It's just that a new performing arts center for the Brook-Haven School would be a much better investment."

"It's just that we all love you the way you are."

"Of course you do, darling. Fat in other people is a very comforting thing."

"It's not just fat," she protested helplessly, letting go of his hand and throwing up her own. "It's you." She reached for the door handle. "Oh, I don't know how to say what I mean! If I were one of your students instead of just your friend, there might be some hope for me. As it is, I'm just a silly ole thing." She blew him a kiss and dashed out of the car, whirling around almost gaily in a twirl of silk and sparkling sequins to shut the door and wave good-bye before running inside like a high school girl trying to make curfew after a date.

In spite of his exhaustion, Norman was deeply moved by her words and sat for some moments in the driveway before trying to crank up his car. "It's not just fat," she had said. "It's you." Notwithstanding her self-deprecation, she had expressed herself quite well, even to the point of reminding him why he loved her. She was not just a vain and empty creature of society, as she had been brought up to be and tried her best to be in the misguided belief that this was the key to her happiness. She possessed a genuine warmth and depth of feeling which was precisely why he loved her.

Norman pumped his gas pedal and turned the key in the ignition with no result. He pumped again and waited a few seconds before turning the key. Still no result. No doubt he had flooded the engine as he was prone to do with his big mastodon's foot on the gas. There was nothing to do but wait it out a few more minutes.

On the other hand, her husband Frank Keller, in his own polite way, was a barbarian. He belonged to that worst species of Alabama male, who worshipped hunting, fishing, and Alabama football. It was even more unforgivable in Frank, a man of money and means, than it was in the working class men of Norman's home town. There were plenty of Alabama rednecks who lived for hunting, fishing, and Alabama football. Men in Mountain Brook with money needed to be civilized and lead the way. With all his fortune, Frank had never once, for example, taken Fee to dinner at Highlands Bar and Grill. His idea of eating out was prime rib and corn pones at the Mountain Brook Country Club. His idea of a vacation was a weekend at his lake place, where he would spend all day in a Goddamned boat holding a fishing pole. He'd never once been to Europe. Fee had declared (to Norman if not to Frank) that she would not be a slave to the two hours Frank was home every evening. But she had made the mistake of assuming that she was loved for who she was rather than who she had married. She had forgotten that her legitimacy came from the mere fact of her marriage. And while Frank might be a bore to his wife, in Mountain Brook, money was never boring, and a man who had money was always regarded as a dazzling genius, regardless of where his money came from or what his mind was made of.

Without even touching the pedal, he tried the key, but the car wouldn't start, although it made a few choking sounds. Lightly tapping the pedal, he tried again, but this time, there wasn't even the choking noise. He sighed and leaned back. Through the curtain of one of the windows in the Keller house he could see the shadowy silhouettes of Fee and Frank, and the restraining hand she had on his arm, holding him back. Probably Frank wanted to come out and help him with the car, and Fee was trying to prevent him. She'd already experienced the ordeal of his car twice tonight, and her social instincts were for pretending not to notice when the man you were with was engaged in anything less than manly behavior.

For all her supposed bubble brain, Fee had articulated his own most private thoughts about himself and his fat. His grotesque obesity was a kind of hideous deformity, especially in a culture which prized the thin and the beautiful above everyone else, including the good and the smart. But instead of letting this deformity become a disabling weakness, he had turned it into his source of strength and power. In return, it was his job now to show all the others who were not thin or beautiful or generously endowed with the benefits of the world how to derive their own strength and power from whatever dubious blessings had been bestowed on them. The real secret was that he had not merely accepted his handicap—his fat—but embraced it. The source of his whole identity and personality flowed largely—in more ways than one—from his uniquely sensational fat. He didn't hide behind it or lose himself in it: he was it.

"You'll be a new man," the doctor had told him, if he had the surgery. Well, that was just it. Losing his weight would be like losing his job: he would lose himself as he knew it. His fat had been his ticket in to the most exclusive society in Alabama. Once he was in, he was allowed and even begged to stay on the basis of who he was. He thought. He hoped. But he was not eager to put it to the test. He couldn't be entirely sure that if he lost his fat he wouldn't lose his acceptance. So he didn't want to be a new man. And he hadn't ever wanted to be anybody other than who he was since surviving the crucible of childhood and adolescence as a fat boy in a blue collar town more prone to wanton cruelty than tolerance and compassion.

Early on he had learned how to make his fat work for him, exactly as he had once explained to Mira Vernon. In school the other children had inevitably taunted and jeered at him until he demonstrated that he could be funny in more ways than one. Soon enough, their mean-spirited laughter turned into appreciative amusement. Although he could neither run, jump, nor climb the jungle gym on the playground, he could imitate all of their teachers. Later he did Jackie Gleason imitations that even the teachers would come to watch. He knew how to perform; he was entertainment. And he realized then that if he entertained his audience properly, they would forgive him anything, even for being fat.

By high school, his classmates didn't even notice his fat anymore; nor did they realize he was their valedictorian until the graduation ceremony. To them, he was simply the beloved class clown, who could always dispel their boredom or divert the teachers' attention away from the lesson. In his valedictory address, he synthesized his roles as star pupil by night and court jester by day into a self-deprecating, class celebrating dramatic monologue that had everyone laughing, clapping and stomping their approval throughout. Pratt City High had never seen anything like it before, and never would again.

At Birmingham-Southern he had found his niche and made his mark in the drama department; it was the first of many times he was to play Falstaff in *Henry IV, Part One* and *Two.*

For the most part, he had indeed used his fat to his advantage, and while it might have prevented him from leading anything like a normal life, he had used it in turn as his own private barge into rare and wonderful waters unknown to regular folk. In exchange for not having a normal life, he had enjoyed an exceptional one. On the whole, he had to acknowledge it was a fair enough trade. In other words, he was happy. For a fat boy who came from Pratt City, Alabama, made less money than a starting sanitation worker and lived with his mother to be able to say he was happy: this was success indeed. He didn't want any other. Most emphatically, he did not want to be a new man.

But he did want sleep. No doubt he had been pushing it, as he always did, to attend the party when he was already exhausted before even going. When he turned the key this time, the car cranked almost noiselessly. Not wanting to take any chances, he put his foot down so rapidly on the gas that the car practically sailed down the driveway.

On the drive home he reflected that Elizabeth would probably say important progress had been made in furthering "the strategy." However, he had been alarmed at how quickly news about him of a private nature could spread. Of course, as Elizabeth had advised, he had not asked Larry Plumlee to keep the interview confidential. She wanted the word to get out, and did not want Dr. Plumlee thinking that Norman was merely angling for a raise at Brook-Haven. But Larry Plumlee was not a member of Mountain Brook society—didn't live there, didn't work there, didn't travel in those circles. Nevertheless, the word was out much sooner than he'd expected.

And he utterly failed to comprehend how the news of his medical consultation could be all over town. Valerie would never betray his confidence on anything, and certainly not on a medical matter. Nevertheless, word of his doctor's appointment had gotten out somehow, and it was disturbing to think what other secrets he tried to harbor might be already out in the open. The town was a fishbowl if ever there was one; and he was a whale if ever there was one. It was not a comfortable position to be in: a whale in a fishbowl.

At home his mother was taking brownies out of the oven, and he ate half a dozen off the cooling rack before she shooed him out of the kitchen and sent him straight to bed.

~ 8 ~

Mr. Laney lived in one of the several apartment complexes in Mountain Brook occupied almost exclusively by "the newly-wed and the nearly dead," according to the popular expression in town. Unlike most of the newer, quickly and cheaply constructed condominiums and apartment buildings sprouting up all over the city, these structures possessed a certain dignity that came not only from their age but from their stately red brick exteriors and lofty interiors of high ceilings and hardwood floors. They blended in nicely with the houses they often resembled and adjoined in neighborhoods near Crestline, English and Mountain Brook villages. It was the only way to live in Mountain Brook without paying the usual price of Mountain Brook real estate. And it was considered an acceptable location for young couples saving up to purchase their first home or elderly widows no longer interested in maintaining a house. The rents were reasonable and the waiting lists were as long as they were secret. Procuring a place in one of these complexes was mostly a matter of who you were and who you knew, and could be as complicated as getting into the country club.

When Norman Laney had first moved from Pratt City years ago, the only place he could find and afford that wasn't unbearably barbaric was right off the Red Mountain Expressway, all the way out near Vestavia. Nine months later, Bella Whitmire got lost when she tried to "run something over" to his "house." When she finally found where he lived, she was appalled and immediately took the necessary steps to find him "a more suitable place to live." After their trip to Europe that summer, he moved into the apartment building next to Crestline Village where he'd been ever since. The location was mercifully near the school, and not far from the Piggly Wiggly, or "the Pig," where his mother preferred to shop for her groceries. Over time she made friends with Phyllis, another elderly resident who still had her car and took Norma to "the Pig" nearly every day. The buildings were well maintained and

133

the rent was mysteriously lower than what he'd paid for his first apartment which had none of the charm or convenience of location. Altogether, Norman felt he couldn't complain about the small size of the rooms or the lack of a second bathroom, especially since his was a corner unit with a bit of extra space that allowed for a separate den as well as living room.

Although some of his students had visited relatives in the building, most had never been inside his own apartment. It was a special privilege for the members of the "Art in the 20th Century" class to be invited there in December for a salon such as Gertrude Stein and Alice B. Toklas might have hosted at 27 Rue de Fleurus. All of them had heard about his place, and believed they knew what to expect from having been in his office, with its unruly clutter of art and books filling every available space on the floor, walls, desk and shelves. However, none of them found they had been quite prepared for what they encountered as soon as they stepped into Mr. Laney's tiny foyer.

For one thing, the already small apartment was made even smaller by the magnitude of Mr. Laney's mountainous girth and the voluminous collection of art and books literally covering every inch of space. There seemed to be little room for any other occupant. Heavy gilt frames as well as large unframed canvases jutted out from the walls; vases, sculptures and objets d'art sprouted up from the tables. With Mr. Laney standing in the foyer, beaming widely with the two rosy balls of flesh on either side of his smile, there didn't seem to be any way for the first wave of students to enter. Apart from the enormity of Mr. Laney in the center of the narrow hallway, there was a huge canvas painted on all sides on the wall to his right, and on his left was a table with a sculpture of a young girl on a swing, with her legs stretched out in front, her hair flying out behind, and her back arched in the childhood ecstasy of soaring through the air. Either you bumped your head on the canvas, had your skin pricked by the girl's metal feet, or ran smack into the abdominous protrusion of Mr. Laney's middle. Yet somehow the first four crowded in without mishap to themselves or the contents of the apartment.

"Is she having an orgasm?" said Luke Pendarvis, looking down with amusement at the girl whose feet threatened to jab him in the arm.

"Not the kind you would understand," retorted Mr. Laney.

"How many kinds are there?" said Luke, with growing amusement, while his three classmates stood scandalized and tried to stifle their laughter and horror. Luke was always pushing it and going too far, but he'd never gone so far as to use the word "orgasm" in the classroom in front of one of their teachers, and they weren't sure how Mr. Laney would take it in his own home as soon as they'd walked through the door.

"There are many kinds of intellectual and spiritual rapture which you'd know about if you ever came to class or did your work," said Mr. Laney, with continued good humor.

Luke shrugged while his classmates laughed openly now. "This looks pretty physical to me," he said, yelling "Ouch!" as the girl's foot finally got him.

"You must not have been paying attention during Gayle's lessons on metaphor," said Mr. Laney, steering these four toward his living room as the slamming of a car door indicated more arrivals.

The twenty students who eventually crowded into Mr. Laney's apartment for the two o'clock salon all found themselves literally face to face with the collection of art they had so often heard about. Luke made a joke of it, as he made a joke of everything, and asked if this was what Mr. Laney meant when he spoke of intense encounters with art and culture. For emphasis and further laughs, he rubbed his arm where the sculpture had poked him. But there was something undeniably special about being so close to all the pictures that had an immediate impact, visual and otherwise. The apartment seemed all art, and nothing else. With pictures jammed up next to one another so that the frames were actually touching and even threatening to overlap, no wall space was actually visible. And as all the walls were similarly covered, one wall disappeared into another until they all disappeared and there was no sense of walls anywhere in the apartment. Contributing to this effect was the placement of the pictures, which seemed haphazard and inapt at first glance, but proved a clever optical trick. Oils, watercolors, pen and ink drawings, lithographs and guaches were as crazily juxtaposed as the cubist, the abstract, the pictorial and the impressionistic. Ornate, formal frames hung side by side with works that had no frames or prints with metal frames. The hodge-podge arrangement served to showcase each piece by preventing one work from blending into another, and further prevented the walls of solid art from seeming like walls. And as the walls vanished, what had at first seemed like an impossibly tiny apartment was magically transformed into an arena of beauty and light that encouraged the soul to soar like the girl in the sculpture was soaring on her swing.

Mr. Laney's students got it. Here the lessons he expounded in his class-room were evident all over his apartment, as the art and culture which abounded crowded out everything else to the point of banishing it alto-gether. They could see what he meant about earthly limitations falling away, and the mind taking flight, powered by art and culture. His whole apart-ment, like he himself, was a monument to Art and Culture. The way the entire space overflowed with splendors suggested a spirit set free and joyfully transcending its physical boundaries.

When Mr. Laney retreated for a moment into the kitchen, Luke Pendarvis picked up a Venetian Carnivale mask from the table next to him and placed it over his face. Karen Ritchie, who had been invited to capture the occasion for inclusion in the yearbook, snapped a picture and a flashbulb went off. Taking a bow, Luke replaced the mask just as Mr. Laney returned bearing a tray with miniature watercress sandwiches. There was already an extensive spread on the dining room table, most of which, Mr. Laney said, came straight out of Alice's cookbook.

After Karen took that first picture, something seemed to snap also in the students. The unique spectacle of Mr. Laney's apartment along with the unique sensation of being treated as his equals had initially confounded them. But here they were, in Mr. Laney's apartment at last. Half of their senior year was behind them, as were their exams and college applications, and the experiences they had heard about forever were soon to be theirs—graduation, college, adulthood, the freedom to live their own lives on their own terms. As they bit into watercress sandwiches and Alice B. Toklas brownies, they felt they were getting their first taste of these freedoms, of what it felt like to hear the word "orgasm" used in conversation or Mrs. Naughton referred to as "Gayle." A sudden hilarity seized the group as if Mr. Laney had, after all, spiked the famous brownies with hashish.

"Which one is the Jasper Johns?" asked Luke, looking around and bouncing on his toes while crunching into watercress. He was rarely known to sit down, even in Mrs. Naughton's class.

Mr. Laney indicated a small, rather unremarkable canvas next to the Picasso drawing. Several of the students went over to inspect it more closely; they had all heard the story of Mr. Laney's first acquisition from his first trip to New York, made when he was a student at Birmingham-Southern. Jasper Johns was unknown at the time, but as soon as Mr. Laney had spied his work in that Manhattan gallery, he had perceived its quality and immediately pulled out all the money he needed for his week in New York to purchase a small piece. In time his judgment was ratified by the art world, and he took this as a sign that he should always trust his vision and yield to his impulses. He could point to many other now valuable works of art—including a Robert Rauschenberg—as well as his own life's work as a result.

"How much is it worth now?" asked Malcolm, as everyone laughed at such a typical Malcolm question.

In the classroom, Mr. Laney would normally have reproved Malcolm for approaching art on such commercial terms, but they weren't in the classroom and Mr. Laney wasn't really treating them like his students anymore. They were being elevated in more ways than one by being in his apartment, and Mr. Laney responded respectfully to Malcolm's question.

"If I sold that piece tomorrow," he said, "I could buy any house I wanted in Mountain Brook."

Malcolm blinked as if taken by surprise, and an admiration for Mr. Laney he'd never shown before spread visibly across his face. He had always been the most sardonic and skeptical of the 20th Century Art students when Mr. Laney spoke of the value of art. Now he was encountering a kind of value he could appreciate. And the kind of person who knew how to invest, who had the vision that enabled him to buy low and be able to sell high later on was the kind of person he was hoping to become.

"Why don't you sell then?" asked Malcolm. "If you could buy a house in Mountain Brook?"

The others waited to see if Malcolm had now finally gone too far, just as they feared Luke had earlier.

"Sell my Jasper Johns?" said Mr. Laney, as if no sane person would consider such an act of barbarity. "Why would I sell the work of a great artist just so I could buy a house in Mountain Brook?"

Mr. Laney had not come close to exploding, but was feigning an amused bafflement designed to cast Malcolm's question in the light of lunacy. Malcolm, however, refused to be deterred.

"Not just so you could *buy* a house in Mountain Brook," he explained, as if he too, were talking to an idiot child. "But so you could *live* in a house. Wouldn't you rather live in a house instead of an apartment?"

"Not without my Jasper Johns I wouldn't," Mr. Laney declared flatly. "Life in a small apartment with my art on the walls is infinitely preferable to life in any house in Mountain Brook without my art on the walls."

Everyone including Malcolm was impressed into a deep silence. Never before had they contemplated this kind of power in art, to make life in a small apartment better than life in a big house. Their parents would be scandalized, they realized happily.

"Should I take a picture, do you think?" fretted Karen, fiddling with her camera.

"No, you should not, said Mr. Laney emphatically. "Put that thing up and forget about it. That's not why I invited you."

Karen looked abashed, as if she'd done something wrong and incurred his displeasure. Dammit, thought Norman. He couldn't get it right with this child. Here she was becoming more rather than less withdrawn—the opposite of what he'd intended. The college trip hadn't helped much either on that score. And naturally, the early decision rejection from Harvard hadn't helped at all. Still, this didn't entirely explain why she didn't feel she could join the group she'd been going to school with for years. It was obviously not just because she wasn't in 20th Century Art. Everyone had always respected Karen—who would most likely be their valedictorian—and since her mother's death had gone out of their way to be kind to her. Still, she hung back as if she didn't think herself good enough, as if she didn't want to impose her inadequacies on anyone else.

Ginger Cooley was gesticulating theatrically as usual in the corner by the Frohock where the other Frenchies had gathered along with Malcolm Fielding and Glenn Daniels. Some story about running out of gas the day before the National French Exam when she'd taken a vow to speak only French during the twenty-four hours before the test. Fortunately the car had stalled just outside of Mountain Brook village, so she had been able to walk to the Shell station, but unable to communicate successfully with the attendant, who naturally spoke no French.

Norman sat down in his accustomed chair to rest for a moment and enjoy the performance. It really was a most amusing story, and Ginger was, like her mother, a comically self-dramatizing personality. They were both about six feet tall, rail-thin, with a page boy hairstyle that seemed cut out of black silk. Not quite beautiful, they were better than beautiful because they were so striking, and once they had your attention, they knew exactly what to do with it, launching into a story, pantomiming dramatically, and reproducing dialogue exactly and hilariously. In this case, the Shell serviceman's puzzled and desperate English—expertly rendered by Ginger in a heavy redneck accent—was the perfect foil for her own volley of elegant French, which was naturally just so much gibberish to the poor guy.

Mme Boyer's protégés this year were the best in a long while. Ginger would have no trouble getting into Yale, and Claire would probably end up at Smith. Even Rebecca, whose grades were not as good as the others, would easily be accepted at Emory. It would remain to be seen what Ginger would do with her Ivy League degree once she had it. Norman could easily imagine her using her four years in the Ivy League simply to obtain an Ivy League husband, in a sort of late 20th century version of what Southern girls used to do when they spoke of getting their MRS degrees from Bama or Ole Miss. In ten years she could be the hit of cocktail parties just like her mother was now, waving her stick-thin, heavily bangled arms frantically in the air as she acted out some story, while an appreciative audience laughed uproariously and her husband beamed from across the room with pride at his talented wife. And there was tons of talent involved, the way they seized on some gaffe or mishap as if putting themselves down, while actually they were dramatizing some aspect of their superiority, like this fluency in French.

A week ago Norman had been at a party with Virginia Cooley, who had regaled the whole room with some story about leading her half-blind mother-in-law into the men's bathroom at the Mountain Brook Country Club; but the underlying point of the story was not—as Virginia insinuated—that she herself was half-blind from having drunk a bit too much on this occasion, but that her husband was now the president of the Mountain Brook Country Club, as the gentleman in the men's room who encountered his mother had made clear when he congratulated her on her son's recent appointment. However, Norman couldn't help but adore Ginger as he adored her mother and anyone else who knew how to perform as well as they did.

Out of the corner of his eye, Norman watched Luke approach the group surrounding Ginger without looking at her or seeming to pay any attention to her. Instead, he appeared to be giving each individual picture on the wall careful scrutiny. Norman wasn't fooled and no one else would have been either: Luke was still smitten with Ginger. He allowed himself only a certain amount of proximity before continuing on around the apartment, bouncing on his toes like a dancer or marathon runner flexing before the day's event. Soon he was out of sight, and Norman could hear him speaking to his mother in the den, where she was smoking and watching television. Luke was an old favorite of hers; they shared a completely irreverent candor and sense of humor. She was planning to join the party later in the afternoon, after she had rested a bit from her exertions in preparing the food. She'd already met all of his students previously from her regular attendance at all the major school functions.

Then Luke was in the hall leading to the bedrooms, pulling books off the shelves lining the walls there and leafing through the pages. He was easily the most brilliant member of the senior class, but Norman had had more trouble getting a single completed application out of him than he had with Lori Wagner or Christopher Johns. If Luke had been as studious as he was brilliant, he would be bound for the Ivy League like so many of his classmates. But Luke never studied, did his homework or turned his assignments in on time. He was usually late to class, and when asked to hand in his work, he invariably needed to be reminded what the work was he needed to hand in. He had always read everything—not last night or last week in preparation for the assignment—but two summers ago out of his own curiosity and on his own initiative. His memory of the work would be good enough, and he'd rip a sheet of paper out of a notebook, dash off a page or two while the day's lesson was underway, and bring his work up to the teacher's desk half-way through the class period. Afterwards, he might go sit back down, or he might not. He liked to roam around the classroom just as he was roaming around Mr. Laney's apartment at the moment. His intellectual energy was expressed through physical movement; it unfortunately wasn't something he expressed on paper unless forced to do so. If the class discussion interested him, he might contribute to it, but if he was bored, he'd just pull a book off a shelf and start flipping through it. Even Gayle Naughton had had no choice but to accept his behavior. Fortunately he was not only brilliant but utterly charming in an impish way, with a head full of loose curls along with the mischievous, unfettered curiosity, boundless energy and short, athletic body of a young boy. Norman fervently hoped that NYU would take him.

One thing was for certain: he could forget about Ginger Cooley. If Luke was unconcerned, or even—as was likely—unaware of their extreme differ-ence in height, it was the first thing she would have noticed and rejected about him years ago. She would never subject herself to the indignity of a date, an escort or a husband shorter than she was, and would no doubt regard short men as failures of manhood. Furthermore, she would want any man by her side to have an Ivy League degree matching her own, and would most likely, Norman guessed, end up with a husband who wasn't averse to living in Birmingham and becoming part of her father's ever-expanding commercial construction company. With two daughters, her father would no doubt wel-come a son-in-law interested in joining the business. If Ginger ever yielded or responded to Luke in any way, he would have lost interest soon enough. But she cleverly kept him on a string, like a pet monkey, and Norman suspected that Luke, as a performer himself, was a sucker for Ginger's comic opera. Norman was too, and found himself laughing out loud at her impersonation of the gas station attendant just as the doorbell rang.

He was disagreeably surprised to find Lori Wagner outside his door, apologizing for being late and chewing gum as if her immediate survival de-pended on it. Until that very moment, he had not been aware of her absence, but if he had been, would not have been sorry. She was irritating to him in the extreme; even the illiterate spelling of her name annoyed him no end. She didn't belong in this group at his house any more than she belonged at the school itself. The mere fact that her family lived just outside the Mountain Brook city limits and didn't want to send her to the Birmingham public schools accounted for her attendance at Brook-Haven. Her father owned a prosperous string of rental furniture stores found all over the less prosperous parts of Birmingham and outlying areas, like Pratt City, where Norman's own brother was the manager of one such store. The Wagners could certainly have afforded any house in Mountain Brook, but had chosen instead to renovate a rambling mansion in the oldest section of Birmingham proper. If that indicated a certain amount of class, it wasn't so much because they possessed any, (because they didn't), but because they quite rightly suspected they'd never really be accepted in Mountain Brook and most certainly would never be accepted into the country club.

Tip Wagner always wore an open necked shirt with a gold chain glinting beneath a mound of grizzled, graying chest hair. His wife was always wearing what looked to Norman like a very short tennis skirt which just barely succeeded in covering her crotch. Her original hair color was insufficiently buried beneath the inexpertly applied peroxide administered by a hairdresser who obviously didn't know what she was doing and did not have access to the best hair color products. It wasn't that Norman was a snob, but he was a lover of beauty and a man of taste, and he simply could not abide tackiness.

Even so, if Lori had possessed the smallest scrap of intelligence, ambition, or talent, he would readily have embraced her and taken her under his wing. But she was just a gum-snapping, crotch-flaunting vulgarian like her mother, and it was best for him to ignore her presence like he did with Priscilla Bradley and the pot-smoking contingent. When he had complained once to Elizabeth Elder that a Brook-Haven education was wasted on the likes of Lori Wagner, she had remarked sharply that it certainly wasn't wasted, since Lori would soon enough be a mother. At first he had stared at her in serious alarm, afraid that Lori's crotch was going to bring forth the immediate fruit of her labors. (Which would be a catastrophic blow to Brook-Haven's reputation, as Mountain Brook High School had not to anyone's knowledge produced a teenage pregnancy.) But to Norman's immense relief, Elizabeth had been speaking only in abstract terms, about the need for future mothers to have an education worthy of their most important task of raising the world's children. Nevertheless, Norman was as unable to conjure interest in Lori's future as in Lori herself. He tried his best to welcome her in and usher her forward into the living room without betraying his dislike.

In his brief absence, Karen had nervously retrieved her camera and was positioning herself to photograph Ginger against the backdrop of the Frohock as she entertained the other Frenchies and whoever else she could hold in thrall. Glenn Daniels had moved on, as most people of deep intelligence did with Ginger, and was now helping himself from the dining room table as he spoke with Dylan Elmore and Jason Simmons. Norman sat back down with a small sigh of resignation at Karen's camera. It was probably best to let her proceed with taking pictures if that was the only way she could manage to enter into the occasion. Dylan, Glenn and Jason, now the focal point for her next photograph, were probably talking about the upcoming chess tournament. Dylan and Glenn would have ended up at Harvard together, Norman thought, if Elizabeth Elder had not exerted her influence over Glenn and his parents. Just as well, he conceded. Harvard was going to be among their list of acceptances. Might as well have Glenn add another prestigious name, like Williams or Amherst, to the list he had managed to get published in the paper every year. Glenn could always go from Williams or Amherst to Harvard Law, which was where he belonged, and from there to Washington, which was probably where he'd end up. In what capacity Norman wasn't sure. Justice Department? Clerk for the Supreme Court? No doubt it would be some sort of public service, like his father performed, but on a grander scale and not in Birmingham. As for Dylan, Norman could see him remaining at Harvard for the rest of his life. The world didn't produce many Sanskrit scholars. Jason Simmons no doubt had a brilliant career ahead doing whatever people did who were brilliant with math.

Bebe Bannon came toward him with a plate of his food and a smile as large and dilated somehow, as her round, looping penmanship.

"You look hungry, Mr. Laney," she said. "So I brought you this."

"Oh, thank you, darling," he said with sincere gratitude. "And thank *you,* darling," he said to Sally Lindgren, as she came up with a glass of iced tea sprouting a sprig of mint just like she knew he liked it.

These two had not the faintest beginnings of the intellect possessed by the likes of Glenn Daniels or Dylan Elmore, but they knew enough to know they should learn all they could about Art and Culture, and they worked seriously and earnestly. Knowing they would never be his star students, these two dear children had opted instead to be his handmaidens, and Lord knew, he needed them. If it weren't for them, he would never have been able to direct the spring play year after year, and he had no idea what in the world he would do without them next year. He didn't even have to open his mouth for them to know what he wanted and execute it, like bringing him food and drink when he was suddenly starving but too exhausted to get up from his chair.

Unwisely, he had stayed up till four in the morning—not reviewing the faculty recommendations or grading exams as he should have done—but reading *A Confederacy of Dunces,* which Edward Allison had given him last night at Libba's party, saying Norman *had* to read it because he was the living incarnation of Ignatius Reilly, the novel's protagonist. With the best of intentions, people were always doing this to him—saying he had to read or go see something or other because someone or other in it reminded them of him. Ignatius Reilly was by no means the worst thing he'd been compared to: that distinction would probably go to the fat redneck named Junior on *Hee Haw,* who resembled Norman Laney only in physical amplitude. But for some reason, this latest comparison offended him most deeply.

It was exactly like Edward Allison to seize on a superficial parallel and miss the fundamental differences that ruled out any real comparison. True, he and the elephantine anti-hero of John Kennedy Toole's novel shared a love of food, though Norman would never eat the jelly doughnuts or frozen pizzas that Ignatius consumed. True, they both lived alone with their mothers, who were similar blue collar personalities with a similar blue collar kind of candor. And true, there was a certain lordly grandiosity in their personalities, in keeping with the grandiosity of their physique. But there the resemblance ended and the more important differences began. The most obvious of which was: Ignatius Reilly was a medievalist while Norman Laney was most decidedly a Renaissance man. (Trust Edward Allison to be completely insensible to the significance of this disparity.) There were dozens of other divergences he could catalog, but the most crucial of these was: when Ignatius Reilly had been a teacher—for a brief and disastrous period of time—he had dumped all his students' *ungraded* exams and essays out the window.

Naturally, Norman often wished he could do exactly the same thing with his students' exams and papers, especially the ones he had *not* been grading while he was reading the Toole novel last night. Of course, he hated grading as much as Ignatius Reilly did. Who wouldn't? Of all those demands placed on a teacher, this was the worst, especially for an English teacher, who had to become like a dentist of the mind, inspecting the mental rot and intellectual cavities he would greatly prefer to avoid. *But as much as he might hate it, he did it anyway.* That was the point. He took on that job, and he did it. Not without grumbling, but he did it. He confronted those untended brains and did his best to stop the decay, fill the cavities, straighten and polish up the rest till it was as close to gleaming perfection as it could get.

The polite, pleasant and attractive faces—even beautiful or handsome faces—that came into the dentists' offices for their routine visits were often only covering up a world of rottenness underneath their appealing façades. Did the dentist lose his respect for these people, he had often wondered, when they opened their mouths and revealed the foulness within? As a teacher, he was constantly struggling to maintain his respect for students who could appear so bright, so eager, so precocious and wise in the classroom; and yet when he peered into the inner workings of their minds through the medium of their own often poorly written words, he found the shocking results of laziness and neglect, the dreadful corrosion caused by overindulgence in harmful substances, like television and pop music. He would much rather deal with just the faces, which were presentable enough, especially in Mountain Brook; but it was his job to get at the brains.

It was work. Hard work. He was not as diligent as Gayle at poking into all the soft spots; he would never be the type who circled comma splices. And he was not as stalwart as Elizabeth, who could stare down the dark corners with the strong light of her superior and implacable reason. He chose to treat through example and inspiration. So he was by no means perfect, and in the eyes of many, was by no means the best at what he did. But he did it. Again, that was the point that Edward Allison so shamefully failed to see. He did not, like Ignatius, lie around in bed all day—though he might have liked to sometimes—filling up Big Chief notebooks while nursing his bloating stomach and tending to his absurd erections. He was out there doing far more important work than Edward Allison did, though naturally, Edward Allison's bow ties, downtown corner office and extremely limited intelligence would prevent him from perceiving this particular truth. His work was a lot harder too: kindling the soggy brain of someone like Edward Allison's son— much harder than anything Edward Allison had attempted. (And if he *had* attempted to fuel his son's mental development, there was no evidence that he had succeeded whatsoever.)

Norman had never asked to be rewarded appropriately for the work he did. No true teacher ever expected that: not in this country or this lifetime, anyway. But he did expect not to be ridiculed. Of course, behind his back, he was ridiculed all the time. But usually, no one dared ridicule him to his face, especially if they owed him deepest gratitude for educating their dull-witted son and doing his damnedest to get him into a decent college. Comparing him to the farcical Ignatius was outright mockery. Was Edward so dim-witted himself that he couldn't see that? As if his problem with the headmaster weren't enough, along came Edward Allison to add insult to injury and give him no choice but to read the book he'd been deliberately avoiding during the four years since it was first published. And this was a Christmas present too.

As good as he was at making other people laugh and helping them see the humor in almost anything, his own life was certainly no comedy and definitely not the kind of exaggerated farce in the novel he'd read last night. He was not a performing elephant and his life was no circus. Of course, if he were in the mood to be honest, he'd have to admit that he often carried on like a performing elephant whenever it suited his purpose. But he wasn't in the mood to be honest. He disguised a sudden yawn by pretending to sigh deeply.

This was Bebe Bannon's cue. "Here," she said, taking his mysteriously empty plate. "Let me get you some more."

"I enjoyed seeing your mother last night," he lied half-heartedly to Sally.

She nodded. "I can't believe what they're saying about you, Mr. Laney," she said, tears forming in her eyes.

"What on earth, darling?" he said, much too loudly and with naked concern. Was he finally going to find out what Turbyfill had on him? From a student?

Sally was shaking her head as Ginger, sensing the drama elsewhere, began moving toward it with her coterie. "I just can't believe it," Sally repeated.

"What?" demanded Ginger. "What are you talking about?" Since Ginger knew how to project her voice so it carried throughout a room and dominated any given situation, everyone now became aware that something was up and began to crowd toward the chair where Mr. Laney was sitting.

"What could you possibly have heard to upset you like this?" said Mr. Laney, forcing his voice into nonchalance.

While Sally hesitated as if unable to utter a terrible truth, total silence descended on the group of students, who exchanged uneasy shrugs or shakes of the head.

"Tell us, Sally," commanded Ginger sharply.

Sally turned around to face her. "Mr. Laney is leaving Brook-Haven!" she declared tremulously.

The silence which followed was the kind that could only be produced by profound shock or dismay.

"Oh, for the love of God," said Mr. Laney, with just that mix of disgust and relief that instantly dispelled the rumor Sally had repeated.

"Norman leave Brook-Haven?" scoffed his mother, who had been drawn out of the den by the unnatural quiet in the living room. "The only way

Norman will leave that school is in a coffin!" It was a tired old joke among students, alumnae, and even other faculty, but delivered in Mrs. Laney's rasping, Pratt City drawl, it seemed freshly funny and new. The students laughed with relieved appreciation. (If Mr. Laney's mother knew nothing about it, then there was nothing to know. He told her everything and often quoted back to them the outrageous responses his mother had made in between puffs on her cigarette.)

"How could such a ridiculous rumor get started?" demanded Mrs. Laney. "Everybody knows that even if that school catches on fire, Norman Laney will be the last to leave, and not because he's a few pounds overweight."

Norman shrugged his shoulders, bored and tired, while the students laughed again at his mother's delivery of another stale joke. "Doesn't take much to start a rumor in Mountain Brook," he said.

His mother narrowed her eyes. "But rumors start somewhere, somehow," she said.

Norman shifted in his seat, which was quite a production requiring that his hands actually lift the weight of his stomach and carry it from one side of the chair to another. "I was invited to come see the new building at Shelby State, Mother," he said with asperity. "And out of politeness, I went." He shrugged again. "Apparently, that's all it takes to get gossip going in Mountain Brook."

"But my mother said they're going to offer you a job!" wailed Sally, as if thoroughly distressed and flabbergasted to learn that Norman Laney had options in life.

"Darlin'," he said, as gently as he could. "They're always offering me a job. The chair of English has been trying to get me to join his department for ten years."

This had the effect of an atomic bomb. It was clear that the thought had never occurred to any of his students—even his most gifted—that he could be doing something else in life besides being their teacher. It wasn't that they didn't respect his intelligence or abilities, but they simply assumed that he— like their devoted parents—was put on this earth to serve their needs, that he was completely happy to spend his entire life doing so, and desired no other form of happiness.

As smart as many of them were, they were also equally sheltered. Only one out of the thirty-three in this senior class came from a broken home. It was probably no coincidence that this one—Malcolm Fielding—was the one headed for Wall Street. But even Malcolm had two loving if not married parents, and not one of these students had yet learned the hard fact of life that nothing and no one was put on this earth to serve their needs. They were all too ready to dismiss the glimmer of an unpleasant truth about Mr. Laney's rumored free will. (Because after all, if he had willingly chosen to be their teacher, and just as deliberately had chosen and continued to choose not to exercise other options in life, then they owed him far more respect and gratitude than they were capable of demonstrating or perhaps even feeling. It was far easier to believe that those who were their teachers were there simply because they had no choice.)

No one noticed Karen creeping into the corner vacated by Ginger and her crowd until she snapped a picture of Mr. Laney in his chair surrounded by a group of students, many literally sitting at his feet. She was fairly certain she'd managed to capture the girl on the swing just beyond the chair as well. But once again she also managed to break the tension in the room and unleash the party spirit with the flashing of her bulb. Conversations broke out everywhere all at once, it seemed, and laughter bubbled up as if alcohol were being served rather than the exquisitely made iced tea from Mrs. Laney's family recipe. Like a backlash to the moment of profound quiescence, a madcap mood took hold of the group and no crumb was remaining by the time the last student left Mr. Laney's apartment at the unexpected hour of five-thirty.

Just as unexpected, this last student to leave was Luke Pendarvis.

"Glad you could make it," said Mr. Laney, with the playful sarcasm he usually employed with Luke.

"Wouldn't miss it," said Luke, pausing at the threshold.

"Unless the plane ticket for Italy had been for today," countered Mr. Laney.

"But didn't you know?" said Luke. "It *was* for today. Until we found out about your party."

Puzzled, Mr. Laney cocked his head sideways.

"I told my father I didn't want to miss this, and he agreed," explained Luke. "Said it would probably be the most significant event of my senior year. So he changed our tickets." He held out his hand. "See you next year," he said, pumping Mr. Laney's hand once and then darting off as if a flare had just announced the start of a fifty-yard dash.

Mr. Laney remained standing on the threshold of his apartment door, staring intently into the vacant stairwell beyond the corridor, echoing with Luke's thunderous steps. For a fat man and a high school English teacher, the kind of explicit validation he had just received from his student was not often forthcoming, and he needed a minute to absorb the shock and compose himself. After all, if *he* had been given a chance to be on a plane going to Italy yesterday . . . he would most certainly have been on that plane.

147

PART TWO

Spring Semester
The Brook-Haven School
1984

JANUARY

~ 9 ~

The students in the library for study hall at ten A.M. on January 3rd at the Brook-Haven School were surprised to hear the slamming of Norman Laney's office door. Usually this door was left open when he was in there, the better to prevent any disturbances from happening in the library and to provide more immediate redress should they occur. (Sometimes it seemed that Mr. Laney actually enjoyed storming out of his office, all his bodily weight shaking with rage, and venting this wrath upon the captive students, Jimmy Kuhn in particular.) Glances of surprise were exchanged and a low buzz filled the air. It was clear Mr. Laney had much more important matters on his mind than their behavior during study hall. But what could that be? And how could anything possibly have already happened to provoke the fury that was so clearly expressed in the slamming of the door? The new semester was only two hours old, and last night, his movie had premiered in Birmingham. Their parents had shown them the article in today's newspaper as they ate breakfast. As far as they could see, Mr. Laney should have been in the best of humors.

If this had been a typical school year, Norman Laney would indeed have been in the best of moods right now. With all college applications completed and posted, all faculty recommendations vetted and ready to go, the most important work of his year was over and done. Come April he could probably expect that an unprecedented percentage of his senior class would receive acceptances from Ivy League schools. In two and a half months he would enjoy a glorious, luxurious week in New York, and another two and a half months after that, he would spend his summer travelling first class on a slow trip through several well-chosen European capitals, namely London, Paris, Florence and Rome. But this year Norman Laney had much more on his mind than the fate of his thirty-odd students vaulting into their futures or his own well-earned reward for helping to make those futures possible. It was his own fate at stake this time.

Somehow in the fall he had managed to defer his anxiety and push his concern to the back of his mind. And the false promise of the Christmas season had fooled and lulled him just as it did when he was a boy. With no rational basis for this belief whatsoever, he had always believed he would somehow get whatever he wanted under the tree, though he rarely, if ever, did. As an adult, this belief was still there, though it had morphed into a seasonal sensation of general well-being, as if all sore spots were being healed and all wrongs were being put right. No doubt the additional quantities of alcohol he consumed at one party after another fueled this feeling. But as early as January 1 of every year, he began to realize that he was in possession of nothing he really wanted or needed. This year was no different. Only worse. Much, much worse.

With a violence matching the vehemence of his mood, he snatched his wastebasket from where it was wedged under the corner of his desk and thrust it down on the floor in front of the chair where he was sitting. Then he began hurling all the detritus of last semester into the can, as he would have liked to hurl the headmaster along with it all. Memo after useless memo. Post-it notes with the phone numbers of panicked parents, hysterical at the prospect of their child attending Rhodes rather than Sewanee. Rough drafts of application essays. Teacher evaluation forms he had "forgotten," once again, to hand out to his students. In two minutes his bin was full.

Norman Laney hurled himself out of the office next, and further shocked the study hall students by failing to look even once in their direction and saying nothing to either reprove or squelch the undeniable hum which had developed beyond his so firmly closed door. Some students even had the confidence to remark out loud that Mr. Laney's back side bore an exact resemblance to an elephant's rear end, minus the tail. Elizabeth Elder was herself slightly surprised that Norman was not coming to see her and neither poked his head in to say "hello, Happy New Year" or even glance her way as he passed her open door. But she knew him better than anyone did, except maybe his mother, and could guess what he was feeling. She knew he could not possibly be upset at her failure to attend last night's premiere or the party following. Even if the movie had not been dreadful—as she'd heard from Norman himself—it would not have been her thing and he could not have reasonably expected her to go. He knew quite well that she never went to movies. Still, she would have liked to make contact with him and shear some of the force off the tropical storm brewing within before it turned into a hurricane. He could say or do some of the most regrettable things when he was in this frame of mind. But the look on his face when he passed back by a

154

few seconds later, holding two large green trash bags from the janitor's closet, forestalled even Elizabeth Elder from getting in his path. When she heard the second slamming of his office door that morning, she hoped she'd made the right decision, and not merely lost her nerve.

Back in his office, Norman Laney began filling one of the trash bags with the art history text books sent by publishers who never dreamed that he had no use for such books and even considered their use to be the mark of a second-rate teacher. Normally it was not his policy to throw away any of these books, but today it was. If only he could rid himself as easily of the extra pounds he'd put on over the holidays, not to mention the uncalled-for quandary the headmaster had put him in. Or the multiplicity of improprieties, indiscretions, wrongs and trespasses he himself had committed. Oh, yes! It wasn't just a matter of one student's abortion he'd facilitated two years ago. Who had he been kidding? It was a lifetime of lapses. Lapses of judgment, lapses of common sense, lapses in his own moral and ethical code, his own ideals and principles. He was guilty. Guilty as hell of everything. Including what the headmaster was accusing him of. Whatever that was. He didn't know what it was, but whatever it was, he was sure he was guilty. Indeed, Tom Turbyfill wasn't even the problem at all; Norman Laney was his own worst enemy.

The last book from the pile made a satisfying smack as it joined the others in the bag. He'd have to get Rosy in with his hand-cart to haul it all off. Unless . . . he caught sight of a box in the corner. Going over to inspect it, he found it contained utterly obsolete exam papers from three years ago. Dumping these into the second trash bag, he then dumped the books into the box. He'd still have to get Rosy in to take it away, but at least he would do so with a lot less grumbling.

The concept of being innocent until proven guilty was just another one of those naïve American notions that quickly evaporated into the fairy dust it was when grim reality occurred. Human beings were guilty and that was that. The older cultures—the Europeans—knew this. Proving innocence was not the issue. No one was innocent. He'd been guilty since as early as he could remember. Guilty of eating too much; guilty of being fat; guilty of wanting to read books instead of hunting, fishing or playing football like the other boys as his father had wished. Guilty of being what he wasn't supposed to be, doing what he wasn't supposed to do. You could never prove your innocence because you weren't innocent. You could only hope to earn, or achieve, a state of grace.

No doubt this was why he'd become a Catholic. Though born a Baptist in the great redneck tradition of his poor white background, he had been confirmed a Catholic while in college, and it was more than just the gorgeousness of Catholic ritual and pageantry, or the storied cultural heritage of the Catholic church which had drawn him. Sometimes—like today—he even wished he'd stuck with his original intention to attend seminary and take orders as a Catholic priest. He had always viewed his work as a teacher as a different kind of priesthood—one that afforded him a place in the world more suited to his temperament—but perhaps he'd been wrong.

He prodded at the box of books with his toe to move it over to the side, near the shelves, but it didn't budge. Would he have to tip Rosy to move it out of the office? Probably. The box proved to need a series of rather forceful kicks which Norman was happy to supply before turning his attention to the more ambiguous items on his desk demanding a more nuanced decision regarding their fate. This he was definitely not in the mood for. The ringing of the phone pierced his eardrum just as he sat down and pulled himself up to his desk. He was not in the mood for that either, no matter who it was. It could be the Queen of England herself inviting him to tea at Buckingham Palace when he was next in London, and he would not want to take the call. Of course, it could be Fee calling with a report on the New Year's Eve party; he'd been expecting to hear from her these past two days. And he *was* curious. But not curious enough! It was time for him to tend to his own problems. He seized a stack of hand-outs he'd neglected to hand out and flung them into the bag while briefly wondering if he should save them for next year. Absolutely not! he decided. If he was going to restore order, he needed to make a clean sweep. And he might well not even be here next year. He should clear out his office with that prospect in mind.

Because when it came to the question of what he'd done wrong, he'd done it all. Example after example after example kept popping up in his brain like the painful throbs of a hangover's headache on January 1. One such example was Kevin Forney. He used to come into Norman's office after school, heavy with the burden of his impossible adolescent existence, and sit down across from Norman with every intention of laying this burden down on the desk between them. Except poor Kevin never could even open his mouth. He just sat there and stared helplessly at Norman, unable to speak. Norman was adept at drawing students out, but in Kevin's case, he didn't want to. He simply let Kevin sit there silently WITH THE DOOR WIDE OPEN while he graded papers or did other paperwork until a phone call, a colleague or another student prompted Kevin to leave the office. Norman knew from the start exactly what Kevin's problem was and thought it infinitely better if this problem were never named by either of them.

Instead, one day he simply told Kevin that he should take Latin next semester. Kevin was surprised, but he complied. And then it was Mr. Carroway who had Kevin in his office in the afternoons. This worked out just as Norman had thought it might, Carroway being, at age forty-five, only a slightly more adult version of Kevin Forney. It wasn't long before Kevin had not only joined the Latin Club but become its president, and his parents were proclaiming him "a different person." How different, Norman hoped they didn't yet know, and he himself didn't want to know. But he had a good enough idea. One Saturday afternoon he had run into the Forneys at the museum; Kevin was with the Latin Club, they told him. Norman hadn't known of any Latin Club outing scheduled for Saturday, and later saw Kevin and Carroway coming out of a movie theater together. Of course, he could claim ignorance and innocence as he had with Alexandra Sanders, but the truth is, he had supported a young man's homosexuality just as surely as he had arranged for an abortion.

Kevin was now in college; had come home for Christmas this year with one pierced ear and a brazen self-assertiveness which made it perfectly clear to everyone that he was what he was. Norman could now claim credit for getting a young man to the point of wearing an earring stud. But this was his job.

At an early age, he himself had realized that he could either go with what he was or try to go up against it. Thanks to his mother, who had always loved and supported every ounce of him, he had been able to go—and go happily —with what he was. Going up against the mountain of his own impossible flesh would have resulted only in defeat and despair. So he had gone with his fat, not against it, and it had worked out amazingly well. In return, in thanks to the universe which had allowed him to thrive and flourish, it was his responsibility to help other youngsters learn how to go with whatever they were, no matter how problematic.

But still! Abortion and homosexuality! Perhaps the two most inflammatory social issues of the day! And Norman had been on the wrong side of both, at least as far as the state of Alabama—if not the entire country itself—was concerned. And here he was, trying to crack open a closed society by sending its sons and daughters who were meant to stay locked inside out into the wider world to encounter its broader ideas and bring those ideas back home. In this he knew he was exceeding his mandate to a treacherous degree. He understood perfectly well that he was supposed to render his young charges super-fit for their Southern society; not get them out of it altogether. So far he'd been able to manage it so that he did it with everyone's blessing, which was the only way in the South to achieve anything that involved change.

This lesson was written in the history books and it never paid to forget it: Southerners would sooner fight a bloody war than adapt to progress they didn't want to accept. Not only that: They loathed carpetbaggers of any kind and would sooner kill them than tolerate "meddling." For any revolution to occur, it would need to rise from within and remain perfectly quiet and utterly invisible until after it had been accomplished. Although he himself was neither quiet nor invisible, somehow the extravagances of his exuberant personality had provided camouflage for the seriousness of his purpose. But clearly someone had finally tumbled to what he was really up to and was trying to stop him.

If he had been able to argue his case before the highest court of Truth and Justice, he knew he would have been acquitted. He had made dubious decisions and taken even more dubious action which he had honestly deemed both best and necessary for the health and happiness of the students who came before him. As a teacher and guidance counselor to high school students, he was placed in one of life's most difficult positions, and his actual job was, above all, to secure the future well-being of these fledgling individuals. He had not shied away from this challenge or pawned it off on others. He had met it head-on. But he'd be dead before he reached the highest court of Truth and Justice. Here on earth it was the court of parental opinion and the headmasters with their Ed.Ds he had to contend with.

But the reason he felt so guilty actually had little to do with any of these actions, not even with that stupid, stupid time he'd accepted a large loan from the Morelands, whose son was later stopped for speeding and then arrested for possession of cocaine. Norman had been placed in the embarrassing position of arguing that since the incident had not occurred on school grounds during school hours, the boy shouldn't be expelled. The handbook was—at that time, anyway—ambiguous on that point, but everyone had expected Norman to argue the opposite point of view. It was abjectly humiliating when news of the Moreland's loan to him became common knowledge. Some even thought the loan was made after the incident happened, which made it appear more of a bribe than a loan. But even the simple truth of the matter had been bad enough.

No, he was guilty just for being who he was. It was that existential guilt Kafka had dramatized so well, and the same situation, in which a mediocre, mid-level bureaucrat comes to arrest you simply for being who you are. And what was he? A teacher who never really taught—just gave his students bits of himself. Choice bits, yes, but no real instruction. A teacher who had no notes, no lectures, no lesson plans and never once actually prepared for a class—except by living his life in a certain way. A teacher who often arrived ten minutes late and let out ten minutes early, thus shaving twenty minutes off an unmanageable fifty and making it a much more manageable thirty. A teacher who might even cut a class altogether when it was his turn to speak at Adelaide Whitmire's book club, which always met at two o'clock in the afternoon, because Adelaide insisted that two o'clock was the only proper ladies' meeting time. And he never notified the front office of these cancellations of class, just told his "Giotto" students to go to study hall tomorrow. Often the seniors just left campus for the day, as he well knew. It was true, too, that sometimes he used class period and his students to get the invitations to his Orange Bowl Gallery exhibits finished. And as for his work as a "guidance counselor," he belonged in hell just for his use of hyperbole on student recommendations. If Tom Turbyfill wanted to get him on something, he didn't have to make it up or look very far. Of course he fudged his receipts for expenses because he always lost the originals. Was that embezzlement? What made it all so much the worse was that he did not know who had accused him of what. So he felt accused of everything by everybody. And he was guilty of it all.

He knew very well what most of his enemies thought he was, beyond being unfit for Mountain Brook society in general. They thought he was a buffoon, a clown; therefore a homosexual, and therefore a pedophile. He was so grossly abnormal in his corporeal shape that it was assumed he harbored further abominations within. Of course the suspicious human mind couldn't see the obvious: that a body like his had no choice but celibacy. Nobody had ever wanted to do anything with it, and he, thank God, had never wanted to do much of anything with it either.

Who could accept at face value the idea that he had dedicated his life to young people? Parents of teenagers knew better than anyone how thankless a job that was. So they assumed there must be some ulterior agenda of his own that was both perverse and sexual; therefore, sexually perverse. Again it was so American—to demand sainthood of everyone while secretly believing that everyone was the worst kind of sinner. There were many affinities he had with European society above and beyond the art and culture it had produced, and one was its matter-of-fact acceptance that everyone was naturally a sinner. And that when someone sinned, it was no big surprise. The big surprise was when someone managed to do some form of good in the world regardless of his own flawed nature.

A tentative knock on his door interrupted what had become a prolonged reverie in which not one further scrap of paper from his cluttered desk had been either filed or thrown away. He was clutching two such scraps in his hands while simply staring into space. "Come in," he said in a voice so angry it was almost a snarl.

Ellis. The last person he wanted to see.

"What is it?"

The face Ellis poked around the door was obviously disconcerted at Mr. Laney's unexpectedly dark mood. He remained on the threshold, afraid to venture further.

"Just wanted to congratulate you on your film debut." Ellis managed a nervous laugh.

"That piece of crap is destined for utter oblivion!" Norman Laney balled up the paper in his hands and savagely consigned it to this exact fate in the trash bag by his desk.

Ellis did not know whether to argue the point or not, but on the whole thought it better to leave the immediate vicinity of Norman Laney as soon as possible after thanking him for being invited to the premiere. Ellis had been prepared to be effusive in his thanks, but swallowed most of it and barely stammered out the minimum before scuttling off like a frightened beetle.

With the door of his office shut once more, Norman Laney rose to his feet and began pacing while contemplating the speckled linoleum of his floor. The phone rang again, and again he ignored it. He *would* like to hear about Palm Beach, he decided, but it was probably another well-wisher who'd been to last night's premiere, and he just didn't want to hear it.

The sight of Ellis had infuriated him, and provided his free-floating anger another target to seize on. Last night Ellis had hardly glanced at Valerie Whitmire even as Norman was pointedly introducing him to her. Instead his eyes had kept darting over to her cousin James, while greeting Valerie only in the most perfunctory way that might or might not have passed for polite according to Yankee standards. By the standards of the Deep South WHERE HE NOW LIVED, he had been downright rude. Fortunately, Valerie had simply shrugged the whole episode off. No doubt she had been able to size up Ellis right away as a man a few years younger than herself and therefore at least a decade behind her in actual maturity. And James, of course, had relished the attention. He depended on fawning fans because he certainly wasn't a critic's darling. So he was quite happy to have Ellis bounding beside him like an eager puppy while fielding introductions, greetings and congratulations from the other guests. Ellis had obviously not been in the South long enough to

160

learn that you didn't monopolize the guest of honor or ignore everyone else, especially the attractive heiress Norman Laney had made a point of introducing you to.

A sudden revelation had exploded like a bomb in Norman's brain and shattered any possibility of enjoyment in the occasion that was supposed to be a triumph, of sorts, for him. Ellis was a homosexual. That had to be it. Norman had grabbed Valerie's arm, put on his biggest grin, and bulldozed through the circle surrounding the Hollywood director responsible for creating the abomination they were all about to be subjected to. Normally Norman's sixth sense alerted him immediately when he was in the presence of a homosexual man, but his radar had failed to register Ellis. James was certainly no homosexual himself, with three ex-wives and now a young blonde barely half his age, an intern at *Vanity Fair* he'd recently met when the magazine did a profile to dovetail with the film based on his first book. She wouldn't last long, Norman could tell. Clearly bored with Birmingham, and just let Adelaide get a hold of her, interrogating her about her parentage and background. That "relationship," such as it was, probably wouldn't last the whole week of James's visit, and she'd fly back early to New York. Or perhaps she was merely a prop, persuaded or even rented in some way, just for this occasion. Yes, of course that was it.

"What? You've never been down South? I can't believe it. You must come. I'll tell you what: why don't you come with me to Alabama when the movie premiere's in my home town? I'll show you around, we'll go to the party, you can see the South? My way of saying thank you . . ."

James just needed a blonde nearby to complete his self-image, the way some women needed a one thousand dollar handbag to complete their look. Hence the three ex-wives. All had originally completed his image at one time, until another blonde came along who completed his image more fully or willingly. Norman, of course, remembered the days when James was teased for being a nerd who couldn't play sports and never went to the prom because he couldn't get a date. Now he was having the nerd's revenge.

But even in the absence of an alert from his radar, he should have guessed about Ellis. In no way effeminate at all, he was still too good-looking in the way of some gay men, and had a bit too much very good hair—like a soap opera star. And it would explain why Ellis never even seemed to notice all the female students who tried to flirt with him. But dear Lord! Norman stared so hard at the linoleum that it now looked black with white speckles instead of white with black speckles. Ellis damn well better keep it to himself. The school couldn't get away with *three* suspect teachers. Then there was Dennis

161

Morton, getting chummy with Kaye Beasley, and Dan Riley, soccer coach, sex ed instructor and confidante at large.

"I didn't see anything wrong with it. I thought it was part of my job. She's going through a really tough time at home, just needs someone to talk to and I . . ."

"Once is one thing!" he had thundered. "But every afternoon? With the door closed? What were you thinking? You're not a licensed counselor! You could get the school sued into bankruptcy! It wouldn't be just you! We would all lose our jobs!"

Not to mention what people thought of him, Norman Laney. They praised him, thanked him, congratulated him. And behind his back, they speculated that he was a pedophile. Either that, or Ignatius Reilly. He didn't know which was worse: pedophilia, or Ignatius Reilly.

When the phone rang yet again, he snatched it up. He was ready to hear about Palm Beach. He needed to hear about Palm Beach.

"Norman, you really need your own phone line."

It was Adelaide Whitmire. He groped for his chair and swiveled it around. "Oh, hey, darlin'," he said. Although Adelaide was no one's idea of a darling, she *was* on the Brook-Haven board, and he needed her help.

"I've called two times already this morning, and the girl in the office insisted she put me through."

"I've been in a meeting and just this minute walked through the door." He extended his leg and rocked it back and forth. He had somehow forgotten that Adelaide was calling "first thing, right after New Year's." She had wagged her finger in his face while reminding him last night.

"You need your own phone line and an answering machine in your office. It's outrageous that anyone who wants to speak to you has to go through that imbecile female in the front office. She swore she took down my messages but of course she didn't since I never heard back. We'll never get that fund-raiser planned at this rate."

Interesting use of the word "we." Norman cleared his throat in a business-like manner and pulled himself up to his desk as if Adelaide were at the other end of it. As chair of the board for the Birmingham Museum of Art, she was in charge of the big fund-raiser this year. "Of course I'll need your help," she had informed him months ago. That was her way of asking. Norman could picture her at the other end of the line, with her reading glasses at the end of her no-nonsense nose, her notepad and pen ready for action as if she were the CEO of a Fortune 500 company. Indeed, Adelaide would have made a perfect CEO, with her autocratic personality and that complete sense of entitlement that others would do all the work that needed to be done, including her own. But as she was one of Norman's strongest allies and supporters, he couldn't afford not to take her as seriously as she took herself.

"Did you manage to get hold of the guest list for the last fund-raiser?" Norman tried his best to make this task sound like a herculean undertaking, when really it was a matter of a simple phone call he had suggested months ago.

"Norman, you know I couldn't possibly call that woman. And anyway, didn't I hear that she's in Palm Beach right now?"

"Actually, the guest list should be in one of the files you inherited when you became chair last year." He hoped he sounded as if this idea had just occurred to him. But she should know quite well—apart from the fact that he'd told her—that there was a file containing all the information and invoices from the museum's last fund-raiser organized by Felicia Keller five years ago. Adelaide did not have to invent the wheel; she just had to follow the template provided by the contents of the file. The guest list, the menu, the caterers, the musicians, the florists, the printers—it was all there. She could tweak it where she wanted and put it on automatic pilot where she wanted. In any case, putting it all together was mainly a matter of making the phone calls and running the errands.

"What file? I don't know what you're talking about. I haven't seen any such file."

He tried not to sigh audibly. "Let me see what I can find out," he said.

He could sense her relaxing as the burden shifted to someone else's shoulders. "You'll need to get right on it," she warned. "There's not a moment to lose."

"Darling, we've got four months." In agitation he began tapping a pencil against a blank notepad on his desk.

"We'll need every bit of it," she said sternly.

"I'll go down there tomorrow," he promised. On his lunch hour, when technically he wasn't supposed to leave campus except on official school business. "Tell them to expect me, okay?" He knew just where to look, having helped Fee with the fund-raiser five years ago.

"Don't be ridiculous. Everybody knows who you are down there."

"Yes, but if I'm going to go rifling through the filing cabinets . . ."

"I see what you mean," she said. "I'll do what I can."

As if it weren't a matter of a simple phone call.

"Good," he said, hoping that concluded that and the conversation could come to an end. Adelaide truly was one of the most tiresome people, thinking herself so much smarter and more important than she was. If born in a different time and place, she might have actually become a CEO instead of simply impersonating one. Still, it would have been through force of will and sheer ambition, not because of any ability or intelligence.

"Who on earth was that young man you introduced to Valerie last night?" she said.

He played dumb and looked at his watch. Ten forty-two. He didn't dare tell Adelaide he had to leave for class. She knew quite well he didn't teach again till eleven.

"The tall one. With the wavy blond hair. He was wearing that tacky sports jacket."

"Oh!" he said. "You mean Ellis. Mark Ellis."

"Who's that?"

"Our new lower school English teacher. He—"

"Where is he from?"

"Indiana, I think. But he—"

"Valerie will never be interested in a boy like that. A teacher. From Indiana." Her voice dripped disdain.

"Oh, no. Of course not." He pulled open a drawer as silently as he could and removed an apple from his stash. He didn't dare bite into it, but looked at it longingly.

"From what I could gather it appeared that you were trying to introduce them to each other."

"Darling, I *did* introduce them to each other. He came with me, she was standing there *all alone* when we walked up. What else was I to do?" Against his better judgment, he bit into the apple. "Just being polite. I wouldn't *dream* of trying to arrange Valerie's love life. If you can't do it, then no one can. Our Valerie seems quite resistant to influence and positively resentful of interference."

Unable to decide whether she was being praised or mocked, Adelaide abruptly changed the subject. "What are we to make of this person James brought with him?"

Again he played dumb, just for the fun of it and to allow himself another bite of apple. "Person? What person? Who are you talking about?"

As Adelaide exhaled her exasperation, Norman took yet another bite of apple.

"That little teenage girl he had with him. You saw her."

"I assure you I didn't meet any teenage girl," he professed.

"You most certainly did. You put your arm around her. I saw you."

"Oh, you mean Heather Moore," he said.

"Yes. Heather Moore. What is she? What is she doing here?"

"She's an intern for *Vanity Fair*. James met—"

"A secretary? Why does a secretary for a magazine need to come down here to the premiere of a movie? And that child doesn't even look old enough to have a driver's license."

"Well, actually she's got a college degree. In journalism. And she's just starting out—"

"You know I don't read idle nonsense like that magazine. Valerie showed me the article on James months ago. She tried to get me to read it but I refused. I threw it away as soon as she left the house. It was all about James's marriages and divorces—as if I wanted to have that lying around the house and be reminded of the way he's chosen to live his life and reflect poorly on his family name. And I fail to see what his personal life has to do with either the book or that stupid movie. I also fail to see why a secretary for the magazine had to come down here months after the piece has already been published. Am I expected to include her in the dinner party this evening?"

"Well, you certainly don't want anyone going back to New York and saying they didn't receive any of the famous Southern hospitality from the Whitmire family. Especially not someone who works for a national magazine. You never know what will end up being printed about you and your dinner party."

"Oh, heavens. Of course she's invited. Of course she is. I never said she wasn't. I never told James that either. It's just that he never told me he was bringing anyone. You know how particular I am about my seating arrangements, and the place cards have already been made out. They were done three weeks ago. I doubt I can get that same calligrapher. As you well know, I use only the best people, and they can't be had at a moment's notice."

"But probably for you, darling, they'll make an exception if you get onto them right away." He pulled himself even closer toward his desk and looked longingly at his telephone cradle as he had once gazed at the now ravaged apple.

"Yes, I'll need to get hold of her immediately. I've got a thousand things to do, so I'll have to call you later. I can't afford to lose any more time chatting on the phone. I'll probably need to get that leaf for the table out of the closet."

"Oh, don't worry about calling me back," he said, generously. "There wasn't anything else you needed to tell me, was there?"

Adelaide was uncharacteristically silent. "Actually, I do think there was one other thing," she said. "But I can't think what it was." She paused again. "I don't think it was that important."

"No," he agreed. "The important thing right now is your dinner party."

"Oh, I know!" she exclaimed suddenly. "It *isn't* very important, really, but I wanted you to know I heard the most ridiculous rumor."

"What's that?" he said sharply, clamping the phone back to his ear.

"Someone told me—can't think who—it might have been Jan Lindgren —no, it must have been Libba Albritton. I see so many people over the holidays, you know, Norman. We get invited to everything and would be out every night if I didn't put my foot down."

"Of course," he murmured, elbows on his desk, head staring down, bracing for the moment Elizabeth Elder had told him to seize when it came.

"But someone—I do think it was Libba—told me you were thinking of leaving Brook-Haven School. I told her not to be absurd; I hadn't heard a thing; and I'd be the first to know, so it couldn't be true. I just wanted to let you know what people are saying. How on earth could such an absurd piece of gossip get started?"

"I think I know," he said confidentially, lowering his voice to the conspiratorial whisper that was so effective with Midge Elmore. "But you don't have time to go into this now," he continued dismissively in his normal voice. "It can wait, though I *did* want you to be the first to know."

"What in the world? Tell me this instant."

"No, no, darling. It's not that important. You need to hang up and call the calligrapher right away."

"I will the minute we're through. Now what is all this about?"

"I'm just guessing," he said doubtfully, "and I don't know if I should even pass along my own idle speculation. . . ."

"Out with it, Norman!"

"Well, all right," he capitulated reluctantly. "But you should choose carefully what you do with this. It isn't information; it's just speculation. I must make that clear."

"Of course," she bristled. "You know quite well I have no time or inclination for gossip."

Norman well knew that despite her illusions of self-importance, Adelaide liked nothing better than a good gossip, unless it was to be the first to hear a good piece of gossip and the first to pass it along.

"Here's what happened." He lowered his voice again. "As you know, almost every time I run into him, Larry Plumlee offers me a job in the English Department at Shelby State."

"I had no earthly idea of any such thing!" she said, outraged. "Who is this person—Plumlee? What kind of a name is that? He sounds ridiculous. I don't even know who this man is!"

166

"Oh, yes, you do. Anyway, it's not important. Only this year, for whatever reason, Larry is going so far as to present me with a formal contract."

"How dare he!" she exclaimed indignantly. "He has no right to try to take you away from us! Is that even legal? Who is he, anyway? I don't believe I've met this person."

"None of that matters. What does matter," he lowered his voice even further, "is that Tom Turbyfill got wind of it and urged me to take the job."

"He did WHAT?"

"You heard me."

"But why? Why would he want you to leave?"

"I don't have the slightest idea," he said, suppressing a fake yawn, as if the whole subject were boring him.

"I can't believe it. He must have given you some reason."

"Oh, he made some remark about my master's degree being in English instead of education. And that as assistant headmaster—"

"I've never heard anything so silly in my life! You could have been the headmaster if you'd taken the job! That nonsense about your degree can't be his real reason."

"Adelaide, you're a very smart woman. I don't think it *is* his real reason. But I—"

"What? What is it?"

"Again, this is pure guesswork on my part. The last thing I want to do is hurt the school in any way, but if rumors are getting around . . ."

"You know you can trust me. I am not like your other friends, Norman. This town is full of frivolous women who have nothing but time to spend chattering on the phone. I'm a serious person with important work to do, and nothing is more important than the school. You should tell me immediately anything you know."

"Well, that's just it. I don't *know* anything. I only suspect—"

"What do you suspect?"

"Here it is: Tom Turbyfill knows that Elizabeth and I are not pleased with him as headmaster. He would like to see me leave the school before I bring my concerns about him to the Board."

There was silence for a prolonged moment. "You know something?" Adelaide said finally. "I have never liked that man. After that party I gave to introduce him to the community? The one you helped me with? Remember?"

"Oh, yes." Having done most of the work for it, he remembered it very well indeed.

"I have never ever received a thank-you note," she said.

"Putting it nicely, he doesn't do this school any favors," said Norman.

167

"No, he doesn't. Why didn't you come to the Board—or to me—with your concerns before now?"

"Well," he said judiciously. "I wanted to give the man every chance. But if rumors are starting to fly, the time has come for me to speak up before it affects our enrollment next year."

"Enrollment?" She was puzzled by this new turn the conversation was taking.

"I've never wanted to take myself too seriously," said Norman modestly, "but if word gets around that I'm not coming back . . ."

"Oh, good gracious! I hadn't even thought of that! What a disaster."

"Yes," he concurred. "I think the Board should step in before it's too late."

"You're absolutely right. Only what's to be done, do you think?"

"Can I count on you?" He feigned hesitation. "Or should I take it to Dirk Pendarvis?"

"Oh, you can count on me," she assured him. "Just tell me what to do."

He knew he better spell it out for her, just as Elizabeth had instructed.

"Just call Tom Turbyfill," he said with the utmost nonchalance he could muster. "Let him know that the Board has heard rumors that I'm being encouraged to take another position, and that the Board does not want to see me leave under any circumstances. If he tries to indicate any problems, you could let him know that the Board is behind me one hundred percent, has complete faith in me, is not interested in hearing anything against me, et cetera et cetera." He paused as if to consider. "You might even go so far as to point out that the Board considers me vital to the school's success, and if he does anything to interfere with the job I'm doing, he'll find that he's the one who needs to look for a new position. You'll know exactly what to say," he concluded breezily. "It's after eleven, now, darling. I've got to go."

"Wait a minute, Norman," she commanded.

He waited.

"Should I tell the other Board members?"

"Oh, I think so," he said casually. "Tom Turbyfill is a bit thick-headed, and it may take more than one person to get the message through to him."

"What about Dirk Pendarvis?"

He considered. "Dirk probably needs to call me first. As chairman of the Board, he needs to hear it from me before speaking to Turbyfill. Now good luck with your dinner party, and call me tomorrow to let me know how it all goes." He hung up abruptly and headed toward the door while seizing his briefcase from the chair as he passed by.

FEBRUARY

~ 10 ~

His mother had told him it would take a miracle to get Mountain Brook to come downtown to the Sloss Furnaces on a Sunday. After all, she pointed out, the whole purpose of Mountain Brook was so the people who lived there would never have to go near places like Sloss Furnaces in their entire lives.

"This is different, Mother," he had said.

"Just because they slap a National Historic Landmark plaque on something and call it a museum doesn't make it different," she had said. "It's still just a blast furnace. You can't tell me that people in Mountain Brook are going to dress in their best and come downtown for a party in a *blast furnace*. That will take a miracle."

The weather had delivered his miracle in the form of one of those magical amalgams of all four seasons concentrated into one day, as sometimes happens in the Deep South. The sun was as bright and dazzling as the summer sun of June or July—it wasn't the pale, weak sun of February. Yet the smell of wood smoke in the air was the very fragrance of winter at its best. The crispness of the temperature was that of fall, but the mild breeze that had been blowing all day was pure spring.

But the occasion itself was simply an Orange Bowl Gallery opening, not in the Orange Bowl at the Brook-Haven School, but at the Visitor's Center of the Sloss Furnaces, because the works being displayed were photographs by Karen Ritchie and her grandfather Jared. It was a retrospective of his work as well as the best way to get a newspaper article and a Harvard acceptance out of hers. And what more appropriate venue than the one where many of the original Pulitzer Prize-winning photographs had been taken? Sloss Furnaces had been much in the news since its opening as a museum in September, and it all just seemed like the right thing in the right place at the right time, what with the weather providing that perfect combination of sunlight and cool air for touring a defunct blast furnace in a mink coat. Because of the climate,

Mountain Brook ladies did not have enough occasions on which to wear their furs for a prolonged period, and he had just given them all a golden opportunity.

Only fifteen minutes in, and already the party was a huge success. Among the throng was the reporter from the *Birmingham News,* along with Lil Nolan, the society columnist. The photographer was expected any minute, and the art critic was supposed to show as well.

Here were Sally and Bebe threading their way importantly through the crowd with the extra trays of fried chicken he had ordered that morning as soon as he saw what a beautiful day it was going to be, and realized his turnout could exceed a hundred percent. Thank God for Brody's! Sally giggled as she tried to pry the plastic covering off one of the trays.

"How did you get yours off?" she stage whispered to Bebe.

"I didn't yet," said Bebe, giggling in response and tugging at the remaining lip of the cover still attached to her tray.

"Here, let me," said Norman, lunging toward the refreshment table like a big black bear whose huge paws easily ripped off both covers in no time.

The girls were in their element. Sally especially looked almost radiant. Had she lost weight? Norman looked around for the trash can.

"I'll take that, Mr. Laney," said Bebe.

"You girls are my guardian angels," he said. "This is the first time I haven't wanted to see everyone in the senior class graduate to bigger and better things. I don't want to lose my angels."

"Is there anything else?" Sally asked him.

There was something different about her hair today, but he couldn't put his finger on it. He gazed up and down the table.

"We're going to run out of wine before the day is over," he said.

Sally and Bebe exchanged glances. Bebe shrugged.

"Not much we can do about that," she said.

How terribly true. Because the state of Alabama was still living in the dark ages of a barbaric era, it wasn't possible to buy beer, wine or alcohol of any kind on Sundays anywhere in the state. He only noticed that Elizabeth Elder was standing beside him when she suddenly spoke.

"I've got a case of wine back at the house," she said. "Should I turn around and go get it?"

"Brilliant," he said. "Bebe will go get it. Give me your house key. You know where Mrs. Elder's house is?" he said to Bebe, who nodded. "Where's the wine?" he turned back to Elizabeth.

"Where you'd expect to find it," she said to Bebe. "In the kitchen pantry. I'm happy to go myself, Norman."

"No, no, don't be ridiculous. I need you here. Bebe, hurry back. I need you here too." He dispatched her with a nod. "Sally, you keep an eye on the table. If the food gets low, either you or Bebe just go to the nearest store and get whatever you can find. Sandwiches, fruit, cheese—anything. Keep your receipts and I'll pay you back."

She nodded happily from behind the table, where she seemed content to play hostess. It was definitely not the usual gallery party for his two gallery assistants. Sally was wearing an attractive A-line skirt of brown wool, cut on the bias. The thickness of the wool minimized her middle, and the long skirt danced right below her calves. Her ankles looked positively slim. Had she indeed lost weight? Or could it be that the rumors he'd heard were true, that she'd taken up with Jimmy Kuhn, and was happier than she'd ever been in her life?

"Now Elizabeth, darling. You *must* have one of Mother's lemon squares. She said to make sure you had one before they were all gone."

"Your mother's not here herself?"

"Oh, no," he said. "Did you really think I'd be able to convince her to come?" He lowered his voice. "She said nothing on this earth could entice her to come downtown even if I told her that the statue of Vulcan was going to fuck the Statue of Liberty. That's more or less an exact quote. Now let's go get us a lemon square."

He had to shed his dear Elizabeth immediately. He thanked God she was here: her presence conferred gravitas on any occasion because she was not one of those people who went to just anything. And he owed everything to her; she was a brilliant political strategist. If he had been a black man running for governor of Alabama, he would have hired Elizabeth Elder to manage his campaign. Also, she insisted on excellent wine, and soon enough, they would be drinking it. All of it. But he had to get rid of her. If there was one thing she wasn't good at, if there was one situation in which she found herself at a complete and total loss, it was parties. Elizabeth had no talent at all for making small talk with people whose IQ was far below hers. She was constitutionally unequipped for saying nothing at all with hearty enthusiasm while standing around eating and drinking dubious substances of dubious quality. For Elizabeth, food, drink and conversation were for the dinner table and intimate friends and family. The only way she knew how to negotiate an occasion full of people she didn't know well and didn't wish to know at all was to cling to him throughout the ordeal like the odd couple they were. If his mother had been there, Elizabeth would have clung to her, which no doubt explained her distress at his mother's absence. But Elizabeth would have to do the best she could without him today. And here was one reason why.

The man coming straight toward him had a camera around his neck and a PHOTOGRAPHER tag from the Birmingham *News*. Norman placed his plastic cup of wine down on the table, put on his biggest grin, and shook hands vigorously with Brad Staples, who wanted to know where he could find Karen Ritchie and her father. Without another word, Norman turned away from Elizabeth and Sally and led the photographer back through the crowd. Hands waved or grabbed at him as he went, but he was a man on a mission, and the man beside him made that mission clear.

With the camera trained on him, Warren Ritchie was as eagerly compliant as Norman had ever known him to be, and Karen was as compliant as ever while the photographer positioned them in front of the pair of photographs Norman had selected: one taken by Karen's grandfather of a former worker from this very same Sloss Furnaces in the 1940s, and the other taken by Karen herself of this worker's grandson, now employed at an auto repair shop in Ensley. Norman turned around to find the Vernon family—dressed for church—huddled obediently if uneasily where he had stationed them when they first arrived. He stopped himself just in time from beckoning them over with an impatient flick of his wrist. Instead he went to fetch them and led them back slowly as if on a royal progression. Whoever said that the best place to give a party was a room too small for the crowd was absolutely right. The Visitor's Center at the Sloss Furnaces was nothing special and had just barely the amount of wall space needed for the pairings of photographs, just barely the amount of floor space for the number of people who were still showing up. Yet it was the bodies in proximity to one another that sparked a real party. It was clear this was *the* place to be on this Sunday afternoon in February.

Lee Vernon was not actually the biological grandson of one of the factory workers photographed by Jared Ritchie in his prize-winning series. But as Karen had discovered in her research, he was the son of the son of this man's second wife, whose husband had adopted her children. The last name was the same, and that was enough. It was a stroke of pure luck, and Norman was a big believer in recognizing luck when it fell in your lap and using it for all it was worth. What good was a gift from the gods if you didn't put it to good use? And why risk the wrath of the gods by rejecting their gift? So Lee Vernon stood stiffly next to Warren Ritchie on one side of the two photographs, while Mira and Karen stood more naturally together on the other side. The flashbulb from the big professional camera went off with a bang.

* * *

"Both have applied to Harvard and both stand a chance of becoming valedictorian of their senior high school class. This is a new day. A new day for Birmingham, for the state of Alabama. A new day for the South and the rest of our country. And I'm proud that the Brook-Haven School has played a part in bringing on this new day. I don't know of another school in this state that was the capital of the Confederacy where a white girl of privilege vies to be valedictorian with a black girl whose ancestors were slaves, sharecroppers, and factory workers."

The slaves part was true and the factory worker part was almost true. He had made up the sharecropper part, and hoped it might be true. As for Karen Ritchie, she *was* in fact, a daughter of privilege, even if her family were not exactly Southern aristocracy but "Yankee" liberals. Let the reporter look into all the nuances if he wanted to! That was his job. And he, Norman Laney, had done his job. Now he was going to enjoy the party.

He shook hands with the reporter and turned to go back for a glass of wine. Elizabeth Elder was right there at his elbow.

"Oh, Elizabeth!" he said. "There you are. Just the person I was looking for." He lowered his voice. "The Vernons are over there in the corner." He nodded in their direction. "They don't know what to do with themselves and don't look like they're having a very good time. Take care of them for me, will you? Introduce them, get them some food, make them feel like they belong. I leave it up to you." As soon as she glanced in the direction he'd indicated, he was gone without another word.

"Norman!" screeched a female voice he feared was Sally's mother Jan.

Who was that coming toward him? Terrible bloated woman three dress sizes too large wearing big fat pearls that actually looked real. (The whole point of *real* pearls, someone needed to tell her, was to project simple, understated elegance.) Who was she?

"Jim Kuhn, Norman," said her husband, thrusting his hand out in a business-like way. He was likewise dressed in a business suit, and his entire demeanor, from the soberness of his craggy, unsmiling face to the stiffness of his body, suggested a quarterly Monday morning meeting with the shareholders of AmSouth Bank, of which he was president. Either that, or a funeral. He seemed completely unaware of the party going on around him, the photographs on the wall, or the unique location in which he found himself. He

175

also appeared to have run out of conversation after introducing himself, and was looking to Norman for further instructions.

Meanwhile his wife was prattling away. "The change in him is unbelievable. You cannot even begin to imagine. He's like a totally different child. Jim and I are so grateful for everything you've done. You have transformed him. You have worked an absolute miracle. We have never seen anything like it. I never dreamed he had this in him and it's all thanks to you—"

"Now, I did warn him," said Norman, adopting his best assistant headmaster's voice, "that if any of his grades ever dropped below a C, he was out of the play, no second chances."

"Best thing anyone has ever done for him," said Dixie Kuhn, seizing his hand and pulling him close as if for a tête-à-tête. "His grades have never been so good in his entire life." He could smell the wine on her breath and wondered if what he'd heard was true: that she was as big a lush as she was a fool. "The first thing he does when he comes home from school is head straight to his room and finish his homework. I've never known him to be so motivated. I'm telling you—I don't recognize my own son. The other day I was—"

"Now you *are* coming to see the play?" said Norman. "Both of you?"

"Oh!" Dixie threw her head back and looked up at the ceiling. "Are we coming to see the *play*?! Honey—" she clutched even tighter on the hand she had seized. "We will be in the front row of every performance! We have heard about nothing but the play, the play, the play, for the past three weeks. He rehearses his lines at the dinner table, and you know what Norman?" She pulled him close again and said in her wine-soaked voice, *"I think studying his lines has helped to teach him how to study for school!"* She leaned back dramatically and pursed her lips as if to give him time and space to process this dazzling aperçu before she unfurled any others. She was one of those women who still frosted her hair, so her head was a crazy quilt of light and dark patches. It really was one of the most unfortunate hairstyles ever invented, and he was so glad most of his female friends had abandoned it years ago in favor of the much more sophisticated look created by foil highlights.

"I must admit," said Norman, looking from husband to wife, "that Jimmy has shown me depths I didn't know he had."

"Oh!" exclaimed Dixie again, this time closing her eyes for emphasis as she thrust her head back and her face toward the ceiling. "That play is utterly beyond me; I don't understand a word of it and half the time I think Jimmy's got his lines all wrong because it all just sounds so absurd. Not to say—" she held up the plastic cup of wine in one hand while the other dug yet deeper, with fingernails this time, into his arm—"I don't mean to say there's anything

176

wrong with the play. How would I know? I never did have a brain in my head. Anything the least bit intellectual just sounds like gibberish to me."

Norman did not think this was the moment to launch into an explanation of theater of the absurd, or explain the fact that the dialogue was supposed to sound like gibberish. Or how it had suddenly struck him on the way to his office one day, that Jimmy Kuhn and his genuine aura of obtuse befuddlement would make for the perfect Rosencrantz.

"As long as you're in the audience, that's all I care about," said Norman.

"Oh, we'll be there!" she shrieked, looking at her husband, who nodded solemnly. In his own way, he was as big a fool as she. "Don't you worry about that! I just wish there were something else we could do to help you, to thank you—"

"No, no, no," said Norman. "It's all taken care of."

"That's what Jimmy says. No sets to speak of, no real costumes . . ."

"I *am* sorry that we don't yet have our new performing arts center. You'll be watching this in the gym, and if ever there were a play that needed a real theater so we could stage it properly . . . but we do the best we can with what we have!" he concluded grandly. "Now you better excuse me so—"

"Oh, of course, of course!" shrilled Dixie. "We've cornered you way too long. We're just so grateful for all you've done."

Again her husband nodded solemnly and thrust out his arm for a businessman's handshake. He had not uttered one word throughout the conversation but had remained rigid with the most formal posture, and nodded sagely from time to time as if his wife's mindless chatter were of the greatest importance. He was Princeton and Harvard MBA, and supposedly brilliant. Norman knew nothing of this couple except through hearsay, as all of their five daughters had attended Mountain Brook High School. Jim was apparently a financial wizard and a social dunce, which Norman had just been able to corroborate for himself. The story was that he'd barely had so much as a date when the beautiful but stupid Dixie Thornton—who had never managed to graduate from Bama—caught his eye and agreed to go out with him, although he wasn't at all good-looking and came from no family to speak of. On top of this, his future success was purely theoretical, based entirely on degrees from institutions celebrated in a different part of the country. Unfortunately, none of the children had inherited his brains, but it didn't seem to matter so much because they were all daughters who had inherited their mother's beauty. None showed any inclination to live anywhere but Mountain Brook, where a girl could achieve a very high standard of living based on her beauty alone. But equally unfortunate, the parents were both Catholic and also determined to have a son, with Jimmy as the result. He bore all the hallmarks of being the last gasp of conjugal energy, and was even dumber than his sisters, though he too had inherited his mother's former looks.

"Oh, Norman! I almost forgot!" It was Dixie Kuhn grabbing his arm again while wine sloshed out of her plastic cup. "Please show me who Sally Lindgren is. I hear about her night and day."

"She's over there." He nodded toward the refreshment table. "Come on; I'll introduce you. If I don't get a glass of wine right this minute I'm going to faint."

So it was true: Jimmy Kuhn, one of the leads of the play, had taken up with Sally Lindgren, his stage manager. It might not be a bad match; he'd have to think about it later. But if Sally got into Middlebury and didn't go, he'd kill her.

On the way over to Sally he was gratified to see many of the guests actually studying the photographs. He nodded at the Forneys, who seemed embarrassed to see him for some reason and moved on hurriedly to the next grouping of pictures. What was that about? A twinge of the fear and paranoia which were now chronic conditions flared within like a stab of pain. Were they the ones . . . ? Was that it . . . ? Had their son spoken up to tell them who he was? Had their son told them it was Mr. Laney who had helped him "discover" himself? He smiled bravely and waved as he caught the eye of the Daniels, who had brought Glenn.

Turning around, he was surprised and pleased to spy Virginia Cooley over by the wall. He would not have expected her to attend an occasion like this, which she could not attempt to dominate in her usual ways. What with the photographs on the one hand and the furnace on the other, there was no stage for her to occupy and too much else that commanded the attention she liked to monopolize at any social gathering. Nevertheless, here she was, and it meant he really *had* created the sensation of the year.

"Darling!" he cried out.

She ran over in equal delight, exclaiming over him as if she hadn't seen him in months, when in fact they had been at a party together last night. After hugging him and air-kissing both cheeks, she took him by the hand and led him over to the wall.

"You must explain this to me!" she said emphatically. "I know there's something important about this photograph I'm just not getting! I even feel like I've seen it somewhere before!" She gestured in front of her with both long, tapering arms and all ten tapering fingers outstretched extravagantly toward the picture. Today those remarkable arms were clad in skin-tight lavender silk with gold thread twinkling here and there. A dozen gold bracelets of various shapes and designs intermingled on each arm. The flashbulb that went off nearly blinded him and startled him so much that he almost stumbled on the photographer. Virginia appeared not to even notice this man's presence, though it now explained to Norman her own presence at the party.

"Look!" she commanded him, extending her arms even further toward the photograph. "What is it I'm seeing here?"

The photographer positioned himself for further shots. This must be for the society page, thought Norman. He needed candids. Virginia understood this instinctively, her arms still gesturing toward the party's central focus and supposed reason for being, her face in a perfect expression of stimulation, interest and curiosity.

No less a performer, Norman grasped his role immediately as the straight man who gazed with unbroken concentration at the actual art on the wall. It *was* art, there was no doubt about that, and Virginia Cooley was no fool, much as she frittered away her intelligence and talents like some people frittered away money. It was undoubtedly one of the best photos in the exhibit, and perhaps his own personal favorite: a black man with his wife and children sitting on the stoop of a house in the company "Quarters" where the factory workers lived. Another flashbulb, but still the photographer wasn't through, as he remained crouching and experimenting with different angles of his camera.

"In a way you *have* seen this photograph before," he told her. "It's intentionally reminiscent of the photographs Walker Evans took a decade earlier of the sharecroppers who lived not a hundred miles from where we're standing right now. One of those Walker Evans images is of a white family grouped on the front porch of their farm shack in a portrait much like the one of this black family in the photograph we see before us."

The squatting photographer, the flash of his camera and the authoritativeness of Norman's speech were drawing other guests toward the spot. Virginia now shifted her position, put her arm around Norman and gazed at his face with that rapt absorption sorority girls used on their dates in the 1950s. Another flash.

"Jared Ritchie set out to document the urban Southern counterpart to Walker Evans' portrait of the rural, agricultural South," continued Norman.

He could see Lil Nolan busily scribbling down the names of those standing around him as he spoke. Someone else was writing industriously in a notebook as well, but it wasn't Clyde Barnaby, the art critic. Probably the hard news reporter Norman had spoken to earlier. Just as well, since Norman was improvising his lecture as he went along, and the art critic might recognize the errors and fabrications, whereas the news reporter probably wouldn't.

"If you look at the Walker Evans photographs of sharecropper families, you'll find amazing similarities to the faces we're seeing here, though one set of families was white and this family was black. He's attempting to erase the distinction between white and black and show the common ground, the common fate, of the working poor." He nodded toward the wall. "You can see part of the porches of the houses on either side and realize how crammed the living conditions were in the Quarters, and the smokestacks in the distance indicate the urban landscape. In contrast, Agee's sharecropper shacks were in isolated fields where there was often nothing but cotton for miles around. Nevertheless, these people share the same socioeconomic class, the same experience of poverty, though they have been taught by their culture to hate and fear one another. It's a beautiful, powerful, *necessary* photograph."

Hadn't he read somewhere that jobs in the steel industry were coveted positions in the 1940s, and that factory workers then were actually fairly well paid? Oh, well. If it was true, hopefully the news reporter wouldn't look into that little detail. He turned around to face his audience, and another flash went off. This time the photographer rose, stretched out his legs, adjusted his camera, and strolled away, causing most members of the group to do the same while murmuring in appreciation of Norman's erudition. Virginia reached up to embrace him again and leaned forward to whisper in his ear.

"You are wonderful," she said.

He was under no illusion that she referred to his impromptu lecture rather than his ability to get her name and picture on the society page of the newspaper.

"There is no way we are going to lose you. We'll pay whatever you want and Tom Turbyfill is history. Just please don't leave us."

Before turning to go, she winked at him and waved gaily at Libba, who had already laid her hand on Norman's arm and her claim on his attention.

"Who is that boy over there with Kevin and Alicia Forney?" She nodded in their direction.

"You mean their son?"

Libba's eyes bulged wide and her lips formed a deliberate O. "I never would have recognized him," she said. "So it's true, then. I heard the rumors all during Christmas."

He shrugged. "Well, darling," he said. "Most people have to do something with somebody. As long as it doesn't involve animals or minors, I couldn't care less."

She laughed wryly. "I doubt the boy's parents will be so cavalier about it."

"Of course they won't be," he snapped. "It's always hard on the parents when a child doesn't turn out to be what they wanted. That's why the rest of us have no business making it any harder."

Indeed, he knew, it was his business now to help these parents come to terms with what their son had turned out to be; just as it had been his business to help the son figure out who he was. This was not something he always got thanked for, and it was certainly something he never got paid for; nevertheless, it was his job, for as long as they would all let him have it—a high-risk tightrope walk no one else wanted to do—and he did it. After he recovered from today he'd have to call Alicia and make plans for lunch. Or rather, drinks and dinner. And more drinks. After catching a glimpse of their son, whom he hadn't noticed earlier, he believed he understood now why the Forneys had avoided him earlier: they were embarrassed to be seen with their own child, who had a silver hoop dangling from one ear and his hair gelled into savage spikes sticking straight up on his head. It might or might not be an announcement of his sexual orientation, but it was certainly a gesture of defiance and rebellion which was making his parents extremely uncomfortable. Yet here they were in public with their son by their side. Still, it was clear they needed help, and what's more, they deserved it. As soon as possible, Norman intended to give them all the help he could. This wasn't going to be easy, like the time Kaye Beasley's mother had telephoned tearfully to ask him what he knew about dykes.

Apparently Cammie did not know exactly what these were, but her daughter Kaye had just "hatefully" flung the announcement in her mother's face that she was a DYKE in such a way that Cammie knew it was a very bad thing. Cammie had begun sobbing after reproducing for Norman's benefit the exact way in which Kaye had "hatefully" spit the word DYKE in her mother's face.

"Oh, she'll get over it," Norman had been able to assure Cammie right away. "But here's what you *have* to do," he said. "First of all: Don't tell a soul. And I mean: not a soul. Not even Neil. Are you with me? NOT ONE SOUL."

Sharp intake of breath on the other end of the line. Not tell Neil? Not even Neil? It must be Serious. It must be Very Serious. Cammie knew that now. She had known it at the time, although she had been hoping Norman would tell her it was all nothing. Unfortunately it was as bad as she feared—possibly even worse—so she had to do exactly as he said if she wanted this to go away.

"Most of all," Norman said, "Do Not Bring This Subject Up again with Kaye. EVER. Do you hear me? Say nothing. Not one word. And try your best just to Stay Out of Her Way. LEAVE HER ALONE. If you do exactly as I tell you, my guess is you'll never hear another word about dykes."

Norman had been right, as he knew he would be, because two weeks earlier, Gayle Naughton had shown him certain portions from Kaye's creative writing journal containing explicit descriptions of sexual encounters—*heterosexual* encounters—in which a certain part of the male anatomy had been described in graphic—and poetic—detail. Whatever else this writing was, it was not the work of a dyke. That much he knew, so he had been able to make the Beasley problem go away. With the Forneys, it was different. It was up to him to convince them that their problem was not a problem. This would be the work of a lifetime.

Meanwhile, he narrowed his eyes at Libba as if to telegraph a reminder about her own son, who once had hair past his shoulders and followed a guru around India for two years. Just because her son had finally cut his hair, gone to law school and become a husband, father and tax attorney did not entitle her to forget there was a time when she'd rather he didn't come home for Christmas with his ponytail and flip flops for all the world to see. One of the many reasons he loved her: he could talk tough to her and she took it well, perhaps even took it to heart. She was one of the smartest women of his acquaintance. And her fur coat was his favorite: the mink mainly on the inside, where it kept her warm, and only along the seams of the exterior, which consisted of a leather that looked like raw animal hide. Gorgeous.

She acknowledged his point by changing the subject. "Tom Turbyfill isn't here, I see."

"Considering that he tried to shut down my Orange Bowl Gallery two years ago, I wouldn't expect him to be. Don't you want some wine?"

He knew she didn't. Libba and Milton were naturally wine snobs who drank only the best and never out of plastic cups. But he wanted some wine, and moved toward the table. She didn't bother to reply but went with him.

"What could he possibly have against your Orange Bowl Gallery?"

"Oh, something about a non-profit institution needing to avoid even the appearance of engaging in for-profit activity."

Libba rolled her eyes while Norman grabbed the nearest bottle and poured to the brim of his fat little plastic cup. He turned back around. "I don't think Tom could believe I was running the gallery for the pure purpose of promoting art, artists and the Brook-Haven School. He was convinced I was lining my pockets. How else could I account for my luxury automobile and my gracious home?" He treated himself to a large slurp of wine. "Sure you don't want any? This is from Elizabeth Elder's own private stash."

"No, thanks," she shook her head curtly.

"I had to show him the books, the bank account statements, everything. Naturally I like to have a surplus to fund the next show. That doesn't mean I'm making a profit, or using it for my own personal gain. And today, of course"—he gestured around the room with his plastic cup—"today will wipe me out totally. And that's with Warren paying for all the prints. Of course, it might not matter if I'm gone next year."

"What in the world does that man think he's up to?"

"Oh, who knows?" said Norman, waving his hand carelessly as if he'd never given the matter much thought. "Tom is really the worst sort of barbarian: he doesn't care about anything beyond his own advancement. I don't think he gives a good God-damn about either the school or the town where it's located."

"But he didn't realize that the one thing guaranteed to rile the Board would be to try to snuff you out."

"Well," he said as judiciously as he could fake, "the school *is* up for re-accreditation next year, and SACS *is* becoming more and more strict in their regulations about credentials . . ."

"Oh, please," she said. "Do you think that's the real reason he advised you to take the other job?"

Norman shrugged and pretended to be most intrigued by the assortment of cheeses Bebe Bannon was hastily unwrapping and placing on the table. A quarter wheel of Brie, a thick wedge of Parmiggiano-Reggianno, a slab of some kind of blue, either Stilton or Gorgonzola. Good girl! he thought. No cheese cubes from you!

"Save your receipts!" he called over to her. "I'll pay you back."

"Sure thing, Mr. Laney," she said cheerfully, enjoying her role to the hilt as she always did, even when only a dozen guests showed up for the gallery opening. She would never present him with any receipts, and he would of course "forget" to ask again, instead accepting her expenditures as one of the many ways his well-to-do students and their parents contributed to the functioning of their special school.

"What's that, darling?" he turned back to Libba.

"Apparently Adelaide confronted him directly, and he said he'd elaborate more fully at the meeting of the Board in the spring."

"Thank you, darling," he said, as Bebe handed him a plate containing a generous selection of all three cheeses on Carr's Table Wafer crackers—his favorite—as she well knew.

"I wish Milton were still on the Board; I'd know more then," sighed Libba, eyeing his plate of cheese.

He held it out. "Take some," he urged with his mouth full. He knew she wouldn't. She never ate between meals and had the trim figure of a young woman to show for it.

"But you've got everybody on the Board in your camp, except possibly that Bible banshee's husband. Can't think of his name."

"Bradley?"

"That's it. Don Bradley. Who knows what he thinks? And who cares? The Board belongs to you, and that's what counts."

"Well, darling, perhaps it's time for me to move on. Make more money, work fewer hours. And I don't exactly relish the prospect of remaining in a job where the boss wants me out."

"But he isn't the boss. The Board is. And they'll be demonstrating that in two months. Luckily for everybody his contract is up this year. So you just sit tight, hold your breath, and don't do anything impulsive." She looked at her watch. "Now where is Milton?"

When Libba was done she was done, and often didn't bother with good-bye, just like him. He turned around first to get another chunk of that Brie, and was surprised to feel her hand again on his arm.

"Oh, and congratulations, Norman," she said.

"It *is* rather a success, isn't it?" he agreed, while slicing imperfectly into the cheese with a white plastic knife.

She pulled closer to him and whispered in his ear. "That too," she said. "But what I meant was: it's the first time I've ever seen white people and black people together at a party. Black people who weren't pouring drinks and serving food, that is." She raised her eyebrows meaningfully when he turned to look at her.

He only nodded, his mouth too full.

"Leave it to you to pull that off," she said. "Now I've got to run. Tennis at four," she explained, and she was gone.

His eyes scanned the crowd until he found the Vernons, the only black people in the room except for the ones in the photographs on the wall. They appeared no more comfortable or glad to be there than they had earlier, but at least Elizabeth Elder was looking after them. At the moment she was introducing them to Craig and Melinda Daniels, who couldn't have been a more perfect couple—social worker and civil rights attorney—to take the Vernons off Elizabeth's hands and give her a breather. He hoped they understood their social obligations.

New faces were still arriving and many others were reappearing after touring the furnace. Apparently the official guided tour took a full hour, and Liza

Sloss had offered to make sure a guide was available, though normally the museum wasn't open on Sundays. But that would have taken the focus away from the exhibit, and as long as the guests were free to wander through the site on their own, that would serve his purposes. Fortunately Liza had stepped in and made the arrangements free of cost after that woman of low IQ and even less imagination in charge of "museum events" had told him that under no circumstances could he host a party in the Visitor's Center, hang pictures on the wall, serve alcohol of any kind, and most definitely not on a Sunday or without paying the usual "event fee" for using the space. Luckily for him Liza Sloss was a graduate of the Brook-Haven School.

Catching sight of Adelaide Whitmire lowering her head like a bull charging in his direction, he crammed the remainder of the cheese in his mouth, downed his last swallow of wine, dusted the crumbs off his hands and prepared for the encounter. The formidable head of hair coming at him was the perfect appurtenance for the battering ram of Adelaide Whitmire's personality. Although she went to the same beauty parlor as all her friends to get her hair "fixed" into the usual carapace worn by most women in Mountain Brook of a certain age, somehow the hair of these other women appeared fluffy, with spongelike breaches revealing an inner airness. It was clear there was nothing inside but a total vacancy underneath the artfully engineered soufflé which deflated more and more as the days passed between hair appointments. But Adelaide's hair seemed molded from a solid piece of brass, as if it were a true force to contend with. It was hard to remember that her hair was just as insubstantial and air-built as all the other hairdos, especially because her face was physiologically incapable of producing a smile. The deep lines around her mouth formed only a frown that could deepen or lengthen, but never disappear. Fortunately he had remembered to get the proofs back to the printer on Friday.

"Hey, darlin'," he said.

"Norman, I must ask you," she began, ignoring his greeting. "What is Valerie doing with that young man from the school?"

"What young man?" His obviously genuine bewilderment softened her somewhat.

But she said, "You know very well who I'm talking about. The one you brought to the movie premiere."

"Oh," he said, with equally genuine enlightenment. "You mean Mark Ellis. I thought at first you were referring to a student."

"Don't be absurd," she said impatiently, waving her hand imperiously. "I ask you again: What is she doing with him?"

"Well, I don't know. I didn't know she *was* doing anything with him."

"See for yourself." Adelaide jerked her thumb to indicate the wall on the other side of the room behind her. "They're right over there."

As Norman stepped sideways to get a better view, Adelaide turned to follow his gaze. Valerie was at the moment studying one of the photographs in solitary intensity, while several photographs away, Mark Ellis was listening dutifully as Warren Ritchie held forth. Warren had stationed himself at the entrance of the Visitor's Center to greet all incoming guests, the better to intercept them and secure his best chance for social interaction. No one who could help it talked to Warren of their own free will.

"Doesn't look to me like Valerie's got anything to do with Mark Ellis," said Norman, turning back around and deciding that he needed a refill of his wine.

"I saw them arrive together!" said Adelaide accusingly.

"Well, maybe they got here at the same time," suggested Norman reasonably. "It doesn't mean they came together."

"I'm telling you, Norman," she shook her finger at him. "That young man has no business with Valerie."

"Darling, don't tell *me*. What have *I* got to do with it?"

"You're the one who suggested I invite him to that dinner party for James."

"I did?"

"You remember," she insisted. "I had to put the leaf in the table because of that silly girl James brought with him—that I knew nothing about—and then I needed another man to balance the numbers. You told me to invite this young man. I didn't know what else to do—I couldn't insult any of my *friends* by asking *them* at the last minute, and you refused to come."

With her reading glasses parked at the end of her nose, the black cord attached to the glasses dangling across her face, and her pocketbook clutched in front of her like a battle shield, Adelaide projected the appearance not of someone rehashing the petty annoyances of last month's dinner party, but of Margaret Thatcher discussing important matters of state.

"Well, darling, since you didn't invite *me* until the last minute, I already had a prior engagement for that evening." (Dinner at home in front of the television with his mother.) "Ellis was passing by my door as I was on the phone with you, and the idea just popped into my head."

"I'm going to hold you accountable if anything unpleasant comes of this," she warned.

"Are you telling me that Valerie and Ellis hit it off at the party?"

The frown on her face deepened. "Well, actually, he spent most of his time talking with James."

"Oh really? About what?"

"How should I know? Something about a literary agent or editor or something like that. I don't pay attention to James's nonsense. I do my family duty by him and that's it."

"Well it doesn't sound to me like there's anything going on between Valerie and Ellis, at any rate."

"There better not be. That would be most inappropriate. He's a highly unsuitable young man."

"Of course, Valerie *is* over thirty," he said musingly, twirling his cup and staring into the middle distance, where he could see Ellis and Valerie standing together in front of one of the photographs. "She *does* need to settle down with someone sometime soon."

Silently Adelaide absorbed this blow with the stoic, dignified fortitude she mustered whenever her abject failure as a mother was pointed out to her.

"You got the proofs to the printer," she stated flatly.

"I got the proofs to the printer," he confirmed.

"And I'm going to need you again next month for the book club."

"I just did the book club *last* month!"

"The March speaker cancelled," she muttered. "That new guy from UAB. I knew he wouldn't work out. You'll have to do it."

"If I'm in town," he said. "You know I'm headed to New York with the Albrittons."

"You'll be in town," she said, and then turned on her heels and left. Fortunately her view of Valerie and Ellis, obviously together, was blocked by the crowd.

Trying to disappear quickly in case Adelaide charged back in his direction, Norman turned around so abruptly and forcefully that he bumped into the man next to him and caused him to spill his wine.

"Oh, I'm so sorry," said Norman, as the man mopped the back of his hand with a napkin.

"Doesn't matter," said Larry Plumlee, holding out that hand and smiling amiably. "I was wondering what I was going to do to get your attention with everyone else clamoring for it."

"I never dreamed this would draw such a crowd," said Norman, who had sent out twice the normal number of invitations and told everyone he came across about the event.

"You really have done something significant here, Norman," said Dr. Plumlee, his eyes sweeping the room, surveying the well-heeled crowd, the prize-winning photographs, the smokestacks of the furnace visible through the windows.

Norman shrugged as if it had all been effortless. "The photographer's granddaughter is one of my seniors. I expect she'll be among several of our students headed to Harvard next year."

Larry Plumlee nodded. "Wonderful idea," he said. "To pair her work with his, follow up on the descendants of the factory workers. Your brainchild, I imagine?"

"Well . . ." Norman hedged.

Dr. Plumlee lowered his voice. "The contract went in the mail on Friday," he said. "I think you'll be pleasantly surprised to see that the—ah—compensation being offered is a bit more than we discussed."

Norman nodded.

"We have ample room in our new building for you to continue your gallery. I hope you'll do so. We—"

"Norman?" a voice broke in. "Quite a coup here. Dirk Pendarvis," said the newcomer, offering his hand to Larry Plumlee.

"Dr. Plumlee is the chair of the English Department at Shelby State," explained Norman.

"Ah," said Dirk. "I've heard good things about you and your department."

"Dirk is the chair of the Board of the Brook-Haven School," said Norman.

"I'm a great admirer of your school," said Dr. Plumlee. "It's a tremendous asset to the community."

Dirk nodded in accepting the compliment. "We couldn't do it without this man here," he said, clapping Norman on the back.

"Norman can single-handedly raise the consciousness of an entire community just by lifting his little finger," agreed Dr. Plumlee.

Norman could feel the genuine glow of admiration radiating from both of these intelligent, worldly, *decent* men, and wondered what their opinion of him would be if they knew the dirt on him. Whatever it was. There was plenty of it: unsavory, unpleasant, unethical, sinful, possibly illegal or criminal, and just plain *wrong*. He had done it all. This moment right here was the climax of his day's triumph, and yet he was utterly unable to enjoy it. Why did there always have to be a pebble in his shoe?

"Well, Norman," said Dr. Plumlee, edging away from the table. "Good to see you. And nice to meet you," he inclined his head toward Dirk Pendarvis. "I need to pay my respects to these photographs."

"Thank you for coming," Norman called after him.

Norman and Dirk stood in a meaningful silence until Larry Plumlee was out of earshot.

"There must have been three dozen urgent messages waiting for me when I got back from Italy," said Dirk. "All about you leaving Brook-Haven."

"All from Adelaide Whitmire."

Dirk shouted with unrestrained laughter. "Two dozen at least from Adelaide," he concurred. "The gist I gathered is that Tom Turbyfill got wind of your offer from Shelby State, and for reasons known only to himself, urged you to take the position."

"That's about it."

"How did he find out?"

Norman shrugged. "How did *you* find out? How does everybody find out everything about everybody else in this town?"

Dirk chuckled. "Got a point there," he said. "Have you actually received the formal contract yet?"

"Went in the mail on Friday, apparently."

Dirk scratched his chin thoughtfully and perched his lanky body on the edge of the table, now littered with abandoned plates, napkins and plastic cups.

"Any idea why Turbyfill would want you to take the job?"

"No, but you know as well as I do: I don't have any education degrees, and technically I'm not qualified to be the assistant headmaster."

Dirk remained thoughtfully stroking his chin while Norman signaled to Sally, who frowned in embarrassment and dashed over to clear the mess Dirk was almost sitting on. Events seemed to be unfolding as Elizabeth Elder had predicted when she devised his strategy. Last month Turbyfill had sent the receptionist, Elaine, to summon him to his office.

"Tell him if he wants to talk he'll have to come to me instead," Norman had growled. They were beyond mere suspension of the rules of engagement; it was guerilla warfare now. Next thing he knew, Turbyfill was tapping on his door and gliding smoothly into his office.

"I have received several calls from several of our Board members," he began pleasantly in his automaton's voice. "They have heard the news that you are considering a position elsewhere, and believe I am to blame. I think the time has come for you to make an official announcement. Otherwise, you are putting the school in an awkward position."

"It's not the school that's in an awkward position; it's you," said Norman, shifting the piles of paper on his desk without even glancing at the headmaster. "And you put yourself there. What did you think was going to happen? You can't expect to be the iceberg that goes up against the Titanic without some shock to your own system. And this time—" he looked over at the headmaster for the first time and leaned into his face—"the Titanic is not going down. It's the iceberg that's going to crack."

"Am I to understand that you would prefer me to explain to the Board why your contract here should not be renewed?"

"What I would prefer," snapped Norman, "is to get on with my job while you get on with yours. If you have any concerns about my performance, I'll be happy to address them at any time. But I have no intention of leaving this school."

Turbyfill had shaken his head. "I think you will regret this, Norman. If I go public with the Board in the spring, no school anywhere will hire you. The Board will not have a choice but to let you go, and your new job will be over before it begins."

"So you've said. But if what you have on me is so alarming, why wait till the spring to tell the Board? Why not tell them now?"

"I do not like dropping bombshells in the middle of the school year. And contrary to what you may believe, I do not wish to destroy your career or your reputation."

"I'll just have to take my chances with the Board in the spring."

Turbyfill had bowed his head ceremoniously and said, "That is your choice," before leaving the room.

Meanwhile, Tom Turbyfill was still in his "awkward position." Everyone believed that Norman had been sought after by Shelby State, which was actually true, and that Tom Turbyfill had then urged him to accept the position, which wasn't actually wrong. But Norman was beginning to feel like Anaïs Nin, who told so many lies she needed a little black book to remind her of what she had told to what person at what time. And Anaïs Nin was not a good thing to feel like.

Dirk waited for Sally to leave and looked around before speaking. "No one was crazy about Turbyfill when we hired him," he said. "We thought he was competent enough, and harmless. Have you ever had a conflict with him?"

"Oh, he's tried to rein me in, of course. Even tried to derail the college tour this year. Said I had to get twenty-five students, make it pay for itself completely, or it would be cancelled. I just ignored him and went right on about my business like I always do. Like I did when he tried to shut down the Orange Bowl Gallery two years ago."

"The college tour?" said Dirk, puzzled. "We're making a name for our-selves with the college tour. It's become part of the school's signature."

"And this," said Norman, sweeping his arm widely to indicate the room. "This is the Orange Bowl Gallery. You can't tell me this doesn't advance the reputation of the school. If I'm not mistaken, we'll get credit for this in three different parts of the *Birmingham News*."

"They've been here?"

"A photographer, a reporter, and Lil Nolan. The art critic hasn't shown yet, but he may come later. He might not necessarily want to attend the opening."

Dirk rose and patted Norman on the arm. "Just hold on," he said. "The headmaster's contract is up for renewal this year, and the Board will have a chance to revisit his suitability for the Brook-Haven School. If he doesn't want you as his colleague, that can be easily solved, though not necessarily in the way he envisions."

"Don't forget to come see your son play the lead in the spring play," said Norman.

"Oh, yes," said Dirk vaguely. "Luke mentioned something about that. I'll be there."

He eased off, clearly bothered by something, probably the same thing that Norman was bothered by: the fear that Tom Turbyfill had the goods on Norman Laney.

The crowd was beginning to thin, and Warren Ritchie was enthusiasti-cally shaking the hands of all departing guests like a politician thanking his supporters. Warren appeared so pleased he seemed ready to explode with bursting pride. "Full as a tick," Norman's mother would have said. In a way, Warren *was* a kind of tick, feeding on the lifeblood of others. To look at him, anyone would have thought the day's event had showcased Warren, instead of his father and daughter, and no one would have guessed that his wife had died unexpectedly a mere six months ago. Warren himself clearly thought that everyone had come to pay homage to him. The idea that all these people might have come for any other reason—to promote the school, to support Norman Laney, to view the photographs, to tour Sloss Furnaces, to be writ-ten up by the society columnist—none of these possibilities had even crossed Warren's mind. He thought Mountain Brook society was embracing him at last. He had done everything he could to gain acceptance, and must have believed it had finally paid off. The poor s.o.b. didn't realize there was noth-ing he could ever do to gain full acceptance in a town as close-minded as Birmingham, where all non-Southerners were Yankees, and all Yankees were

Jews, and no Jews would ever be truly accepted. Today Warren thought he was being celebrated; he was merely being tolerated. To Norman's dismay, Warren went so far as to put his arm around him in an excess of gratitude for having orchestrated this triumphant moment. Karen was nowhere to be seen, of course. Typically of the girl, she had effaced herself completely.

At least it was over; he could go home and put his feet up. He had not sat down for the last four hours.

The next thing he knew, a camera crew from Channel 6 News was wheeling its equipment into the room.

MARCH

~ 11 ~

Norman Laney hitched up his stomach, shifted in his chair, and seemed on the verge of launching into his talk, when suddenly he shook his head apologetically and said sheepishly, "I'm sorry. But I just can't do this with that man staring me in the face."

As he was the only man in the room, all the ladies turned in a twitter of curiosity to see who he could possibly be referring to. There was no man in the room. The ladies now looked at each other. Had Norman Laney lost his mind? They looked back at Norman, and when they followed his gaze, it led them to the framed photograph of the Haskins family with Ronald Reagan in the White House. This portrait occupied a place of prominence on the secretary in the Haskins' living room, on the wall directly opposite where the largest, sturdiest chair in the Haskins' household had been placed for Norman's use during the meeting of the book club.

Norman shook his head again and laughed in self-deprecation. "There are three things about myself I've never tried to hide," he said, smiling hugely. "I'm fat, I'm poor, and I'm a Democrat!"

The ladies erupted into laughter: Norman Laney was always a hoot. As far as they were concerned, he could lead every meeting of their monthly book club, if only he would.

"I mean, maybe he does something for you all," said Norman. "But he sure doesn't do anything for me."

The ladies positively cackled with glee, as Hailey Haskins scurried over to remove the photograph and place it in one of the drawers to the secretary. She was young; she didn't understand what she'd done wrong, why all the ladies were laughing, or what Norman Laney was talking about. It was a stroke of bad luck for her that he'd been asked to substitute for the other speaker who'd backed out. Norman Laney was such a wild card. Of course, this could turn out in her favor, especially if he told that hilarious Fannie Flagg story someone had recounted last week, about Norman Laney and Fannie Flagg in the back seat of a Buick driven by Miss Alabama's parents, all the way from Birmingham to Atlantic City to see Birmingham's own Miss Alabama, Delores Hodgens, compete for Miss America. Hailey Haskins had always loved watching Fannie Flagg on *Hollywood Squares,* and her opinion of Norman Laney had risen accordingly. Otherwise, she had never understood why some people were so crazy about the man.

But as for the photograph of Ronald Reagan: all she knew was that several of her husband's business partners at Hammond Coal had framed pictures of their family with Ronald Reagan in the White House, but not everybody did, so it seemed to her quite a score to have such a prized memento of their trip to Washington last year and their generous donations to the Republican Party every year.

Norman, on the other hand, understood quite well that he had a Fool's license and was expected to use it, that the ladies loved it when he was outrageous, when he said and did things no one else they knew would ever dream of saying or doing. It gave them something to recount to those who weren't there, as if they had witnessed something scandalous. And it gave them something to tell their husbands at the dinner table, as if they, too, had been out in the real world that day. But at the same time, Norman thought, it wouldn't hurt if even one of these ladies had been made to think twice about Ronald Reagan and the Republicans. Norman considered himself an educator in the broadest sense of the word, and used any opportunity that came to hand for spreading enlightenment.

"Now. Have I ever told y'all my favorite story about Flannery O'Connor?"

The ladies shook their heads in happy anticipation. They would much rather hear Norman's stories than any talk about the book they had not had time to read.

"She was the guest speaker once at Birmingham-Southern when I was a student there. I won't say how long ago this was."

The ladies tittered as he knew they would.

"She was a pitiful looking thing then, on crutches," he continued. "The lupus had really hobbled her, though she could still get around. And the poor woman was afflicted with more than just a dread disease." He paused for effect, as if trying to find the right words. "Let's just say," he continued, "that her physical appearance created no mystery as to why she died an old maid."

The ladies laughed in appreciation, as their own major accomplishment in life had been to achieve marital status. Further, they all harbored the view that those women who "did" things, like Flannery O'Connor, were the ones who couldn't get a husband.

"But I adored her! I adored her!" Norman was quick to assure them. "After her talk, she took questions from the audience. This one young man stood up and said: "Miss O'Connor." Here Norman adopted the officious manner of a self-satisfied know-it-all. "Miss O'Connor," he repeated in the new voice. "Do you think the shift away from teaching humanities in the public educational system has discouraged too many of our young people from pursuing creative writing?"

Now Norman changed into his Pratt City drawl, which was close enough to Flannery O'Connor's rural Georgia accent. "'Naw-aw-aw-aw,'" he said, dragging out that classic Southern syllable while endowing Flannery with a pronounced overbite. "'Naw-aw-aw-aw, I don't think the public educational system has discouraged *enough* of our young people from pursuing creative writing!'"

This time the ladies laughed because they knew they were expected to. This was obviously the punch line, though they didn't quite get it. Norman could tell that his story had fallen flat—he should have known this was not the right audience for it, which was undoubtedly why he'd never told it before to this particular group. But he just couldn't whip out his Fannie Flagg story for the ten thousandth time. He'd told it again last week at some other ladies' meeting club—he'd already forgotten which one it was, but he knew that many of those same ladies were sitting in front of him now. So he quickly veered into his prescribed talk, and the ladies switched into their dutiful listening mode, sitting a bit too still with their eyes a bit too absolutely focused on their speaker. (They did not want to be accused later of nodding off during Norman Laney's talk.) This part of the occasion was actually expected to be a bit dull, or it would not qualify as educational, and the ladies would not feel as if they'd earned the treats Hailey Haskins' maid was bringing in from the kitchen and placing on the table in the dining room as Norman Laney spoke about Flannery O'Connor's story "Everything that Rises Must Converge," in the living room.

It was only when he began his discussion of the violent confrontation be-tween a white lady and a black woman on a Georgia bus that he realized his mistake. What four A.M. demon had driven him to pick this particular story when there were so many others in the collection? No doubt at that mystical hour of the night/day, he had flattered himself that Flannery needed him now every bit as much as she'd once needed her editor and publisher. Because it was the likes of him that took the ideas from her pages and crammed them through the thick skulls of those who would never read them. But at the unmagical hour of two-thirty in the afternoon, he was overcome with regret that he had chosen one of the more provocative stories, guaranteed to chafe the sensibilities of both the white ladies and the black help who were there for an event over which he alone presided at the moment. Why did he always have to take these huge risks and push things to the very brink, the absolute limit? His mother was right; this particular form of excess would be the undoing of him one day, if it had not undone him already.

Briefly he looked up from the book he was using, made a swift scan of the room, and quickly determined that he needn't worry, at least as far as the white ladies were concerned. Years of slavery, racial injustice, the Civil Rights Movement and the Montgomery bus boycott might as well not have happened. The burden of Southern history was not lying heavily on anyone's consciousness in the room today. In fact, there was very little consciousness at all. The eyelids of some of the ladies *were* actually flickering as he spoke, but apparently not in recognition that the story's themes had any bearing on the reality of their lives. Rather, they appeared to be dozing. Really, thought Norman with disgust, not even Cheever could have done justice to the mentality that lay sleeping before him. It was one thing not to understand why the plane had crashed near Philadelphia because it hadn't rained in Shady Hill. Surely it was quite another not to be aware of the race riots in Birmingham because you lived in Mountain Brook.

"Just as well," Norman tried to console himself. Perhaps some of his ideas or words would drift unnoticed into some of the sleeping brains and take root, sprout, even flourish and bloom despite the unfertilized soil. This was a phenomenon not unknown to him in his paying job as a teacher of young people. It was like scattering wildflower seeds in untended gardens. And given that he would never marry and have children, this was the only way that he would ever spread any of his own seeds. All he could do was throw whatever he had as far and wide as he could, and hope that some of it produced blossoms. Invariably it actually did, and sometimes in the most unexpected places. Seeds that landed in the cracks of the sidewalk, for example, could still produce beautiful flowers that were even more important than the ones in the garden because these offset and sometimes even redeemed the dull concrete. The seeds that lodged beneath the concrete were actually the most important of all, because these had the potential to break through the hardened crust and change the landscape. And this, after all, was his mission in life.

As soon as he had concluded, the ladies rose with a grateful sigh and followed quickly after their hostess, who knew that her moment had finally arrived. Only old Dot Trimble, bless her heart, came up to him instead.

It wasn't clear whether she had read the assigned book either, but she said, "It makes me so sad when a creative genius like Flannery O'Connor or Proust or Keats suffers from a terminal illness. I wonder why those who have so much to offer have to have their lives cut short. Then there's me, who has lived forever and never been a bit of good to anybody."

"Hush, darling," said Norman, leaning over to her good ear. "I'll tell you a secret." He lowered his voice. "If this house caught on fire in the next five minutes, and I had to choose one person to save from the burning building, it would be you." And this was true, too, or almost, since Libba Albritton was among the group, and she was taking him with her to New York in two days' time.

"You are nothing but a shameless flatterer," said Dot, delighted nonetheless.

"Am not," said Norman firmly. "You know what else?" he said confidentially. "The longer she's gone, the more I miss Bella Whitmire."

Dot nodded sympathetically. She missed her dearest friend more than she missed her departed husband.

"I hate to sound like an old crank," said Norman, "but I think after your generation, they must have changed the baby formula and left out a key ingredient. Because the younger generations of ladies do not equal yours."

"It's your mother," said Dot graciously if somewhat inexplicably. "You put the younger generation next to her, and of course they don't measure up. No one does."

"You do, darling," he patted her hand. "You do."

By now they could hear the exclamations of delight coming from the dining room as the other ladies spied the food. When Norman and Dot Trimble joined them, he could see at a glance why. It was not the usual spread found at the other homes hosting the monthly book club meetings. Nothing offered on the table was homemade, and nothing came from Brody's, as far as he could tell. As the ladies quizzed their hostess, Norman learned that Hailey Haskins had ordered from that new bakery in Vestavia, of all places, and from a caterer who had recently opened up way out 280. He tried a lemon square. "Delicious!" he proclaimed with his mouth full, but only because Hailey Haskins had been eyeing him anxiously. His was the most important verdict in the room. But really, his mother's lemon squares were superior, and any good Southern hostess really should make her own. The food so proudly displayed on the starched linen tablecloth and the gleaming silver trays was just like the rest of the house: too perfect. Even the lace cookies were somehow perfectly round instead of imperfect and irregular, as lace cookies were supposed to be.

He had never been to the Haskins home before, and it was the kind of Mountain Brook house he detested, furnished in that generic upper middle class taste produced by items of décor from shops specializing in bridal registries and expensive wedding gifts. There was no work of art and not a single book anywhere in the living room except for the large atlas on the coffee table. And no doubt that was there because some decorator had told Hailey she needed a book for the table, and Hailey had thought any big book would do. The walls had lavishly framed prints of ducks and birds. Obviously the prized object was the photograph of Reagan, and he had made her put that away. Everything else he could do his best to ignore, but he simply could not countenance that. He thought he also might point out to her as he was leaving that the shelves which flanked her fireplace were not for mass-produced though pricey knickknacks, but for books—preferably ones which had been read.

Alarmed to see Norman Laney scowling while standing empty-handed in front of a table full of food in her dining room, Hailey hurried over with a plate containing a choice selection of delicacies.

"Oh, thank you," he said with perfect politeness. "I've been trying to resist, because I really must get back to campus."

Hailey only nodded and left quickly, as if afraid to attempt a conversation she knew she would not be equal to. In a sense she was exactly like her house: perfect in a bland, generic way, and utterly lacking in any individual appeal or attraction. Everything about her figure was ultra petite and in exact proportion to everything else. "Cute" was the word that came to Norman's mind, and he hated cute. Not a single hair was out of place in her blonde bob, which was her generation's equivalent of the bouffant hairstyle favored by the older ladies. But her hair had been sprayed into place just as thoroughly, and the blonde was a single uniform shade with no alternation of high and lowlights. Clearly she was not capable of understanding the need for the subtle variations which produced the best effect. Her clothes were impeccable and her makeup was meticulous, especially as she refrained from eating any of the goodies which inevitably smeared the lipstick and left traces of powdered sugar in the strangest places. The diamond solitaire of her wedding ring was not over-large in and of itself, but was accompanied by so many stone-studded bands that her finger looked like it had been colonized by diamonds. It was what Norman privately called the Junior League ring finger. Even her very name had that cutesy effect. Of course, she could hardly be blamed for that, but with her, he couldn't help wondering if one of the things she had looked for in a husband was how well his name would go with hers. Norman despised cutesy names and could have throttled Bebe Bannon's parents, for example, who had given their daughter the stately and lovely name of Elizabeth, only to vulgarize it unforgivably.

Hailey was thirty to forty years younger than most of the ladies in this particular book club, who belonged to a generation of women who didn't read a book from cover to cover any more than they washed their own hair. But it was Adelaide Whitmire's book club, and therefore the only one Hailey had wanted to join. To a degree Norman pitied her, because she came from Opelika, Alabama, and had all the insecurity of the small town girl who needed to prove herself equal to Mountain Brook. Norman had once been in a similar position himself, when he needed to make it in Mountain Brook. But at least he'd had the good sense to know that the only way he was going to make it was by being who he was, and not by trying to pretend that he'd always been one of them.

This poor woman was trying too hard in all the wrong ways. As he bit into a beautiful but boring brownie, he was reminded of Food Rule #1 in the Deep South: Taste was more important than looks. Southerners would serve or eat the most hideous-looking glop as long as it tasted good. This food looked too good and didn't taste good enough. She was trying to impress them, trying to make her mark—instead of trying to feed them well. That was a costly mistake in more ways than one, as clearly all the food was expensive and designed to look like it. Then the way she hovered around the table—as if to facilitate and gauge her success—without eating, drinking, chatting, or seeming to enjoy herself in any way—was all wrong. As if she were merely part of the help. She would never make it in Mountain Brook this way.

He would have his work cut out for him with her children, who were currently in the lower school at Brook-Haven. Of course she had the perfect millionaire's family, a boy and a girl, whose first names both started with H. He'd have to see to it that they both took his "Art in the 20th Century" class. Perhaps some of its instruction would educate the parents as well as the children. Often he could reach the parents by reaching their children. Parents always had a second chance at education when their children were in school, and he did his best to make his lessons penetrate beyond the boundaries of his classroom. By the time he got through with the Haskins children, he sincerely hoped the parents would have something else on their living room wall besides ducks and birds, and something else on the shelves next to the mantel besides empty vases and glass figurines.

"We were wondering, Norman, if anybody had heard anything from poor Fee Keller."

It was Sissy Lockhart, one of his least favorite people, though everyone else loved her as much as they pitied her for the way her three daughters had turned out: one a suicide, one an alcoholic, and the other a serial divorcée who had lost custody of Sissy's only grandchildren two divorces ago. These grandchildren now lived in Louisiana, and if she ever saw them, no one heard about it. What everyone else loved was what he couldn't stand: the perpetual cheerfulness that never dimmed even as tragedy struck again and again and again. She was the party girl who never grew up, for whom disaster was no more than a bad grade on a test that would not deter her from attending the fraternity party tonight or dampen her spirits while there. If she had no other invitations, she would be at the Mountain Brook Country Club tonight playing bridge, as she did on any of her "free" nights. The dire struggles and sad fates of her grown children had impacted her no more than had their presence in her life as children, whose needs and desires had never curtailed her social schedule. To Norman, this was not a heroic sunny disposition. This was utter inner vacancy. This was the meaning of the word "vapid." Today she was clearly enjoying herself as much as always, her lipstick smudged beyond repair and her upper lip twinkling with sugar crystals.

"Haven't heard a word," said Norman, wiping his own mouth fiercely.

"You don't mean it," said Sissy, taking a large bite from a chocolate petit four, which left dark crumbs lodging contentedly in the corners of her mouth. "I thought if anybody knew anything, it would be you."

"Oh, I didn't say I didn't *know* anything," said Norman provocatively. "Just that I haven't heard from *her*."

"Oh, so you *do* know something," said Sissy, placing her china dessert plate on the table. "Wait a minute." She turned around and snagged the arm of Grace Newcomb. "Norman knows something about Fee!"

This news travelled fast, and the ladies who had earlier avoided Norman on the subject of Flannery O'Connor now gathered near him as the subject had changed to Felicia Keller. Gossip trumped literature every time.

He shrugged noncommittally. "Finally I just picked up the phone and called her sister."

A collective "ah" rippled through the group.

"Said I was worried I hadn't heard from Fee and just wanted to check in."

As he paused, the anticipation of the ladies mounted almost palpably. "You all remember Monica."

The ladies murmured and nodded expectantly, though Monica had not lived in Birmingham since going away to college many many years ago—decades ago—and almost never came back to visit. Still, she had been "Zsa-Zsa Gabor," and as such, was of course utterly unforgettable.

"She's Monica van Hook now. As in van Hook Pharmaceuticals."

Everybody knew that. What they had not known was that Fee would just up and move in with her sister like that. She had told some of her "friends" that she would be visiting her sister at New Year's. They had thought nothing of it; she visited her sister fairly regularly throughout the year. But she had not told them she wasn't planning to come back. It was a bold, brave move that had taken them all by surprise.

"Monica just laughed and said she hardly heard from Fee either."

Now there was a collective gasp. The ladies didn't know what to expect at this point.

"I thought Fee was staying with her sister," said Libba Albritton sharply.

"Well, she is," said Norman. "But they're hardly under the same roof. And the guest house on the van Hook estate in Palm Beach is bigger than most residences in Mountain Brook, even on the most exclusive streets."

This sobering reminder of the larger world outside Mountain Brook actually silenced the ladies.

"No need to worry about Fee, I was told. She's the belle of the ball whose only concern is which invitations to accept. Supposedly she's got three suitors vying for her attention already. And one of them is a van Hook. A cousin of Monica's husband. His wife died last year. Apparently he is absolutely smitten with Fee and has been for some time. Long before his wife finally passed away. She'd had leukemia for years, I'm told, and lived like an invalid."

There was a moment of profound, thunderstruck silence before a buzz broke out all over the room as the ladies turned to one another for help in processing this startling information. But now that Fee was once again the object of male attention and desire, one thing was automatically established: it was no longer "poor" Fee but "darling" Fee. And no doubt about it: van Hook was a better name than Keller. The "van" conjured the notion of European aristocracy, if not royalty. And the van Hook fortune made Frank Keller look like a mere pauper.

"I just hope she *enjoys* herself," said Sissy to no one in particular and everyone at large. "That's what my mother told me, and I wish I'd listened. Just go out with all of them, keep them guessing, make each one think he's your

203

favorite, and do it as long as you can get away with it. Because as soon as you pick one, you have to settle down with him, and then all the fun stops."

The ladies were glad to be able to vent their confused emotions into a big giggle.

"I just think it's absolutely grand that Fee is getting a second chance like this," continued Sissy. "She should make the most of it she can, and when it comes time to make a decision, pick the one with the most money and hope the good times last forever!"

This pronouncement was nothing more than a statement of the philosophy by which all the ladies had guided their young lives. However, they murmured in approval of Sissy's sweetness and uncomplicated good nature. She had suffered a series of mortal blows in her own life, and yet managed to be so kindhearted; it was a lesson to them all. Most were now dealing with some degree of envy that Fee had gained a second chance to make it work out even better for herself than it had her first time around. Most would have welcomed such a second chance themselves, if only because their lives as sought-after belles had been so much more fun than their lives as married women. Despite the joys they had known as wives, mothers and grandmothers, the happiest time of their lives had taken place when they were teenagers. The idea that a middle-aged woman could reprise that whirlwind girlhood of parties, dances, dates and dinners had never occurred to them. The fact that Felicia Keller was actually reliving those years, and they were not, was mildly devastating.

Norman popped a dark chocolate truffle in his mouth and decided on one cup of coffee before heading back to the school. Sissy Lockhart always depressed him, and just now he felt his spirits plummet to the point he even wondered if life weren't trying to usher him away from Mountain Brook for his own good as it had with Fee. Of course Fee had her faults—who didn't?— but nothing like the complete hollowness of Sissy Lockhart. At least Fee had raised her children, and had three successful sons to show for it. One on Wall Street, one in the MBA program at Northwestern in Chicago, and one a vice president in the Hong Kong office of a Fortune 500 company whose name momentarily escaped him.

True, it was much easier to raise sons than daughters in this Southern society, and Sissy's daughters had been caught in the very gears of social change, raised to live a life like their mother's, but unable either to embrace that existence or reject it fully. Mountain Brook could be treacherous for women. Fee was better off out of it and maybe he would be too if he took the job at Shelby State and used the extra money to buy a house somewhere outside of Mountain Brook. He often wondered why he even bothered with these people, why he didn't follow the advice he offered so forcefully to his students—to think big, to aim high, and above all, get out into that larger world.

But as he gazed around the dining room at the ladies who had put on their silk dresses and pearls and had their hair done for him, he was reminded of why he did bother. They had let him in to their world, misbegotten, malformed, misshapen beast that he was. They had accepted him and embraced him. Not all of them had, but enough had been able to see the worthiness of the soul buried beneath all those layers of fat. This proved there was at least a tiny spark of goodness buried beneath all those layers of injustice in a society engineered for the comfort and prosperity of the white and the rich. But that tiny spark was enough. Its mere existence showed that the whole society was capable of redemption, and now that he was in, his job was to be the agent of change and transformation. It was up to him to show them the path to salvation, and through their sons and daughters, he would deliver them from their own evil. After all, if they could overcome a prejudice against fat people, perhaps they could overcome their other prejudices as well.

Turning around, coffee cup in hand, he saw Adelaide Whitmire sidling up to him, her mouth in downturn as usual.

"I knew it was a mistake to let that girl into the book club," she grumbled.

"Why? What has she done? This looks perfectly lovely to me," said Norman, gesturing at the bounty laid out on the dining room table. When it came to Adelaide, he couldn't stop himself from playing devil's advocate.

"Before we started, I reminded her to ask for any questions and open up the discussion after your talk. You saw what happened. She completely forgot. As if the book club were just an excuse for a social occasion."

"Well, darling," he said mildly. "She's just nervous. It's her first time to be hostess. She'll learn."

Adelaide muttered something unintelligible.

"Was there something *you* wanted to say about Flannery O'Connor?" he asked innocently, popping another dark chocolate truffle into his mouth.

"And you were quite right to make her put that photograph up," said Adelaide.

"I've always said I wouldn't even want to be in the same room as Ronald Reegan," said Norman, "and I'm not about to start making exceptions now, not even for a photograph."

"It's terribly tacky," said Adelaide. "That sort of thing should be in the study, not in the living room."

Norman raised his eyebrows. "What makes you think these people have a study?" he asked. "I don't see any evidence anywhere that they've even read one book, let alone keep a collection of books in a room set aside for that purpose."

"At least he could put it in his office at work."

"Oh, I can think of other places to put that photograph," said Norman.

"Have you talked to Valerie lately?" said Adelaide. It was one of her many prerogatives in life to be able to change subjects abruptly without warning or preamble.

"No, I haven't. Why?" He sipped his coffee. At least this was good and strong. A New Orleans blend, with chicory.

"What about that teacher of yours? What's his name? Have you seen him?"

"Ellis. Mark Ellis. I see him every day." He took another slurp of coffee. And those dark chocolate truffles weren't bad either. Best thing on the table. He popped a third one into his mouth.

Adelaide clenched her jaw. "I need to know what's going on between them," she said.

"No, you don't," he said cheerfully.

"Norman, I insist you tell me everything you know right this minute."

"I don't know anything," he protested, setting his cup down on the sideboard. "And I don't want to know anything. We've been through this before. I make it a point never to get involved with anyone's love life. Those who've never managed to have a love life of their own have no business interfering in anyone else's."

Adelaide grimaced with displeasure.

"Libba only *thinks* it was Mark Ellis she saw with Valerie at Highlands Bar and Grill," he said soothingly. "But it could have been anybody. I didn't even know Libba had ever laid eyes on Ellis. If she has, it's only been once or twice, and she could easily be mistaken."

"Libba Albritton has eagle eyes," said Adelaide grimly. "She's never mistaken."

This was true.

"Look Adelaide," said Norman decisively. "You might as well accept reality. *If* Valerie *ever* gets married at all, it will be on her own terms to the man of her own choice."

"Dirk Pendarvis refuses to give me a copy of your contract," she said.

"That's probably because I shouldn't have given *him* a copy of it. It's not fair of me to abuse Dr. Plumlee's good faith in making me such a generous offer—"

"I think we should sue him. I hardly think it's legal for him to offer you a contract when you're under contract to us. Dirk laughed at me but I made him promise to look into it."

"You wouldn't really dream of going to that other place, would you, Norman?" said Grace Newcomb, breaking into the conversation which a scowling Adelaide tried to indicate was her own and hers alone. "What's the name of the place? I know they've offered you a lot more money—"

"Shelby State," he said.

"Shelby State," she echoed, nodding.

"Oh!" exclaimed Sissy. "I can't imagine Brook-Haven without you." As she bit into an almond cookie which crumbled awkwardly in unexpected ways, the other ladies nearby chimed in agreement.

"Shelby State has made Norman a very generous offer of a position in the English Department which the Brook-Haven School could never hope to match in terms of the salary," said Adelaide, drawing herself up to take command of the conversation. *She* was the one on the Board; *she* was the one who knew the details; *she* was the one who should be doing the talking.

"The only reason Norman would even consider the other position has nothing to do with money. The problem is the current headmaster at Brook-Haven School. He has urged Norman to take the other job—we're not sure why—but we suspect it's because Norman has been critical of his performance, and he wants Norman out of the picture. Naturally, this places Norman in a difficult predicament since the headmaster has made it publicly known he wants Norman to go."

"Can't you just fire the headmaster, then?" said Grace Newcomb, as the other ladies murmured their approval.

Adelaide held up her hand. "I can't go into confidential Board matters," she said grandly. "But I did ask the chair of our Board as much myself. And he said—" she paused and looked out over her audience—"we had to wait for the annual meeting and give the headmaster a chance to explain himself before any action is taken."

"I don't see why," said Libba emphatically. "He was clearly just hoping to shuttle Norman out quickly and quietly without much ado. Now it's blown up in his face and I don't see why we have to give him all this time to come up with some reason for wanting Norman out. He's had plenty of time to come up with some *very* creative reasons."

Adelaide drew herself up in preparation for launching another speech, but a babble of voices took over.

". . . never even met the man, have you?"

". . . don't believe I'd know him if I saw him."

". . . contract is up anyway at the end of this year."

". . . imagine why anyone wouldn't love Norman Laney."

". . . certainly isn't from around here."

Libba's voice broke through. "I think he should have been confronted immediately, and if he couldn't give a valid reason for setting himself up against Norman, he should have been advised that his contract would not be renewed at the end of this school year."

"Oh, Libba," said Sissy. "You are so smart."

"That might have left us without a headmaster in the middle of the year," said a prune-faced Adelaide.

Libba shrugged. "So what? Can't see that this man will be any great loss, whenever he leaves. Old Dr. Meacham meant for Norman to take over when he finally retired three years ago. Norman's the one who runs the school anyway. And *that's* why the headmaster wants him out. Meanwhile, we're giving him ample time to come up with something to say against Norman. This man could cause us a lot of trouble."

This time Adelaide's voice succeeded in rising above the babble. "We don't have to renew his contract no matter what," she stated flatly.

"Yes," agreed Libba. "But if he besmirches Norman's reputation, that could make it hard for Norman to become the headmaster."

That prospect silenced Adelaide, who had clearly never considered this angle before.

"But what could this man possibly say against Norman?" said Sissy.

"He could say I spend too much time off campus leading ladies' book clubs!" said Norman. "When I ought to be in the classroom teaching!"

There was general laughter followed by a cacophony of voices each coming up with their own theory.

"Didn't you take a month off last spring to prepare for the Shakespeare Festival?" said Grace.

"And I know you weren't supposed to use the gym last year when you read 'Christmas Memory,'" said Roberta Birdwell, wagging her finger playfully.

"Not to mention that picture of me in the new brochure is hardly a helpful advertisement for the school," said Norman.

"Is it true this headmaster person—whatever his name is—tried to call off the college tour this year?"

"What did Norman decide about that stomach surgery?" said Sissy.

"I didn't see that headmaster at the Sloss Furnaces exhibit last month."

"He certainly wasn't at the Orange Bowl Gallery opening when I went in September. That was one of the best shows Norman has had in a while."

"I think he must be jealous of Norman."

"He knows how much everyone adores Norman."

"Is Norman still taking me to Europe this summer?" said poor dear old deaf Dot Trimble, who could make out only that something was amiss—something about something being called off—and hoped it wasn't her trip to Europe.

"I just hope we haven't given this man the only weapon he needs," said Libba darkly. "Which is time. Time to come up with something to save his own skin at the expense of Norman's."

"It would take a lot to skin me," said Norman. "I dare anyone even to attempt it!" The ladies thought this was hilarious.

The only one not contributing to the raucous free-for-all was Hailey Haskins, who went around along with her hired help collecting soiled plates, crumpled napkins and lipstick-stained cups half full of cold coffee. Although pleased by a sense of success generated by the chattering voices, she would have preferred it if the ladies had continued to talk about her food, and where she got it, her home furnishings, and where they came from, as they had at the beginning of the social hour. Still, she was confident that her little party had given the ladies much enjoyment in the moment and much to talk about later, and that was the main thing. Her success today as a hostess would be known.

"But you *are* planning to stay at Brook-Haven?" insisted Grace. "The extra money offered by the other place isn't going to tempt *you,* is it?"

"Oh, what do I care about money?" said Norman, whose car would be in the shop for an estimated minimum of $800 in repairs while he was out of town the following week. "But I really can't remain at the school with a headmaster who apparently has taken it into his head to oppose me on so many important fronts. It's either him or me, but one of us has to go. So far the Board has given me every support . . . We'll just have to see what the headmaster has to say for himself next month."

"But honestly, Norman," said Sissy. "What could this man possibly say?"

"Well," sighed Norman. "I haven't murdered anybody and I haven't raped anybody, but otherwise, I'm probably guilty of everything else. So who knows? Now, ladies, I've got to fly, or the headmaster really *will* have something on me."

He blew kisses around the room and grabbed Adelaide's hand to give it a good-bye squeeze. He was also hoping that she, as this year's treasurer of the club, would remember to give him the $100 check he was due for being the speaker this month. But as she had forgotten to give him his check two months ago, he was not surprised when the idea never crossed her mind. It would only be at the end of the year, when there was a large, unexpected surplus in the account, that she would call him up to find out why, and he'd suggest that maybe she'd forgotten to pay the speakers. He would point out off-handedly that he, for example, had never received a check, and assure her that although it didn't matter so very much to *him*, maybe the others. . . . Except he was hoping to have that little extra for his trip to New York.

Well, he had to concede, even without the honorarium, the outing had been worthwhile and had served a purpose. Elizabeth Elder's game plan had now been executed in full. It only remained to be seen what, exactly, Tom Turbyfill was going to reveal, and whether this was enough to turn the tide against Norman Laney.

MAY

~ 12 ~

Whatever ground Norman Laney had gained in cleaning out his office at the beginning of the semester had long since been lost by the end of the semester, and now he needed to vacate his office completely. For a moment he simply stood in the middle of the room and looked around in disgust, not really knowing where, or how, to start. If only his office were like Elizabeth's, this would be easy. Somehow she managed to achieve scrupulous order, rigid organization, and perfect discipline without even one filing cabinet or scrap of so-called office furniture. He never even saw any evidence of trash in the bronze cache pot she used for a waste receptacle. But ask her to produce any essential piece of information, phone number, name or document, and she could pull it out of a drawer like a magician pulling something out of a hat at a children's birthday party. She even seemed to know in advance exactly what he was going to ask her for before he came into her office to ask for it, and to have it right there at her fingertips in the top drawer.

It was definitely a kind of magic he didn't possess, he thought, sighing as he regarded his row of drab gray metal filing cabinets, with their open drawers sprouting files and papers in all directions. He seemed to have everything, and never could find anything. For some reason he couldn't seem to throw anything away—ever—and it was simply not possible for him to maintain the aesthetic ideals and principles he insisted on in his living space in his work space as well. He needed a dumping ground. And that's what this was, he thought, sighing again and taking another survey. A dump. And he knew already, no matter how much bigger and supposedly better his office would be—as befit his new position and higher salary—this next office would quickly become just such another dump. Secretly he suspected Elizabeth Elder had her own dumping ground, it was just that she had the luxury of keeping it at home, in one of those rooms he'd never been invited to enter and whose doors were always kept closed. This enabled her to furnish her office at school more as a living space, and quite naturally too, since she spent most of her day there. How utterly civilized and absolutely Elizabeth. But he didn't have that luxury, living with his mother in a tiny apartment. And so—here was the result.

Tired of standing and contemplating the task before him, he suddenly sat down and decided to tackle the mounds on his desk first. As soon as he had pulled up to it, Ellis appeared at his door. Norman looked up briefly but said nothing, offered no greeting, no invitation to enter. He always found himself treating Ellis with literally unspeakable rudeness, though he liked this young man and identified with him in many ways. It wasn't just that Ellis was entirely too handsome for Birmingham, and Norman distrusted such easy good looks as much as he envied them. Chiefly, he wanted to find out what this young man was made of. Push up against him, test his mettle, go ahead and drive him away and get it over with if that's what he was going to do. If that was the inevitable outcome, then it would be better occurring sooner rather than later.

Ellis tapped at the door as if Norman hadn't seen him.

"May I come in?"

Norman paused a beat before looking up from his desk, where he was busily sorting papers from one pile to another.

"I'm busy," he said gruffly, looking quickly back down as if Ellis were of little to no consequence.

"So I see. Is there anything I can do to help?"

Norman scanned the room without once resting his eyes on Ellis, then again looked down at his desk. "If it were possible for anyone to help me, my office wouldn't look like this in the first place." He leaned across the arm of his chair and threw a stack of papers into his waste can with an emphatic thud. Then abruptly his eyes pierced Ellis. "Is that all you wanted?"

Ellis was momentarily thrown and reached out for the door knob as if for both moral and physical support. After a few swallowed stammers along the lines of "No," "Ah," "I," "Ah," he ultimately managed a complete sentence. "Of course I wanted to congratulate you on your new job."

Norman grunted but said nothing and continued rearranging the contents of various piles on his desk with increased intensity, as if this were absorbing all his attention and he had none left over for the faltering young man in front of him. The faltering young man finally decided to make bold and took a single unbidden step into the office. His all-too-obvious nervousness was in complete contrast to his exceptional good looks, which could have been expected to confer a sense of power and confidence on their possessor. This combination of diffidence and deference, coupled with youth and beauty, was utterly charming and endearing. Here was Michelangelo's David, but he was quaking in his boots. True, Norman was a kind of Goliath in a way, yet did Ellis not know he was Michelangelo's David? Clearly he did not, and that was precisely his charm. A brief thrill went through Norman as he remembered that in a few weeks' time, he would be seeing Michelangelo's actual David in Florence.

"I also wanted to thank you again for introducing me to James Whitmire," he declared, summoning all his might to make an unblinking pronouncement. "His literary agent has managed to find a publisher for my stories."

Norman couldn't stop himself from looking up immediately on hearing this news.

"So you'll be leaving the school, then?" he said, looking back down with an I-knew-it smirk. "Is that what you came here to tell me?" Out of the corner of his eye he watched the confusion and distress cross the young man's face.

"No," he said quickly. "No. Not at all."

"Really?" said Norman, his voice dripping with disbelief, his eyes meeting but mocking the young man. "You won't be heading back to New York to be a published author? You'll get a lot more traction there than you will here, believe me." Norman rose to confront the young man personally with the choice in front of him. His voice rose also, as if he were angry and fault-finding.

"This is the land of the Crimson Tide and the mullet toss at the Flora-Bama Lounge! And at this school, you've only seen a very rarefied version of what this state has to offer! The other 99.999 percent is deep frying, deer hunting, fish rodeoing and church going to places where they practically drown you so that born again takes on a nearly lit-e-ral meaning! None of these people will ever know about your book! And they wouldn't care about it if they knew! Most couldn't afford it, wouldn't consider buying it even if they could, and wouldn't read it if it were wrapped in gold paper and left under their Christmas tree by Santa Claus himself!"

Abruptly Norman turned back to his desk and changed his tone. "I think you ought to head back to New York. Don't you? That's where you belong."

Mark Ellis's face looked like it had just been slapped.

"Well, no," he said uneasily, the conversation not progressing at all the way he had envisioned. "It's not as if I can suddenly afford—"

"Who is it?" said Norman, squeezing his bulk between the arms of his chair and pulling out the drawer where he was sure he'd seen a banana earlier in the day. His supply of both apples and Baby Ruths was totally depleted.

"Who?" echoed Ellis, puzzled.

"Your publisher," said Norman impatiently, thrusting his hand into the back of the drawer and praying that it didn't get stuck like it had once before. "Who is your publisher?"

"Oh," said Ellis. "Scribner. It's Scribner & Sons."

"How much?" said Norman, wincing as he plucked both the banana and his arm, both somewhat mangled, back out of his desk.

Ellis hesitated a moment, then said, "Ten thousand."

"Not enough to live on in New York," said Norman, peeling the prize banana in three rapid strokes.

"Not enough to live on in New York," agreed Ellis. Ill at ease, he wasn't quite sure where to look as Norman devoured the banana in three equally rapid bites and just as swiftly tossed the empty peel into the trash before looking back down at his desk.

Bravely the young man ventured into the silence and further into the room. "Until this movie, James said the only way he could live in New York as a writer was because of his trust fund."

"But you could get a nice teaching position somewhere else," said Norman briskly. He pulled himself even closer to his desk and redoubled his attention to its impressive piles. "You could teach at a college or university. With an MFA from Columbia and a book of stories published by Scribner, you can do far, far better than teach high school kids in a city that didn't know any better than to bomb four little girls in Sunday school dresses or let loose the dogs and the fire hoses on one of the most luminous souls of the 20th century."

Ellis appeared confounded. "But I want to stay here," he protested.

Norman treated this remark as such an obvious lie that it didn't even merit a response.

"I have personal reasons," Ellis persisted nervously.

"I hope they're good ones."

Ellis blushed and his hands fidgeted, finally reaching out for one of the visitor's chairs he had not been asked to sit in.

"Depending on who she is," said Norman, coolly, not bothering to look up, "depending on what she does, she might be happy to move with you if it furthers your career. Which it would." He slapped a stack of envelopes down on the far corner of his desk.

Ellis blushed more deeply and stammered "We—I—like it here. I don't want to move. I've been happy."

"You want to stay in this town?" Norman's eyes looked like they wanted to pierce right through Ellis to detect the truth for himself lodged deep in the young man's brain.

Ellis nodded vigorously.

"At this school?"

Ellis nodded again. Norman's eyes narrowed as if he still suspected a lie, but had to acknowledge that the young man had withstood the interrogation.

"In that case," he said, attempting to thrust himself up from the chair. Part of his bulk had become wedged under the arm as it tended to do once a certain number of thrusts had pushed the chair's arms too far down toward the seat. He went through a chair every two or three months, but this one was now no matter. He'd have a new one in his new office soon enough. After extracting himself finally, he went over to his filing cabinets. "You can have all my material for senior English." He tossed a bulging manila folder onto one of the empty seats. "I'm going to recommend that you take over that course." Just as he started to rifle through the drawer for the remainder of the relevant files, the telephone rang. Norman looked up in annoyance at Ellis, as if it were the young man's fault. "Sit down," he ordered. Norman himself remained standing while picking up the receiver. He didn't want to fight with the chair all over again so soon, and clearly hoped to be able to dispense with this caller in short order. But when he heard the voice at the other end, it immediately commanded his attention and he appeared to forget all about Mark Ellis.

"That's right," he said. "Eleven. Out of a senior class of thirty-three. So that means *one third* of the Brook-Haven School's graduating class of 1984 received acceptances from Ivy League institutions. I've got the list right here in front of me."

Trailing the extra-long phone cord he'd paid for himself, he moved back around to sit at his desk and began rummaging through papers, destroying all the order he had so far achieved. Ellis raised his eyebrows and indicated the door, wordlessly asking if he should leave. Norman frowned and shook his head.

"Three of those acceptances are from Harvard," he said, pulling out the top drawer on his left. "And one went to an African-American student who was on minority scholarship." Norman did not believe he needed to inform the reporter that Mira Vernon had declined her position in Harvard's freshman class along with the full scholarship offered her. That was one of the battles he'd lost this year, and it was as bitter as any.

Shutting the top drawer and opening the middle one on the left, he spelled out the names of those who'd received fat envelopes from Harvard.

"Two from Yale," he continued, shutting the middle drawer with almost a bang of frustration. "Now get this right: T-h-e-o-p-h-i-l-u-s Jackson. He's another African-American student, so whatever you do, don't misspell his name. He was the lead in our fall play. Go back in your archives and you can see the article the *News* did about that six months ago."

Reaching down precariously to grab the handle on the third and last drawer on the left, he spied the list he was seeking in the trash can where he'd thrown it with the stack of papers for dramatic effect while putting Ellis on the rack. Clearly he'd have to go through that whole stack after Ellis had left the room.

"Theo Jackson's father is the president of a life insurance company in Birmingham's black community," he said, reaching unsuccessfully for the list in the trash. "And the father of our other Yale acceptance is president of the Mountain Brook Country Club. So that tells a tale right there."

He had to push back from the desk, spread his legs wide in the chair and bend all the way over to achieve successful retrieval of the list in the trash. Meanwhile, he couldn't help but think this would be so much easier if only he could write the article himself. Which he would be happy to do. But with the list finally in front of him, the conversation went much more quickly now that he no longer needed to stall for time. It gave him particular pleasure to mention Columbia, a feather he hadn't thought would be in his cap this year but was anyway, thanks largely to his own machinations. He had told Kaye Beasley to set her sights on Barnard but apply anyway to Columbia, and she'd written some damn fine essays. He had discounted the C he'd given her on the final exam as a wake-up call and given her an A for the course. Hopefully New York would introduce her to the bigger picture and she would lose those silly high school antics. She had a good brain and perhaps even serious writing ability. Before graduation he would try to find an opportunity to point out to her that while the world was full of girls who knew how to smoke pot and have sex, it was not full of super-bright young women with degrees from Columbia.

Another pleasant surprise was the acceptance from Brown for Brett Peet, a rather dull, slow-witted, plodding boy who commuted forty-five minutes from Trussville every day, and who made very good grades thanks to his very plodding nature. His father was a minister at the First Baptist Church in Trussville, though fortunately not the kind of Baptist as those dreadful Bradleys. Brett was big into youth fellowship and Young Christians, and led all those good works and community service projects and volunteer efforts that Young Christians liked to do. His was clearly one of those geographical and sociological diversity acceptances, but Norman would take it any way he could get it.

The rest had been pretty much as expected: Glenn Daniels to Amherst, Jason Simmons to M.I.T., Malcolm Fielding to the Wharton School at the

University of Pennsylvania. Smith for Claire Markham was not officially the Ivy League, but it was close enough for the Birmingham *News,* and it really did help if people could hear that "one third" of the class was headed for the Ivy League. That made so much more of an impact, stuck in the brain and came out easily on the tongue. As he well knew, word of mouth was everything. So he needed eleven Ivy Leaguers.

"And we have several other acceptances from other fine schools in the Northeast." He held up one finger to indicate to Ellis that he was almost through. "NYU and Middlebury." He spelled out "Lindgren," laying careful emphasis on the "d." Misspelled names were like fingernails on the chalkboard to him.

"Finally, I do want to point out that one hundred percent of our graduating class applied to college." He paused out of habit instilled by the catalog copy, from which he had just quoted an exact sentence verbatim. "And one hundred percent received acceptances. Call me back any time if you have any questions."

Norman hung up the phone and managed to stand up from his chair in a smooth movement without getting part of himself stuck under one of the arms this time. But instead of going back over to the filing cabinets, he astonished Ellis by walking right past him and saying "Wait right here. I'll be back in a minute."

With similar suddenness and without warning or greeting he materialized in Elizabeth Elder's office and ignored the hand gesturing for him to take his accustomed seat in the big leather armchair.

"Did Karen Ritchie come to see you?" he demanded.

"She did," acknowledged Elizabeth imperturbably.

"What did you tell her?"

Elizabeth removed her reading glasses, the better to return Norman Laney's accusing stare.

There was a moment of stalemate between her ice and his fire.

"Sit down, Norman," she said.

Reluctantly he complied. Still she waited until he had composed himself in such a way that he was no longer menacing.

"That's better," she said.

"What did you tell her?" he repeated.

"I didn't tell her anything," said Elizabeth. "I simply asked her if she was prepared to wear a button on her blouse for the rest of her life saying: 'I Could Have Gone to Harvard.'"

Now there was a moment of tense silence.

"What did she say?"

"She laughed. First time I've heard the girl laugh since her mother died."
Another moment of tense silence.

"Then?"

"Then," said Elizabeth calmly, "I told her she best better go to Harvard."

Norman exhaled a large amount of breath that could have become an explosion if the answer had not been to his liking. "Good," he said, rising from his chair.

Elizabeth blinked. "Good?"

"I was afraid you would tell her she ought to go to RISD," he said sheepishly, suddenly shedding the defiant demeanor he'd brought with him into the room.

"The poor girl was afraid *you* wanted her to go to RISD."

"I just wanted her to know that she has choices in life besides the ones her father has mapped out for her that are hers to make. But of course I wanted her to go to Harvard. Who wouldn't? Except for you, maybe."

"As you know," said Elizabeth primly, restoring her reading glasses. "There are several schools of higher education I prefer to Harvard. But the Rhode Island School of Design is not one of them. As far as I'm concerned, if an individual has artistic ability, she can develop that ability after she has obtained the best general education available to her."

"Thank God," said Norman, turning to go. "Don't forget you're taking me home," he called as he exited the room and wondered if he should phone that reporter back and mention RISD as one of the other prominent Northeastern schools which had offered places in the freshman class to Brook-Haven students. This was the school's first RISD acceptance, and with Alexandra Sanders a few years ago going to Juilliard, he could work a fine arts angle that was certainly in keeping with his own reputation. He hoped also that he'd remembered to emphasize—as he'd intended—the first M.I.T. acceptance with Jason Simmons. He couldn't overlook the math and science people just because it wasn't his thing. On the whole he thought he better make that phone call, and right away too. For all he knew, the reporter could be writing up the story this red-hot minute, and it would be much easier for him to incorporate the new material while the piece was in the works. After it was written—forget it. It would be like trying to penetrate the Kremlin with a ping-pong ball.

He was startled and annoyed to find Mark Ellis sitting in a chair in his office waiting for him. What was he doing there? Then he caught sight of the manila folder in the young man's hand and remembered. He went straightaway to the filing cabinets and luckily spied the "Senior English" tab immediately. Some of Elizabeth Elder's magic must have rubbed off on him while in her office. It took several tugs to extract all the files before he could plunk them unceremoniously into Ellis's lap.

"You can do whatever you want with all that, including throw it into the Dumpster at the Jitney Jungle," he said, moving toward his chair and the telephone. But the one thing I insist on"—he turned toward Ellis and wagged his finger at the young man. "You must find a way to teach. And I mean *really* teach. If it means you can't write a single world except in the summer, then that's what it means. Are we understood?"

Ellis nodded and began moving to the edge of his seat in preparation for departure. Norman was just about to dismiss him and reach for the phone when it suddenly rang, as if anticipating his hand. But it wasn't the reporter from the *Birmingham News;* it was the travel agent who'd been working heroically to make the necessary rearrangements for the trip to Europe. Norman didn't want to, but unfortunately, he had to take this call. The details had to be squared away immediately.

"Darling, I'm afraid so. If I'm going to be the headmaster of the Brook-Haven School, I really can't go around looking like a circus elephant anymore."

Privately, Norman was not so sure that the bypass surgery he'd agreed to wasn't a mistake. His fat was a handicap he'd not only overcome, but used to his advantage. As he never wanted to lose his advantage, perhaps it was a bad idea to lose his fat—his unique, one-of-a-kind identity as the fattest person anyone had ever seen—no matter how often the doctors assured him he couldn't lose it soon enough. But when he was named headmaster instead of being fired, Norman figured the time had come to abandon the performing animals' body in which he had cloaked himself, and step forth as the leading man he was. After all, he would not be abandoning all he had gained from struggling with that body, especially the self-confidence and self-acceptance he had fought so hard for. But he had fought and won, just like he had fought for his job and won that battle as well. Now he needed to move forward and build on his victories and accomplishments. Of course this was a risk: he might get invited to far fewer parties. But as headmaster of the Brook-Haven School, he needed to lead with something other than his stomach—he needed to lead with his inner rather than outer qualities. But naturally these had become so intertwined he feared if he gave up one, he'd lose the other too. Or simply become invisible. Who wanted to become average or ordinary, when you could be special? Like who would choose the dull Midwest over the eccentric South? Unfortunately, the new bariatric surgeon to whom he'd posed this completely rhetorical question was actually from the dull Midwest. He had simply stared at Norman with dull, Midwestern eyes which indicated he preferred the dull Midwest to the eccentric South. And he'd taken Norman's question literally.

"But there's a lot about the South that needs to change," the doctor had declared, as if articulating an original thought never before expressed.

"Oh, that's hardly a news flash," Norman said airily.

"I've only been here a few months," the doctor went on, heedless of Norman, "but it seems to me that the South clings to the worst things about itself simply because it's afraid it will lose what makes it unique if it changes. But we all have to have the courage to change when it will make us better. Don't you agree? Isn't that what you teach your students?"

Meanwhile the travel agent from the eccentric South had been chattering away on the other end of the line as Norman had lapsed into reverie. In a rural Alabama accent not unlike his own Pratt City voice, she was teasing and flattering him, asking if he was really determined to have the surgery, because she liked him just the way he was, et cetera et cetera. This was not a good sign. It meant she was preparing to tell him that she hadn't been able to rework the plane tickets or juggle the hotel reservations. And sure enough, that was the news: when she had made the plans initially, she had secured group rates dependent on no changes or cancellations. She simply had not been able to get around that. If the ladies were willing to pay extra . . . He calculated rapidly. Of course, they could all easily afford any additional expense, but it really was too much to ask them to pay a few thousand more for one *less* week of Europe. Even he didn't feel comfortable trying to pull that one off.

"Are you sure you have to cut that week out?" she was asking.

"Oh, yes, yes," he said impatiently. "I would never have put either of us through this otherwise. The recovery is six to eight weeks, so even if I'm back mid-July, I'm pushing it to be ready for the fall semester. But you know me—I wouldn't mind pushing it, only the doctor is leaving for his own vacation that third week in July." Norman sighed. "So I really must come back a week earlier than we planned."

"Forgive me for asking this," she giggled. "I don't mean to be rude. But is there someone who could come over and take your place for that week?" She giggled again. "I know there's no one who can really take your place—"

"No," he agreed. "No one can occupy the space I do. But that's a brilliant idea. Brilliant. When I come to get the tickets I'm going to present you with the Albert Einstein award for the year. Then I'll take you to lunch. Change my plane ticket but leave everything else exactly as it is. And I'm going to pay the difference on my ticket. Hear? Thanks a million, darling."

He hung up the phone.

"Listen," he said to Ellis, who was leafing through the pages on his lap. "Are you doing anything in particular this summer?"

The question took Ellis by surprise. He shrugged. "Just visiting my parents for a few days . . ."

"Good. How would you like to travel first class to Europe for a week in July? All expenses paid—the best hotels, meals in five star restaurants, museum tickets, spending money. You pay your own air fare. That's it."

It took Ellis a while to assimilate the extent of this opportunity; for the moment he was speechless.

"Your only responsibility would be to look after half a dozen old ladies who will worship you the minute they lay eyes on your Scandinavian cheekbones and your curly blond hair."

Still Ellis was speechless.

"Why don't you get Valerie to join you? I'm sure she could use a vacation, and God knows, she can afford it."

As Ellis nodded, a blush suffused his cheeks. No doubt he had thought Valerie was his own little secret. He had a lot to learn about the Southern town he was trying to live in.

"She can help you with the old ladies, and you can make sure she enjoys Europe as it is meant to be enjoyed."

Ellis nodded again and the blush deepened.

"Think it over this weekend and let me know on Monday morning. I'll need a definite answer by then. No later. Now I've got to make a phone call."

Ellis seemed only too happy to gather himself and leave the room without having to engage in any further conversation.

But yet again Norman Laney was thwarted in making his own call by the ringing of the telephone. He could hear Adelaide Whitmire's voice coming through the receiver before he could even get it to his ear.

". . . Garden Club and she knew the whole story. *I've* certainly never breathed a word to anybody, but *someone* obviously did. And if I find out *who*—"

"Well, darling, I wouldn't worry about it," said Norman. "It was bound to get out. You know how this town is."

"But it's very embarrassing for the Board and I don't like being embarrassed. Grace was actually laughing. She thought the whole thing was hilarious."

"I don't see anything embarrassing for the *Board* in all of this—"

"You don't think it's embarrassing that the headmaster we hired for the Brook-Haven School is either a pathological liar or certifiably insane?"

"I think hiring mistakes are made all the time, even in the most successful Fortune 500 companies. And the man at the top is often the worst mistake of all. Look at Reegan," he said, deliberately mispronouncing the president's name in his habitual show of disrespect. "I'm convinced he has early onset Alzheimer's, and no one even seems to care."

Adelaide sighed in exasperation at this change of subject.

"Look," said Norman. "We're just lucky the man's contract was up for renewal and we didn't have to get into any messy termination struggles. We can move on swiftly, and that's what I think we should do, without dwelling on the past."

Lucky indeed. At the annual two day meeting of the Board two weeks ago, there were many items on the agenda, but none so highly charged and anticipated as Tom Turbyfill's long-awaited explanation for advising Norman Laney to take another job. He had begun by advising the Board not to renew Norman Laney's contract. And then, in the dumbstruck silence which followed, he had explained why.

It appeared that in the fall of that school year, after his conference with Norman Laney regarding his daughter's applications to college, an enraged Warren Ritchie had stormed into the headmaster's office, threatening legal action and lawsuits because, he alleged, Norman Laney had attempted to extort him by demanding a quid pro quo: if Karen wanted to apply early decision to Harvard, then her father had to send her on the college tour. And earlier that morning, Tom Turbyfill had informed Norman Laney that unless he got the full twenty-five students to sign up for the trip, it would be called off this year. Turbyfill had attempted to calm Warren down, offered to mediate, said he was sure Norman had been misinterpreted, of course Karen could apply early decision without going on the trip, and Turbyfill would personally see to it. The whole misunderstanding could be resolved right away, this afternoon.

But Warren most emphatically would not hear of it. He said he knew Norman wouldn't do his best for Karen in the college application process—wouldn't pull out all the stops in his usual way—if he were crossed. In fact, Warren did not want Norman to know of his complaint until the end of the school year, so as not to jeopardize Karen's chances of becoming the valedictorian. But unless Norman Laney was removed from his job after this year was over, Warren Ritchie intended to take legal action. Turbyfill had had no choice as he saw it but to assure Warren Ritchie that either Norman would resign or he, Tom Turbyfill, would recommend that Norman's contract not be renewed. And he assured the Board that he had no other agenda besides the continued success of the Brook-Haven School, which he hoped to spare from any scandal or blight on its reputation, not to mention an expensive and protracted legal ordeal the school could ill afford, either in terms of its coffers or its standing in the community. Warren Ritchie's litigiousness as well as his prowess as a plaintiff's attorney were well-known even to himself, a relative newcomer in the city. For this reason he had advised Norman Laney to take the other position he had so fortuitously been offered. He had hoped that either Norman would announce his resignation or the whole matter could be kept under wraps, but unfortunately, he could not prevent gossip and rumor from spreading. He concluded by saying that he knew Warren Ritchie expected and wanted an opportunity to go before the Board and make his complaint known himself.

Accordingly, Dirk Pendarvis, as chair of the Board, had contacted Warren Ritchie and asked if he could come before the Board on the second day of its scheduled meeting. Warren had responded with an eager alacrity that had Dirk fearing the worst, especially because he could easily imagine Norman Laney doing exactly what he'd been accused of. These fears only escalated the next day as Warren sat there smug and self-satisfied while being introduced at the board meeting. When Dirk said "I understand you have a serious accusation to make against Norman Laney," Warren's face had darkened so ominously that every other board member also began fearing the worst and gripped their chairs in alarm.

The cataclysm occurred; Warren exploded.

"I don't know what you're talking about!" he had shouted.

The board members looked at each other in bafflement. Warren's wrath was not directed at Norman Laney, but at everyone else: Dirk Pendarvis, Tom Turbyfill, and themselves.

"Is this some sort of joke?" Warren had spluttered, enraged. "Are you mocking me? Here I am, thinking you're about to ask me to join the Board, and then you throw this stuff and nonsense at me?"

"You have no complaint to make against Norman Laney?" Dirk had asked him.

"Are you out of your minds?!" Warren had cried. "Norman Laney is the best thing that ever happened to this school! Norman Laney *is* this school! He does more for this whole town than anyone I know! He got my daughter into Harvard! He's worth his entire weight in gold!"

Given Norman's actual weight, combined with the enormous relief of the Board members, this trite joke elicited laughter and applause, which soon turned into a standing ovation. Assuming it was meant for him, Warren Ritchie was appeased and finally pleased with the situation in front of him. Yes, he thought, he had truly arrived.

For the first time since he'd known Warren Ritchie, Norman was profoundly grateful for the amnesia which prevented the man from remembering any of his outbursts. Or was he unaware that his tantrums did not constitute civilized discourse? Perhaps he was even unaware of the tantrums themselves. Maybe when he lost his temper, it was like temporarily losing his mind, and thus his memory. It didn't matter. Clearly he had no recollection of his fit of rage in Turbyfill's office or the threats he'd issued.

The upshot was that Tom Turbyfill was thanked for his three years of service to the school and told that his contract would not be renewed. Once again, Norman Laney was offered the position of headmaster of the Brook-Haven School, and this time, he accepted, with one proviso: Elizabeth Elder must be made the co-head. Norman could not do this without her, and besides, he intended to give up none of his current duties except for senior English. He *must* teach "From Giotto to Talleyrand," he *must* teach "Art in the 20th Century," and he *had* to continue as guidance counselor.

Lucky indeed. Especially that Karen Ritchie had been named valedictorian.

"As for that young man at your school . . ." Adelaide was saying.

"What about him?"

"I think you're right," she said. "I haven't heard another word about it and no one *I* know has seen a thing, except for Libba that one time, and that was *months* ago. If there *was* anything going on between them—which I seriously doubt—it's all over now. However different her ideas are from mine, Valerie knows better than to associate herself with an absolute nobody from nowhere."

"Mark Ellis was in my office just a minute ago," said Norman. "Right before you called. He certainly didn't say a word about Valerie to me."

"See? I knew it!" cried Adelaide triumphantly.

"So it would certainly be a shock to me if anything's going on between them," said Norman.

"Oh, there isn't," she assured him. "And there never was. The very idea is so silly I don't know why you even brought it up to me in the first place."

"Just always looking out for you, darling."

"Oh, and Norman," she said. "You are such a natural wonder. How ever did you manage to get that man to donate all that money for the new performing arts center?"

"Oh, I've been working on that a long time," he told her. "Just didn't want to say anything in case nothing came of it."

"I thought Libba told me you were as shocked as anybody."

"Well . . . I do think it's better if most people believe Jim Kuhn made a spontaneous, unprompted gesture out of the generosity of his heart and his strong belief in the Brook-Haven School. Don't you? But I can let one or two of my closest friends know the truth."

"I won't tell a soul," she promised.

It would be all over town tomorrow.

"Love you," he said, hanging up but holding onto the receiver, trying to remember who it was he'd intended to call before getting sidetracked.

He sighed and looked at his watch. Ten after five. He was tired, hungry, and there was nothing to eat anywhere in his office. He'd been down to his last brown banana, and he'd devoured that *hours* ago. Besides, Elizabeth Elder was giving him a ride home since his own rattletrap was in the shop again, and she always left the campus promptly at five. Come to think of it: strange she hadn't fetched him from his office ten minutes ago, and spared him Adelaide Whitmire at the same time. Wearily he stood up, patted his pants' pocket to make sure of his keys, collected his briefcase and left the room without even bothering to shut the door. Although he was a long way from clearing it out, there was at least nothing worth stealing in there anymore, and he could afford not to lock it up every time he left.

But when he reached Elizabeth Elder's office, he encountered her own firmly and unaccountably closed and locked door. This was stranger still. Unlike the current president of the United States, Elizabeth was most decidedly not suffering from Alzheimer's, and she never forgot anything. How could she possibly forget she was taking him home? Perhaps, he thought, she was in the ladies room, the faculty lounge, or the front office. But when he reached the main corridor, there was no sign of anyone anywhere, and the hollow echo of his footsteps indicated total desertion. Sticking his head out the entrance, he could see that her car was gone from her faculty parking place, as in fact, all the cars were. There was only a single vehicle he didn't recognize parked at the curb right out front. Someone, at least, was somewhere in the building, and could perhaps be persuaded to give him a ride home. Luckily he didn't live too far away.

But after traversing the main hallways both upstairs and down, calling out "hello" at regular intervals, he could only conclude that someone else was *not* in the building after all. He could always call for his mother's friend Phyllis to come and get him—which she'd graciously done several times this spring—but he could hardly lock and leave the school with a strange automobile parked right out front as if someone else were clearly on the premises if not in the building. He *was* the headmaster now, and this sort of custodial headache was his burden to bear.

Trudging back up the stairs, he hoped the car would be gone, and then he would be too. But no, when he peered again out the front door, the car was still there. Who did it belong to? He thought he better go try to find out. Reaching the end of the walkway, he squinted through the passenger door window to see if there were any telltale signs of the car's owner, as there always was in his car—magazines, mail, bills needing stamps. But the car was immaculate inside, as if brand-new, quite a contrast to his own junk heap. There *was* one scrap of something on the passenger floorboard; it appeared to be an envelope. Leaning closer, he saw to his surprise that it had his name on it. Hastily he looked around to make sure he was alone before opening the door and snatching up the card. He looked around again before he opened it.

"Thank you from the Brook-Haven Class of 1984," it said. There was a crowd of names which blurred strangely before his eyes. There were keys in the ignition.

Apparently the automobile—a powder blue Buick—belonged to him.

As he stowed his briefcase into the spotless back seat, he reflected it was a good thing after all that David Allison had been accepted by UVA, because Edward Allison's brother owned a Buick dealership. Furthermore, he realized, this probably meant that Edward Allison's loyalties were with him rather than against him. It was always gratifying to be able to add to the "Friends" column.

* * *

When his new car reached the bottom of the hill and the driveway leading to the school, he encountered a crowd of people blocking the way. They appeared to be cheering and clapping. They appeared to be his students. And many of their parents. Also his colleagues. Although his vision went blurry again, he could still somehow see that all these people were his darlings.

Epilogue
Four Years Later
The Brook–Haven School
September, 1988

If Mr. Laney wasn't in his own office, he could usually be found in Mrs. Elder's. At least, that's what the new secretary told visitors who came looking for Mr. Laney. The only trouble was, on this particular Friday afternoon in September, Mrs. Elder's office door was closed, and the voices raised behind it indicated they would not react positively to an interruption.

Mr. Laney had thrust his hands on the arms of the big leather armchair as if preparing to hoist himself up, but had so far remained seated. With elbows akimbo and his face jutting forward, he had the aggressive, even menacing posture of a great ape. But his anger, it appeared, was directed at himself.

"I should either never have meddled at all, or done a much more thorough job of it! I violated my own Golden Rule: First do no harm. She would have made a perfectly good doctor, just as her father wished. Though I still fail to understand why that barbarian was so opposed to an art history degree."

Elizabeth raised her shoulders ever so slightly in the suggestion of a shrug.

"His own father made a name for himself as an artist," Norman went on, musing to himself as much as to Elizabeth.

"But art isn't success in Mountain Brook," explained Elizabeth. "For that you need at least a law degree or a medical degree, if not a family fortune or business."

"What you're telling me is: I should have known better than to suggest his daughter's life belonged to her rather than to her father's ego."

Elizabeth shook her head at Norman's stubborn determination to blame himself. "Remember what you said to me almost four years ago to the day?" she asked.

He shook his head miserably.

"He killed her, you said."

Norman gave no indication that he recognized the words she quoted back to him.

"If anybody is to blame for this, it's him," she continued. "Not you."

"Who did I think I was?" said Norman, shaking his head as if he hadn't heard her. "I didn't even know the girl. I had absolutely no business interfering in her life."

"You weren't interfering. You were doing your job."

"I didn't do that job!" he shouted, leaning forward in his chair. "The job I meant to do was focus on her and get her through! Not just her mother's death and the school year! Not just into Harvard! But get her through, period. I didn't do that job! If I had, a young girl might still be alive today!"

"The person who did not do his job is her father. In the limited way available to you, you attempted to compensate for his failure. In this, you failed. But you did not kill her."

Norman relaxed his arms and sank back in his chair with a deep sigh. Elizabeth was more alarmed by this development than by his shouting or his hostile glare.

"You're right," he said. "I'm a failure."

Elizabeth thought it best not to grace this bit of self-indulgent nonsense with a reply. Instead, she waited a few seconds and then pointed out: "It's not as if you didn't have your own serious problems during that poor girl's senior year."

"Yes," he concurred grimly, through gritted teeth. "I had to focus on the barbarian who was trying to wreck my life rather than the one who was busy wrecking a young girl's life. But I should have known," he sat up again and wagged a finger in Elizabeth's imperturbable face. "After what happened to his wife—suicide or not—I should have seen it coming with his daughter. I simply underestimated the extent of damage that one barbarian could do. He killed two people—one in the name of marriage and one in the name of fatherhood. And all the world just sat idly by and let it happen. Myself included."

"As you know," said Elizabeth calmly, "it is my firm belief—which I've expressed to you many times—that parents who fail to parent properly—for whatever reason—are at the root of most, if not all, of the world's troubles. And unfortunately, when a parent fails to be a proper parent to a serious degree, there is only so much any of the rest of us can do to redeem the situation."

She sighed and Norman remained silent in honor of what he privately called one of her Elizabethan pronouncements. But ultimately he couldn't restrain himself and finally blurted out: "At least we could have kept her alive, Elizabeth!"

Elizabeth bowed her head in eloquent acknowledgement of the tragedy that had unfolded in front of them. When she looked back up again, she said quietly, "You are a rare soul, Norman Laney. In a world full of false priests, you are one of the very few true priests I've ever encountered. Still. It's not your job to save the world, Norman."

"Oh, yes it is!" he declared fiercely, his voice rising. "That is *precisely* what my job is!" he shouted, although up until that moment, not even he had thought to define his job in quite those terms.

Elizabeth believed the time had come to change the subject with a choice bit of news she had been saving for a final attempt to cheer him up.

"You'll never guess what I learned today," she said.

Norman said nothing and appeared lost in his own thoughts in the inner recesses of his capacious chair.

"Do you remember Mira Vernon?" she persisted.

"Of course I do," he said sharply. "Do I look like Reegan? Alzheimer's is not yet among my list of medical problems." (But Mira Vernon was another one of his failures.)

"Glenn Daniels' father—who teaches law school in Tuscaloosa—called me today." She waited patiently for Norman to muster self-control and exhibit some curiosity. Finally he looked at her with sufficient interest, and she continued. "Mira is going to law school," she said.

Norman raised his eyebrows as if to say "So what?"

"Harvard Law School," she said.

"Did you say *Harvard* Law School?"

"Harvard Law School."

"How do you know?" said Norman suspiciously.

"I just told you," said Elizabeth patiently. "She's in the first-year class with Glenn Daniels this fall."

Norman clasped the arms of his chair and moved up to the edge of his seat. A gleam came into his eye. "So I got through to her after all," he said.

She nodded. "You got through to her after all."

"Well," he said, heaving himself up and out of the chair. "Let's hope my influence has a more positive outcome in this case." He opened the door and was on the threshold of her office when he turned back around. "Don't forget I'm picking you up on Sunday," he said.

She inclined her head. "Ten-thirty."

"Did I say ten-thirty?"

"Mark Ellis told me ten-thirty," she said.

"We better make it ten," he sighed. "Since we're the godparents, we better get there early or Adelaide will never forgive us for being late to her grandson's christening."

As soon as he left, Elizabeth Elder opened the bottom drawer of her desk to retrieve her purse. It was five o'clock and time to go.

Norman Laney was hoping there were no messages awaiting him so he could also lock up and leave with Elizabeth, but when he reached his office, an attractive young woman sitting in one of his chairs turned around and smiled. He had seen her at the memorial service that morning, and she had looked vaguely familiar, but he couldn't place her. The voice that greeted him sounded vaguely familiar as well, but he couldn't place that either.

"You don't remember me, do you, Mr. Laney?" she said, still smiling.

"It's been a long day," he said, moving slowly into his office. "A long week."

She rose from her chair. "I'm Lori Wagner," she said, extending her hand. "I graduated with Karen four years ago. I saw you today at the service, but there were too many other people trying to talk to you."

"Of course I remember you," he said brusquely. Lori Wagner! He would never in a million years have recognized her. She was not chewing gum and her crotch was nowhere in evidence. On the contrary, she was dressed with taste and care in the navy blue raw silk skirt and jacket he'd seen her in at John's Ride-Outs. She stood before him now with confident poise and looked him in the eye with polite determination. The blonde highlights in her hair looked so natural they could have indeed been the real thing. She was almost beautiful. In fact, he had to admit, she *was* beautiful.

"If you're here to talk about Karen," he said wearily, "I can't. I just can't. I've run out of tears, I've run out of words, I've just plain run out."

Indeed, it had been the most exhausting week of his entire life. Late Monday afternoon, when everyone but Norman had left school for the day, Warren Ritchie had stormed into his office while Norman was still on the phone hearing the horrible news from Midge Elmore: Karen Ritchie's dead body had been discovered by her roommate in medical school.

As Norman swiveled around in his chair, Warren had started shouting:

"This is all your fault!" he screamed. "Do you know what you did?! You killed my daughter! That's what you did! If she hadn't come under your influence, she'd still be alive today! If you hadn't filled her head with all that stuff and nonsense about an art history degree! When you knew she was already starting medical school! You killed her!" he shouted.

Something told Norman not to hang up the phone, but simply to put the receiver down on the desk so that Midge Elmore could hear every word of the

234

confrontation. If his own dead body were discovered later that day, he would want there to be at least one person who could go all over town and tell the whole story, with appropriate embellishment.

Something also told Norman to remain seated at his desk, and to speak in a voice of icy calm, the exact counterpart to Warren. "If anybody killed that girl besides her own self," he said quietly, "it was you. And I'm not alone in having that opinion, either."

"Me?! Are you crazy?!" Warren yelled and gesticulated in a wild, frenzied fashion. "I loved her! She was all I had left, and I loved her! How dare you say such a thing?! You're crazy! You're the last person on earth who should be allowed around young people! I'm going to sue you into bankruptcy! I'm suing the school! You've got to be stopped before you do this to somebody else's child! I'm calling a press conference and taking this to the media, too! Somebody's got to see to it that you're stopped in your tracks! Since no one else has seen fit to do so, it will be my pleasure! If it's the last thing I do! I'm going to put an end to you for once and for all!"

By this point, Warren was bent halfway over the desk. If the desk had not been there, Norman suspected that he himself would no longer be there either. And he wasn't sure he didn't agree with Warren; perhaps he shouldn't be there.

"If anyone needs to be stopped, Warren, it's you," he said, sighing.

"What are you talking about?! You're the sociopath! She was my daughter, and I loved her! I never hurt a hair on her head! I never so much as raised my voice to her!" he shouted.

Rendered speechless, Norman simply gaped at the man. Warren had all the righteous, if enraged, indignation of a man telling the absolute truth. Once again Norman found himself astounded at the man's complete lack of both self-awareness and memory. In every possible way, he forgot himself. It was as if there were a black hole inside, where nothing he said or did either registered or remained, and there was no trace of a civilized soul. Was this the source of the evil he inflicted on others?

"At a time like this, you dare to try to turn the tables on me?!" Warren continued yelling, ever more frenzied and out of control. "It was you, I tell you! You! And I'm going to put a stop to it! I'll put an end to you and all your evil for once and for all!"

Warren's tirade went on and on for what seemed like hours until there was a quiet but persistent tap on the open office door. Both Norman and Warren looked over to where two uniformed policemen stood on the threshold of the room.

"Is there a problem here?" said one of the officers, in an accent that instantly identified him as a native of that part of Alabama most often associated with the state of Alabama.

"There certainly is!" yelled Warren, moving toward the policemen. "Officers! Arrest this man!" he pointed over to Norman. "He's a menace to society! He killed my daughter!"

"Calm down, sir," said the officer who seemed designated to do all the talking. "We understand you've been making threats against the headmaster here."

"Me?!" said Warren, genuinely puzzled. "I'm not making any threats!" he shouted, quickly recovering the normal decibel level for his speaking voice. "This man is the threat!" He pointed again in a wild way over to Norman. If his arm had been a weapon, Norman would have been dead by now.

"We've received a report that you were making threats against the headmaster's life here," stated the officer calmly.

"Ha!" shouted Warren, now directing his rage at the policemen. "Me?! Making threats?! What utter nonsense! Did *he* tell you that?!" he ranted, flinging his arm back over in Norman's direction. "The man is crazy! Crazy, I tell you! He killed my daughter! He should be arrested and locked up for the rest of his life! He's a public menace! A danger to society! He's a liar and a murderer and I tell you he made a false report if he told you I was threatening him! This man is the threat, I tell you!"

"Actually, sir," said the officer, consulting a notebook. "It was a Mrs.—" he peered more closely—"a Mrs. Perry Elmore who called in the report. And we've now heard the threats you've made against this man with our own ears."

Warren was momentarily thrown, unaware how Midge Elmore could possibly have been motivated to call in a report. "This is a conspiracy!" he screamed.

It was the last intelligible thing he said, as a violent, incoherent stream of language spewed from his lips. His face bursting with a red rage, his forehead plastered with damp strands of hair and his skin flecked with spit, he looked like nothing so much as a man who belonged in a straight jacket, especially as his arms flailed savagely in all directions. When the distraught Warren advanced toward the officers, threatening to sue, inform their superiors, get their badges revoked, get them fired and otherwise put an end to *them,* the officers even thought that at the very least, Warren needed to be in handcuffs, and proceeded to do just that. For the first time since Norman had known him, Warren was speechless.

"What are you doing?!" he demanded when he found his voice. "What in the world do you think you're doing?!"

"We're taking you down to the station, sir."

"Me? What have *I* done?"

With his hands cuffed in front of him, Warren's anger was that much less able to vent or express itself, and was gradually replaced by the look of genuine incomprehension he shot in Norman's direction. There was pleading in his eyes. "Norman," he whined, as if Norman were his best friend and staunchest ally. "Tell them who I am."

As the officers led him away, one on either side leading him by the arms, he looked like a startled three-year-old boy who had just been caught in the act of hitting another child over the head with a block of wood. He had felt at the time that what he had done was justified and necessary, but as he was being taken away to the principal's office, it began to dawn on him that perhaps he'd hit the other child a bit too hard.

Norman snatched up the receiver from his desk. "Thank you, darling," he said, into the phone. "You saved my life."

"Oh, Norman," she said. "As soon as I realized what was happening, I told Pearl to go next door and have Libba call the police."

"I only wish there had been a way to call the cops on him sooner. Then Karen might still be alive."

Nevertheless, Norman declined to press charges. By the time of the memorial service this morning, Warren characteristically appeared to have forgotten the whole episode. And when he stood up to deliver the eulogy for his daughter, his face suddenly collapsed. Tears streamed down his face. He couldn't move from the pew. Finally he looked over to where Norman was sitting on the front row, where Norman always had a seat to everything, Warren or no Warren. It was the prerogative of the fat man.

"Will you do the eulogy?" he whispered.

Although Norman was usually prepared to speak on any subject at any occasion on a moment's notice, for the first time in his life, he didn't know what to say, and no words would come. For a moment he just stood there at the podium and mopped his brow. His mother later told him it was the best thing he'd had to say.

"I don't know if I'm the right one to give Karen's eulogy," he had said. "Because I didn't really know Karen."

He had heard a gasp—a sharp intake of breath—from more than one source besides his mother on the row in front of him.

"I loved her," he continued defiantly. "But I did not know her. And I do not know why she did what she did. The best way we can honor the life Karen took is to try to learn from her death the lessons we need to know to support all the young people in our lives. The last thing I'm going to do is pretend this is easy. And I should know."

For entirely different reasons, Warren Ritchie and his mother both had their heads in their hands.

"I do not believe in that nonsense that anybody can be what they want to be," he continued forcefully. "That can end up killing a person's spirit just as surely—though not as quickly—as telling a young person *they can only be what we want them to be.*"

He was well aware that this was not the traditional eulogy. But if he was going to be pressed into service, he was going to tell Warren Ritchie and all those parents out there what they needed to hear.

"Our job is to help these young people be who they are, *whatever that is.* If we do anything else, we are committing a sin against nature. And *that* is the lesson of Karen's death."

He knew his audience was expecting a conclusion, so he swept on quickly.

"I stand before you as a prime example of exactly what I'm talking about. Anyone who looked in the mirror and saw what I saw every day I was growing up—this misshapen monstrosity of a human body—might have been headed for hari-kari on day one. But when I looked in my mother's eyes, I never saw anything but love. That love is the reason I'm standing here today. That love is the reason I've dedicated my life to giving young people the support I once received that has made my whole life possible."

Back at their apartment, his mother, of course, had been furious.

"When a young girl is found floating in a bathtub full of her own blood, people only want to hear about how beautiful and wonderful she was!" his mother declared, blowing cigarette smoke directly into his face as she pushed her plate toward him, suggesting that *he* could clear the table before he headed back to school. "At a time like that, people don't want to hear all that philosophical crap!"

"Mother," he had remonstrated. "I did have some hopes that you of all people would find something to like in all that 'philosophical crap.'"

"Oh, shut up, Norman," she had interrupted. "Don't think I don't know exactly what you were doing. You've always wanted to beat the man to a pulp, and you finally got your chance. At his daughter's funeral." Her voice exuded contempt along with cigarette smoke.

Norman sighed as he rose and began removing the remains of their lunch.

"You'll be interested to know," his mother called into the kitchen. He could hear her taking a deep drag on her cigarette. "His law partners have told him to take a leave of absence from the firm."

"He needs to take a leave of absence from life!" Norman shot back as the dishes clattered in the sink.

"If he does, it'll be on your head!"

But Norman's conscience was clear. People like that never killed themselves; they only killed others. His conscience was totally clear.

But now, late on Friday afternoon following one of the most difficult weeks of his life, his body was utterly exhausted. He heaved a sigh as big as the stomach it came from and tried to refocus his attention on the young woman sitting in front of him in his office.

"I completely understand you can't talk about Karen," Lori Wagner was saying. "There *is* something else I wanted to discuss, but if now is not a good time, I can come back whenever you want."

He looked at his watch by way of pointing out that it *was* five-fifteen on the Friday afternoon following the Sunday evening when Karen Ritchie had committed suicide.

"I'll bet I'm the last person you ever expected to see visiting your office," she said, a grin stealing slowly over her face.

This was so completely true and she was so remarkably transformed, he found himself curious enough to prolong the encounter.

"What can I do for you?" he said, less graciously than he intended. However, it gratified him to see that she lost none of her poise. He wanted to think that four years of high school with him had taught her at least that much.

"I probably don't have to remind you that I wasn't one of your Ivy Leaguers," she began, grinning again in a charming, self-deprecating way. "I went to UAB and majored in business, probably because my father wanted me to. But I did get my degree."

Norman stifled a yawn. This was proving less interesting than he'd hoped, and he wished he hadn't sat down in his chair. Getting back up, even with several hundred fewer pounds than he used to have, was never as easy.

"I notice you're no longer doing the Orange Bowl Gallery," she was saying.

"No, I'm not," he said, a bit uneasily, realizing he'd missed something while his mind wandered. "When I became headmaster, I couldn't continue to do everything. I either had to give up the gallery or stop being the guidance counselor. So . . ." He looked again at his watch.

"But you're still teaching 'Art in the 20th Century,'" she noted.

He nodded. "Not senior English, but yes, 'Art in the 20th Century.'"

He was just about to begin the arduous ordeal of extricating himself from his chair when she said, "Your 'Art in the 20th Century' class changed my life."

All he could do was stare, stunned and transfixed, as she continued on about the art history degree she was currently pursuing, the start-up capital her father had given her when she completed her business degree, the space he had leased for her in Mountain Brook Village where the Boutique Bootery used to be, and her idea to reopen the Orange Bowl Gallery, with Norman Laney as her consultant, her scout, her curator, or whatever he wanted to call it.

"About Karen," she said shyly on her way out, after he'd agreed to meet her at noon on Monday, to have lunch and look over the space. "I hope you don't blame yourself for anything. You tried your best to save her. If you couldn't do it, nobody could."

If only he'd known he'd had Karen's life in his hands, he reflected grimly, as he walked slowly down the lonely hall of his empty school. Until this moment, he had honestly not realized how much power he had in the world, for good or ill. He had thought he was just an obscure, if obese, schoolteacher in a benighted Southern city. Obscure he might be, and obese he definitely still was, but he wielded tremendous power nonetheless. In fact, he had the only kind of power that mattered: the power to change the world. Not many people really had this kind of power. And of course, with great power came great responsibility.

In the back of his mind, he could hear his mother's voice. Whenever she wanted to take him down a peg or three, she always said: "Who do you think you are, Norman Laney? The most important person in the world?"

"Well, yes, Mother," he argued with the voice inside. "I *am* the most important person in the world. Because I am a teacher. And my job is to save the souls of the damned."

At least from now on, he knew. He had all these lives in his hands. They were all his darlings whether they knew it or not. And he had to make sure, first and foremost, that he had done his utmost to save each and every one of them from the barbarians. Then, and only then, could he turn his attention to making sure they embarked on a lifelong journey toward higher civilization. After all, it wasn't just a matter of Art and Culture. It was a matter of life itself.

AUTHOR'S NOTE AND ACKNOWLEDGMENTS

Temple Tutwiler planted the first seed of this book when he suggested that I add to my "canon" of oral biographies by doing one with the extraordinary man who had been an English teacher and mentor to us both, Carl Martin Hames.

Next was Doug Pepper, the editor for my book *Milking the Moon,* an oral biography of the Truman Capote-esque Eugene Walter. I did not meet Doug until after a year of phone calls and emails discussing the editing of this manuscript. Then he came from New York to attend a literary conference in New Orleans, where I invited him for dinner at my house. We hit it off so well I was truly sorry to decline his invitation to Sunday brunch in the French Quarter.

"My high school English teacher is in town for a convention of private school principals," I explained. "Sunday at noon is the only time I can see him."

"And your English teacher from Birmingham takes precedence over your editor from New York?" Doug teased. "Let me guess," he said. "This man was the most important teacher in your life. He transformed your existence and inspired your future like no one else."

Everything he said was true, but I thought Doug was just pulling clichés out of the hat until he said, "And this man weighed at least 600 pounds."

Flabbergasted, I could only stare at him. "How on earth did you know?"

Then he told me something I'll never forget. "I have three authors who came from Birmingham, Alabama," he said. "And they all had that same damn English teacher."

I shouldn't have been bowled over like I was, because after all, Martin Hames has inspired many more than the three published authors my editor was referring to. When I recovered from my amazement, Doug remarked, perhaps jokingly, "Maybe your next book should be about this English teacher."

He may or may not have been joking, but the idea that Temple Tutwiler had first planted in my brain began to take serious root. But before I could even begin to convince him to undertake such a project with me, Mr. Hames passed away, leaving behind a huge hole that no one could ever fill, and not just because of the outrageous amount of physical space he took up when he was still among us.

Mr. Hames's death made a book about him all the more imperative. And since I could no longer do the kind of nonfiction book I wanted, I switched to fiction. The great thing about fiction is that no one can blame me for all the deviations from the factual record in which this novel abounds. Instead of trying to re-create any literal or biographical truth, I spent my efforts trying to capture in words the large body and spirit of my beloved Mr. Hames. Then I made up a plot and a cast of other characters, as is necessary for a work of fiction.

Since nothing can fill the void created by Mr. Hames's absence, my attempted tribute no doubt fails to do justice to the man or the now-empty place he occupied in his community. Those who loved Mr. Hames as much as I did may wonder why I endowed his fictional counterpart with so many flaws. My own belief is that a great man's flaws are as integral to his success and greatness as his more positive attributes. While perfect saints can be heroes, most heroes accomplish their heroic mission because they are not perfect saints. Also, to whitewash someone's character is to pay the ultimate insult. In any case, I'm sure there are much better tributes than my novel that can be offered to the memory of Carl Martin Hames, and I sincerely encourage all those who want to do better than me to do so immediately, if not in fiction, then in nonfiction, poetry, painting, sculpture, or a donation to the scholarship fund at The Altamont School in Birmingham, Alabama. Meanwhile, there is already another book that pays homage to Mr. Hames, and that is Carolyn Sloss Ratliff's choice compilation of testimonials, collected in *Larger Than Life: Memories of Carl Martin Hames*.

There are several people responsible for making sure that what I've written has a public life. The first is the unbelievable person who got this book into print. His name is Pat Conroy. He read my novel when it was still just a Kinko's manuscript that arrived unexpectedly on his South Carolina island, un-recommended, un-agented, and unbidden. He had never once met me and did not know me. Ordinarily I would never have had the gumption to approach a famous author with my own un-famous work, but I suspected from having read Pat's novels many times that he possessed a soul as large and generous as that of my teacher. I was right. This famous author I'd never met actually read my Kinko's manuscript. Then he *called* me to discuss it. He suggested ways to make it better. And ultimately, now he is publishing it through his Story River Books imprint at the University of South Carolina Press. Pat Conroy has become reader, editor, mentor, publisher, and most of all, friend, and not just to me, either, but to countless other authors. Thank you, Pat, for being who you are: human being extraordinaire.

Pat Conroy would not, and could not, attempt what he's doing with Story River Books if not for the incomparable Jonathan Haupt, director of USC Press. Together, Jonathan and Pat have taken up the task of seeking and publishing quality Southern fiction, and I'm deeply honored that my novel was chosen for the imprint.

I would never have had the nerve to show my work to either of these literary superiors if not for my dearest friend and first reader, Tom Uskali, whose trenchant analysis of a manuscript's problems and shortcomings arrives in the form of praise and compliments. In his brilliant offhand manner, he politely and subtly indicates major changes and revisions that need to be made. If I need to talk for hours about my work, Tom will always oblige, and in the process, tell me more about my own novel than I knew myself. With his insight, I can then go back and make the book live up to what Tom has shown me it can be. I have come to rely on him so completely that I would never put anything I write out there before showing it first to Tom. My next reader is Sean Smith, who wields the alchemy of an ideal audience. As soon as I'm ready to send a manuscript to Sean, I suddenly think of a dozen improvements I need to make in order to reach my reader. As soon as I've made these improvements and sent the manuscript, I think of a dozen more. This process repeats itself every time I send a new version. I don't show what I write to my husband, Brandon, because he deserves a break. He supports me in all ways, without which I wouldn't have written anything. I would rather present him with the polished and published final product, which he has made possible. Kathe Telingator is the agent who has represented me without tangible hope of being compensated financially for her tremendous investment of time and effort. Thank you all.

ABOUT THE AUTHOR

KATHERINE CLARK holds an A.B. degree in English from Harvard and a Ph.D. in English from Emory. She is the coauthor of the oral biographies *Motherwit: An Alabama Midwife's Story* with Onnie Lee Logan and *Milking the Moon: A Southerner's Story of Life on This Planet* with Eugene Walter (a finalist for the National Book Critics Circle Award). A former student of Martin Hames, the inspiration for the character of Norman Laney, Clark has written three additional Mountain Brook novels featuring Laney and his students—*All the Governor's Men, The Harvard Bride,* and *The Ex-suicide*—all forthcoming from the University of South Carolina Press imprint Story River Books. Clark is currently collaborating with Pat Conroy on his oral biography, also forthcoming from the University of South Carolina Press. She lives on the Gulf Coast.